Queed
A Novel

by

Henry Sydnor Harrison

Double 9
BOOKS

Queed
A Novel
by Henry Sydnor Harrison

Copyright © 2024

All Rights reserved.

ISBN: 978-93-64285-73-5

Published by

DOUBLE 9 BOOKS

2/13-B, Ansari Road
Daryaganj, New Delhi – 110002
info@double9books.com
www.double9books.com
Tel. 011-40042856

ABOUT THE AUTHOR

Henry Sydnor Harrison (1880-1930) was an American novelist known for his works that often explored themes of personal transformation, social engagement, and the importance of human connections. Harrison was born on November 5, 1880, in Sewanee, Tennessee. His notable works include Queed perhaps his best-known work. The novel tells the story of a reclusive scholar's journey of self-discovery and social integration, reflecting Harrison's interest in personal transformation and social responsibility, **V.V.'s Eyes (1913):** a popular novel that deals with themes of personal growth and the importance of empathy and human connection and **Angela's Business (1915):** A novel that explores the challenges faced by a young woman in a male-dominated business world, highlighting issues of gender and social expectations and **Saint Teresa (1922):** A novel that delves into the complexities of personal faith and the quest for spiritual fulfillment. Harrison's novels are often characterized by their realistic portrayal of characters and settings. He had a keen eye for detail and an ability to capture the nuances of everyday life. Harrison's novels often include commentary on contemporary social issues, such as gender roles, social responsibility, and the importance of community. Harrison's works continue to be appreciated for their insightful exploration of human nature and social issues. His ability to create compelling characters and engaging narratives has earned him a respected place in the literary world.

CONTENTS

CHAPTER I 7

CHAPTER II 16

CHAPTER III 25

CHAPTER IV 37

CHAPTER V 46

CHAPTER VI 56

CHAPTER VII 68

CHAPTER VIII 80

CHAPTER IX 89

CHAPTER X 97

CHAPTER XI 107

CHAPTER XII 115

CHAPTER XIII 122

CHAPTER XIV 135

CHAPTER XV 143

CHAPTER XVI 152

CHAPTER XVII 163

CHAPTER XVIII 176

CHAPTER XIX 194

CHAPTER XX 201

CHAPTER XXI 208

CHAPTER XXII 222

CHAPTER XXIII 235

CHAPTER XXIV 243

CHAPTER XXV 253

CHAPTER XXVI 267

CHAPTER XXVII 279

CHAPTER XXVIII 293

CHAPTER XXIX 303

CHAPTER XXX 313

CHAPTER XXXI 321

CHAPTER XXXII 335

CHAPTER I

First Meeting between a citizen in Spectacles and the Great Pleasure-Dog Behemoth; also of Charles Gardiner West, a Personage at Thirty.

It was five of a November afternoon, crisp and sharp, and already running into dusk. Down the street came a girl and a dog, rather a small girl and quite a behemothian dog. If she had been a shade smaller, or he a shade more behemothian, the thing would have approached a parody on one's settled idea of a girl and a dog. She had enough height to save that, but it was the narrowest sort of squeak.

The dog was of the breed which are said to come trotting into Alpine monasteries of a winter's night with fat American travelers in their mouths, frozen stiff. He was extremely large for his age, whatever that was. On the other hand, the girl was small for her age, which was twenty-four next month; not so much short, you understand, for she was of a reasonable height, as of a dainty slimness, a certain exquisite reticence of the flesh. She had cares and duties and even sober-sided responsibilities in this world, beyond the usual run of girls. Yet her hat was decidedly of the mode that year; her suit was smartly and engagingly cut; her furs were glossy and black and big. Her face, it may be said here as well as later, had in its time given pleasure to the male sex, and some food for critical conversation to the female. A good many of the young men whom she met along the way this afternoon appeared distinctly pleased to speak to her.

The girl was Sharlee Weyland, and Sharlee was the short for Charlotte Lee, as invented by herself some score of years before. One baby-name in a hundred sticks through a lifetime, and hers was the one in that particular hundred. Of the young men along the way, one was so lucky as to catch her eye through a large plate-glass window. It was Semple and West's window, the ground-floor one in the great new Commonwealth Building, of which the town is rightly so proud, and the young man was no other than West, Charles Gardiner himself. A smile warmed his good-looking face when he met the eye of the girl and the dog; he waved a hand at them. That done, he immediately vanished from the window and reached for his hat and coat; gave hurried directions to a clerk and a stenographer; and sallying forth, overtook the pair before they had reached the next corner.

"Everything's topsy-turvy," said he, coming alongside. "Here you are frivolously walking downtown with a dog. Usually at this time you are most earnestly walking uptown, and not a sign of a dog as far as the eye can see. What on earth's happened?"

"Oh, how do you do?" said she, apparently not displeased to find herself thus surprised from the rear. "I too have a mad kind of feeling, as though the world had gone upside down. Don't be amazed if I suddenly clutch out at you to keep from falling. But the name of it—of this feeling—is having a holiday. Mr. Dayne went to New York at 12.20."

"Ah, I see. When the cat's away?"

"Not at all. I am taking this richly earned vacation by his express command."

"In that case, why mightn't we turn about and go a real walk—cease picking our way through the noisome hum of commerce and set brisk evening faces toward the open road—and all that? You and I and the dog. What is his name? Rollo, I suppose?"

"Rollo! No! Or Tray or Fido, either! His name is Bee, short for Behemoth—and I think that a very captivating little name, don't you? His old name, the one I bought him by, was Fred—Fred!—but already he answers to the pretty name of Bee as though he were born to it. Watch." She pursed her lips and gave a whistle, unexpectedly loud and clear. "Here, Bee, here! Here, sir! Look, look. He turned around *right away*!"

West laughed. "Wonderfully gifted dog. But I believe you mentioned taking a walk in the November air. I can only say that physicians strongly recommend it, valetudinarians swear by it—"

"Oh—if I only could!—but I simply cannot think of it. Do you know, I never have a holiday without wondering how on earth I could have gotten on another day without it. You can't imagine what loads of things I've done since two o'clock, and loads remain. The very worst job of them all still hangs by a hair over my head. I must cross here."

West said that evidently her conception of a holiday was badly mixed. As they walked he paid for her society by incessantly taking off his hat; nearly everybody they met spoke to them, many more to him than to her. Though both of them had been born in that city and grown up with it, the girl had only lately come to know West well, and she did not know him very well now. All the years hitherto she had joined in the general admiration of him shyly and from a distance, the pretty waiting-lady's attitude toward the dazzling young crown prince. She was observant, and so she could not fail to observe now the cordiality with which people of all sorts saluted him, the touch of deference in the greeting of not a few. He was scarcely thirty, but it would have been clear to a duller eye that he was already something of a personage. Yet he held no public office, nor were his daily walks the walks of philanthropic labor for the common good. In fact Semple & West's was merely a brokerage establishment, which was understood to be cleaning up a tolerable lot of money per annum.

They stood on the corner, waiting for a convenient chance to cross, and West looked at her as at one whom it was pleasant to rest one's eyes upon. She drew his attention to their humming environment. For a city of that size the life and bustle here were, indeed, such as to take the eye. Trolley cars clanged by in a tireless procession; trucks were rounding up for stable and for bed; delivery wagons whizzed corners and bumped on among them; now and then a chauffeur honked by, grim eyes roving for the unwary pedestrian. On both sides of the street the homeward march of tired humans was already forming and quickening.

"Heigho! We're living in an interesting time, you and I," said West. "It isn't every generation that can watch its old town change into a metropolis right under its eyes."

"I remember," said she, "when it was an exciting thing to see anybody on the street you didn't know. You went home and told the family about it, and very likely counted the spoons next morning. The city seemed to belong to *us* then. And now—look. Everywhere new kings that know not Joseph. Bee!"

"It's the law of life; the old order changeth." He turned and looked along the street, into the many faces of the homeward bound. "The eternal mystery of the people.... Don't you like to look at their faces and wonder what they're all doing and thinking and hoping and dreaming to make out of their lives?"

"Don't you think they're all hoping and dreaming just one thing?—how to make more money than they're making at present? All over the world," said Miss Weyland, "bright young men lie awake at night, thinking up odd, ingenious ways to take other people's money away from them. These young men are the spirit of America. We're having an irruption of them here now ... the Goths sacking the sacred city."

"Clever rascals they are too. I," said West, "belong to the other group. I sleep of nights and wake up in the morning to have your bright young Goths take my money away from me."

He laughed and continued: "Little Bobby Smythe, who used to live here, was in my office the other day. I was complimenting him on the prosperity of the plumbers' supply manufacture—for such is his mundane occupation, in Schenectady, N.Y. Bobby said that plumbers' supplies were all well enough, but he made his real money from an interesting device of his own. There is a lot of building going on in his neighborhood, it seems, and it occurred to him to send around to the various owners and offer his private watchman to guard the loose building materials at night. This for the very reasonable price of $3.50 a week. It went like hot cakes. 'But,' said I, 'surely your one watchman can't look after thirty-seven different places.' 'No,' said Bobby, 'but they think he does.' I laughed and commended his ingenuity. 'But the best part of the joke,' said he, 'is that *I haven't got any watchman at all.*'"

Sharlee Weyland laughed gayly. "Bobby could stand for the portrait of young America."

"You've been sitting at the feet of a staunch old Tory Gamaliel named Colonel Cowles. I can see that. Ah, me! My garrulity has cost us a splendid chance to cross. What are all these dreadful things you have still left to do on your so-called holiday?"

"Well," said she, "first I'm going to Saltman's to buy stationery. Boxes and boxes of it, for the Department. Bee! Come here, sir! Look how fat this purse is. I'm going to spend all of that. Bee! I wish I had put him to leash. He's going to hurt himself in a minute—you see!—"

"Don't you think he's much more likely to hurt somebody else? For a guess, that queer-looking little citizen in spectacles over the way, who so evidently doesn't know where he is at."

"Oh, do you think so?—Bee!... Then, after stationery, comes the disagreeable thing, and yet interesting too. I have to go to my Aunt Jennie's, dunning."

"You are compelled to dun your Aunt Jennie?"

She laughed. "No—dun for her, because she's too tender-hearted to do it herself. There's a man there who won't pay his board. Bee! Bee!—BEE!-O heavens—It's happened!"

And, too quick for West, she was gone into the mêlée, which immediately closed in behind her, barricading him away.

What had happened was a small tragedy in its way. The little citizen in spectacles, who had been standing on the opposite corner vacantly eating an apple out of a paper bag, had unwisely chosen his moment to try the crossing. He was evidently an indoors sort of man and no shakes at crossing streets, owing to the introspective nature of his mind. A grocery wagon shaved him by an inch. It was doing things to the speed-limit, this wagon, because a dashing police patrol was close behind, treading on its tail and indignantly clanging it to turn out, which it could not possibly do. To avoid erasing the little citizen, the patrol man had to pull sharply out; and this manoeuvre, as Fate had written it, brought him full upon the great dog Behemoth, who, having slipped across the tracks, stood gravely waiting for the flying wagon to pass. Thus it became a clear case of *sauve qui peut*, and the devil take the hindermost. There was nothing in the world for Behemoth to do but wildly leap under the hoofs for his life. This he did successfully. But on the other side he met the spectacled citizen full and fair, and down they went together with a thud.

The little man came promptly to a sitting posture and took stock of the wreck. His hat he could not see anywhere, the reason being that he was sitting on it. The paper bag, of course, had burst; some of the apples had rolled to amazing distances, and newsboys, entire strangers to the fallen gentleman, were eating them with cries of pleasure. This he saw in one pained glance. But on the very heels of the dog, it seemed, came hurrying a girl with marks of great anxiety on her face.

"Can you possibly forgive him? That fire-alarm thing scared him crazy—he's usually so good! You aren't hurt, are you? I do hope so much that you aren't?"

The young man, sitting calmly in the street, glanced up at Miss Weyland with no sign of interest.

"I have no complaint to make," he answered, precisely; "though the loss of my fruit seems unfortunate, to say the least of it."

"I know! The way they fell on them," she answered, as self-unconscious as he—"quite as though you had offered to treat! I'm very much mortified— But—*are* you hurt? I thought for a minute that the coal cart was going right over you."

A crowd had sprung up in a wink; a circle of interested faces watching the unembarrassed girl apologizing to the studious-looking little man who sat so calmly upon his hat in the middle of the street. Meantime all traffic on that side was hopelessly blocked. Swearing truck drivers stood up on their seats from a block away to see what had halted the procession.

"But what is the object of a dog like that?" inquired the man ruminatively. "What good is he? What is he for?"

"Why—why—why," said she, looking ready to laugh—"he's not a utilitarian dog at all, you see! He's a pleasure-dog, you know—just a big, beautiful dog to give pleasure!—"

"The pleasure he has given me," said the man, gravely producing his derby from beneath him and methodically undenting it, "is negligible. I may say non-existent."

From somewhere rose a hoarse titter. The girl glanced up, and for the first time became aware that her position was somewhat unconventional. A very faint color sprang into her cheeks, but she was not the kind to retreat in disorder. West dodged through the blockade in time to hear her say with a final, smiling bow:

"I'm so glad you aren't hurt, believe me ... And if my dog has given you no pleasure, you may like to think that you have given him a great deal."

A little flushed but not defeated, her gloved hand knotted in Behemoth's gigantic scruff, she moved away, resigning the situation to West. West handled it in his best manner, civilly assisting the little man to rise, and bowing himself off with the most graceful expressions of regret for the mishap.

Miss Weyland was walking slowly, waiting for him, and he fell in beside her on the sidewalk.

"Don't speak to me suddenly," said she, in rather a muffled voice. "I don't want to scream on a public street."

"Scratch a professor and you find a Tartar," said West, laughing too. "When I finally caught you, laggard that I was, you looked as if he were being rude."

Miss Weyland questioned the rudeness; she said that the man was only superbly natural. "Thoughts came to him and he blabbed them out artlessly. The only things that he seemed in the least interested in were his apples and Bee. Don't you think from this that he must be a floral and faunal naturalist?"

"No Goth, at any rate. Did you happen to notice the tome sticking out of his coat pocket? It was *The Religion of Humanity*, unless my old eyes deceived me. Who under heaven reads Comte nowadays?"

"Not me," said Miss Weyland.

"There's nothing to it. As a wealthy old friend of mine once remarked, people who read that sort of books never make over eighteen hundred a year."

On that they turned into Saltman's. There much stationery and collateral stuff was bought for cash paid down, and all for the use of the Department. Next, at a harness-store, a leash was bargained for and obtained, and Behemoth bowled over no more young men that day. Thereafter, the two set their faces westerly till they came to the girl's home, where the dog was delivered to the cook, and Miss Weyland went upstairs to kiss her mother. Still later they set out northward through the lamp-lit night for the older part of town, where resided the aunt on whose behalf there was dunning to be done that night.

Charles Gardiner West asserted that he had not a thing in all this world to do, and that erranding was only another way of taking a walk, when you came to think of it. She was frankly glad of his company; to be otherwise was to be fantastic; and now as they strolled she led him to talk of his work, which was never difficult. For West, despite his rising prosperity, was dissatisfied with his calling, the reason being, as he himself sometimes put it, that his heart did not abide with the money changers.

"Sometimes at night," he said seriously, "I look back over the busy day and ask myself what it has all amounted to. Suppose I did all the world's stock-jobbing, what would I really have accomplished? You may say that I could take all the money I made and spend it for free hospitals, but would I do it? No. The more I made, the more I'd want for myself, the more all my interest and ambition would twine themselves around the counting-room. You can't serve two masters, can you, Miss Weyland? Uplifting those who need uplifting is a separate business, all by itself."

"You could make the money," laughed she, "and let me spend it for you. I know this minute where I could put a million to glorious advantage."

"I'm going to get out of it," said West. "I've told Semple so—though perhaps it ought not to go further just yet. I'd enjoy," said he, "just such work as yours. There's none finer. You'd like me immensely as your royal master, I suppose? Want nothing better than to curtsy and kowtow when I flung out a gracious order?—as, for instance, to shut up shop and go and take a holiday?"

"Delicious! Though I doubt if anybody in the world could improve on Mr. Dayne." Suddenly a new thought struck her, and she made a faint grimace. "There's nothing so very fine about my present work—oh me! I'll give you that if you want it."

"I see I must look this gift horse over very closely. What is it?"

"They call it dunning."

"I forgot. You started to tell me, and then your dog ran amuck and began butting perfect strangers all over the place."

"Oh," said she, "it's the commonest little story in the world. All landladies can tell them to you by the hour. This man has been at Aunt Jennie's nearly a month, and what's the color of his money she hasn't the faintest idea. Such is the way our bright young men carve out their fortunes—the true Gothic architecture! Possibly Aunt Jennie has thrown out one or two delicate hints, carefully insulated to avoid hurting his feelings. You know the way our ladies of the old school do—the worst collectors the world has ever seen. So she telephoned me this morning—I'm her business woman, you see—asking me to come and advise her, and I'm coming, and after supper—"

"Well, what'll you do?"

"I'm going to talk with him, with the man. I'm simply going to *collect that money*. Or if I can't—"

"What's the horrid alternative?"

"I'm going to *fire* him!"

West laughed merrily. His face always looked most charming when he smiled. "Upon my word I believe you can do it."

"I *have* done it, lots of times."

"Ah! And is the ceremony ever attended by scenes of storm and violence?"

"Never. They march like little lambs when I say the word. Hay-foot—straw-foot!"

"But then your aunt loses their arrears of board, I suppose."

"Yes, and for that reason I never fire except as a last desperate resort. Signs of penitence, earnest resolves to lead a better life, are always noted and carefully considered."

"If you *should* need help with this customer to-night—not that I think you will, oh no!—telephone me. I'm amazingly good at handling bright young men. This is your aunt's, isn't it?"

"No, no—next to the corner over there. O heavens! Look—*look!*"

West looked. Up the front steps of Miss Weyland's Aunt Jennie's a man was going, a smallish man in a suit of dusty clothes, who limped as he walked. The electric light at the corner illumined him perfectly—glinted upon the spectacles, touched up the stout volume in the coat-pocket, beat full upon the swaybacked derby, whereon its owner had sat what time Charlotte Lee Weyland apologized for the gaucherie of Behemoth. And as they watched, this man pushed open Aunt Jennie's front door, with never so much as a glance at the door-bell, and stepped as of right inside.

Involuntarily West and Miss Weyland had halted; and now they stared at each other with a kind of wild surmise which rapidly yielded to ludicrous certainty. West broke into a laugh.

"Well, do you think you'll have the nerve to fire *him*?"

CHAPTER II

Mrs. Paynter's Boarding-House: which was not founded as an Eleemosynary Institution.

There was something of a flutter among the gathered boarders when Miss Weyland was seen to be entering the house, and William Klinker, who announced the fact from his place by the window, added that that had ought to help some with the supper. He reminded the parlor that there had been Porterhouse the last time. Miss Miller, from the sofa, told Mr. Klinker archly that he was *so* material. She had only the other day mastered the word, but even that is more than could be said for Mr. Klinker. Major Brooke stood by the Latrobe heater, reading the evening paper under a flaring gas-light. He habitually came down early to get it before anybody else had a chance. By Miss Miller on the sofa sat Mr. Bylash, stroking the glossy moustache which other ladies before her time had admired intensely. Despite her archness Miss Miller had heard with a pang that Miss Weyland was coming to supper, and her reason was not unconnected with this same Mr. Bylash. In earlier meetings she had vaguely noted differences between Mrs. Paynter's pretty niece and herself. True, she considered these differences all in her own favor, as, for example, her far larger back pompadour, with the puffs, but you never could tell about gentlemen.

"I'm surprised," she said to Mr. Klinker, "Mr. Bylash didn't go out to give her the glad hand, and welcome her into our humble *coturee.*"

Mr. Bylash, who had been thinking of doing that very thing, said rather shortly that the ladies present quite satisfied *him.*

"And who do you think brought her around and right up to the door?" continued William Klinker, taking no notice of their blandishments. "Hon. West—Charles Gardenia West—"

A scream from Miss Miller applauded the witty hit.

"Oh, it ain't mine," said Mr. Klinker modestly. "I heard a fellow get it off at the shop the other day. He's a pretty smooth fellow, Charles Gardenia is—a little too smooth for my way of thinking. A fellow that's always so smilin'—Oh, you Smithy!" he suddenly yelled out the window—"Smithy!

Hey!—Aw, I can beat the face off you!—Awright—eight sharp at the same place.—Go on, you fat Mohawk you!... But say," he resumed to the parlor, "y'know that little woman is a stormy petrel for this house—that's right. Remember the last time she was here—the time we had the Porterhouse? Conference in the dining-room after supper, and the next morning out went the trunks of that red-head fellow—from Baltimore—what's his name?— Milhiser."

"Well, she hasn't got any call to intrude in my affairs," said Mr. Bylash, still rather miffed. "I'm here to tell you that!"

"Oh, I ain't speakin' of the reg'lars," answered Klinker, "so don't get nervous. But say, I got kind of a hunch that here is where the little Doc gets his."

Klinker's hunch was not without foundation; this very question was being agitated at that moment in the room just over his head. Miss Weyland, having passed the parlor portières with no thought that her movements were attracting interest on the other side of them, skipped up the stairs, rapped on her Aunt Jennie's door, and ran breathlessly into the room. Her aunt was sitting by the bureau, reading a novel from the circulating library. Though she had been sitting right here since about four o'clock, only getting up once to light the gas, she had a casual air like one who is only killing a moment's time between important engagements. She looked up at the girl's entrance, and an affectionate smile lit her well-lined face.

"My dear Sharlee! I'm so glad to see you."

They kissed tenderly.

"Oh, Aunt Jennie, tell me! Is he—this man you telephoned me about— is he a little, small, dried young man, with spectacles and a brown derby, and needing a hair-cut, and the gravest, drollest manner in the world? Tell me—is he?"

"My dear, you have described him to the life. Where did you see him?"

Sharlee collapsed upon the bed. Presently she revived and outlined the situation to Aunt Jennie.

Mrs. Paynter listened with some interest. If humor is a defect, as they tell us nowadays, she was almost a faultless woman. And in her day she had been a beauty and a toast. You hear it said generously of a thousand, but it happened to be true in her case. The high-bred regularity of feature still survived, but she had let herself go in latter years, as most women will who have other things than themselves to think about, and hard things at that.

Her old black dress was carelessly put on; she could look at herself in the mirror by merely leaning forward an inch or two, and it never occurred to her to do it—an uncanny thing in a woman.

"I'm sure it sounds quite like him," said Mrs. Paynter, when her niece had finished. "And so Gardiner West walked around with you. I hope, my dear, you asked him in to supper? We have an exceptionally nice Porterhouse steak to-night. But I suppose he would scorn—"

The girl interrupted her, abolishing and demolishing such a thought. Mr. West would have been only too pleased, she said, but she positively would not ask him, because of the serious work that was afoot that night.

"The pleasure I've so far given your little man," laughed she, patting her aunt's cheeks with her two hands, "has been negligible—I have his word for that—and to-night it is going to be the same, only more so."

Sharlee arose, took off her coat and furs, laid them on the bed, and going to the bureau began fixing her hair in the back before the long mirror. No matter how well a woman looks to the untrained, or man's, eye, she can always put in some time pleasurably fixing her hair in the back.

"Now," said Sharlee, "to business. Tell me all about the little dead-beat."

"It is four weeks next Monday," said Mrs. Paynter, putting a shoe-horn in her novel to mark the place, "since the young man came to me. He was from New York, and just off the train. He said that he had been recommended to my house, but would not say by whom, nor could he give references. I did not insist on them, for I can't be too strict, Sharlee, with all the other boarding-places there are and that room standing empty for two months hand-running, and then for three months before that, before Miss Catlett, I mean. The fact is, that I ought to be over on the Avenue, where I could have only the best people. It would be infinitely more lucrative— why, my dear, you should hear Amy Marsden talk of her enormous profits! And Amy, while a dear, sweet little woman, is not clever! I remember as girls—but to go back even of that to the very heart of the matter, who ever heard of a clever *Wilkerson*? For she, you know, was born ..."

"Never you mind Mrs. Marsden, Aunt Jennie," said the girl, gently drawing her back to the muttons,—"we'll make lots more money than she some day. So you gave him the room, then?"

"Yes, the room known as the third hall back. A small, neat, economical room, entirely suitable for a single gentleman. I gave him my lowest price, though I must say I did not dream then that he would spend all his time in his room, apparently having no downtown occupation, which is certainly not what one expects from gentlemen, who get low terms on the silent understanding that they will take themselves out of the house directly after breakfast. Nevertheless—will you believe it?—ten days passed and not a word was said about payment. So one morning I stopped him in the hall, as though for a pleasant talk. However, I was careful to introduce the point, by means of an anecdote I told him, that guests here were expected to pay by the week. Of course I supposed that the hint would be sufficient."

"But it wasn't, alas?"

"On the contrary, ten days again passed, and you might suppose there was no such thing as money in all this world. Then I resolved to approach him directly. I knocked on his door, and when he opened it, I told him plainly and in so many words that I would be very much gratified if he would let me have a check whenever convenient, as unfortunately I had heavy bills due that must be met. I was very much mortified, Sharlee! As I stood there facing that young man, dunning him like a grocer's clerk, it flashed into my mind to wonder what your great-grandfather, the Governor, would think if he could have looked down and seen me. For as you know, my dear, though I doubt if you altogether realize it at all times, since our young people of to-day, I regret to have to say it—though of course I do except you from this criticism—"

By gentle interruption and deft transition, Sharlee once more wafted the conversation back to the subject in hand.

"And when you went so far as to tell him this, how did he take it?"

"He took it admirably. He told me that I need feel no concern about the matter; that while out of funds for the moment, doubtless he would be in funds again shortly. His manner was dignified, calm, unabashed—"

"But it didn't blossom, as we might say, in money?"

"As to that—no. What are you to do, Sharlee? I feel sure the man is not dishonest,—in fact he has a singularly honest face, transparently so,—but he is only somehow queer. He appears an engrossed, absent-minded young man—what is the word I want?—an eccentric. That is what he is, an engrossed young eccentric."

Sharlee leaned against the bureau and looked at her aunt thoughtfully. "Do you gather, Aunt Jennie, that he's a gentleman?"

Mrs. Paynter threw out her hands helplessly. "What does the term mean nowadays? The race of gentlemen, as the class existed in my day, seems to be disappearing from the face of the earth. We see occasional survivals of the old order, like Gardiner West or the young Byrd men, but as a whole—well, my dear, I will only say that the modern standards would have excited horror fifty years ago and—"

"Well, but according to the modern standards, do you think he is?"

"I *don't* know. He is and he isn't. But no—no—no! He is *not* one. No man can be a gentleman who is utterly indifferent to the comfort and feelings of others, do you think so?"

"Indeed, no! And is that what he is?"

"I will illustrate by an incident," said Mrs. Paynter. "As I say, this young man spends his entire time in his room, where he is, I believe, engaged in writing a book."

"Oh, me! Then he's penniless, depend upon it."

"Well, when we had the frost and freeze early last week, he came to me one night and complained of the cold in his room. You know, Sharlee, I do not rent that room as a sitting-room, nor do I expect to heat it, at the low price, other than the heat from the halls. So I invited him to make use of the dining-room in the evenings, which, as you know, with the folding-doors drawn, and the yellow lamp lit, is converted to all intents and purposes into a quiet and comfortable reading-room. Somewhat grumblingly he went down. Fifi was there as usual, doing her algebra by the lamp. The young man took not the smallest notice of her, and presently when she coughed several times—the child's cold happened to be bad that night—he looked up sharply and asked her please to stop. Fifi said that she was afraid she couldn't help it. He replied that it was impossible for him to work in the room with a noise of that sort, and either the noise or he would have to vacate. So Fifi gathered up her things and left. I found her, half an hour later, in her little bedroom, which was ice-cold, coughing and crying over her sums, which she was trying to work at the bureau. That was how I found out about it. The child would never have said a word to me."

"How simply outrageous!" said the girl, and became silent and thoughtful.

"Well, what do you think I'd better do, Sharlee?"

"I think you'd better let me waylay him in the hall after supper and tell him that the time has come when he must either pay up or pack up."

"My dear! Can you well be as blunt as that?"

"Dear Aunt Jennie, as I view it, you are not running an eleemosynary institution here?"

"Of course not," replied Aunt Jennie, who really did not know whether she was or not.

Sharlee dropped into a chair and began manicuring her pretty little nails. "The purpose of this establishment is to collect money from the transient and resident public. Now you're not a bit good at collecting money because you're so well-bred, but I'm not so awfully well-bred—"

"You *are*—"

"I'm bold—blunt—brazen! I'm forward. I'm resolute and grim. In short, I belong to the younger generation which you despise so—"

"I don't despise *you*, you dear—"

"Come," said Sharlee, springing up; "let's go down. I'm wild to meet Mr. Bylash again. Is he wearing the moleskin vest to-night, do you know? I was fascinated by it the last time I was here. Aunt Jennie, what is the name of this young man—the one I may be compelled to bounce?"

"His name is Queed. Did you ever—?"

"Queed? *Queed?* Q-u-e-e-d?"

"An odd name, isn't it? There were no such people in my day."

"Probably after to-morrow there will be none such once more."

"Mr. Klinker has christened him the little Doctor—a hit at his appearance and studious habits, you see—and even the servants have taken it up."

"Aunt Jennie," said Sharlee at the door, "when you introduce the little Doctor to me, refer to me as your business woman, won't you? Say 'This is my niece, Miss Weyland, who looks after my business affairs for me,' or something like that, will you? It will explain to him why I, a comparative stranger, show such an interest in his financial affairs."

Mrs. Paynter said, "Certainly, my dear," and they went down, the older lady disappearing toward the dining-room. In the parlor Sharlee was greeted cordially and somewhat respectfully. Major Brooke, who appeared to have taken an extra toddy in honor of her coming, or for any other reason why, flung aside his newspaper and seized both her hands. Mr. Bylash, in the moleskin waistcoat, sure enough, bowed low and referred to her agreeably as "stranger," nor did he again return to Miss Miller's side on the sofa. That young lady was gay and giggling, but watchful withal. When Sharlee was not looking, Miss Miller's eye, rather hard now, roved over her ceaselessly from the point of her toe to the top of her feather. What was the trick she had, the little way with her, that so delightfully unlocked the gates of gentlemen's hearts?

At supper they were lively and gay. The butter and preserves were in front of Sharlee, for her to help to; by her side sat Fifi, the young daughter of the house. Major Brooke sat at the head of the table and carved the Porterhouse, upon which when the eyes of William Klinker fell, they irrepressibly shot forth gleams. At the Major's right sat his wife, a pale, depressed, nervous woman, as anybody who had lived thirty years with the gallant officer her husband had a right to be. She was silent, but the Major talked a great deal, not particularly well. Much the same may be said of Mr. Bylash and Miss Miller. Across the table from Mrs. Brooke stood an empty chair. It belonged to the little Doctor, Mr. Queed. Across the table from Sharlee stood another. This one belonged to the old professor, Nicolovius. When the meal was well along, Nicolovius came in, bowed around the table in his usual formal way, and silently took his place. While Sharlee liked everybody in the boarding-house, including Miss Miller, Professor Nicolovius was the only one of them that she considered at all interesting. This was because of his strongly-cut face, like the grand-ducal villain in a ten-twenty-thirty melodrama, and his habit of saying savage things in a soft, purring voice. He was rude to everybody, and particularly rude, so Sharlee thought, to her. As for the little Doctor, he did not come in at all. Half-way through supper, Sharlee looked at her aunt and gave a meaning glance at the empty seat.

"I don't know what to make of it," said Mrs. Paynter *sotto voce*. "He's usually so regular."

To the third floor she dispatched the colored girl Emma, to knock upon Mr. Queed's door. Presently Emma returned with the report that she had knocked, but could obtain no answer.

"He's probably fallen asleep over his book," murmured Sharlee. "I feel certain it's that kind of book."

But Mrs. Paynter said that he rarely slept, even at night.

"... Right on my own front porch, mind you!" Major Brooke was declaiming. "And, gentlemen, I shook my finger in his face and said, 'Sir, I never yet met a Republican who was not a rogue!' Yes, sir, that is just what I told him—"

"I'm afraid," said Nicolovius, smoothly,—it was the only word he uttered during the meal,—"your remark harrows Miss Weyland with reminders of the late Mr. Surface."

The Major stopped short, and a silence fell over the table. It was promptly broken by Mrs. Paynter, who invited Mrs. Brooke to have a second cup of coffee. Sharlee looked at her plate and said nothing. Everybody thought that the old professor's remark was in bad taste, for it was generally known that Henry G. Surface was one subject that even Miss Weyland's intimate friends never mentioned to her. Nicolovius, however, appeared absolutely unconcerned by the boarders' silent rebuke. He ate on, rapidly but abstemiously, and finished before Mr. Bylash, who had had twenty minutes' start of him.

The last boarder rising drew shut the folding-doors into the parlor, while the ladies of the house remained to superintend and assist in clearing off the supper things. The last boarder this time was Mr. Bylash, who tried without success to catch Miss Weyland's eye as he slid to the doors. He hung around in the parlor waiting for her till 8.30, at which time, having neither seen nor heard sign of her, he took Miss Miller out to the moving-picture shows. In the dining-room, when Emma had trayed out the last of the things, the ladies put away the unused silver, watered the geranium, set back some of the chairs, folded up the white cloth, placing it in the sideboard drawer, spread the pretty Turkey-red one in its stead, set the reading lamp upon it; and just then the clock struck eight.

"Now then," said Sharlee.

So the three sat down and held a council of war as to how little Doctor Queed, the young man who wouldn't pay his board, was to be brought into personal contact with Charlotte Lee Weyland, the grim and resolute collector. Various stratagems were proposed, amid much merriment. But the collector herself adhered to her original idea of a masterly waiting game.

"Only trust me," said she. "He can't spend the rest of his life shut up in that room in a state of dreadful siege. Hunger or thirst will force him out; he'll want to buy some of those apples, or to mail a letter—"

Fifi, who sat on the arm of Sharlee's chair, laughed and coughed. "He never writes any. And he never has gotten but one, and that came to-night."

"Fifi, did you take your syrup before supper? Well, go and take it this minute."

"Mother, it doesn't do any good."

"The doctor gave it to you, my child, and it's going to make you better soon."

Sharlee followed Fifi out with troubled eyes. However, Mrs. Paynter at once drew her back to the matter in hand.

"Sharlee, do you know what would be the very way to settle this little difficulty? To write him a formal, businesslike letter. We'll—"

"No, I've thought of that, Aunt Jennie, and I don't believe it's the way. A letter couldn't get to the bottom of the matter. You see, we want to find out something about this man, and why he isn't paying, and whether there is reason to think he can and will pay. Besides, I think he needs a talking to on general principles."

"Well—but how are you going to do it, my dear?"

"Play a Fabian game. Wait!—be stealthy and wait! If he doesn't come out of hiding to-night, I'll return for him to-morrow. I'll keep on coming, night after night, night after night, n—Some one's knocking—".

"Come in," said Mrs. Paynter, looking up.

The door leading into the hall opened, and the man himself stood upon the threshold, looking at them absently.

"May I have some supper, Mrs. Paynter? I was closely engaged and failed to notice the time."

Sharlee arose. "Certainly. I'll get you some at once," she answered innocently enough. But to herself she was saying: "The Lord has delivered him into my hand."

CHAPTER III

Encounter between Charlotte Lee Weyland, a Landlady's Agent, and Doctor Queed, a Young Man who wouldn't pay his Board.

Sharlee glanced at Mrs. Paynter, who caught herself and said: "Mr. Queed, my niece—Miss Weyland."

But over the odious phrase, "my business woman," her lips boggled and balked; not to save her life could she bring herself to damn her own niece with such an introduction.

Noticing the omission and looking through the reasons for it as through window-glass, Sharlee smothered a laugh, and bowed. Mr. Queed bowed, but did not laugh or even smile. He drew up a chair at his usual place and sat down. As by an involuntary reflex, his left hand dropped toward his coat-pocket, whence the top edges of a book could be descried protruding. Mrs. Paynter moved vaguely toward the door. As for her business woman, she made at once for the kitchen, where Emma and her faithful co-worker and mother, Laura, rose from their supper to assist her. With her own hands the girl cut a piece of the Porterhouse for Mr. Queed. Creamed potatoes, two large spoonfuls, were added; two rolls; some batterbread; coffee, which had to be diluted with a little hot water to make out the full cup; butter; damson preserves in a saucer: all of which duly set forth and arranged on a shiny black "waiter."

"Enough for a whole platform of doctors," said Sharlee, critically reviewing the spread. "Thank you, Emma."

She took the tray in both hands and pushed open the swing-doors with her side, thus making her ingress to the dining-room in a sort of crab-fashion. Mrs. Paynter was gone. Mr. Queed sat alone in the dining-room. His book lay open on the table and he was humped over it, hand in his hair.

Having set her tray on the side-table, Sharlee came to his side with the plate of steak and potatoes. He did not stir, and presently she murmured, "I beg your pardon."

He looked up half-startled, not seeming to take in for the first second who or what she was.

"Oh ... yes."

He moved his book, keeping his finger in the place, and she set down the plate. Next she brought the appurtenances one by one, the butter, coffee, and so on. The old mahogany sideboard yielded knife, fork, and spoon; salt and pepper; from the right-hand drawer, a fresh napkin. These placed, she studied them, racked her brains a moment and, from across the table—

"Is there anything else?"

Mr. Queed's eye swept over his equipment with intelligent quickness. "A glass of water, please."

"Oh!—Certainly."

Sharlee poured a glass from the battered silver pitcher on the side-table—the one that the Yankees threw out of the window in May, 1862—and duly placed it. Mr. Queed was oblivious to the little courtesy. By this time he had propped his book open against the plate of rolls and was reading it between cuts on the steak. Beside the plate he had laid his watch, an open-faced nickel one about the size of a desk-clock.

"Do you think that is everything?"

"I believe that is all."

"Do you remember me?" then asked Sharlee.

He glanced at her briefly through his spectacles, his eyes soon returning to his supper.

"I think not."

The girl smiled suddenly, all by herself. "It was my dog that—upset you on Main Street this afternoon. You may remember ...? I thought you seemed to—to limp a little when you came in just now. I'm awfully sorry for the—mishap—"

"It is of no consequence," he said, with some signs of unrest. "I walk seldom. Your—pleasure-dog was uninjured, I trust?"

"Thank you. He was never better."

That the appearance of the pleasure-dog's owner as a familiar of his boarding-house piqued his curiosity not the slightest was only too evident. He bowed, his eyes returning from steak to book.

"I am obliged to you for getting my supper."

If he had said, "Will you kindly go?" his meaning could hardly have been more unmistakable. However, Mrs. Paynter's resolute agent held her ground. Taking advantage of his gross absorption, she now looked the delinquent boarder over with some care. At first glance Mr. Queed looked as if he might have been born in a library, where he had unaspiringly settled down. To support this impression there were his pallid complexion and enormous round spectacles; his dusty air of premature age; his general effect of dried-up detachment from his environment. One noted, too, the tousled mass of nondescript hair, which he wore about a month too long; the necktie-band triumphing over the collar in the back; the collar itself, which had a kind of celluloid look and shone with a blue unwholesome sheen under the gas-light. On the other hand there was the undeniably trim cut of the face, which gave an unexpected and contradictory air of briskness. The nose was bold; the long straight mouth might have belonged to a man of action. Probably the great spectacles were the turning-point in the man's whole effect. You felt that if you could get your hands on him long enough to pull those off, and cut his hair, you might have an individual who would not so surely have been christened the little Doctor.

These details the agent gathered at her leisure. Meantime here was the situation, stark and plain; and she, and she alone, must handle it. She must tell this young man, so frankly engrossed in his mental and material food, which he ate by his watch, that he must fork over four times seven-fifty or vacate the premises.... Yes, but how to do it? He could not be much older than she herself, but his manner was the most impervious, the most impossible that she had ever seen. "I'm grim and I'm resolute," she said over to herself; but the splendid defiance of the motto failed to quicken her blood. Not even the recollection of the month's sponge for board and the house-rent due next week spurred her to action. Then she thought of Fifi, whom Mr. Queed had packed off sobbing for his good pleasure, and her resolution hardened.

"I'm afraid I must interrupt your reading for a moment," she said quietly. "There is something I want to say...."

He glanced up for the second time. There was surprise and some vexation in the eyes behind his circular glasses, but no sign of any interest.

"Well?"

"When my aunt introduced you to me just now she did not—did not identify me as she should—"

"Really, does it make any difference?"

"Yes, I think it does. You see, I am not only her niece, but her business woman, her agent, as well. She isn't very good at business, but still she has a good deal of it to be done. She runs this boarding-place, and people of various kinds come to her and she takes them into her house. Many of these people are entirely unknown to her. In this way trouble sometimes arises. For instance people come now and then who—how shall I put it?—are very reserved about making their board-payments. My aunt hardly knows how to deal with them—"

He interrupted her with a gesture and a glance at his watch. "It always seems to me an unnecessary waste of time not to be direct. You have called to collect my arrearage for board?"

"Well, yes. I have."

"Please tell your aunt that when I told her to give herself no concern about that matter, I exactly meant what I said. To-night I received funds through the mail; the sum, twenty dollars. Your aunt," said he, obviously ready to return to his reading matter, "shall have it all."

But Sharlee had heard delinquent young men talk like that before, and her business platform in these cases was to be introduced to their funds direct.

"That would cut down the account nicely," said she, looking at him pleasantly, but a shade too hard to imply a beautiful trust. She went on much like the firm young lady enumerators who take the census: "By the way—let me ask: Have you any regular business or occupation?"

"Not, I suppose, in the sense in which you mean the interrogation."

"Perhaps you have friends in the city, who—"

"Friends! Here! Good Lord—*no!*" said he, with exasperated vehemence.

"I gather," was surprised from her, "that you do not wish—"

"They are the last thing in the world that I desire. My experience in that direction in New York quite sufficed me, I assure you. I came here," said he, with rather too blunt an implication, "to be let alone."

"I was thinking of references, you know. You have friends in New York, then?"

"Yes, I have two. But I doubt if you would regard them as serviceable for references. The best of them is only a policeman; the other is a yeggman by trade—his brother, by the way."

She was silent a moment, wondering if he were telling the truth, and deciding what to say next. The young man used the silence to bolt his coffee at a gulp and go hurriedly but deeply into the preserves.

"My aunt will be glad that you can make a remittance to-night. I will take it to her for you with pleasure."

"Oh!—All right."

He put his hand into his outer breast-pocket, pulled out an envelope, and absently pitched it across the table. She looked at it and saw that it was postmarked the city and bore a typewritten address.

"Am I to open this?"

"Oh, as you like," said he, and, removing the spoon, turned a page.

The agent picked up the envelope with anticipations of helpful clues. It was her business to find out everything that she could about Mr. Queed. A determinedly moneyless, friendless, and vocationless young man could not daily stretch his limbs under her aunt's table and retain the Third Hall Back against more compensatory guests. But the letter proved a grievous disappointment to her. Inside was a folded sheet of cheap white paper, apparently torn from a pad. Inside the sheet was a new twenty-dollar bill. That was all. Apart from the address, there was no writing anywhere.

Yet the crisp greenback, incognito though it came, indubitably suggested that Mr. Queed was not an entire stranger to the science of money-making.

"Ah," said the agent, insinuatingly, "evidently you have *some* occupation, after all—of—of a productive sort...."

He looked up again with that same air of vexed surprise, as much as to say: "What! You still hanging around!"

"I don't follow you, I fear."

"I assume that this money comes to you in payment for some—work you have done—"

"It is an assumption, certainly."

"You can appreciate, perhaps, that I am not idly inquisitive. I shouldn't—"

"What is it that you wish to know?"

"As to this money—"

"Really, you know as much about it as I do. It came exactly as I handed it to you: the envelope, the blank paper, and the bill."

"But you know, of course, where it comes from?"

"I can't say I do. Evidently," said Mr. Queed, "it is intended as a gift."

"Then—perhaps you have a good friend here after all? Some one who has guessed—"

"I think I told you that I have but two friends, and I know for a certainty that they are both in New York. Besides, neither of them would give me twenty dollars."

"But—but—but," said the girl, laughing through her utter bewilderment—"aren't you interested to know who *did* give it to you? Aren't you *curious?* I assure you that in this city it's not a bit usual to get money through the mails from anonymous admirers—"

"Nor did I say that this was a usual case. I told you that I didn't *know* who sent me this."

"Exactly—"

"But I have an idea. I think my father sent it."

"Oh! Your father ..."

So he had a father, an eccentric but well-to-do father, who, though not a friend, yet sent in twenty dollars now and then to relieve his son's necessities. Sharlee felt her heart rising.

"Don't think me merely prying. You see I am naturally interested in the question of whether you—will find yourself able to stay on here—"

"You refer to my ability to make my board payments?"

"Yes."

Throughout this dialogue, Mr. Queed had been eating, steadily and effectively. Now he slid his knife and fork into place with a pained glance at his watch; and simultaneously a change came over his face, a kind of tightening, shot through with Christian fortitude, which plainly advertised an unwelcome resolution.

"My supper allowance of time," he began warningly, "is practically up. However, I suppose the definite settlement of this board question cannot be postponed further. I must not leave you under any misapprehensions. If this money came from my father, it is the first I ever had from him in my life. Whether I am to get any more from him is problematical, to say the least. Due consideration must be given the fact that he and I have never met."

"Oh!... Does—he live here, in the city?"

"I have some reason to believe that he does. It is indeed," Mr. Queed set forth to his landlady's agent, "because of that belief that I have come here. I have assumed, with good grounds, that he would promptly make himself known to me, take charge of things, and pay my board; but though I have been here nearly a month, he has so far made not the slightest move in that direction, unless we count this letter. Possibly he leaves it to me to find him, but I, on my part, have no time to spare for any such undertaking. I make the situation clear to you? Under the circumstances I cannot promise you a steady revenue from my father. On the other hand, for all that I know, it may be his plan to send me money regularly after this."

There was a brief pause. "But—apart from the money consideration—have you no interest in finding him?"

"Oh—if that is all one asks! But it happens not to be a mere question of my personal whim. Possibly you can appreciate the fact that finding a father is a tremendous task when you have no idea where he lives, or what he looks like, or what name he may be using. My time is wholly absorbed by my own work. I have none to give to a wild-goose chase such as that, on the mere chance that, if found, he would agree to pay my board for the future."

If he had been less in earnest he would have been grotesque. As it was, Sharlee was by no means sure that he escaped it; and she could not keep a controversial note out of her voice as she said:—

"Yours must be a very great work to make you view the finding of your father in that way."

"The greatest in the world," he answered, drily. "I may call it, loosely, evolutionary sociology."

She was so silent after this, and her expression was so peculiar, that he concluded that his words conveyed nothing to her.

"The science," he added kindly, "which treats of the origin, nature, and history of human society; analyzes the relations of men in organized communities; formulates the law or laws of social progress and permanence; and correctly applies these laws to the evolutionary development of human civilization."

"I am familiar with the terms. And your ambition is to become a great evolutionary sociologist?"

He smiled faintly. "To become one?"

"Oh! Then you are one already?"

For answer, Mr. Queed dipped his hand into his inner pocket, produced a large wallet, and from a mass of papers selected a second envelope.

"You mention references. Possibly these will impress you as even better than friends."

Sharlee, seated on the arm of Major Brooke's chair, ran through the clippings: two advertisements of a well-known "heavy" review announcing articles by Mr. Queed; a table of contents torn from a year-old number of the

Political Science Quarterly to the same effect; an editorial from a New York newspaper commenting on one of these articles and speaking laudatorily of its author; a private letter from the editor of the "heavy" urging Mr. Queed to write another article on a specified subject, "Sociology and Socialism."

To Sharlee the exhibit seemed surprisingly formidable, but the wonder in her eyes was not at that. Her marvel was for the fact that the man who was capable of so cruelly elbowing little Fifi out of his way should be counted a follower of the tenderest and most human of sciences.

"They impress me," she said, returning his envelope; "but not as better than friends."

"Ah? A matter of taste. Now—"

"I had always supposed," continued the girl, looking at him, "that sociology had a close relation with life—in fact, that it was based on a conscious recognition of—the brotherhood of man."

"Your supposition is doubtless sound, though you express it so loosely."

"Yet you feel that the sociologist has no such relation?"

He glanced up sharply. At the subtly hostile look in her eyes, his expression became, for the first time, a little interested.

"How do you deduce that?"

"Oh!... It is loose, if you like—but I deduce it from what you have said—and implied—about your father and—having friends."

But what she thought of, most of all, was the case of Fifi.

She stood across the table, facing him, looking down at him; and there was a faintly heightened color in her cheeks. Her eyes were the clearest lapis lazuli, heavily fringed with lashes which were blacker than Egypt's night. Her chin was finely and strongly cut; almost a masculine chin, but unmasculinely softened by the sweetness of her mouth.

Mr. Queed eyed her with some impatience through his round spectacles.

"You apparently jumble together the theory and what you take to be the application of a science in the attempt to make an impossible unit. Hence your curious confusion. Theory and application are as totally distinct as the poles. The few must discover for the many to use. My own task—since the matter appears to interest you—is to work out the laws of human society for those who come after to practice and apply."

"And suppose those who come after feel the same unwillingness to practice and apply that you, let us say, feel?"

"It becomes the business of government to persuade them."

"And if government shirks also? What is government but the common expression of masses of individuals very much like yourself?"

"There you return, you see, to your fundamental error. There are very few individuals in the least like me. I happen to be writing a book of great importance, not to myself merely, but to posterity. If I fail to finish my book, if I am delayed in finishing it, I can hardly doubt that the world will be the loser. This is not a task like organizing a prolonged search for one's father, or dawdling with friends, which a million men can do equally well. I alone can write my book. Perhaps you now grasp my duty of concentrating all my time and energy on this single work and ruthlessly eliminating whatever interferes with it."

The girl found his incredible egoism at once amusing and extremely exasperating.

"Have you ever thought," she asked, "that thousands of other self-absorbed men have considered their own particular work of supreme importance, and that most of them have been—mistaken?"

"Really I have nothing to do with other men's mistakes. I am responsible only for my own."

"And that is why it is a temptation to suggest that conceivably you had made one here."

"But you find difficulty in suggesting such a thought convincingly? That is because I have not conceivably made any such mistake. A Harvey must discover the theory of the circulation of the blood; it is the business of lesser men to apply the discovery to practical ends. It takes a Whitney to invent the cotton gin, but the dullest negro roustabout can operate it. Why multiply illustrations of a truism? Theory, you perceive, calls for other and higher gifts than application. The man who can formulate the eternal laws of social evolution can safely leave it to others to put his laws into practice."

Sharlee gazed at him in silence, and he returned her gaze, his face wearing a look of the rankest complacence that she had ever seen upon a human countenance. But all at once his eyes fell upon his watch, and his brow clouded.

"Meantime," he went on abruptly, "there remains the question of my board."

"Yes.... Do I understand that you—derive your living from these social laws that you write up for others to practice?"

"Oh, no—impossible! There is no living to be made there. When my book comes out there may be a different story, but that is two years and ten months off. Every minute taken from it for the making of money is, as you may now understand, decidedly unfortunate. Still," he added depressedly, "I must arrange to earn something, I suppose, since my father's assistance is so problematical. I worked for money in New York, for awhile."

"Oh—did you?"

"Yes, I helped a lady write a thesaurus."

"Oh...."

"It was a mere fad with her. I virtually wrote the work for her and charged her five dollars an hour." He looked at her narrowly. "Do you happen to know of any one here who wants work of that sort done?"

The agent did not answer. By a series of covert glances she had been trying to learn, upside down, what it was that Mr. Queed was reading. "Sociology," she had easily picked out, but the chapter heading, on the opposite page, was more troublesome, and, deeply absorbed, she had now just succeeded in deciphering it. The particular division of his subject in which Mr. Queed was so much engrossed was called "Man's Duty to His Neighbors."

Struck by the silence, Sharlee looked up with a small start, and the faintest possible blush. "I beg your pardon?"

"I asked if you knew of any lady here, a wealthy one, who would like to write a thesaurus as a fad."

The girl was obliged to admit that, at the moment, she could think of no such person. But her mind fastened at once on the vulgar, hopeful fact that the unsocial socioloologist wanted a job.

"That's unfortunate," said Mr. Queed. "I suppose I must accept a little regular, very remunerative work—to settle this board question once and for all. An hour or two a day, at most. However, it is not easy to lay one's hand on such work in a strange city."

"Perhaps," said Miss Weyland slowly, "I can help you."

"I'm sure I hope so," said he with another flying glance at his watch. "That is what I have been approaching for seven minutes."

"Don't you always find it an unnecessary waste of time not to be direct?"

He sat, slightly frowning, impatiently fingering the pages of his book. The hit bounded off him like a rubber ball thrown against the Great Wall of China.

"Well?" he demanded. "What have you to propose?"

The agent sat down in a chair across the table, William Klinker's chair, and rested her chin upon her shapely little hand. The other shapely little hand toyed with the crisp twenty dollar bill, employing it to trace geometric designs upon the colored table-cloth. Mr. Queed had occasion to consult his watch again before she raised her head.

"I propose," she said, "that you apply for some special editorial work on the *Post*."

"The *Post*? The *Post*? The morning newspaper here?"

"One of them."

He laughed, actually laughed. It was a curious, slow laugh, betraying that the muscles which accomplished it were flabby for want of exercise.

"And who writes the editorials on the *Post* now?"

"A gentleman named Colonel Cowles—"

"Ah! His articles on taxation read as if they might have been written by a military man. I happened to read one the day before yesterday. It was most amusing—"

"Excuse me. Colonel Cowles is a friend of mine—"

"What has that got to do with his political economy? If he is your friend, then I should say that you have a most amusing friend."

Sharlee rose, decidedly irritated. "Well—that is my suggestion. I believe you will find it worth thinking over, Good-night."

"The *Post* pays its contributors well, I suppose?"

"That you would have to take up with its owners."

"Clearly the paper needs the services of an expert—though, of course, I could not give it much time, only enough to pay for my keep. The suggestion is not a bad one—not at all. As to applying, as you call it, is this amiable Colonel Cowles the person to be seen?"

"Yes. No—wait a minute." She had halted in her progress to the door; her mind's eye conjured up a probable interview between the Colonel and the scientist, and she hardly had the heart to let it go at that. Moreover, she earnestly wished, for Mrs. Paynter's reasons, that the tenant of the third hall back should become associated with the pay-envelope system of the city. "Listen," she went on. "I know one of the directors of the *Post*, and shall be glad to speak to him in your behalf. Then, if there is an opening, I'll send you, through my aunt, a card of introduction to him and you can go to see him."

"Couldn't he come to see me? I am enormously busy."

"So is he. I doubt if you could expect him to—"

"H'm. Very well. I am obliged to you for your suggestion. Of course I shall take no step in the matter until I hear from you."

"Good-evening," said the agent, icily.

He bowed slightly in answer to the salute, uttering no further word; for him the interview ended right there, cleanly and satisfactorily. From the door the girl glanced back. Mr. Queed had drawn his heavy book before him, pencil in hand, and was once more engrossed in the study and annotation of "Man's Duty to His Neighbors."

In the hall Sharlee met Fifi, who was tipping toward the dining-room to discover, by the frank method of ear and keyhole, how the grim and resolute collector was faring.

"You're still alive, Sharlee! Any luck?"

"The finest in the world, darling! Twenty dollars in the hand and a remunerative job for him in the bush."

Fifi did a few steps of a minuet. "Hooray!" said she in her weak little voice.

Sharlee put her arms around the child's neck and said in her ear: "Fifi, be very gentle with that young man. He's the most pitiful little creature I ever saw."

"Why," said Fifi, "I don't think he feels that way at all—"

"Don't you see that's just what makes him so infinitely pathetic? He's the saddest little man in the world, and it has never dawned on him."

It was not till some hours later, when she was making ready for bed in her own room, that it occurred to Sharlee that there was something odd in this advice to her little cousin. For she had started out with the intention to tell Mr. Queed that he must be very gentle with Fifi.

CHAPTER IV

*Relating how Two Stars in their Courses fought for Mr. Queed;
and how he accepted Remunerative Employment under Colonel
Cowles, the Military Political Economist.*

The stars in their courses fought for Mr. Queed in those days. Somebody had to fight for him, it seemed, since he was so little equipped to fight for himself, and the stars kindly undertook the assignment. Not merely had he attracted the militant services of the bright little celestial body whose earthly agent was Miss Charlotte Lee Weyland; but this little body chanced to be one of a system or galaxy, associated with and exercising a certain power, akin to gravitation, over that strong and steady planet known among men as Charles Gardiner West. And the very next day, the back of the morning's mail being broken, the little star used some of its power to draw the great planet to the telephone, while feeling, in a most unstellar way, that it was a decidedly cheeky thing to do. However, nothing could have exceeded the charming radiance of Planet West, and it was he himself who introduced the topic of Mr. Queed, by inquiring, in mundane language, whether or not he had been fired.

"No!" laughed the star. "Instead of firing him, I'm now bent on *hiring* him. Oh, you'd better not laugh! It's to you I want to hire him!"

But at that the shining Planet laughed the more.

"What have I done to be worthy of this distinction? Also, what can I do with him? To paraphrase his own inimitable remark about your dog, what is the object of a man like that? What is he for?"

Sharlee dilated on the renown of Mr. Queed as a writer upon abstruse themes. Mr. West was not merely agreeable; he was interested. It seemed that at the very last meeting of the *Post* directors—to which body Mr. West had been elected at the stockholders' meeting last June—it had been decided that Colonel Cowles should have a little help in the editorial department. The work was growing; the Colonel was ageing. The point had been to find the help. Who knew but what this little highbrow was the very man they were looking for?

"I'll call on him—at your aunt's, shall I?—to-day if I can. Why, not a bit of it! The thanks are quite the other way. He may turn out another Charles A. Dana, cleverly disguised. When are you going to have another half-holiday up there?"

Sharlee left the telephone thinking that Mr. West was quite the nicest man she knew. Ninety-nine men out of a hundred, in his position, would have said, "Send him to see me." Mr. West had said, "I'll call on him at your aunt's," and had absolutely refused to pose as the gracious dispenser of patronage. However, a great many people shared Sharlee's opinion of Charles Gardiner West. One of them walked into his office at that very moment, also petitioning for something, and West received him with just that same unaffected pleasantness of manner which everybody found so agreeable. But this one's business, as it happened, completely knocked from Mr. West's head the matter of Mr. Queed. In fact, he never gave it another thought. The following night he went to New York with a little party of friends, chiefly on pleasure bent; and, having no particularly frugal mind, permitted himself a very happy day or so in the metropolis. Hence it happened that Sharlee, learning from her aunt that no Post directors had called forcing remunerative work on Mr. Queed, made it convenient, about five days after the telephone conversation, to meet Mr. West upon the street, quite by accident. Any girl can tell you how it is done.

"Oh, by the way," she said in the most casual way, "shall I send my little Doctor Queed to call upon you some day?"

West was agreeably contrite; abused himself for a shiftless lackwit who was slated for an unwept grave; promised to call that very day; and, making a memorandum the instant he got back to the office, this time did not fail to keep his word.

Not that Mr. Queed had been inconvenienced by the little delay. The minute after his landlady's agent left him, he had become immersed in that great work of his, and there by day and night, he had remained. Having turned over to the agent the full responsibility for finding work for him, he no longer had to bother his head about it. The whole matter dropped gloriously from his mind; he read, wrote, and avoided practicing sociology with tremendous industry; and thus he might have gone on for no one knows how long had there not, at five o'clock on the fifth day, come a knock upon his door.

"Well?" he called, annoyed.

Emma came in with a card. The name, at which the young man barely glanced, conveyed nothing to him.

"Well? What does he want?"

Emma did not know.

"Oh!" said Mr. Queed, irritably—"tell him to come up, if he must."

The *Post* director came up—two flights; he knocked; was curtly bidden to enter; did so.

He stepped into one of the smallest rooms he had ever seen in his life; about nine by five-and-a-half, he thought. A tiny single bed ran along one side of it; jammed against the foot of the bed was a tiny table. A tiny chair stood at the table; behind the chair stood a tiny bureau; beside the bureau, the tiniest little iron wash-stand in the world. In the chair sat a man, not tiny, indeed, but certainly nobody's prize giant. He sat in a kind of whirling tempest of books and papers, and he rode absorbedly in the whirlwind and majestically directed the storm.

West was intensely interested. "Mr. Queed?" he asked, from just inside the door.

"Yes," said the other, not looking up. "What can I do for you?"

West burst out laughing; he couldn't help it.

"Maybe you can do a great deal, Mr. Queed. On the other hand maybe I can do some little trifle for you. Which leg the boot is on nobody on earth can say at this juncture. I have ventured to call," said he, "as an ambassador from the morning *Post* of this city."

"The *Post*?"

The name instantly started Queed's memory to working; he recalled something about the *Post*—as yet, so it happened, only the copy of it he had read; and he turned and looked around with slow professorial amusement kindling in his eyes.

"Ah!" said he. "Possibly you are Colonel Cowles, the military political economist?"

West was more amused than ever. "No," said he, "on the contrary, West is the name, C.G. West—to correspond, you know, with the one on that card you have in your hand. I'll sit down here on the bed—shall I?—so that we can talk more comfortably. Sitting does help the flow of ideas so remarkably, don't you find? I am trespassing on your time," said he, "at the suggestion of—an acquaintance of yours, who has been telling me great things about your work."

Queed looked completely puzzled.

"The *Post*, Mr. Queed," went on West agreeably, "is always looking for men who can do exceptional work. Therefore, I have come to consider with you whether we might not make an arrangement to our mutual advantage."

At that the whole thing came back to the young man. He had agreed to take light remunerative work to pay his board, and now the day of reckoning was at hand. His heart grew heavy within him.

"Well," said he, exactly as he had said to the agent, "what have you to propose?"

"I thought of proposing, first, that you give me some idea of what you have done and can do on lines useful for a daily newspaper. How does that method of procedure strike you?"

Queed produced his celebrated envelope of clippings. Also he hunted up one or two stray cuttings which proved to be editorials he had written on assignment, for a New York newspaper. West ran through them with intelligent quickness.

"I say! These are rather fine, you know. This article on the income tax now—just right!—just the sort of thing!"

Queed sat with his hand clamped on his head, which was aching rather badly, as indeed it did about three fourths of the time.

"Oh, yes," he said wearily.

"I take off my hat to you!" added West presently. "You're rather out of my depth here, but at least I know enough political economy to know what is good."

He looked at Queed, smiling, very good-humored and gay, and Queed looked back at him, not very good-humored and anything but gay. Doubtless it would have surprised the young Doctor very much to know that West was feeling sorry for him just then, for at that moment he was feeling sorry for West.

"Now look here," said West.

He explained how the *Post* desired a man to write sleep-inducing fillers—"occasional articles of weight and authority" was the way he put it—and wanted to know if such an opening would interest Mr. Queed. Queed said he supposed so, provided the *Post* took little of his time and paid his board in return for it. West had no doubt that everything could be satisfactorily arranged.

"Colonel Cowles is the man who hires and fires," he explained. "Go to see him in a day or two, will you? Meantime, I'll tell him all about you."

Presently West smiled himself out, leaving Queed decidedly relieved at the brief reprieve. He had been harried by the fear that his visitor would insist on his stopping to produce an article or so while he waited. However, the time had come when the inevitable had to be faced. His golden privacy must be ravished for the grim god of bread and meat. The next afternoon he put on his hat with a bad grace, and went forth to seek Colonel Cowles, editor-in-chief of the leading paper in the State.

The morning *Post* was an old paper, which had been in the hands of a single family from A.D. 1846 till only the other day. It had been a power during the war, a favorite mouthpiece of President Davis. It had stood like a wall during the cruelties of Reconstruction; had fought the good fight for white man's rule; had crucified carpet-baggism and scalawaggery upon a cross of burning adjective. Later it had labored gallantly for Tilden; denounced Hayes as a robber; idolized Cleveland; preached free trade with pure passion; swallowed free silver; stood "regular," though not without grimaces, through Bryanism. The *Post* was, in short, a paper with an honorable history, and everybody felt a kind of affection for it. The plain fact remained, however, that within recent years a great many worthy persons had acquired the habit of reading the more hustling *State*.

The *Post*, not to put too fine a point upon it, had for a time run fast to seed. The third generation of its owners had lost their money, mostly in land speculations in the suburbs of New York City, and in the State of Oregon. You could have thrown a brick from their office windows and hit far better land speculations, but they had the common fault of believing that things far away from home are necessarily and always the best. The demand rose for bigger, fatter newspapers, with comic sections and plenty of purple ink, and the *Post's* owners found themselves unable to supply it. In fact they had to retort by mortgaging their property to the hilt and cutting expenses to rock-bottom. These were dark days for the *Post*. That it managed to survive them at all was due chiefly to the personality of Colonel Cowles, who, though doubtless laughable as a political economist, was yet considered to have his good points. But the Hercules-labor grew too heavy even for him, and the paper was headed straight for the auctioneer's block when new interests suddenly stepped in and bought it. These interests, consisting largely of progressive men of the younger generation, thoroughly overhauled and reorganized the property, laid in the needed purple ink, and were now gradually driving the old paper back to the dividend-paying point again.

Colonel Cowles, whose services had, of course, been retained, was of the old school of journalism, editor and manager, too. Very little went into the *Post* that he had not personally viséd in the proof: forty galleys a night were child's play to him. Managing editor there was none but himself; the city editor was his mere office-boy and mouthpiece; even the august business manager, who mingled with great advertisers on equal terms, was known to take orders from him. In addition the Colonel wrote three columns of editorials every day. Of these editorials it is enough to say at this point that there were people who liked them.

Toward this dominant personality, the reluctant applicant for work now made his way. He cut an absent-minded figure upon the street, did Mr. Queed, but this time he made his crossings without mishap. Undisturbed by dogs, he landed at the *Post* building, and in time blundered into a room described as "Editorial" on the glass-door. A friendly young girl sitting there, pounding away on a typewriter, referred him to the next office, and the young man, opening the connecting door without knocking, passed inside.

A full-bodied, gray-headed, gray-mustached man sat in his shirt-sleeves behind a great table, writing with a very black pencil in a large sprawling hand. He glanced up as the door opened.

"Colonel Cowles?"

"I am the man, sir. How may I serve you?"

Queed laid on the table the card West had given him with a pencilled line of introduction.

"Oh—Mr. Queed! Certainly—certainly. Sit down, sir. I have been expecting you.—Let me get those papers out of your way."

Colonel Cowles had a heavy jaw and rather too rubicund a complexion. He looked as if apoplexy would get him some day. However, his head was like a lion's of the tribe of Judah; his eye was kindly; his manner dignified, courteous, and charming. Queed had decided not to set the Colonel right in his views on taxation; it would mean only a useless discussion which would take time. To the older gentleman's polite inquiries relative to his impressions of the city and so forth, he for the same reason gave the briefest possible replies. But the Colonel, no apostle of the doctrine that time is far more than money, went off into a long monologue, kindly designed to give the young stranger some idea of his new surroundings and atmosphere.

"... Look out there, sir. It is like that all day long—a double stream of people always pouring by. I have looked out of these windows for twenty-five years, and it was very different in the old days. I remember when the cows used to come tinkling down around that corner at milking-time. A twelve-story office building will rise there before another year. We have here the finest city and the finest State in the Union. You come to them, sir, at a time of exceptional interest. We are changing fast, leaping forward very fast.

I do not hold with those who take all change to be progress, but God grant that our feet are set in the right path. No section of the country is moving more rapidly, or, as I believe, with all our faults, to better ends than this. My own eyes have seen from these windows a broken town, stagnant in trade and population and rich only in memories, transform itself into the splendid thriving city you see before you. Our faces, too long turned backward, are set at last toward the future. From one end of the State to another the spirit of honorable progress is throbbing through our people. We have revolutionized and vastly improved our school system. We have wearied of mud-holes and are laying the foundations of a network of splendid roads. We are doing wonders for the public health. Our farmers are learning to practice the new agriculture—with plenty of lime, sir, plenty of lime. They grasp the fact that corn at a hundred bushels to the acre is no dream, but the most vital of realities. Our young men who a generation ago left us for the irrigated lands of your Northwest, are at last understanding that the finest farmlands in the country are at their doors for half the price. With all these changes has come a growing independence in political thought. The old catchwords and bogies have lost their power. We no longer think that whatever wears the Democratic tag is necessarily right. We no longer measure every Republican by Henry G. Surface. We no longer ..."

Queed, somewhat interested in spite of himself, and tolerably familiar with history, interrupted to ask who Henry G. Surface might be. The question brought the Colonel up with a jolt.

"Ah, well," said he presently, with a wave of his hand, "you will hear that story soon enough." He was silent a moment, and then added, sadly and somewhat sternly: "Young man, I have reserved one count in the total, the biggest and best, for the last. Keep your ear and eye open—and I mean the inner ear and eye as well as the outer—keep your mind open, above all keep your heart open, and it will be given you to understand that we have here the bravest, the sweetest, and the kindliest people in the world. The Lord has been good to you to send you among them. This is the word of a man in the late evening of life to one in the hopeful morning. You will take it, I hope, without offense. Are you a Democrat, sir?"

"I am a political economist."

The Colonel smiled. "Well said, sir. Science knows no party lines. Your chosen subject rises above the valley of partisanry where we old wheel-horses plod—stinging each other in the dust, as the poet finely says. Mr. West has told me of your laurels."

He went on to outline the business side of what the *Post* had to offer. Queed found himself invited to write a certain number of editorial articles, not to exceed six a week, under the Colonel's direction. He had his choice of working on space, at the rate of five dollars per column, payment dependent upon publication; or of drawing a fixed honorarium of ten dollars per week, whether called on for the stipulated six articles or for no articles at all. Queed decided to accept the fixed honorarium, hoping that there would be many weeks when he would be called on for no articles at all. A provisional arrangement to run a month was agreed upon.

"I have," said the Colonel, "already sketched out some work for you to begin on. The legislature meets here in January. It is important to the State that our whole tax-system should be overhauled and reformed. The present system is a mere crazy-quilt, unsatisfactory in a thousand ways. I suggest that you begin with a careful study of the law, making yourself familiar with—"

"I am already familiar with it."

"Ah! And what do you think of it?"

"It is grotesque."

"Good! I like a clean-cut expression of opinion such as that, sir. Now tell me your criticisms on the law as it stands, and what you suggest as remedies."

Queed did so briefly, expertly. The Colonel was considerably impressed by his swift, searching summaries.

"We may go right ahead," said he. "I wish you would block out a series of articles—eight, ten, or twelve, as you think best—designed to prepare the public mind for a thorough-going reform and point the way that the reform should take. Bring this schedule to me to-morrow, if you will be so good, and we will go over it together."

Queed, privately amused at the thought of Colonel Cowles's revising his views on taxation, rose to go.

"By the bye," said the Colonel, unluckily struck by a thought, "I myself wrote a preliminary article on tax reform a week or so ago, meaning to follow it up with others later on. Perhaps you had best read that before—"

"I have already read it."

"Ah! How did it strike you?"

"You ask me that?"

"Certainly," said Colonel Cowles, a little surprised.

"Well, since you ask me, I will say that I thought it rather amusing."

The Colonel looked nettled. He was by nature a choleric man, but in his age he had learned the futility of disputation and affray, and nowadays kept a tight rein upon himself.

"You are frank sir—'tis a commendable quality. Doubtless your work will put my own poor efforts to the blush."

"I shall leave you to judge of that, Colonel Cowles."

The Colonel, abandoning his hospitable plan of inviting his new assistant to sup with him at the club, bowed with dignity, and Queed eagerly left him. Glancing at his watch in the elevator, the young man figured that the interview, including going and coming, would stand him in an hour's time, which was ten minutes more than he had allowed for it.

CHAPTER V

Selections from Contemporary Opinions of Mr. Queed; also concerning Henry G. Surface, his Life and Deeds; of Fifi, the Landlady's Daughter, and how she happened to look up Altruism in the Dictionary.

A month later, one icy afternoon, Charles Gardiner West ran into Colonel Cowles at the club, where the Colonel, a lone widower, repaired each day at six P.M., there to talk over the state of the Union till nine-thirty.

"Colonel," said West, dropping into a chair, "man to man, what is your opinion of Doctor Queed's editorials?"

"They are unanswerable," said the Colonel, and consulted his favorite ante-prandial refreshment.

West laughed. "Yes, but from the standpoint of the general public, Constant Reader, Pro Bono Publico, and all that?"

"No subscriber will ever be angered by them."

"Would you say that they helped the editorial page or not?"

"They lend to it an academic elegance, a scientific stateliness, a certain grand and austere majesty—"

"Colonel, I asked you for your opinion of those articles."

"Damn it, sir," roared the Colonel, "I've never read one."

Later West repeated the gist of this conversation to Miss Weyland, who ornamented with him a tiny dinner given that evening at the home of their very good friends, Mr. and Mrs. Stewart Byrd.

It was a beautiful little dinner, as befitted the hospitable distinction of the givers. The Stewart Byrds were hosts among a thousand. In him, as it further happens, West (himself the beau ideal of so many) had from long ago recognized his own paragon and pattern; a worthy one, indeed, this tall young man whose fine abilities and finer faiths were already writing his name so large upon the history of his city. About the dim-lit round of his table there were gathered but six this evening, including the host and hostess; the others, besides Sharlee Weyland and West, being Beverley Byrd and Miss Avery: the youngest of the four Byrd brothers, and heir with them to one of the largest fortunes in the State; and the only daughter of old Avery, who came to us from Mauch Chunk, Pa., his money preceding him in a special train of box cars, especially invented for the transportation of Pennsylvania millions to places where the first families congregate.

"And I had to confess that I'd never read one either. I did begin one," said West—"it was called 'Elementary Principles of Incidence and Distribution,' I remember—but the hour was eleven-thirty and I fell asleep."

"I know exactly how you felt about it," said Sharlee, "for I have read them all—*moi!*"

He looked at her with boundless admiration. "His one reader!"

"There are two of us, if you please. I think of getting up a club—Associated Sons and Daughters of Mr. Queed's Faithful Followers; President, Me. I'll make the other member Secretary, for he is experienced in that work. He's at present Secretary of the Tax Reform League in New York. Did Colonel Cowles show you the wonderful letter that came from him, asking the name of the man who was writing the *Post's* masterly tax articles, et cetera, et cetera?"

"No—really! But tell me, how have you, as President, enjoyed them?"

"I haven't understood a single word in any of them. Where on earth did he dig up his fearful vocabulary? Yet it is the plain duty of both of us to read these articles: you as one of his employers, I as the shrewd landlady's agent who keeps a watchful eye upon the earning power of her boarders."

West mused. "He has a wonderful genius for crushing all the interest out of any subject he touches, hasn't he? Yet manifestly the first duty of an editorial is to get itself read. How old do you think he is?"

"Oh—anywhere from twenty-five to—forty-seven."

"He'll be twenty-four this month. I see him sometimes at the office, you know, where he still treats me like an intrusive subscription agent. In some ways, he is undoubtedly the oldest man in the world. In another way he hasn't any age at all. Spiritually he is unborn—he simply doesn't exist at all. I diagnose his complaint as ingrowing egoism of a singularly virulent variety."

It was beyond Sharlee's power to controvert this diagnosis. Mr. Queed had in fact impressed her as the most frankly and grossly self-centred person she had ever seen in her life. But unlike West, her uppermost feeling in regard to him was a strong sense of pity. She knew things about his life that

West did not know and probably never would. For though the little Doctor of Mrs. Paynter's had probably not intended to give her a confidence, and certainly had no right to do so, she had thus regarded what he said to her in the dining-room that night, and of his pathetic situation in regard to a father she never meant to say a word to anybody.

"I sized him up for a remarkable man," said she, "when I saw the wonderful way he sat upon his hat that afternoon. Don't you remember? He struck me then as the most natural, unconscious, and direct human being I ever saw—don't you think that?—and now think of his powers of concentration. All his waking time, except what he gives to the *Post*, goes to that awful book of his. He is ridiculous now because his theory of life is ridiculous. But suppose it popped into his head some day to switch all that directness and concentrated energy in some other direction. Don't you think he might be rather a formidable young person?"

West conceded that there might be something in that. And happening to glance across the flower-sweet table at the moment, he was adroitly detached and re-attached by the superbly "finished" Miss Avery.

The little dinner progressed. Nor was this the only spot in town where evening meals were going forward amid stimulating talk. Far away over the town, at the same hour, the paying guests of Mrs. Paynter's were gathered about her hospitable board, plying the twin arts of supping and talking. And as Sharlee's fellow-diners talked of Mr. Queed, it chanced that Mr. Queed's fellow-suppers were talking of Sharlee, or at any rate of her family's famous misfortune. Mr. Queed, it is true, did not appreciate this fact, for the name of the female agent who had taken his Twenty from him could not have been more unknown to him if she had been a dweller in Phrygia or far Cappadocia.

Major Brooke told, not by request, one of his well-known stories about how he had flouted and routed the Republicans in 1875. The plot of these stories was always the same, but the setting shifted about here and there, and this one had to do with a county election in which, the Major said, the Republicans and negroes had gone the limit trying to swindle the Democrats out of the esteemed offices.

"And I said, 'You'—the ladies will excuse me, I'm sure—'You lying rascal,' s' I, 'don't you dare to contradict me! You're all tarred with the same pitch,' s' I. 'Everything you touch turns corrupt and rotten. Look at Henry G. Surface,' s' I. 'The finest fellow God ever made, till the palsied hand of Republicanism fell upon him, and now cankering and rotting in jail—'"

"But Henry G. Surface wasn't rotting in jail in 1875," said William Klinker, and boldly winked at the little Doctor.

The Major, disconcerted for an instant by his anachronism, recovered superbly. "My vision, sir, was prophetic. The stain was upon him. The cloven foot had already been betrayed...."

"And who was Henry G. Surface?" inquired Mr. Queed.

"What! You haven't heard that infamous story!" cried the Major, with the surprised delight of the inveterate raconteur who has unexpectedly stumbled upon an audience.

A chair-leg scraped, and Professor Nicolovius was standing, bowing in his sardonic way to Mrs. Paynter.

"Since I have happened to hear it often, madam, through Major Brooke's tireless kindness, you will perhaps be so good as to excuse me."

And he stalked out of the room, head up, his auburn goatee stabbing the atmosphere before him, in rather a heavy silence.

"Pish!" snapped the Major, when the door had safely shut. And tapping his forehead significantly, he gave his head a few solemn wags and launched upon the worn biography of Henry G. Surface.

Tattered with much use as the story is, and was, the boarders listened with a perennial interest while Major Brooke expounded the familiar details. His wealth of picturesque language we may safely omit, and briefly remind the student of the byways of history how Henry G. Surface found himself, during the decade following Appomattox, with his little world at his feet. He was thirty at the time, handsome, gifted, high-spirited, a brilliant young man who already stood high in the councils of the State. But he was also restless in disposition, arrogant, over-weeningly vain, and ambitious past all belief—"a yellow streak in him, and we didn't know it!" bellowed the Major. Bitterly chagrined by his failure to secure, from a legislature of the early seventies, the United States Senatorship which he had confidently expected, young Surface, in a burst of anger and resentment, committed the unforgivable sin. He went over bag and baggage to the other side, to the "nigger party" whom all his family, friends, and relations, all his "class," everybody else with his instincts and traditions, were desperately struggling, by hook and by crook, to crush.

In our mild modern preferences as between presidents, or this governor and that, we catch no reminiscence of the fierce antagonisms of the elections of reconstruction days. The idolized young tribune of the people became a Judas Iscariot overnight, with no silver pieces as the price of his apostasy.

If he expected immediate preferment from the other camp, he was again bitterly disappointed. Life meantime had become unbearable to him. He was ostracized more studiously than any leper; it is said that his own father cut him when they passed each other in the street. His young wife died, heartbroken, it was believed, by the flood of hatred and vilification that poured in upon her husband. One man alone stood by Surface in his downfall, his classmate and friend of his bosom from the cradle, John Randolph Weyland, a good man and a true. Weyland's affection never faltered. When Surface withdrew from the State with a heart full of savage rancor, Weyland went every year or two to visit him, first in Chicago and later in New York, where the exile was not slow in winning name and fortune as a daring speculator. And when Weyland died, leaving a widow and infant daughter, he gave a final proof of his trust by making Surface sole trustee of his estate, which was a large one for that time and place. Few have forgotten how the political traitor rewarded this misplaced confidence. The crash came within a few months. Surface was arrested in the company of a woman whom he referred to as his wife. The trust fund, saving a fraction, was gone, swallowed up to stay some ricketty deal. Surface was convicted of embezzlement and sentenced to ten years at hard labor, and every Democrat in the State cried, "I told you so." What had become of him after his release from prison, nobody knew; some of the boarders said that he was living in the west, or in Australia; others, that he was not living anywhere, unless on the shores of perpetual torment. All agreed that the alleged second Mrs. Surface had long since died—all, that is, but Klinker, who said that she had only pretended to die in order to make a fade-away with the gate receipts. For many persons believed, it seemed, that Surface, by clever juggling of his books, had managed to "hold out" a large sum of money in the enforced settlement of his affairs. At any rate, very little of it ever came back to the family of the man who had put trust in him, and that was why the daughter, whose name was Charlotte Lee Weyland, now worked for her daily bread.

That Major Brooke's hearers found this story of evergreen interest was natural enough. For besides the brilliant blackness of the narrative, there was the close personal connection that all Paynterites had with some of its chief personages. Did not the sister-in-law of John Randolph Weyland sit and preside over them daily, pouring their coffee morning and night with her own hands? And did not the very girl whose fortune had been stolen, the bereft herself, come now and then to sit among them, occupying that identical chair which Mr. Bylash could touch by merely putting out his hand? Henry G. Surface's story? Why, Mrs. Paynter's wrote it!

These personal bearings were of course lost upon Mr. Queed, the name Weyland being utterly without significance to him. He left the table the moment he had absorbed all the supper he wanted. In the hall he ran upon Professor Nicolovius, the impressive-looking master of Greek at Milner's Collegiate School, who, already hatted and overcoated, was drawing on his gloves under the depressed fancy chandelier. The old professor glanced up at the sound of footsteps and favored Queed with a bland smile.

"I can't resist taking our doughty swashbuckler down a peg or two every now and then," said he. "Did you ever know such an interminable ass?"

"Really, I never thought about it," said the young man, raising his eyebrows in surprise and annoyance at being addressed.

"Then take my word for it. You'll not find his match in America. You show your wisdom, at any rate, in giving as little of your valuable time as possible to our charming supper-table."

"That hardly argues any Solomonic wisdom, I fancy."

"You're in the hands of the Philistines here, Mr. Queed," said Nicolovius, snapping his final button. "May I say that I have read some of your editorials in the *Post* with—ah—pleasure and profit? I should feel flattered if you would come to see me in my room some evening, where I can offer you, at any rate, a fire and a so-so cigar."

"Thank you. However, I do not smoke," said Doctor Queed, and, bowing coldly to the old professor, started rapidly up the stairs.

Aloft the young man went to his scriptorium, happy in the thought that five hours of incorruptible leisure and unswerving devotion to his heart's dearest lay before him. It had been a day when the *Post* did not require him; hour by hour since breakfast he had fared gloriously upon his book. But to-night his little room was cold; unendurably cold; not even the flamings of genius could overcome its frigor; and hardly half an hour had passed before he became aware that his sanctum was altogether uninhabitable. Bitterly he faced the knowledge that he must fare forth into the outer world of the dining-room that night; irritably he gathered up his books and papers.

Half-way down the first flight a thought struck Queed, and he retraced his steps. The last time that he had been compelled to the dining-room the landlady's daughter had been there—(it was all an accident, poor child! Hadn't she vowed to herself never to intrude on the little Doctor again?)— and, stupidly breaking the point of her pencil, had had the hardihood to ask him for the loan of his knife. Mr. Queed was determined that this sort of thing should not occur again. A method for enforcing his determination, at once firm and courteous, had occurred to him. One could never tell when trespassers would stray into the dining-room—his dining-room by right of his exalted claim. Rummaging in his bottom bureau drawer, he produced a placard, like a narrow little sign-board, and tucking it under his arm, went on downstairs.

The precaution was by no means superfluous. Disgustingly enough the landlady's daughter was once more in his dining-room before him, the paraphernalia of her algebra spread over half the Turkey-red cloth. Fifi looked up, plainly terrified at his entrance and his forbidding expression. It was her second dreadful blunder, poor luckless little wight! She had faithfully waited a whole half-hour, and Mr. Queed had shown no signs of coming down. Never had he waited so long as this when he meant to claim the dining-room. Mrs. Paynter's room, nominally heated by a flume from the Latrobe heater in the parlor, was noticeably coolish on a wintry night. Besides, there was no table in it, and everybody knows that algebra is hard enough under the most favorable conditions, let alone having to do it on your knee. It seemed absolutely safe; Fifi had yielded to the summons of the familiar comforts; and now—

"Oh—how do you do?" she was saying in a frightened voice.

Mr. Queed bowed, indignantly. Silently he marched to his chair, the one just opposite, and sat down in offended majesty. To Fifi it seemed that to get up at once and leave the room, which she would gladly have done, would be too crude a thing to do, too gross a rebuke to the little Doctor's Ego. She was wrong, of course, though her sensibilities were indubitably right. Therefore she feigned enormous engrossment in her algebra, and struggled to make herself as small and inoffensive as she could.

The landlady's daughter wore a Peter Thompson suit of blue serge, which revealed a few inches of very thin white neck. She was sixteen and reddish-haired, and it was her last year at the High School. The reference is to Fifi's completion of the regular curriculum, and not to any impending promotion to a still Higher School. She was a fond, uncomplaining little thing, who had never hurt anybody's feelings in her life, and her eyes, which were light blue, had just that look of ethereal sweetness you see in Burne-Jones's women and for just that same reason. Her syrup she took with commendable faithfulness; the doctor, in rare visits, spoke cheerily of the time when she was to be quite strong and well again; but there were moments when Sharlee Weyland, looking at her little cousin's face in repose, felt her heart stop still.

Fifi dallied with her algebra, hoping and praying that she would not *have* to cough. She had been very happy all that day. There was no particular reason for it; so it was the nicest kind of happiness, the kind that comes from inside, which even the presence of the little Doctor could not take away from her. Heaven knew that Fifi harbored no grudge against Mr. Queed, and she had not forgotten what Sharlee said about being gentle with him. But how to be gentle with so austere a young Socrates? Raising her head upon the pretext of turning a page, Fifi stole a hurried glance at him.

The first thing Mr. Queed had done on sitting down was to produce his placard, silently congratulating himself on having brought it. Selecting the book which he would be least likely to need, he shoved it well forward, nearly halfway across the table, and against the volume propped up his little pasteboard sign, the printed part staring straight toward Fifi. The sign was an old one which he had chanced to pick up years ago at the Astor Library. It read:

SILENCE

Arch-type and model of courteous warning!

When Fifi read the little Doctor's sign, her feelings were not in the least wounded, insufficiently subtle though some particular people might have thought its admonition to be. On the contrary, it was only by the promptest work in getting her handkerchief into her mouth that she avoided laughing out loud. The two of them alone in the room and his *Silence* sign gazing at her like a pasteboard Gorgon!

Fifi became more than ever interested in Mr. Queed. An intense and strictly feminine curiosity filled her soul to know something of the nature of that work which demanded so stern a noiselessness. Observing rigorously the printed Rule of the Dining-Room, she could not forbear to pilfer glance after glance at the promulgator of it. Mr. Queed was writing, not reading, to-night. He wrote very slowly on half-size yellow pads, worth seventy-five cents a dozen, using the books only for reference. Now he tore off a sheet only partly filled with his small handwriting, and at the head of a new sheet inscribed a Roman numeral, with a single word under that. Like her cousin Sharlee at an earlier date, Fifi experienced a desire to study out, upside down, what this heading was. Several peeks were needed, with artful attention to algebra between whiles, before she was at last convinced that she had it. Undoubtedly it was

XVIII

ALTRUISM

There was nothing enormous about Fifi's vocabulary, but she well knew what to do in a case like this. Behind her stood a battered little walnut bookcase, containing the Paynter library. After a safe interval of absorption in her sums, she pushed back her chair with the most respectful quietude and pulled out a tall volume. The pages of it she turned with blank studious face but considerable inner expectancy: Af—Ai—Al—Alf....

A giggle shattered the academic calm, and Fifi, in horror, realized that she was the author of it. She looked up quickly, and her worst fears were realized. Mr. Queed was staring at her, as one scarcely able to credit his own senses, icy rebuke piercing through and overflowing his great round spectacles.

"I beg your pardon!—Mr. Queed. It—it slipped out, really—"

But the young man thought that the time had come when this question of noise in his dining-room must be settled once and for all.

"Indeed? Be kind enough to explain the occasion of it."

"Why," said Fifi, too truthful to prevaricate and completely cowed, "it—it was only the meaning of a word here. It—was silly of me. I—I can't explain it—exactly—"

"Suppose you try. Since your merriment interrupts my work, I claim the privilege of sharing it."

"Well! I—I—happened to see that word at the head of the page you are writing—"

"Proceed."

"I—I looked it up in the dictionary. It *says*," she read out with a gulp and a cough, "it means 'self-sacrificing devotion to the interests of others.'"

The poor child thought her point must now be indelicately plain, but the lips of Doctor Queed merely emitted another close-clipped: "Proceed."

At a desperate loss as she was, Fifi was suddenly visited by an idea. "Oh! I see. You're—you're writing *against* altruism, aren't you?"

"What leads you to that conclusion, if I may ask?"

"Why—I—I suppose it's the—way you—you do. Of course I oughtn't to have said it—"

"Go on. What way that I do?"

Poor Fifi saw that she was floundering in ever more deeply. With the boldness of despair she blurted out: "Well—one thing—you sent me out of the room that night—when I coughed, you know. I—I don't understand about altruism like you do, but I—should think it was—my interests to stay here—"

There followed a brief silence, which made Fifi more miserable than any open rebuke, and then Mr. Queed said in a dry tone: "I am engaged upon a work of great importance to the public, I may say to posterity. Perhaps you can appreciate that such a work is entitled to the most favorable conditions in which to pursue it."

"Of course. Indeed I understand perfectly, Mr. Queed," said Fifi, immediately touched by what seemed like kindness from him. And she added innocently: "All men—writing men, I mean—feel that way about their work—I suppose. I remember Mr. Sutro who used to have the very same room you're in now. He was writing a five-act play, all in poetry, to show the horrors of war, and he used to say—"

The young man involuntarily shuddered. "I have nothing to do with other men. I am thinking," he said with rather an unfortunate choice of words, "only of myself."

"Oh—I see! Now I understand exactly!"

"What is it that you see and understand so exactly?"

"Why, the way you feel about altruism. You believe in it for other people, but not for yourself! Isn't that right?"

They stared across the table at each other: innocent Fifi, who barely knew the meaning of altruism, but had practiced it from the time she could practice anything, and the little Doctor, who knew everything about altruism that social science would ever formulate, and had stopped right there. All at once, his look altered; from objective it became subjective. The question seemed suddenly to hook onto something inside, like a still street-car gripping hold of a cable and beginning to move; the mind's eye of the young man appeared to be seized and swept inward. Presently without a word he resumed his writing.

Fifi was much disturbed at the effect of her artless question, and just when everything was beginning to go so nicely too. In about half an hour, when she got up to retire, she said timidly:—

"I'm sorry if I—I was rude just now, Mr. Queed. Indeed, I didn't mean to be...."

"I did not say that you were rude," he answered without looking up.

But at the door Fifi was arrested by his voice.

"Why do you think it to your advantage to work in here?"

"It's—it's a good deal warmer, you know," said Fifi, flustered, "and—then of course there's the table and lamp. But it's quite all right upstairs—really!"

He made no answer.

CHAPTER VI

Autobiographical Data imparted, for Sound Business Reasons, to a Landlady's Agent; of the Agent's Other Title, etc.

While all move in slots in this world, Mr. Queed's slot was infinitely more clearly marked than any of his neighbors'. It ran exclusively between the heaven of his room and the hades of the *Post* office; manifesting itself at the latter place in certain staid writings done in exchange for ten dollars, currency of the realm, paid down each and every Saturday. Into this slot he had been lifted, as it were by the ears, by a slip of a girl of the name of Charlotte Lee Weyland, though it was some time before he ever thought of it in that way.

In the freemasonry of the boarding-house, the young man was early accepted as he was. He was promptly voted the driest, most uninteresting and self-absorbed savant ever seen. Even Miss Miller, ordinarily indefatigable where gentlemen were concerned, soon gave him up. To Mr. Bylash she spoke contemptuously of him, but secretly she was awed by his stately manner of speech and his godlike indifference to all pleasures, including those of female society. Of them all, Nicolovius was the only one who seemed in the least impressed by Mr. Queed's appointment as editorial writer on the *Post*. With the others the exalted world he moved in was so remote from theirs that no surprises were possible there, and if informed that the little Doctor had been elected president of Harvard University, it would have seemed all in the day's work to William Klinker. Klinker was six feet high, red-faced and friendly, and Queed preferred his conversation above any heard at Mrs. Paynter's table. It reminded him very much of his friend the yeggman in New York.

What went on behind the door of the tiny Scriptorium the boarders could only guess. It may be said that its owner's big grievance against the world was that he had to leave it occasionally to earn his bread and meat. Apart from this he never left it in those days except for one reason, viz., the consumption three times a day of the said bread and meat. Probably this was one explanation of the marked pallor of his cheek, but of such details as this he never took the smallest notice.

Under the tiny bed were three boxes of books, chief fruit of the savings of an inexpensive lifetime. But the books were now merely the occasional stimulus of a mind already well stored with their strength, well fortified against their weaknesses. Nowadays nearly all of Queed's time, which he administered by an iron-clad Schedule of Hours, duly drawn up, went to the actual writing of his Magnum Opus. He had practically decided that it should be called "The Science of Sciences." For his book was designed to coördinate and unify the theories of all science into the single theory which alone gave any of them a living value, namely, the progressive evolution of a higher organized society and a higher individual type. That this work would blaze a wholly new trail for a world of men, he rarely entertained a doubt. To its composition he gave fifteen actual hours a day on *Post* days, sixteen hours on non-*Post* days. Many men speak of working hours like these, or even longer ones, but investigation would generally show that all kinds of restful interludes are indiscriminately counted in. Queed's hours, you understand, were not elapsed time—they were absolutely net. He was one of the few men in the world who literally "didn't have time."

He sat in Colonel Cowles's office, scribbling rapidly, with his eye on his watch, writing one of those unanswerable articles which were so much dead space to a people's newspaper. It was a late afternoon in early February, soon after the opening of the legislature; and he was alone in the office. A knock fell upon the door, and at his "Come," a girl entered who looked as pretty as a dewy May morning. Queed looked up at her with no welcome in his eye, or greeting on his lip, or spring in the pregnant hinges of his knee. Yet if he had been a less self-absorbed young scientist, it must certainly have dawned on him that he had seen this lady before.

"Oh! How do you do!" said Sharlee, for it was indeed no other.

"Oh—quite well."

"Miss Leech tells me that Colonel Cowles has gone out. I particularly wished to see him. Perhaps you know when he will be back?"

"Perhaps in half an hour. Perhaps in an hour. I cannot say."

She mused disappointedly. "I could hardly wait. Would you be good enough to give him a message for me?"

"Very well."

"Well—just tell him, please, that if he can make it convenient, we'd like the article about the reformatory to go in to-morrow, or the next day, anyway. He'll understand perfectly; I have talked it all over with him. The only point was as to when the article would have the most effect, and we think the time has come now."

"You would like an article written about a reformatory for to-morrow's *Post* or next day's. Very well."

"Thank you so much for telling him. Good-afternoon."

"*You* would like," the young man repeated—"but one moment, if you please. You have omitted to inform me who *you* are."

To his surprise the lady turned round with a gay laugh. Sharlee had supposed that Mr. Queed, having been offended by her, was deliberately cutting her. That her identity had literally dropped cleanly from his mind struck her as both much better and decidedly more amusing.

"Don't you remember me?" she reminded him once again, laughing full at him from the threshhold. "My dog knocked you over in the street one day—surely you remember the pleasure-dog?—and then that night I gave you your supper at Mrs. Paynter's and afterwards collected twenty dollars from you for back board. I am Mrs. Paynter's niece and my name is Charlotte Weyland."

Weyland?... Weyland? Oho! So this was the girl—sure enough—that Henry G. Surface had stripped of her fortune. Well, well!

"Ah, yes, I recall you now."

She thought there was an inimical note in his voice, and to pay him for it, she said with a final smiling nod: "Oh, I am *so* pleased!"

Her little sarcasm passed miles over his head. She had touched the spring of the automatic card-index system known as his memory and the ingenious machinery worked on. Presently it pushed out and laid before him the complete record, neatly ticketed and arranged, the full dossier, of all that had passed between him and the girl. But she was nearly through the door before he had decided to say:

"I had another letter from my father last night."

"Oh!" she said, turning at once—"*Did* you!"

He nodded, gloomily. "However, there was not a cent of money in it."

If he had racked his brains for a subject calculated to detain her—which we may rely upon it that he did not do—he could not have hit upon a surer one. Sharlee Weyland had a great fund of pity for this young man's worse than fatherlessness, and did not in the least mind showing it. She came straight back into the room and up to the table where he sat.

"Does it help you at all—about knowing where he is, I mean?"

"Not in the least. I wonder what he's up to anyway?"

He squinted up at her interrogatively through his circular glasses, as though she ought to be able to tell him if anybody could. Then a thought very much like that took definite shape in his mind. He himself had no time to give to mysterious problems and will-o'-the-wisp pursuits; his book and posterity claimed it all. This girl was familiar with the city; doubtless knew all the people; she seemed intelligent and capable, as girls went. He remembered that he had consulted her about securing remunerative work, with some results; possibly she would also have something sensible to say about his paternal problem. He might make an even shrewder stroke. As his landlady's agent, this girl would of course be interested in establishing his connection with a relative who had twenty-dollar bills to give away. Therefore if it ever should come to a search, why mightn't he turn the whole thing over to the agent—persuade her to hunt his father for him, and thus leave his own time free for the service of the race?

"Look here," said he, with a glance at his watch. "I'll take a few minutes. Kindly sit down there and I'll show you how the man is behaving."

Sharlee sat down as she was bidden, close by his side, piqued as to her curiosity, as well as flattered by his royal condescension. She wore her business suit, which was rough and blue, with a smart little pony coat. She also wore a white veil festooned around her hat, and white gloves that were quite unspotted from the world. The raw February winds had whipped roses into her cheeks; her pure ultramarine eyes made the blue of her suit look commonplace and dull. Dusk had fallen over the city, and Queed cleverly bethought him to snap on an electric light. It revealed a very shabby, ramshackle, and dingy office; but the long table in it was new, oaken, and handsome. In fact, it was one of the repairs introduced by the new management.

"Here," said he, "is his first letter—the one that brought me from New York."

He took it from its envelope and laid it open on the table. A sense of the pathos in this ready sharing of one's most intimate secrets with a stranger took hold of Sharlee as she leaned forward to see what it might say.

"Be careful! Your feather thing is sticking my eye."

Meekly the girl withdrew to a safer distance. From there she read with amazement the six typewritten lines which was all that the letter proved to be. They read thus:

> Your father asks that, if you have any of the natural feelings
> of a son, you will at once leave New York and take up your
> residence in this city. This is the first request he has ever

made of you, as it will be, if you refuse it, the last. But he
earnestly begs that you will comply with it, anticipating that
it will be to your decided advantage to do so.

"The envelope that that came in," said Queed, briskly laying it down.
"Now here's the envelope that the twenty dollars came in — it is exactly like
the other two, you observe. — The last exhibit is somewhat remarkable; it
came yesterday. Read that."

Sharlee required no urging. She read:

Make friends; mingle with people, and learn to like them.
This is the earnest injunction of
Your father.

"Note especially," said the young man, "the initial Q on each of the
three envelopes. You will observe that the tail in every instance is defective
in just the same way."

Sure enough, the tail of every Q was broken off short near the root, like
the rudimentary tail anatomists find in Genus Homo. Mr. Queed looked at
her with scholarly triumph.

"I suppose that removes all doubt," said she, "that all these came from
the same person."

"Unquestionably. — Well? What do they suggest to you?"

A circle of light from the green-shaded desk-lamp beat down on the
three singular exhibits. Sharlee studied them with bewilderment mixed
with profound melancholy.

"Is it conceivable," said she, hesitatingly — "I only suggest this because
the whole thing seems so extraordinary — that somebody is playing a very
foolish joke on you?"

He stared. "Who on earth would wish to joke with me?"

Of course he had her there. "I wish," she said, "that you would tell me
what you yourself think of them."

"I think that my father must be very hard up for something to do."

"Oh — I don't think I should speak of it in that way if I were you."

"Why not? If he cites filial duty to me, why shall I not cite paternal duty
to him? Why should he confine his entire relations with me in twenty-four
years to two preposterous detective-story letters?"

Sharlee said nothing. To tell the truth, she thought the behavior of
Queed Senior puzzling in the last degree.

"You grasp the situation? He knows exactly where I am; evidently he has known it all along. He could come to see me to-night; he could have come as soon as I arrived here three months ago; he could have come five, ten, twenty years ago, when I was in New York. But instead he elects to write these curious letters, apparently seeking to make a mystery, and throwing the burden of finding him on me. Why should I become excited over the prospect? If he would promise to endow me now, to support or pension me off, if I found him, that would be one thing. But I submit to you that no man can be expected to interrupt a most important life-work in consideration of a single twenty-dollar bill. And that is the only proof of interest I ever had from him. No—" he broke off suddenly—"no, that's hardly true after all. I suppose it was he who sent the money to Tim."

"To Tim?"

"Tim Queed."

Presently she gently prodded him. "And do you want to tell me who Tim Queed is?"

He eyed her thoughtfully. If the ground of his talk appeared somewhat delicate, nothing could have been more matter-of-fact than the way he tramped it. Yet now he palpably paused to ask himself whether it was worth his while to go more into detail. Yes; clearly it was. If it ever became necessary to ask the boarding-house agent to find his father for him, she would have to know what the situation was, and now was the time to make it plain to her once and for all.

"He is the man I lived with till I was fourteen; one of my friends, a policeman. For a long time I supposed, of course, that Tim was my father, but when I was ten or twelve, he told me, first that I was an orphan who had been left with him to bring up, and later on, that I had a father somewhere who was not in a position to bring up children. That was all he would ever say about it. I became a student while still a little boy, having educated myself practically without instruction of any sort, and when I was fourteen I left Tim because he married at that time, and, with the quarreling and drinking that followed, the house became unbearable. Tim then told me for the first time that he had, from some source, funds equivalent to twenty-five dollars a month for my board, and that he would allow me fifteen of that, keeping ten dollars a month for his services as agent. You follow all this perfectly? So matters went along for ten years, Tim bringing me the fifteen dollars every month and coming frequently to see me in between, often bringing along his brother Murphy, who is a yeggman. Last fall came this letter, purporting to be from my father. Absurd as it appeared to me, I decided to come. Tim said that, in that case, he would be compelled to cut off the allowance entirely. Nevertheless, I came."

Sharlee had listened to this autobiographical sketch with close and sympathetic attention. "And now that you are here—and settled—haven't you decided to do something—?"

He leaned back in his swivel chair and stared at her. "Do something! Haven't I done all that he asked? Haven't I given up fifteen dollars a month for him? Decidedly, the next move is his."

"But if you meant to take no steps when you got here, why did you come?"

"To give him his chance, of course. One city is exactly like another to me. All that I ask of any of them is a table and silence. Apart from the forfeiture of my income, living here and living there are all one. Do! You talk of it glibly enough, but what is there to do? There are no Queeds in this city. I looked in the directory this morning. In all probability that is not his name anyway. Kindly bear in mind that I have not the smallest clue to proceed upon, even had I the time and willingness to proceed upon it."

"I am obliged to agree with you," she said, "in thinking that your—"

"Besides," continued Doctor Queed, "what reason have I for thinking that he expects or desires me to track him down? For all that he says here, that may be the last thing in the world he wishes."

Sharlee, turning toward him, her chin in her white-gloved hand, looked at him earnestly.

"Do you care to have me discuss it with you?"

"Oh, yes, I have invited an expression of opinion from you."

"Then I agree with you in thinking that your father is not treating you fairly. His attitude toward you is extraordinary, to say the least of it. But of course there must be some good reason for this. Has it occurred to you that he may be in some—situation where it is not possible for him to reveal himself to you?"

"Such as what?"

"Well, I don't know—"

"Why doesn't he say so plainly in his letters then?"

"I don't know."

The young man threw out his hands with a gesture which inquired what in the mischief she was talking about then.

"Here is another thought," said Sharlee, not at all disconcerted. "Have you considered that possibly he may be doing this way—as a test?"

"Test of what?"

"Of you. I mean that, wanting to—to have you with him now, he is taking this way of finding out whether or not you want him. Don't you see what I mean? He appeals here to the natural feelings of a son, and then again he tells you to make friends and learn to like people. Evidently he is expecting something of you—I don't know exactly what. But don't you think, perhaps, that if you began a search for him, he would take it as a sign—"

"I told you that there was no way in which a search, as you call it, could be begun. Nor, if there were, have I the smallest inclination to begin it. Nor, again, if I had, could I possibly take the time from My Book."

She was silent a moment. "There is, of course, one way in which you could find out at any moment."

"Indeed! What is that, pray?"

"Mr. Tim Queed."

He smiled faintly but derisively. "Hardly. Of course Tim knows all about it. He told me once that he was present at the wedding of my parents; another time that my mother died when I was born. But he would add, and will add, not a word to these confidences; not even to assure me definitely that my father is still alive. He says that he has sworn an oath of secrecy. I called on him before I left New York. No, no; I may discover my father or he may discover me, or not, but we can rest absolutely assured that I shall get no help from Tim."

"But you can't mean simply to sit still—"

"And leave matters to him. I do."

"But—but," she still protested, "he is evidently unhappy Mr. Queed—evidently counting on you for something—"

"Then let him come out like a man and say plainly what he wants. I cannot possibly drop my work to try to solve entirely superfluous enigmas. Keep all this in mind—take an interest in it, will you?" he added briskly. "Possibly I might need your help some day."

"Certainly I will. I appreciate your telling me about it, and I'd be so glad to help you in any way that I could."

"How do you like my editorials?" he demanded abruptly.

"I'm afraid I don't understand a line of them!"

He waved his hand indulgently, like a grandfather receiving the just tribute of his little ones. "They are for thinkers, experts," said he, and picked up his pencil.

The agent took the hint; pushed back her chair; her glove was unbuttoned and she slowly fastened it. In her heart was a great compassion for the little Doctor.

"Mr. Queed, I want you to know that if I ever could be of help to you about *anything*, I'd always think it a real pleasure. Please remember that, won't you? Did you know I lived down this way, in the daytime?"

"Lived?"

She made a gesture toward the window, and away to the south and east. "My office is only three blocks away, down there in the park—"

"Your office? You don't work!"

"Oh, don't I though!"

"Why, I thought you were a *lady*!"

They were so close together that she was compelled to laugh full in his face, disclosing two rows of splendid little teeth and the tip of a rosy little tongue. Probably she could have crushed him by another pointing gesture, turned this time toward her honored great-grandfather who stood in marble in the square; but what was the use?

"What are you laughing at?" he inquired mildly.

"At your definition of a lady. Where on earth did you get it? Out of those laws of human society you write every night at my aunt's?"

"No," said he, the careful scientist at once, "no, I admit, if you like, that I used the term in a loose, popular sense. I would not seriously contend that females of gentle birth and breeding—ladies in the essential sense—are never engaged in gainful occupations—"

"You shouldn't," she laughed, "not in this city at any rate. It might astonish you to know how many females of gentle birth and breeding are engaged in gainful occupations on this one block alone. It was not ever thus with them. Once they had wealth and engaged in nothing but delicious leisure. But in 1861 some men came down here, about six to one, and took all this wealth away from them, at the same time exterminating the males. Result: the females, ladies in the essential sense, must either become gainful or starve. They have not starved. Sociologically, it's interesting. Make Colonel Cowles tell you about it some time."

"He has told me about it. In fact he tells me constantly. And this work that you do," he said, not unkindly and not without interest, "what is it? Are you a teacher, perhaps, a ... no!—You speak of an office. You are a clerk, doubtless, a bookkeeper, a stenographer, an office girl?"

She nodded with exaggerated gravity. "You have guessed my secret. I am a clerk, bookkeeper, stenographer, and office girl. My official title, of course, is a little more frilly, but you describe—"

"Well? What is it?"

"They call it Assistant Secretary of the State Department of Charities."

He looked astonished; she had no idea his face could take on so much expression.

"You! *You!* Why, how on earth did you get such a position?"

"Pull," said Sharlee.

Their eyes met, and she laughed him down.

"Who is the real Secretary to whom you are assistant?"

"The nicest man in the world. Mr. Dayne—Rev. George Dayne."

"A parson! Does he know anything about his subject? Is he an expert?—a trained relief worker? Does he know Willoughby? And Smathers? And Conant?"

"Knows them by heart. Quotes pages of them at a time in his letters without ever glancing at the books."

"And you?"

"I may claim some familiarity with their theories."

He fussed with his pencil. "I recall defining sociology for you one night at my boarding-house...."

"I remember."

"Well," said he, determined to find something wrong, "those men whom I mentioned to you are not so good as they think, particularly Smathers. I may as well tell you that I shall show Smathers up completely in my book."

"We shall examine your arguments with care and attention. We leave no stone unturned to keep abreast of the best modern thought."

"It is extraordinary that such a position should be held by a girl like you, who can have no scientific knowledge of the many complex problems.... However," he said, a ray of brightness lightening his displeasure, "your State is notoriously backward in this field. Your department, I fancy, can hardly be more than rudimentary."

"It will be much, much more than that in another year or two. Why, we're only four years old!"

"So this is why you are interested in having editorials written about reformatories. It is a reformatory for women that you wish to establish?"

"How did you know?"

"I merely argue from the fact that your State is so often held up to reproach for lack of one. What is the plan?"

"We are asking," said the Assistant Secretary, "for a hundred thousand dollars—sixty thousand to buy the land and build, forty thousand for equipment and two years' support. Modest enough, is it not? Of course we shall not get a penny from the present legislature. Legislatures love to say no; it dearly flatters their little vanity. We are giving them the chance to say no now. Then when they meet again, two years from now, we trust that they will be ready to give us what we ask—part of it, at any rate. We can make a start with seventy-five thousand dollars."

Queed was moved to magnanimity. "Look here. You have been civil to me—I will write that article for you Myself."

While Sharlee had become aware that the little Doctor was interested, really interested, in talking social science with her, she thought he must be crazy to offer such a contribution of his time. A guilty pink stole into her cheek. A reformatory article by Mr. Queed would doubtless be scientifically pluperfect, but nobody would read it. Colonel Cowles, on the other hand, had never even heard of Willoughby and Smathers; but when he wrote an article people read it, and the humblest understood exactly what he was driving at.

"Why—it's very nice of you to offer to help us, but I couldn't think of imposing on your time—"

"Naturally not," said he, decisively; "but it happens that we have decided to allow a breathing-space in my series on taxation, that the public may digest what I have already written. I am therefore free to discuss other topics for a few days. For to-morrow's issue, I am analyzing certain little understood industrial problems in Bavaria. On the following day—"

"It's awfully good of you to think of it," said Sharlee, embarrassed by his grave gaze. "I can't tell you how I appreciate it. But—but—you see, there's a lot of special detail that applies to this particular case alone—oh, a great lot of it—little facts connected with peculiar State conditions and—and the history of our department, you know—and I have talked it over so thoroughly with the Colonel—"

"Here is Colonel Cowles now."

She breathed a sigh. Colonel Cowles, entering with the breath of winter upon him, greeted her affectionately. Queed, rather relieved that his too hasty offer had not been accepted, noted with vexation that his conversation with the agent had cost him eighteen minutes of time. Vigorously he readdressed himself to the currency problems of the Bavarians; the girl's good-night, as applied to him, fell upon ears deafer than any post.

Sharlee walked home through the tingling twilight; fourteen blocks, and she did them four times a day. It was a still evening, clear as a bell and very cold; already stars were pushing through the dim velvet round; all the world lay white with a light hard snow, crusted and sparkling under the street lights. Her private fear about the whole matter was that Queed Senior was a person of a criminal mode of life, who, discovering the need of a young helper, was somehow preparing to sound and size up his long-neglected son.

CHAPTER VII

*In which an Assistant Editor, experiencing the Common Desire
to thrash a Proof-Reader, makes a Humiliating Discovery; and of
how Trainer Klinker gets a Pupil the Same Evening.*

The industrial problems of the Bavarians seemed an inoffensive thesis enough, but who can evade Destiny?

Queed never read his own articles when they appeared in print in the *Post*. In this peculiarity he may be said to have resembled all the rest of the world, with the exception of the Secretary of the Tax Reform League, and the Assistant Secretary of the State Department of Charities. But not by any such device, either, can a man elude his Fate. On the day following his conversation with Mrs. Paynter's agent, Fortune gave Queed to hear a portion of his article on the Bavarians read aloud, and read with derisive laughter.

The incident occurred on a street-car, which he had taken because of the heavy snow-fall: another illustration of the tiny instruments with which Providence works out its momentous designs. Had he not taken the car—he was on the point of not taking it, when one whizzed invitingly up—he would never have heard of the insult that the Post's linotype had put upon him, and the course of his life might have been different. As it was, two men on the next seat in front were reading the Post and making merry.

"... '*A lengthy procession of fleas harassed the diet.*' Now what in the name of Bob ..."

Gradually the sentence worked its way into the closed fastness of the young man's mind. It had a horrible familiarity, like a ghastly parody on something known and dear. With a quick movement he leaned forward, peering over the shoulder of the man who held the paper.

The man looked around, surprised and annoyed by the strange face breaking in so close to his own, but Queed paid no attention to him. Yes ... it was his article they were mocking at—HIS article. He remembered the passage perfectly. He had written: "A lengthy procession of pleas harassed the Diet." His trained eye swept rapidly down the half column of print. There it was! "A procession of fleas." In *his* article! Fleas, unclean, odious vermin, in His Article!

Relatively, Queed cared nothing about his work on the *Post*, but for all the children of his brain, even the smallest and feeblest, he had a peculiar tenderness. He was more jealous of them than a knight of his honor, or a beauty of her complexion. No insult to his character could have enraged him like a slight put upon the least of these his articles. He sat back in his seat, feeling white, and something clicked inside his head. He remembered having heard that click once before. It was the night he determined to evolve the final theory of social progress, which would wipe out all other theories as the steam locomotive had wiped out the prairie schooner.

He knew well enough what that click meant now. He had got a new purpose, and that was to exact personal reparation from the criminal who had made Him and His Work the butt of street-car loafers. Never, it seemed to him, could he feel clean again until he had wiped off those fleas with gore.

To his grim inquiry Colonel Cowles replied that the head proof-reader, Mr. Pat, was responsible for typographical errors, and Mr. Pat did not "come on" till 6.30. It was now but 5.50. Queed sat down, wrote his next day's article and handed it to the Colonel, who read the title and coughed.

"I shall require no article from you to-morrow or next day. On the following day"—here the Colonel opened a drawer and consulted a schedule—"I shall receive with pleasure your remarks on 'Fundamental Principles of Distribution—Article Four.'"

Queed ascended to the next floor, a noisy, discordant floor, full of metal tables on castors, and long stone-topped tables not on castors, and Mergenthaler machines, and slanting desk-like structures holding fonts of type. Rough board partitions rose here and there; over everything hung the deadly scent of acids from the engravers' room.

"That's him now," said an ink-smeared lad, and nodded toward a tall, gangling, mustachioed fellow in a black felt hat who had just come up the stairs.

Queed marched straight for the little cubbyhole where the proof-readers and copy-holders sweated through their long nights.

"You are Mr. Pat, head proof-reader of the *Post?*"

"That's me, sor," said Mr. Pat, and he turned with rather a sharp glance at the other's tone.

"What excuse have you to offer for making my article ridiculous and me a common butt?"

"An' who the divil may you be, please?"

"I am Mr. Queed, special editorial writer for this paper. Look at this." He handed over the folded *Post*, with the typographical enormity heavily underscored in blue. "What do you mean by falsifying my language and putting into my mouth an absurd observation about the most loathsome of vermin?"

Mr. Pat was at once chagrined and incensed. He happened, further, to be in most sensitive vein as regards little oversights in his department. His professional pride was tortured with the recollection that, only three days before, he had permitted the *Post* to refer to old Major Lamar as "that immortal veterinary," and upon the *Post's* seeking to retrieve itself the next day, at the Major's insistent demand, he had fallen into another error. The hateful words had come out as "immoral veteran."

"Now look here!" said he, "there's nothing to be gained talking that way. Ye've got me—I'll give ye that! But what do ye expect?—eighty columns of type a night and niver a little harmless slip—?"

"You must be taught to make no slips with my articles. I'm going to punish you for that—"

"What-a-at! Say that agin!"

"Stand out here—I am going to give you a good thrashing. I shall whip ..."

Another man would have laughed heartily and told the young man to trot away while the trotting was good. He was nearly half a foot shorter than Mr. Pat, and his face advertised his unmartial customs. But Mr. Pat had the swift fierce passions of his race; and it became to him an unendurable thing to be thus bearded by a little spectacled person in his own den. He saw red; and out shot his good right arm.

The little Doctor proved a good sailer, but bad at making a landing. His course was arched, smooth, and graceful, but when he stopped, he did it so bluntly that men working two stories below looked up to ask each other who was dead. Typesetters left their machines and hurried up, fearing that here was a case for ambulance or undertaker. But they saw the fallen editor pick himself up, with a face of stupefied wonder, and immediately start back toward the angry proof-reader.

Mr. Pat lowered redly on his threshhold. "G'awn now! Get away!"

Queed came to a halt a pace away and stood looking at him.

"G'awn, I tell ye! I don't want no more of your foolin'!"

The young man, arms hanging inoffensively by his side, stared at him with a curious fixity.

These tactics proved strangely disconcerting to Mr. Pat, obsessed as he was by a sudden sense of shame at having thumped so impotent an adversary.

"Leave me be, Mr. Queed. I'm sorry I hit ye, and I niver would 'a' done it—if ye hadn't—"

The man's voice died away. He became lost in a great wonder as to what under heaven this little Four-eyes meant by standing there and staring at him with that white and entirely unfrightened face.

Queed was, in fact, in the grip of a brand-new idea, an idea so sudden and staggering that it overwhelmed him. He could not thrash Mr. Pat. He could not thrash anybody. Anybody in the world that desired could put gross insult upon his articles and go scot-free, the reason being that the father of these articles was a physical incompetent.

All his life young Mr. Queed had attended to his own business, kept quiet and avoided trouble. This was his first fight, because it was the first time that anybody had publicly insulted his work. In his whirling sunburst of indignation, he had somehow taken it for granted that he could punch the head of a proof-reader in much the same way that he punched the head off Smathers's arguments. Now he suddenly discovered his mistake, and the discovery was going hard with him. Inside him there was raging a demon of surprising violence of deportment; it urged him to lay hold of some instrument of a rugged, murderous nature and assassinate Mr. Pat. But higher up in him, in his head, there spoke the stronger voice of his reason. While the demon screamed homicidally, reason coldly reminded the young man that not to save his life could he assassinate, or even hurt, Mr. Pat, and that the net result of another endeavor to do so would be merely a second mortifying atmospheric journey. Was it not unreasonable for a man, in a hopeless attempt to gratify irrational passion, to take a step the sole and certain consequences of which would be a humiliating soaring and curveting through the air?

It was a terrible struggle, the marks of which broke out on the young man's forehead in cold beads. But he was a rationalist among rationalists, and in the end his reason subdued his demon. Therefore, the little knot of linotypers and helpers who had stood wonderingly by while the two adversaries stared at each other, through a tense half-minute, now listened to the following dialogue:—

"I believe I said that I would give you a good thrashing. I now withdraw those words, for I find that I am unable to make them good."

"I guess you ain't—what the divil did ye expect? Me to sit back with me hands behind me and leave ye—"

"I earnestly desire to thrash you, but it is plain to me that I am not, at present, in position to do so."

"Fergit it! What's afther ye, Mr. Queed—?"

"To get in position to thrash you, would take me a year, two years, five years. It is not—no, it is *not* worth my time."

"Well, who asked f'r any av your time? But as f'r that, I'll give ye your chance to get square—"

"I suppose you feel yourself free now to take all sorts of detestable liberties with my articles?"

"Liberties—what's bitin' ye, man? Don't I read revised proof on the leaded stuff every night, no matter what the rush is? When did ye ever before catch me—?"

"Physically, you are my superior, but muscle counts for very little in this world, my man. Morally, which is all that matters, I am your superior—you know that, don't you? Be so good as to keep your disgusting vermin out of my articles in the future."

He walked away with a face which gave no sign of his inner turmoil. Mr. Pat looked after him, stirred and bewildered, and addressed his friends the linotypers angrily.

"Something loose in his belfry, as ye might have surmised from thim damfool tax-drools."

For Mr. Pat was still another reader of the unanswerable articles, he being paid the sum of twenty-seven dollars per week to peruse everything that went into the *Post*, including advertisements of auction sales and for sealed bids.

Queed returned to his own office for his hat and coat. Having heard his feet upon the stairs, Colonel Cowles called out:—

"What was the rumpus upstairs, do you know? It sounded as if somebody had a bad fall."

"Somebody did get a fall, though not a bad one, I believe."

"Who?" queried the editor briefly.

"I."

In the hall, it occurred to Queed that perhaps he had misled his chief a little, though speaking the literal truth. The fall that some *body* had gotten was indeed nothing much, for people's bodies counted for nothing so long as they kept them under. But the fall that this body's self-esteem had gotten was no such trivial affair. It struck the young man as decidedly curious that the worst tumble his pride had ever received had come to him through his body, that part of him which he had always treated with the most systematic contempt.

The elevator received him, and in it, as luck would have it, stood a tall young man whom he knew quite well.

"Hello, there, Doc!"

"How do you do, Mr. Klinker?"

"Been up chinning your sporting editor, Ragsy Hurd. Trying to arrange a mill at the Mercury between Smithy of the Y.M.C.A. and Hank McGurk, the White Plains Cyclone."

"A mill—?"

"Scrap—boxin' match, y' know. Done up your writings for the day?"

"My newspaper writings—yes."

In the brilliant close quarters of the lift, Klinker was looking at Mr. Queed narrowly. "Where you hittin' for now? Paynter's?"

"Yes."

"Walkin'?—That's right. I'll go with you."

As they came out into the street, Klinker said kindly: "You ain't feelin' good, are you, Doc? You're lookin' white as a milk-shake."

"I feel reasonably well, thank you. As for color, I have never had any, I believe."

"I don't guess, the life you lead. Got the headache, haven't you? Have it about half the time, now don't you, hey?"

"Oh, I have a headache quite frequently, but I never pay any attention to it."

"Well, you'd ought to. Don't you know the headache is just nature tipping you off there's something wrong inside? I've been watching you at the supper table for some time now. That pallor you got ain't natural pallor. You're pasty, that's right. I'll bet segars you wake up three mornings out of four feelin' like a dish of stewed prunes."

"If I do—though of course I can only infer how such a dish feels—it is really of no consequence, I assure you."

"Don't you fool yourself! It makes a lot of consequence to you. Ask a doctor, if you don't believe me. But I got your dia'nosis now, same as a medical man that's right. I know what's your trouble, Doc, just like you had told me yourself."

"Ah? What, Mr. Klinker?"

"Exercise."

"You mean lack of exercise?"

"I mean," said Klinker, "that you're fadin' out fast for the need of it."

The two men pushed on up Centre Street, where the march of home-goers was now beginning to thin out, in a moment of silence. Queed glanced up at Klinker's six feet of red beef with a flash of envy which would have been unimaginable to him so short a while ago as ten minutes. Klinker was physically competent. Nobody could insult *his* work and laugh at the merited retribution.

"Come by my place a minute," said Klinker. "I got something to show you there. You know the shop, o' course?"

No; Mr. Queed was obliged to admit that he did not.

"I'm manager for Stark's," said Klinker, trying not to appear boastful. "Cigars, mineral waters, and periodicals. And a great rondy-vooze for the sporting men, politicians, and rounders of the town, if I do say it. I've seen you hit by the window many's the time, only your head was so full of studies you never noticed."

"Thank you, I have no time this evening, I fear—"

"Time? It won't take any—it's right the end of this block. You can't do any studyin' before supper-time, anyhow, because it's near that now. I got something for you there."

They turned into Stark's, a brilliantly-lit and prettily appointed little shop with a big soda-water plant at the front. To a white-coated boy who lounged upon the fount, Klinker spoke winged words, and the next moment Queed found himself drinking a foaming, tingling, hair-trigger concoction under orders to put it all down at a gulp.

They were seated upon a bench of oak and leather upholstery, with an enormous mirror reproducing their back views to all who cared to see. Klinker was chewing a tooth-pick; and either a tooth-pick lasted him a long time, or the number he made away with in a year was simply stupendous.

"Ever see a gymnasier, Doc?"

No; it seemed that the Doc had not.

"We got one here. There's a big spare room behind the shop. Kind of a store-room it was, and the Mercuries have fitted it up as a gymnasier and athletic club. Only they're dead ones and don't use it much no more. Got kind of a fall this afternoon, didn't you, Doc?"

"What makes you think that?"

"That eye you got. She'll be a beaut to-morrow—skin's broke too. A bit of nice raw beefsteak clapped on it right now would do the world and all for it."

"Oh, it is of no consequence—"

"You think nothing about your body is consequence, Doc, that only your mind counts, and that's just where you make your mistake. Your body's got to carry your mind around, and if it lays down on you, what—"

"But I have no intention of letting my body lie down on me, as you put it, Mr. Klinker. My health is sound, my constitution—"

"Forget it, Doc. Can't I look at you and see with my own eyes? You're committing slow suicide by over-work. That's what it is."

"As it happens, I am doing nothing of the sort. I have been working exactly this way for twelve years."

"Then all the bigger is the overdue bill nature's got against you, and when she does hit you she'll hit to kill. Where'll your mind and your studies be when we've planted your body down under the sod?"

Mr. Queed made no reply. After a moment, preparing to rise, he said: "I am obliged to you for that drink. It is rather remarkable—"

"Headache all gone, hey?"

"Almost entirely. I wish you would give me the name of the medicine. I will make a memorandum—"

"Nix," said Klinker.

"Nix? Nux I have heard of, but ..."

"Hold on," laughed Klinker, as he saw Queed preparing to enter Nix in his note-book. "That ain't the name of it, and I ain't going to give it to you. Why, that slop only covers up the trouble, Doc—does more harm than good in the long run. You got to go deeper and take away the cause. Come back here and I'll show you your real medicine."

"I'm afraid—"

"Aw, don't flash that open-faced clock of yours on me. That's your trouble, Doc—matching seconds against your studies. It won't take a minute, and you can catch it up eating supper faster if you feel you got to."

Queed, curious, as well as decidedly impressed by Klinker's sure knowledge in a field where he was totally ignorant, was persuaded. The two groped their way down a long dark passage at the rear of the shop, and into a large room like a cavern. Klinker lit a flaring gas-jet and made a gesture.

"The Mercury Athletic Club gymnasier and sporting-room."

It was a basement room, with two iron-grated windows at the back. Two walls were lined with stout shelves, partially filled with boxes. The remaining space, including wall-space, was occupied by the most curious and puzzling contrivances that Queed had ever seen. Out of the glut of enigmas there was but one thing—a large mattress upon the floor—that he could recognize without a diagram.

"Your caretaker sleeps here, I perceive."

Klinker laughed. "Look around you, Doc. Take a good gaze."

Doc obeyed. Klinker picked up a "sneaker" from the floor and hurled it with deadly precision at a weight-and-pulley across the room.

"There's your medicine, Doc!"

Orange-stick in mouth, he went around like a museum guide, introducing the beloved apparatus to the visitor under its true names and uses, the chest-weights, dumb-bells and Indian clubs, flying-rings, a rowing-machine, the horizontal and parallel bars, the punching-bag and trapeze. Klinker lingered over the ceremonial; it was plain that the gymnasier was very dear to him. In fact, he loved everything pertaining to bodily exercise and manly sport; he caressed a boxing-glove as he never caressed a lady's hand; the smell of witch-hazel on a hard bare limb was more titillating to him than any intoxicant. The introduction over, Klinker sat down tenderly on the polished seat of the rowing-machine, and addressed Doctor Queed, who stood with an academic arm thrown gingerly over the horizontal bar.

"There's your medicine, Doe. And if you don't take it—well, it may be the long good-by for yours before the flowers bloom again."

"How do you mean, Mr. Klinker—there is my medicine?"

"I mean, you need half an hour to an hour's hardest kind of work right here every day, reg'lar as meals."

Queed started as though he had been stung. He cleared his throat nervously.

"No doubt that would be beneficial—in a sense, but I cannot afford to take the time from My Book—"

"That's where you got it dead wrong. You can't afford not to take the time. Any doctor'll tell you the same as me, that you'll never finish your book at all at the clip you're hitting now. You'll go with nervous prostration, and it'll wipe you out like a fly. Why, Doc," said Klinker, impressively, "you don't realize the kind of life you're leading—all indoors and sedentary and working twenty hours a day. I come in pretty late some nights, but I never come so late that there ain't a light under your door. A man can't stand it, I tell you, playing both ends against the middle that away. You got to pull up, or it's out the door feet first for you."

Queed said uneasily: "One important fact escapes you, Mr. Klinker. I shall never let matters progress so far. When I feel my health giving way—"

"Needn't finish—heard it all before. They think they're going to stop in time, but they never do. Old prostration catches 'em first every crack. You think an hour a day exercise would be kind of a waste, ain't that right? Kind of a dead loss off'n your book and studies?"

"I certainly do feel—"

"Well, you're wrong. Listen here. Don't you feel some days as if mebbe you could do better writing and harder writing if only you didn't feel so mean?"

"Well ... I will frankly confess that sometimes—"

"Didn't I know it! Do you know what, Doc? If you knocked out a little time for reg'lar exercise, you'd find when bedtime came, that you'd done better work than you ever did before."

Queed was silent. He had the most logical mind in the world, and now at last Klinker had produced an argument that appealed to his reason.

"I'll put it to you as a promise," said Klinker, eyeing him earnestly. "One hour a day exercise, and you do more work in twenty-four hours than you're doing now, besides feelin' one hundred per cent better all the time."

Still Queed was silent. *One hour a day!*

"Try it for only a month," said Klinker the Tempter.

"I'll help you—glad to do it—I need the drill myself. Gimme an hour a day for just a month, and I'll bet you the drinks you wouldn't quit after that for a hundred dollars."

Queed turned away from Klinker's honest eyes, and wrestled the bitter thing out. *Thirty Hours stolen from His Book!...* Yesterday, even an hour ago, he would not have considered such an outrage for a moment. But now, driving him irresistibly toward the terrible idea, working upon him far more powerfully than his knowledge of headache, even than Klinker's promise of a net gain in his working ability, was this new irrationally disturbing knowledge that he was a physical incompetent.... If he had begun systematic exercise ten years ago, probably he could thrash Mr. Pat to-day.

Yet an hour a day is not pried out of a sacred schedule of work without pains and anguish, and it was with a grim face that the Doc turned back to William Klinker.

"Very well, Mr. Klinker, I will agree to make the experiment, tentatively—an hour a day for thirty days only."

"Right for you, Doc! You'll never be sorry—take it from me."

Klinker was a brisk, efficient young man. The old gang that had fitted out the gymnasium had drifted away, and the thought of going once more into regular training, with a pupil all his own, was breath to his nostrils. He assumed charge of the ceded hour with skilled sureness. Rain or shine, the Doctor was to take half an hour's hard walking in the air every day, over and above the walk to the office. Every afternoon at six—at which hour the managerial duties at Stark's terminated—he was to report in the gym for half an hour's vigorous work on the apparatus. This iron-clad regime was to go into effect on the morrow.

"I'll look at you stripped," said Klinker, eyeing his new pupil thoughtfully, "and see first what you need. Then I'll lay out a reg'lar course for you—exercises for all parts of the body. Got any trunks?"

Queed looked surprised. "I have one small one—a steamer trunk, as it is called."

Klinker explained what he meant, and the Doctor feared that his wardrobe contained no such article.

"Ne'mmind. I can fit you up with a pair. Left Hand Tom's they used to be, him that died of the scarlet fever Thanksgiving. And say, Doc!"

"Well?"

"Here's the first thing I'll teach you. Never mister your sparring-partner."

The Doc thought this out, laboriously, and presently said: "Very well, William."

"Call me Buck, the same as all the boys."

Klinker came toward him holding out an object made of red velveteen about the size of a pocket handkerchief.

"Put these where you can find them to-morrow. You can have 'em. Left Hand Tom's gone where he don't need 'em any more."

"What are they? What does one do with them?"

"They're your trunks. You wear 'em."

"Where? On—what portion, I mean?"

"They're like little pants," said Klinker.

The two men walked home together over the frozen streets. Queed was taciturn and depressed. He was annoyed by Klinker's presence and irritated by his conversation; he wanted nothing in the world so much as to be let alone. But honest Buck Klinker remained unresponsive to his mood. All the way to Mrs. Paynter's he told his new pupil grisly stories of men he had known who had thought that they could work all day and all night, and never take any exercise. Buck kindly offered to show the Doc their graves.

CHAPTER VIII

Formal Invitation to Fifi to share Queed's Dining-Room (provided it is very cold upstairs); and First Outrage upon the Sacred Schedule of Hours.

Queed supped in an impenetrable silence. The swelling rednesses both above and below his left eye attracted the curious attention of the boarders, but he ignored their glances, and even Klinker forbore to address him. The meal done, he ascended to his sacred chamber, but not alas, to remain.

For a full week, the Scriptorium had been uninhabitable by night, the hands of authors growing too numb there to write. On this night, conditions were worse than ever; the usual valiant essay was defeated with more than the usual case. Queed fared back to his dining-room, as was now becoming his melancholy habit. And to-night the necessity was exceptionally trying, for he found that the intrusive daughter of the landlady had yet once again spread her mathematics there before him.

Nor could Fifi this time claim misunderstanding and accident. She fully expected the coming of Mr. Queed, and had been nervously awaiting it. The state of mind thus induced was not in the least favorable to doing algebra successfully or pleasurably. No amount of bodily comfort could compensate Fifi for having to have it. But her mother had ruled the situation to-night with a strong hand and a flat foot. The bedroom was *entirely too cold* for Fifi. She must, positively *must*, go down to the warm and comfortable dining-room,—do you hear me, Fifi? As for Mr. Queed—well, if he made himself objectionable, Sharlee would simply have to give him another good talking to.

Yet Fifi involuntarily cowered as she looked up and murmured: "Oh— good evening!"

Mr. Queed bowed. In the way of conveying displeasure, he had in all probability the most expressive face in America.

He passed around to his regular place, disposed his books and papers, and placed his *Silence* sign in a fairly conspicuous position. This followed his usual custom. Yet his manner of making his arrangements to-night wanted something of his ordinary aggressive confidence. In fact, his promise to give an hour a day to exercise lay on his heart like lead, and the lumps on his eye, large though they were, did not in the least represent the dimensions of the fall he had received at the hands of Mr. Pat.

Fifi was looking a little more fragile than when we saw her last, a little more thin-cheeked, a shade more ethereal-eyed. Her cough was quite bad to-night, and this increased her nervousness. How could she *help* from disturbing him with that dry tickling going on right along in her throat? It had been a trying day, when everything seemed to go wrong from the beginning. She had waked up feeling very listless and tired; had been late for school; had been kept in for Cicero. In the afternoon she had been going to a tea given to her class at the school, but her mother said her cold was too bad for her to go, and besides she really felt too tired. She hadn't eaten any supper, and had been quite cross with her mother in their talk about the dining-room, which was the worst thing that had happened at all. And now at nine o'clock she wanted to go to bed, but her algebra would not, *would not* come right, and life was horrible, and she was unfit to live it anyway, and she wished she was ...

"You are crying," stated a calm young voice across the table.

Brought up with a cool round turn, greatly mortified, Fifi thought that the best way to meet the emergency was just to say nothing.

"What is the matter?" demanded the professorial tones.

"Oh, nothing," she said, winking back the tears and trying to smile, apologetically—"just silly reasons. I—I've spent an hour and ten minutes on a problem here, and it won't come right. I'm—sorry I disturbed you."

There was a brief silence. Mr. Queed cleared his throat.

"You cannot solve your problem?"

"I haven't *yet*," she sniffed bravely, "but of course I will *soon*. Oh, I understand it very well...."

She kept her eyes stoutly fixed upon her book, which indicated that not for worlds would she interrupt him further. Nevertheless she felt his large spectacles upon her. And presently he astonished her by saying, resignedly—doubtless he had decided that thus could the virginal calm be most surely and swiftly restored:—

"Bring me your book. I will solve your problem."

"Oh!" said Fifi, choking down a cough. And then, "Do you know all about algebra, too?"

It seemed that Mr. Queed in his younger days had once made quite a specialty of mathematics, both lower, like Fifi's, and also far higher. The child's polite demurs were firmly overridden. Soon she was established in a chair at his side, the book open on the table between them.

"Indicate the problem," said Mr. Queed.

Fifi indicated it: No. 71 of the collection of stickers known as Miscellaneous Review. It read as follows:

> 71. A laborer having built 105 rods of stone fence, found that if he had built 2 rods less a day he would have been 6 days longer in completing the job. How many rods a day did he build?

Queed read this through once and announced: "He built seven rods a day."

Fifi stared. "Why—how in the world, Mr Queed—"

"Let us see if I am right. Proceed. Read me what you have written down."

"Let x equal the number of rods he built each day," began Fifi bravely.

"Proceed."

"Then 105 divided by x equals number of days consumed. And 105 divided by $x - 2$ equals number of days consumed, if he had built 2 rods less a day."

"Of course."

"And $(105 \div x - 2) + 6$ = number of days consumed if it had taken him six days longer."

"Nothing of the sort."

Fifi coughed. "I don't see why, exactly."

"When the text says 'six days longer,' it means longer than what?"

"Why—longer than ever."

"Doubtless. But you must state it in terms of the problem."

"In terms of the problem," murmured Fifi, her red-brown head bowed over the bewildering book—"in terms of the problem."

"Of course," said her teacher, "there is but one thing which longer can mean; that is longer than the original rate of progress. Yet you add the six to the time required under the new rate of progress."

"I—I'm really afraid I don't quite see. I'm dreadfully stupid, I know—"

"Take it this way then. You have set down here two facts. One fact is the number of days necessary under the old rate of progress; the other is the number of days necessary under the new rate. Now what is the difference between them?"

"Why—isn't that just what I don't know?"

"I can't say what you don't know. This is something that *I* know very well."

"But you know everything," she murmured.

Without seeking to deny this, Queed said: "It tells you right there in the book."

"I don't see it," said Fifi, nervously looking high and low, not only in the book but all over the room.

The young man fell back on the inductive method: "What is that six then?"

"Oh! *Now* I see. It's the difference in the number of days consumed—isn't it?"

"Naturally. Now put down your equation. No, no! The greater the rate of progress, the fewer the number of days. Do not attempt to subtract the greater from the less."

Now Fifi figured swimmingly:—

$(105/(x-2)) - (105/x) = 6$
$105x - 105x + 210 = 6x^2 - 12x$
$6x^2 - 12x - 210 = 0$
$6x^2 - 12x - 210 = 0$
$x^2 - 2x - 35 = 0$
$(x - 7) (X + 5) = 0$
$x = 7$ or -5

She smiled straight into his eyes, sweetly and fearlessly. "Seven! Just what you said! Oh, if I could only do them like you! I'm ever and ever so much obliged, Mr. Queed—and now I can go to bed."

Mr. Queed avoided Fifi's smile; he obviously deliberated.

"If you have any more of these terrible difficulties," he said slowly, "it isn't necessary for you to sit there all evening and cry over them. You ... may ask me to show you."

"Oh, *could* I really! Thank you ever so much. But no, I won't be here, you see. I didn't mean to come to-night—truly, Mr. Queed—I know I bother you so—only Mother made me."

"Your mother made you? Why?"

"Well—it's right cold upstairs, you know," said Fifi, gathering up her books, "and she thought it might not be very good for my cough...."

Queed glanced impatiently at the girl's delicate face. A frown deepened on his brow; he cleared his throat with annoyance.

"Oh, I am willing," he said testily, "for you to bring your work here whenever it is very cold upstairs."

"Oh, how good you are, Mr. Queed!" cried Fifi, staggered by his nobility. "But of course I can't think of bothering—"

"I should not have asked you," he interrupted her, irritably, "if I had not been willing for you to come."

But for all boarders, their comfort and convenience, Fifi had the great respect which all of us feel for the source of our livelihood; and, stammering grateful thanks, she again assured him that she could not make such a nuisance of herself. However, of course Mr. Queed had his way, as he always did.

This point definitely settled, he picked up his pencil, which was his way of saying, "And now, for heaven's sake—good-night!" But Fifi, her heart much softened toward him, stood her ground, the pile of school-books tucked under her arm.

"Mr. Queed—I—wonder if you won't let me get something to put on your forehead? That bruise is so dreadful—"

"Oh, no! No! It's of no consequence whatever."

"But I don't think you can have noticed how bad it is. Please let me, Mr. Queed. Just a little dab of arnica or witch-hazel—"

"My forehead does very well as it is, I assure you."

Fifi turned reluctantly. "Indeed something on it would make it get well so *much* faster. I wish you would—"

Ah! There was a thought. As long as he had this bruise people would be bothering him about it. It was a world where a man couldn't even get a black eye without a thousand busybodies commenting on it.

"If you are certain that its healing will be hastened—"

"Positive!" cried Fifi happily, and vanished without more speech.

One Hour a Day to be given to Bodily Exercise.... How long, O Lord, how long!

Fifi returned directly with white cloths, scissors, and two large bottles.

"I won't take hardly a minute—you see! Listen, Mr. Queed. One of these bottles heals fairly well and doesn't hurt at all worth mentioning. That's witch-hazel. The other heals very well and fast, but stings—well, a lot; and that's turpentine. Which will you take?"

"The turpentine," said Mr. Queed in a martyr's voice.

Fifi's hands were very deft. In less than no time, she made a little lint pad, soaked it in the pungent turpentine, applied it to the unsightly swelling, and bound it firmly to the young man's head with a snowy band. In all of Mr. Queed's life, this was the first time that a woman had ministered to him. To himself, he involuntarily confessed that the touch of the girl's hands upon his forehead was not so annoying as you might have expected.

Fifi drew off and surveyed her work sympathetically yet professionally. The effect of the white cloth riding aslant over the round glasses and academic countenance was wonderfully rakish and devil-may-care.

"Do you feel the sting much so far?"

"A trifle," said the Doctor.

"It works up fast to a kind of—climax, as I remember, and then slowly dies away. The climax will be pretty bad—I'm so sorry! But when it's at its worst just say to yourself, 'This is doing me lots and lots of good,' and then you won't mind so much."

"I will follow the directions," said he, squirming in his chair.

"Thank you for letting me do it, and for the algebra, and—good-night."

"Good-night."

He immediately abandoned all pretense of working. To him it seemed that the climax of the turpentine had come instantly; there was no more working up about it than there was about a live red coal. The mordant tooth bit into his blood; he rose and tramped the floor, muttering savagely to himself. But he would not pluck the hateful thing off, no, no—for that would have been an admission that he was wrong in putting it on; and he was never wrong.

So Bylash, reading one of Miss Jibby's works in the parlor, and pausing for a drink of water at the end of a glorious chapter, found him tramping and muttering. His flying look dared Bylash to address him, and Bylash prudently took the dare. But he poured his drink slowly, stealing curious glances and endeavoring to catch the drift of the little Doctor's murmurings.

In this attempt he utterly failed, because why? Obviously because the Doctor cursed exclusively in the Greek and Latin languages.

In five minutes, Queed was upon his work again. Not that the turpentine was yet dying slowly away, as Fifi had predicted that it would. On the contrary it burned like the fiery furnace of Shadrach and Abednego. But *One Hour a Day to be given to Bodily Exercise!* ... Oh, every second must be made to count now, whether one's head was breaking into flame or not.

Whatever his faults or foibles, Mr. Queed was captain of his soul. But the fates were against him to-night. In half an hour, when the sting—they called this conflagration a sting!—was beginning to get endurable and the pencil to move steadily, the door opened and in strode Professor Nicolovius; he, it seemed, wanted matches. Why under heaven, if a man wanted matches, couldn't he buy a thousand boxes and store them in piles in his room?

The old professor apologized blandly for his intrusion, but seemed in no hurry to make the obvious reparation. He drew a match along the bottom of the mantle-shelf, eyeing the back of the little Doctor's head as he did so, and slowly lit a cigar.

"I'm sorry to see that you've met with an accident, Mr. Queed. Is there anything, perhaps, that I might do?"

"Nothing at all, thanks," said Queed, so indignantly that Nicolovius dropped the subject at once.

The star-boarder of Mrs. Paynter's might have been fifty-five or he might have been seventy, and his clothes had long been the secret envy of Mr. Bylash. He leaned against the mantel at his ease, blowing blue smoke.

"You find this a fairly pleasant place to sit of an evening, I daresay!" he purred, presently.

The back of the young man's head was uncompromisingly stern. "I might as well try to write in the middle of Centre Street."

"So?" said Nicolovius, not catching his drift. "I should have thought that—"

"The interruptions," said Queed, "are constant."

The old professor laughed. "Upon my word, I don't blame you for saying that. The gross communism of a boarding-house ... it does gall one at times! So far as I am concerned, I relieve you of it at once. Good-night."

The afternoon before Nicolovius had happened to walk part of the way downtown with Mr. Queed, and had been favored with a fair amount of his stately conversation. He shut the door now somewhat puzzled by the young man's marked curtness; but then Nicolovius knew nothing about the turpentine.

The broken evening wore on, with progress slower than the laborer's in Problem 71, when he decided to build two rods less a day. At eleven, Miss Miller, who had been to the theatre, breezed in; she wanted a drink of water. At 11.45—Queed's open watch kept accurate tally—there came Trainer Klinker, who, having sought his pupil vainly in the Scriptorium, retraced his steps to rout him out below. At sight of the tall bottle in Klinker's hand Queed shrank, fearing that Fifi had sent him with a second dose of turpentine. But the bottle turned out to contain merely a rare unguent just obtained by Klinker from his friend Smithy, the physical instructor at the Y.M.C.A., and deemed surprisingly effective for the development of the academic bicep.

At last there was blessed quiet, and he could write again. The city slept; the last boarder was abed; the turpentine had become a peace out of pain; only the ticking of the clock filtered into the perfect calm of the dining-room. The little Doctor of Mrs. Paynter's stood face to face with his love, embraced his heart's desire. He looked into the heart of Science and she gave freely to her lord and master. Sprawled there over the Turkey-red cloth, which was not unhaunted by the ghosts of dead dinners, he became chastely and divinely happy. His mind floated away into the empyrean; he saw visions of a far more perfect Society; dreamed dreams of the ascending spiral whose law others had groped at, but he would be the first to formulate; caught and fondled the secret of the whole great Design; reduced it to a rule-of-thumb to do his bidding; bestrode the whole world like a great Colossus....

From which flight he descended with a thud to observe that it was quarter of two o'clock, and the dining-room was cold with the dying down of the Latrobe, and the excellent reading-lamp in the death-throes of going out.

He went upstairs in the dark, annoyed with himself for having overstayed his bedtime. Long experimentation had shown him that the minimum of sleep he could get along with to advantage was six and one-half hours nightly. This meant bed at 1.30 exactly, and he hardly varied it five minutes in a year. To his marrow he was systematic; he was as definite as an adding-machine, as practical as a cash register. But even now, on this exceptional night, he did not go straight to bed. Something still remained to be accomplished: an outrage upon his sacred Schedule.

In the first halcyon days at Mrs. Paynter's, before the board question ever came up at all, the iron-clad Schedule of Hours under which he was composing his great work had stood like this:

8.20 Breakfast
8.40 Evolutionary Sociology

1.30 Dinner
2 Evolutionary Sociology
7 Supper
7.20 to 1.30 Evolutionary Sociology

But the course of true love never yet ran smooth, and this schedule was too ideal to stand. First the *Post* had come along and nicked a clean hour out of it, and now his Body had unexpectedly risen and claimed yet another hour. And, beyond even this ... some devilish whim had betrayed him to-night into offering his time for the service and uses of the landlady's daughter in the puling matter of algebra.

No ... *no!* He would not put that in. The girl could not be so selfish as to take advantage of his over-generous impulse. She *must* understand that his time belonged to the ages and the race, not to the momentary perplexities of a high school dunce.... At the worst it would be only five minutes here and there—say ten minutes a week; forty minutes a month. No, no! He would not put that in.

But the hour of Bodily Exercise could not be so evaded. It must go in. On land or sea there was no help for that. For thirty days henceforward at the least—and a voice within him whispered that it would be for much longer—his Schedule must stand like this:

8.20 Breakfast
8.40 Evolutionary Sociology
1.30 Dinner
2 Evolutionary Sociology
4.45 to 5.15 Open-Air Pedestrianism
5.15 to 6.15 The *Post*
6.15 to 6.45 Klinker's Exercises for all Parts of the Body
7 Supper
7.20 Evolutionary Sociology

Hand clasped in his hair, Queed stared long at this wreckage with a sense of foreboding and utter despondency. Doubtless Mr. Pat, who was at that moment peacefully pulling a pipe over his last galleys at the *Post* office, would have been astonished to learn what havoc his accursed fleas had wrought with the just expectations of posterity.

CHAPTER IX

Of Charles Gardiner West, President-Elect of Blaines College, and his Ladies Fair: all in Mr. West's Lighter Manner.

The closing German of the Thursday Cotillon, hard upon the threshold of a late Lent, was a dream of pure delight. Six of them in the heart of every season since 1871, these Germans have become famous wherever the light fantastic toe of aristocracy trips and eke is tripped. They are the badge of quality, and the test of it, the sure scaling-rod by which the frightened débutante may measure herself at last, to ask of her mirror that night, with who can say what tremors: *"Am I a success?"* Over these balls strangers go mad. They come from immense distances to attend them, sometimes with superciliousness; are instantly captivated; and returning to their homes, wherever they may be, sell out their businesses for a song and move on, to get elected if they can, which does not necessarily follow.

Carriages, in stately procession, disembarked their precious freight; the lift, laden with youth and beauty, shot up and down like a glorious Jack-in-the-Box; over the corridors poured a stream of beautiful maidens and handsome gentlemen, to separate for their several tiring-rooms, and soon to remeet in the palm-decked vestibule. Within the great room, couples were already dancing; Fetzy's Hungarians on a dais, concealed behind a wild thicket of growing things, were sighing out a wonderful waltz; rows of white-covered chairs stood expectantly on all four sides of the room; and the chaperones, august and handsome, stood in a stately line to receive and to welcome. And to them came in salutation Charles Gardiner West and, beside him, the lady whom he honored with his hand that evening, Miss Millicent Avery, late of Maunch Chunk, but now of Ours.

They made their devoirs to the dowagers; silently they chose their seats, which he bound together with a handkerchief in a true lovers' knot; and, Fetzy's continuing its heavenly work, he put his arm about her without speech, and they floated away upon the rhythmic tide.

At last her voice broke the golden silence: "I feel enormously happy to-night. I don't know why."

The observation might seem unnoteworthy to the casual, but it carried them all around the room again.

"Fortune is good to me," said he, as lightly as he could, "to let me be with you when you feel like that."

He had never seen her so handsome; the nearness of her beauty intoxicated him; her voice was indolent, provocative. She was superbly dressed in white, and on her rounded breast nodded his favor, a splendid corsage of orchid and lily-of-the-valley.

"Fortune?" she queried. "Don't you think that men bring these things to pass for themselves?"

They had made the circle on that, too, before West said: "I wonder if you begin to understand what a power you have of bringing happiness to me."

He looked, and indeed, for the transient moment, he felt, like a man who must have his answer, for better or worse, within the hour. She saw his look, and her eyes fell before it, not wholly because she knew how to do that to exactly the best advantage. Few persons would have mistaken Miss Avery for a wholly inexperienced and unsophisticated girl. But how was she to know that that same look had risen in the eyes of West, and that same note, obviously sincere, broken suddenly into his pleasant voice, for many, many of the fair?

The music died in a splendid crash, and they threaded their way to their seats, slowly and often stopped, across the crowded floor. Many eyes followed them as they walked. She was still "new" to us; she was beautiful; she was her own young lady, and something about her suggested that she would be slightly unsafe for boys, the headstrong, and the foolish; rumor made her colossally wealthy. As for him, he was the glass of fashion and the mould of form, and much more than that besides. Of an old name but a scanty fortune, he had won his place by his individual merits; chiefly, perhaps, for so wags the world, by an exterior singularly prepossessing and a manner that was a possession above rubies. His were good looks of the best fashion of men's good looks; not a tall man, he yet gave the effect of tallness, so perfect was his carriage, so handsome his address. And he was as clever as charming; cultured as the world knows culture; literary as the term goes; nor was there any one who made a happier speech than he, whether in the forum or around the festal board. Detractors, of course, he had—as which of those who raise their heads above the dead level have not?—but they usually contented themselves with saying, as Buck Klinker had once said, that his manners were a little too good to be true. To most he seemed a fine type of the young American of the modern South; a brave gentleman; a true Democrat with all his honors; and, though he had not yet been tested in any position of responsibility, a rising man who held the future in his hand.

They took their seats, and at last he freed himself from the unsteadying embarrassment which had shaken him at the first sight of her under the brilliant lights of the ballroom.

"Two things have happened to make this seventh of March a memorable day for me," said he. "Two great honors have come to me. They are both for your ear alone."

She flung upon him the masked battery of her eyes. They were extraordinary eyes, gray and emerald, not large, but singularly long. He looked fully into them, and she slowly smiled.

"The other honor," said Charles Gardiner West, "is of a commoner kind. They want to make me president of Blaines College."

"Oh—really!" said Miss Avery, and paused. "And shall you let them do it?"

He nodded, suddenly thoughtful and serious. "Long before snow flies, Semple & West will be Semple and Something else. They'll elect me in June. I needn't say that no one must know of this now—but you."

"Of course. It is a great honor," she said, with faint enthusiasm. "But why are you giving up your business? Doesn't it interest you?"

He made a large gesture. "Oh, it interests me.... But what does it all come to, at the last? A man aspires to find some better use for his abilities than dollar-baiting, don't you think?"

Miss Avery privately thought not, though she certainly did not like his choice of terms.

"If a man became the greatest stock-jobber in the world, who would remember him after he was gone? Miss Avery, I earnestly want to serve. My deepest ambition is to leave some mark for the better upon my environment, my city, and my State. I am baring my small dream for you to look at, you see. Now this little college ..."

But a daring youth by the name of Beverley Byrd bore Miss Avery away for the figure which was just then forming, and the little college hung in the air for the nonce. Mr. West was so fortunate as to secure the hand of Miss Weyland for the figure, he having taken the precaution to ask that privilege when he greeted her some minutes since. Couple behind couple they formed, the length of the great room, and swung away on a brilliant march.

"It's going to be a delicious German—can't you tell by the *feel*?" began Sharlee, doing the march with a *deux-temps* step. "I'm so glad to see you, for it seems ages since we met, though, you know, it was only last week. Is not that a nice speech for greeting? Only I must tell you that I've said it to four other men already, and the evening is yet young."

"Is there nothing in all the world that you can say, quite new and special, for me?"

"Oh, yes! For one thing your partner to-night is altogether the loveliest thing I ever saw. And for another—"

"I am listening."

"For another, *her* partner to-night is quite the nicest man in all this big, big room."

"And how many men have you said that to to-night, here in the youth of the evening?"

But the figure had reached that point where the paths of partners must diverge for a space, and at this juncture Sharlee whirled away from him. Around and up the room swept the long file of low-cut gowns and pretty faces, and step for step across the floor moved a similar line of swallow-tail and masculinity. At the head of the room the two lines curved together again, round meeting round, and here, in good time, the lovely billow bore on Sharlee, who slipped her little left hand into West's expectant right with the sweetest air in the world.

"Nobody but you, Charles Gardiner West," said she.

The whistle blew; the music changed; and off they went upon the dreamy valse.

There are dancers in this world, and other dancers; but Sharlee was the sort that old ladies stop and watch. Of her infinite poetry of motion it is only necessary to say that she could make even "the Boston" look graceful; as witness her now. In that large room, detectives could have found men who thought Sharlee decidedly prettier than Miss Avery. Her look was not languorous; her voice was not provocative; her eyes were not narrow and tip-tilted; they did not look dangerous in the least, unless you so regard all extreme pleasure derived from looking at anything in the nature of eyes. Nor was there anything in the least businesslike, official, or stenographic about her manner. If her head bulged with facts about the treatment of the deficient classes, no hint of that appeared in her talk at parties. Few of the young men she danced with thought her clever, and this shows how clever she really was. For there are men in this world who will run ten city blocks in any weather to avoid talking to a woman who knows more than they do, and knows it, and shows that she knows that she knows it.

Charles Gardiner West looked down at Sharlee; and the music singing in his blood, and the measure that they trod together, was all a part of something splendid that belonged to them alone in the world. Another man at such a moment would have contented himself with a pretty speech, but West gave his sacred confidence. He told Sharlee about the presidency of Blaines College.

Sharlee did not have to ask what he would do with such an offer. She recognized at sight the opportunity for service he had long sought; and she so sincerely rejoiced and triumphed in it for him that his heart grew very tender toward her, and he told her all his plans; how he meant to make of Blaines College a great enlightened modern institution which should turn out a growing army of brave young men for the upbuilding of the city and the state.

"They elect me the first of June. Of course I am supposed to know nothing about it yet, and you must keep it as a great secret if you please. I give up my business in April. The next month goes to my plans, arranging and laying out a great advertising campaign for the September opening. Early in June I shall sail for Europe, nominally for a little rest, but really to study the school systems of the old world. The middle of August will find me at my new desk, oh, so full of enthusiasms and high hopes!"

"It's splendid.... Oh, how fine!" pæaned she.

Upon the damask wrapping of Sharlee's chair lay a great armful of red, red roses, the gift of prodigal young Beverley Byrd, and far too large to carry. She lifted them up; scented their fragrance; selected and broke a perfect flower from its long stem; and held it out with a look.

"The Assistant Secretary of the State Department of Charities presents her humble duty to President West."

"Ah! Then the president commands his minion to place it tenderly in his buttonhole."

"Look at the sea of faces ... lorgnettes, too. The minion *dassen't*."

"Oh, that we two were Maying!"

"You misread our announcement," said Beverley Byrd, romping up. "No opening for young men here, Gardy! Butt out."

West left her, his well-shaped head in something of a whirl. In another minute he was off with Miss Avery upon a gallant two-step.

Fetzy's played on; the dancers floated or hopped according to their nature; and presently a waltz faded out and in a breath converted itself into the march for supper, the same air always for I don't know how many years.

Miss Avery rose slowly from her seat, a handsome siren shaped, drilled, fitted, polished from her birth for nothing else than the beguiling of lordly man. From the heart of her beautiful bouquet she plucked a spray of perfect lily-of-the-valley, and, eyes upon her own flowers, held it out to West.

"They are beautiful," she said in her languorous voice. "I hadn't thanked you for them, had I? Wear this for me, will you not?" She looked up and her long eyes fell—we need not assume for the first time—upon the flower in his lapel. "I beg your pardon," she said, with the slightest change of expression and voice. "I see that you are already provided. Shall we not go up?"

Laughing, he plucked a red, red rose from his buttonhole and jammed it carelessly in his pocket.

"Give it to me."

"Why, it's of no consequence. Flowers quickly fade."

"Won't you understand?... you maddening lady. I've known all these girls since they were born. When they offer me flowers, shall I hurt their feelings and refuse? Give it to me."

She shook her head slowly.

"Don't you know that I'll prize it—and why?" said he in a low voice. "Give it to me."

Their eyes met; hers fluttered down; but she raised them suddenly and put the flower in his buttonhole, her face so close that he felt her breath on his cheek.

Beside him at supper, she took up the thread of their earlier talk.

"If you must give up your business, why shouldn't it be for something bigger than the college—public life for instance?"

"I may say," West answered her, "that as yet there has not been that sturdy demand from the public, that uproarious insistence from the honest voter ..."

"At dinner the other evening I met one of your fine old patriarchs, Colonel Cowles. He told us that the new Mayor of this city, if he was at all the right sort, would go from the City Hall to the Governorship. And do you know who represents his idea of the right sort of Mayor?"

West, picking at a bit of duck, said that he hadn't the least idea.

"So modest—so modest! He said that the city needed a young progressive man of the better class and the highest character, and that man was—you. No other, by your leave! The Mayoralty, the Governorship, the Senate waiting behind that, perhaps—who knows? Is it wise to bottle one's self up in the blind alley of the college?"

Thus Delilah: to which Samson replied that a modern college is by no means a blind alley; that from the presidential retreat he would keep a close eye upon the march of affairs, doubtless doing his share toward moulding public opinion through contributions to the *Post* and the reviews; that, in fact, public life had long had an appeal for him, and that if at any time a cry arose in the land for him to come forward ...

"For a public career," said Delilah, with a sigh, "I should think you had far rather be editor of the *Post*, for example, than head of this college."

Samson made an engaging reply that had to do with Colonel Cowles. The talk ran off into other channels, but somehow Delilah's remark stuck in the young man's head.

Soul is not all that flows at the Thursday German, and it has frequently been noticed that the dance becomes gayest after supper. But it becomes, too, sadly brief, and *Home Sweet Home* falls all too soon upon the enthralled ear. Now began the movement toward that place, be it never so humble, like which there is none; and amid the throng gathered in the vestibule before the cloak-rooms, West again found himself face to face with Miss Weyland with whom he had stepped many a measure that evening.

"I've been thinking about it lots, President West," said she; "it grows better all the time. Won't you please teach all your boys to be very good, and to work hard, and never to grow up to make trouble for the State Department of Charities."

She had on a carriage-robe of light blue, collared and edged with white fur, and her arms were as full of red roses as arms could be.

"But if I do that too well," said he, "what would become of you? Blaines College shall never blot out the Department of Charities. I nearly forgot a bit of news. Gloomy news. The *Post* is going to fire your little Doctor."

"Ah—*no!*"

"It looks that way. The directors will take it up definitely in April. Colonel Cowles is going to recommend it. He says the Doc has more learning than society requires."

"But don't you think his articles give a—a tone to the paper—and—?"

"I do; a sombre, awful, majestic tone, if you like, but still one that ought to be worth something."

Sharlee looked sad, and it was one of her best looks.

"Ah, me! I don't know what will become of him if he is turned adrift. Could you, *could* you do anything?"

"I can, and will," said he agreeably. "I think the man's valuable, and you may count on it that I shall use my influence to have him kept."

So the Star and the Planet again fought in their courses for Mr. Queed. West, gazing down at her, overcoat on arm, looked like a Planet who usually had his way. The Star, too, had strong inclinations in the same direction. For example, she had noted at supper the lily-of-the-valley in the Planet's buttonhole, and she had not been able to see any good reason for that.

Her eyes became dreamy. "How shall I say thank you?... I know. I must give you one of my pretty flowers for your buttonhole." She began pulling out one of the glorious roses, but suddenly checked herself and gazed off pensively into space, a finger at her lip. "Ah! I thought this gesture seemed strangely familiar, and now I remember. I gave him a flower once before, and ah, look!... the president of the college has tossed it away."

West glanced hastily down at his buttonhole. The lily-of-the-valley was gone; he had no idea where he had lost it, nor could he now stay to inquire. The rose he took with tender carefulness from the upper pocket of his waistcoat.

"What did Mademoiselle expect?" said he, with a courtly bow. "The president wears it over his heart."

Sharlee's smile was a coronation for a man.

"That one was for the president. This new one," said she, plucking it out, "is for the director and—the man."

This new one, after all, she put into his buttonhole with her own hands, while he held her great bunch of them. As she turned away from the dainty ceremony, her color faintly heightened, Sharlee looked straight into the narrow eyes of Miss Avery, who, talking with a little knot of men some distance away, had been watching her closely. The two girls smiled and bowed to each other with extraordinary sweetness.

CHAPTER X

Of Fifi on Friendship, and who would be sorry if Queed died; of Queed's Mad Impulse, sternly overcome; of his Indignant Call upon Nicolovius, the Old Professor.

Could I interrupt you for just a minute, Mr. Queed?"

"No. It is not time yet."

"Cicero's so horrid to-night."

"Don't scatter your difficulties, as I've told you before. Gather them all together and have them ready to present to me at the proper time. I shall make the usual pause," said Mr. Queed, "at nine sharp."

Fifi, after all, had been selfish enough to take the little Doctor at his word. He had both given her the freedom of his dining-room and ordered her to bring her difficulties to him, instead of sitting there and noisily crying over them. And she had done his bidding, night after night. For his part he had stuck manfully by his moment of reckless generosity, no matter how much he may have regretted it. He helped Fifi, upon her request, without spoken protest or censure. But he insisted on doing it after an iron-clad schedule: Absolute silence until nine o'clock; then an interlude for the solving of difficulties; absolute silence after that; then at 9.45 a second interlude for the solving of the last difficulties of the night. The old rule of the dining-room, the *Silence* sign, had been necessarily suspended, but the young man enforced his schedule of hours far more strictly than the average railroad.

"Nine o'clock," he announced presently. "Bring me your difficulties."

Fifi's brain was at low ebb to-night. She came around with several books, and he jabbed his pencil at her open Cicero with some contempt.

"You have a fundamental lack of acquaintance with Latin grammar, Miss—Miss Fifi. You badly need—"

"Why don't you call me Fifi, Mr. Queed? That's what all my friends call me."

He stared at her startled; she thought his eyes looked almost terrified. "My dear young lady! *I'm* not your friend."

A rare color sprang into Fifi's pallid cheeks: "I—I thought you liked me—from your being so good about helping me with my lessons—and everything."

Queed cleared his throat. "I do like you—in a way. Yes—in that way—I like you very well. I will call you F—Fifi, if you wish. But—friends! Oh, no! They take up more time than such a man as I can afford."

"I don't think I would take up one bit more time as your friend than I do now," said Fifi, in a plaintive voice.

Queed, uncomfortably aware of the flying minutes, felt like saying that that was impossible.

"Oh, I know what I'm talking about, I assure you," said the possessor of two friends in New York. "I have threshed the whole question out in a practical way."

"Suppose," said Fifi, "your book came out and you were very famous, but all alone in the world, without a friend. And you died and there was not one single person to cry and miss you—would you think that was a—a successful life?"

"Oh, I suppose so! Yes, yes!"

"But don't—don't you want to have people like you and be your friend?"

"My dear young lady, it is not a question of what I want. I was not put here in the world to frivol through a life of gross pleasure. I have serious work to do in the service of humankind, and I can do it only by rigid concentration and ruthless elimination of the unessential. Surely you can grasp that?"

"But—if you died to-morrow," said Fifi, fearfully fascinated by this aspect of the young man's majestic isolation,—"don't you know of anybody who'd be really and truly sorry?"

"Really, I've never thought of it, but doubtless my two friends in New York would be sorry after their fashion. They, I believe, are all."

"No they aren't! There's somebody else!"

Queed supposed she was going to say God, but he dutifully inquired, "Who?"

Fifi looked decidedly disappointed. "I thought you knew," she said, gazing at him with childlike directness. "Me."

Queed's eyes fell. There was a brief silence. The young man became aware of a curious sensation in his chest which he did not understand in the least, but which he was not prepared to describe as objectionable. To pass over it, and to bring the conversation to an immediate close, he rapped the open book austerely with his pencil.

"We must proceed with the difficulties. Let me hear you try the passage. Come! *Quam ob rem, Quirites*...."

The nine o'clock difficulties proceeded with, and duly cleared up, Fifi did not stay for the second, or 9.45, interlude. She closed *M.T. Ciceronis Orationes Selectæ*, gathered together her other paraphernalia, and then she said suddenly: —

"I may leave school next week, Mr. Queed. I—don't think I'm going to graduate."

He looked up, surprised and displeased. "Why on earth do you think that?"

"Well, you see, they don't think I'm strong enough to keep up the work right now. The Doctor was here to-day, and that's what he says. It's silly, I think—I know I am."

Queed was playing the devil's tattoo with his pencil, scowling somewhat nervously. "Did you want to graduate particularly?"

A look of exquisite wistfulness swept the child's face, and was gone. "Yes, I wanted to—lots. But I won't mind so much after I've had time to get used to it. You know the way people are."

There was a silence, during which the young man wrestled with the sudden mad idea of offering to help Fifi with all her lessons each night—not merely with the difficulties—thus enabling her to keep up with her class with a minimum of work. Where such an impulse came from he could not conjecture. He put it down with a stern hand. Personally, he felt, he might be almost willing to make this splendid display of altruism; but for the sake of posterity and the common good, he could not dream of stealing so much time from the Magnum Opus.

"Well!" he said rather testily. "That is too bad."

"I know you'll be glad not to have me bothering you any more with my lessons, and all."

"I will not say that."

He looked at Fifi closely, examined her face in a searching, personal manner, which he had probably never before employed in reviewing a human countenance.

"You don't look well—no, not in the least. You are not well. You are a sick girl, and you ought to be in bed at this moment."

Fifi colored with pleasure. "No," she said, "I am not well."

Indeed Fifi was not well. Her cheek spoke of the three pounds she had lost since he had first helped her with her difficulties, and the eleven pounds before that. The hand upon the Turkey-red cloth was of such transparent thinness that you were sure you could see the lamplight shining through. Her eyes were startling, they were so full of other-worldly sweetness and so ringed beneath with shadows.

"And if I stopped coming down here to work nights," queried Fifi shamelessly, "would you—miss me?"

"Miss you?"

"You wouldn't—you wouldn't! You'd only be glad not to have me around—"

"I can truthfully say," said the little Doctor, glancing at his watch, "that I am sorry you are prevented from graduating."

Fifi retired in a fit of coughing. She and her cough had played fast and loose with Queed's great work that evening, and, moreover, it took him a minute and a half to get her out of his mind after she had gone. Not long afterwards, he discovered that the yellow sheet he wrote upon was the last of his pad. That meant that he must count out time to go upstairs and get another one.

Count out time! Why, that was what his whole life had come down to now! What was it but a steady counting out of ever more and more time?

The thirty days of hours ceded to Klinker were up, and instead of at once bringing the prodigal experiment to a close, Doctor Queed found himself terribly tempted to listen to his trainer's entreaties and extend by fifty per centum the time allotted to the gymnasium and open-air pedestrianism. He could not avoid the knowledge that he felt decidedly better since he had begun the exercises, especially during these last few days. For a week "the" headache and he had been strangers. Much more important, he was conscious of bringing to his work, not indeed a livelier interest, for that would have been impossible, but an increasing vitality and an enlarged capacity. He kept the most careful sort of tabs upon himself, and his records seemed to show, at least for the past week or two, that his net volume of work had not been seriously lowered by the hour per day wrung from the Schedule. The exercises, then, seemed to be paying their own freight. And besides all this, they were clearly little mile-stones on the path which led men to physical competency and the ability to protect their articles from public affront.

Still, an hour out was an hour out—three hundred and sixty-five hours a year—three months' delay in finishing his book. Making allowance for increased productivity, a month and a half's delay. And that was only a beginning. The *Post*—Klinker's Exercises for All Parts of the Body—Klinker himself, who called frequently—now Fifi (eighteen minutes this very evening)—who could say where the mad dissipation would end? On some uncharted isle in the far South Seas, perchance, a man might be let alone to do his work. But in this boarding-house, it was clear now, the effort was foredoomed and hopeless. Once make the smallest concession to the infernal ubiquity of the race, once let the topmost bar of your gate down never so little, and the whole accursed public descended with a whoop to romp all over the premises. What, oh, what was the use of trying?...

"Ah, Mr. Queed—well met! Won't you stop in and see me a little while? You're enormously busy, I know—but possibly I can find something to interest you in my poor little collection of books."

Nicolovius, coming up the stairs, had met Queed coming down, pad in hand. The impertinence of the old professor's invitation fitted superbly with the bitterness of the little Doctor's humor. It pressed the martyr's crown upon his brow till the perfectness of his grudge against a hateful world lacked nor jot nor tittle.

"Oh, certainly! Certainly!" he replied, with the utmost indignation.

Nicolovius, bowing courteously, pushed open the door.

It was known in the boarding-house that the remodeling of the Second Hall Back into a private bathroom for Nicolovius had been done at his own expense, and rumor had it that for his two rooms—his "suite," as Mrs. Paynter called it—he paid down the sum of eighteen dollars weekly. The bed-sitting-room into which he now ushered his guest was the prettiest room ever seen by Mr. Queed, who had seen few pretty rooms in his life. Certainly it was a charming room of a usual enough type: lamp-lit and soft-carpeted; brass fittings about the fireplace where a coal fire glowed; a large red reading-table with the customary litter of books and periodicals; comfortable chairs to sit in; two uncommonly pretty mahogany bookcases with quaint leaded windows. The crude central identity about all bedrooms that had hitherto come within Queed's ken, to wit, the bed, seemed in this remarkable room to be wanting altogether. For how was he, with his practical inexperience, to know that the handsome leather lounge in the bay-window had its in'ards crammed full of sheets, and blankets, and hinges and collapsible legs?

The young man gravitated instinctively toward the bookcases. His expert eye swept over the titles, and his gloom lightened a little.

"You have some fair light reading here, I see," he said, plucking out a richly bound volume of Lecky's *History of European Morals*.

Nicolovius, who was observing him closely, smiled to himself. "Ah, yes. I'm the merest dilettante, without your happiness of being a specialist of authority."

The old professor was a tall man, though somewhat stooped and shrunken, and his head was as bare of hair as the palm of your hand; which of course was why he wore the black silk skull cap about the house. On the contrary his mustaches were singularly long and luxuriant, they, and the short, smart goatee, being of a peculiar deep auburn shade. His eyes were dark, brilliant, and slightly sardonic; there were yellow pouches under them and deep transverse furrows on his forehead; his nose, once powerfully aquiline, appeared to have been broken cleanly across the middle. Taken all in all, he was a figure to be noticed in any company.

He came forward on his rubber heels and stood at his guest's elbow.

"Your field is science, I believe? This Spencer was bound for me years ago, by a clever devil in Pittsburg, of all places; Huxley, too. My Darwin is hit and miss. Mill is here; Hume; the American John Fiske. By chance I have *The Wealth of Nations*. Here is a fine old book, Sir Henry Maine's *Ancient Law*. You know it, of course?"

"All—all! I know them all," murmured the little Doctor, standing with two books under his arm and plucking out a third. "I look back sometimes and stand amazed at the immensity of my reading. Benjamin Kidd—ha! He won't be in so many libraries when I get through with him. You are rather strong on political economy, I see. Alfred Marshall does very well. Nothing much in philosophy. The *Contrat Social*—absurd."

"Do you care for these?" asked Nicolovius, pointing to a row of well-worn works of Bible criticism. "Of course the Germans are far in the lead in this field, and I am unhappily compelled to rely on translations. Still I have—"

"Here! Look here! I must have this! I must take this book from you!" interrupted Queed, rather excitedly dragging a fat blue volume from a lower shelf. "Crozier's *Civilization and Progress*. What a find! I need it badly. I'll just take it with me now, shall I not? Eh?"

"I shall be only too happy to have you take it," said Nicolovius, blandly, "and as many others as you care for."

"I'll have another look and see," said Queed. "My copy of Crozier disappeared some time before I left New York, and so far I have been unable to replace it. I am showing him up completely.... Why, this is singular—extraordinary! There's not a history among all these books—not a volume!"

Nicolovius's expression oddly changed; his whole face seemed to tighten. "No," he said slowly, "I have some reason to dislike history."

The young man straightened sharply, horrified. "Why don't you say at once that you hate Life—Man—the Evolution of the Race—and be done with it?"

"Would that seem so dreadful to you?" The old man's face wore a sad smile. "I might say even that, I fear. Try one of those chairs by the fire. I shall not mind telling you how I came by this feeling. You don't smoke, I believe! You miss a good deal, but since you don't know it, how does it matter?"

Nicolovius's haughty aloofness, his rigid uncommunicativeness, his grand ducal bearing and the fact that he paid eighteen dollars a week for a suite had of course made him a man of mark and mystery in the boarding-house, and in the romancings of Miss Miller he had figured as nearly everything from a fugitive crown prince to a retired counterfeiter. However, Queed positively refused to be drawn away from the book-shelves to listen to his story, and the old professor was compelled to turn away from the fire and to talk, at that, to the back of the young man's head.

Nicolovius, so he told Queed, was not an American at all, but an Irishman, born at Roscommon, Connaught. His grandfather was a German, whence he got his name. But the lad grew up in the image of his mother's people. He became an intense patriot even for Ireland, an extremist among extremists, a notorious firebrand in a land where no wood glows dully. Equipped with a good education and natural parts, he had become a passionate leader in the "Young Ireland" movement; was a storm-centre all during the Home Rule agitations; and suddenly outgrew Ireland overnight during the "Parnellism and Crime" era. He got away to the coast, disguised as a coster, and once had the pleasure of giving a lift in his cart to the search-party who wanted him, dead or alive. This was in the year 1882.

"You were mixed up in the Phoenix Park murders, I daresay?" interjected Queed, in his matter-of-fact way.

"You will excuse my preference for a certain indefiniteness," said Nicolovius, with great sweetness.

On this side, he had drifted accidentally into school-teaching, as a means of livelihood, and stuck at it, in New York, St. Paul, and, for many years, in

Chicago. The need of a warmer climate for his health's sake, he said, had driven him South, and some three years before an appointment at Milner's Collegiate School had brought him to the city which he and the young man now alike called their own.

Queed, still sacking the shelves for another find, asked if he had never revisited Ireland.

"Ah, no," said Nicolovius, "there was no gracious pardon for my little peccadillo, no statute of limitations to run after me and pat me on the head. I love England best with the sea between us. You may fancy that a refugee Irishman has no fondness for reading history."

He flicked the fire-ash from his cigar and looked at Queed. All the time he talked he had been watching the young man, studying him, conning him over....

"My life ended when I was scarcely older than you. I have been dead while I was alive.... God pity you, young man, if you ever taste the bitter misery of that!"

Queed turned around surprised at the sudden fierceness of the other's tone. Nicolovius instantly sprang up and went over to poke the fire; he came back directly, smiling easily and pulling at his long cigar.

"Ah, well! Forgive the saddening reminiscences of an old man—not a common weakness with me, I assure you. May I say, Mr. Queed, how much your intellect, your culture, your admirable—ah—poise—amazing they seem to me in so young a man—have appealed to me among a population of Brookes, Bylashes, and Klinkers? You are the first man in many a day that has inspired me with an impulse toward friendship and confidence. It would be a real kindness if you'd come in sometimes of an evening."

At the word "friendship" the young man flinched uncontrollably. Was the whole diabolical world in league to spring out and make friends with him?

"Unfortunately," he said, with his iciest bow, "my time is entirely engrossed by my work."

But as his eye went round the pretty, dim-lit room, he could not help contrasting it with the bleak Scriptorium above, and he added with a change of tone and a sigh:—

"You appear wonderfully comfortable here."

Nicolovius shrugged. "So-so," he said indifferently. "However, I shall make a move before long."

"Indeed?"

"I want more space and independence, more quiet—surcease from meeting fellow-boarders at every step. I plan to move into an apartment, or perhaps a modest little house, if I can manage it. For I am not rich, unhappily, though I believe the boarders think I am, because I make Emma a present of a dollar each year at the anniversary of the birth of our Lord."

Queed ignored his little pleasantry. He was struck with the fact that Nicolovius had described exactly the sort of living arrangement that he himself most earnestly desired.

"I should have made the move last year," continued Nicolovius, pulling at his auburn mustaches, "except that—well, I am more sensitive to my loneliness as I grow older, and the fact was that I lacked a congenial companion to share a pleasanter home with."

The eyes of the two men met, and they moved away from each other as by common consent. Apparently the same thought popped simultaneously into both their minds. Queed dallied with his thought, frankly and with the purest unaltruism.

Though this was the first time he had ever been in the old professor's pretty room, it was the third or fourth time he had been invited there. Nothing could be clearer than that Nicolovius liked him enormously,—where on earth did he get his fatal gift for attracting people?—nothing than that he was exactly the sort of congenial companion the old man desired. Why shouldn't he go and live with Nicolovius in his new home, the home of perfect quiet and immunity from boarders? And unbroken leisure, too, for of course Nicolovius would bear all expenses, and he himself would fly from all remunerative work as from the Black Death. Nay more, the old chap would very likely be willing to pay him a salary for his society, or at least, see that he was kept well supplied with everything he needed—books to demolish like this one under his arm, and ...

He looked up and found the sardonic Italian eyes of the old professor fixed on him with a most curious expression.... No, no! Better even Mrs. Paynter's than solitude shared with this stagey old man, with his repellent face and his purring voice which his eyes so belied.

"I must be going," said Queed hastily.

His host came forward with suave expressions of regret. "However, I feel much complimented that you came at all. Pray honor me again very soon—"

"I'll return this book sometime," continued the young man, already at the door. "You won't mind if I mark it, of course?"

"My dear sir—most certainly not. Indeed I hoped that you would consent to accept it for your own, as a—"

"No, I'll return it. I daresay you will find," he added with a faint smile, but his grossest one, "that my notes have not lessened its value exactly!"

In the hall Queed looked at his watch; ten minutes to ten. *Twenty-five minutes to his visit upon the old professor!*

However, let us be calm and just about it. The twenty-five minutes was not a flat loss: he had got Crozier by it. Crozier was worth twenty-five minutes; thirty-five, if it came to that—fifty!... But how to fit such a thing as this into the Schedule—and Klinker's visits—and the time he had given to Fifi to-night and very likely would have to give through an endless chain of to-morrows? Here was the burning crux. Was it endurable that the Schedule must be corrupted yet again?

So far as little Fifi was concerned, it turned out that these agonies were superfluous; he had helped her with her lessons for the last time. She did not appear in the dining-room the next night, or the next, or the next. Inquiries from the boarders drew from Mrs. Paynter the information that the child's cough had pulled her down so that she had been remanded to bed for a day or two to rest up. But resting up appeared not to prove so simple a process as had been anticipated, and the day or two was soon running into weeks.

Halcyon nights Queed enjoyed in the dining-room in Fifi's absence, yet faintly marred in a most singular way by the very absence which alone made them halcyon. It is a fact that you cannot give to any person fifteen minutes of valuable time every night, and not have your consciousness somewhat involved in that person's abrupt disappearance from your horizon. Messages from Fifi on matters of most trivial import came to Queed occasionally, and these served to keep alive his subtle awareness of her absence. But he never took any notice of the messages, not even of the one which said that he could look in and see her some afternoon if he wanted to.

CHAPTER XI

Concerning a Plan to make a Small Gift to a Fellow-Boarder, and what it led to in the Way of Calls; also touching upon Mr. Queed's Dismissal from the Post, and the Generous Resolve of the Young Lady, Charles Weyland.

The State Department of Charities was a rudimentary affair in those days, just as Queed had said. Its appropriation was impossibly meager, even with the niggard's increase just wrung from the legislature. The whole Department fitted cozily into a single room in the Capitol; it was small as a South American army, this Department, consisting, indeed, of but the two generals. But the Secretary and the Assistant Secretary worked together like a team of horses. They had already done wonders, and their hopes were high with still more wonders to perform. In especial there was the reformatory. The legislature had adjourned without paying any attention to the reformatory, exactly as it had been meant to do. But a bill had been introduced, at all events, and the *Post* had carried a second editorial, expounding and urging the plan; several papers in the smaller cities of the State had followed the *Post's* lead; and thus the issue had been fairly launched, with the ground well broken for a successful campaign two years later.

The office of the Department was a ship-shape place, with its two desks, a big one and a little one; the typewriter table; the rows and rows of letter-files on shelves; a sectional bookcase containing Charities reports from other States, with two shelves reserved for authoritative books by such writers as Willoughby, Smathers, and Conant. Here, doubtless, would some day stand the colossal work of Queed. At the big desk sat the Rev. Mr. Dayne, a practical idealist of no common sort, a kind-faced man with a crisp brown mustache. At the typewriter-table sat Sharlee Weyland, writing firm letters to thirty-one county almshouse keepers. It was hard upon noon. Sharlee looked tired and sad about the eyes. She had not been to supper at Mrs. Paynter's for months, but she went there nearly every afternoon from the office to see Fifi, who had been in bed for four weeks.

The Department door opened, with no premonitory knock, and in walked, of all people, Mr. Queed.

Sharlee came forward very cordially to greet the visitor, and at once presented him to the Secretary. However Queed dismissed Mr. Dayne very easily, and gazing at Sharlee sharply through his spectacles, said:

"I should like to speak to you in private a moment."

"Certainly," said Sharlee.

"I'll step into the hall," said kind-faced Mr. Dayne.

"No, no. Indeed you mustn't. We will."

Sharlee faced the young man in the sunlit hall with sympathetic expectancy and some curiosity in her eyes.

"There is," he began without preliminaries, "a girl at the house where I board, who has been confined to her bed with sickness for some weeks. It appears that she has grown thin and weak, so that they will not permit her to graduate at her school. This involves a considerable disappointment to her."

"You are speaking of Fifi," said Sharlee, gently.

"That is the girl's name, if it is of any interest to you—"

"You know she is my first cousin."

"Possibly so," he replied, as though to say that no one had the smallest right to hold him responsible for that. "In this connection, a small point has arisen upon which advice is required, the advice of a woman. You happen to be the only other girl I know. This," said Queed, "is why I have called."

Sharlee felt flattered. "You are most welcome to my advice, Mr. Queed."

He frowned at her through glasses that looked as big and as round as butter-saucers, with an expression in which impatience contended with faint embarrassment.

"As her fellow-lodger," he resumed, precisely, "I have been in the habit of assisting this girl with her studies and have thus come to take an interest in her—a small interest. During her sickness, it seems, many of the boarders have been in to call upon her. In a similar way, she has sent me several messages inviting me to call, but I have not been in position to accept any of these invitations. It does not follow that, because I gave some of my time in the past to assisting her with her lessons, I can afford to give more of it now for purposes of—of mere sociability. I make the situation clear to you?"

Sharlee, to whom Fifi had long since made the situation clear, puckered her brow like one carefully rehearsing the several facts. "Yes, I believe that is all perfectly clear, Mr. Queed."

He hesitated visibly; then his lips tightened and, gazing at her with a touch of something like defiance, he said: "On the other hand, I do not wish this girl to think that I bear her ill-will for the time I have given her in the past. I—ahem—have therefore concluded to make her a present, a small gift."

Sharlee stood looking at him without a reply.

"Well?" said he, annoyed. "I am not certain what form this small gift had best take."

She turned away from him and walked to the end of the hall, where the window was. To Queed's great perplexity, she stood there looking out for some time, her back toward him. Soon it came into his mind that she meant to indicate that their interview was over, and this attitude seemed extremely strange to him. He could not understand it at all.

"I fear that you have failed to follow me, after all," he called after her, presently. "This was the point—as to what form the gift should take—upon which I wanted a woman's advice."

"I understand." She came back to him slowly, with bright eyes. "I know it would please Fifi very much to have a gift from you. Had you thought at all, yourself, what you would like to give?"

"Yes," he said, frowning vaguely, "I examined the shop windows as I came down and pretty well decided on something. Then at the last minute I was not altogether sure."

"Yes? Tell me what."

"I thought I would give her a pair of silk mitts."

Sharlee's eyes never left his, and her face was very sweet and grave.

"White silk ones," said he—"or black either, for that matter, for the price is the same."

"Well," said she, "why did you select mitts, specially?"

"What first attracted me to them," he said simply, "was that they came to precisely the sum I had planned to spend: seventy-five cents."

The little corrugation in Sharlee's brow showed how carefully she was thinking over the young man's suggestion from all possible points of view. You could easily follow her thought by her speaking sequence of expressions. Clearly it ran like this: "Mitts—splendid! Just the gift for a girl who's sick in bed. The one point to consider is, could any other gift possibly be better? No, surely none.... Wait a minute, though! Let's take this thing slowly and be absolutely sure we're right before we go ahead.... Run over carefully all the things that are ever used as gifts. Anything there that is better than mitts? Perhaps, after all ... Mitts ... Why, look here, isn't there one small objection, one trifling want of the fulness of perfection to be raised against the gift of mitts?"

"There's this point against mitts," said Sharlee slowly. "Fifi's in bed now, and I'm afraid she's likely to be there for some time. Of course she could not wear the mitts in bed. She would have to tuck them away in a drawer somewhere. Don't you think it might be a good idea to give her something that she could enjoy at once—something that would give her pleasure *now* and so help to lighten these tedious hours while she must be in her room?"

The mitts were the child of Queed's own brain. Unconsciously he had set his heart on them; but his clock-like mind at once grasped the logic of this argument, and he met it generously.

"Your point is well taken. It proves the wisdom of getting the advice of a woman on such a matter. Now I had thought also of a book—"

"I'll tell you!" cried Sharlee, nearly bowled over by a brilliant inspiration. "A *great* many men that I know make it a rule to send flowers to girls that are sick, and—"

"*Flowers!*"

"It does seem foolish—*such* a waste, doesn't it?—but really you've no idea how mad girls are about flowers, or how much real joy they can bring into a sick-room. And, by changing the water often, and—so on, they last a *long* time, really an incredible time—"

"You recommend flowers, then? Very well," he said resolutely—"that is settled then. Now as to the kind. I have only a botanical knowledge of flowers—shall we say something in asters, perhaps, chrysanthemums or dahlias? What is your advice as to that?"

"Well, I advise roses."

"Roses—good. I had forgotten them for the moment. White roses?"

A little shiver ran through her. "No, no! Let them be the reddest you can find."

"Next, as to the cost of red roses."

"Oh, there'll be no trouble about *that*. Simply tell the florist that you want seventy-five cents' worth, and he will give you a fine bunch of them. By the way, I'd better put his name and address down on a piece of paper for you. Be sure to go to this one because I know him, and he's extremely reliable."

He took the slip from her, thanked her, bowed gravely, and turned to go. A question had risen involuntarily to the tip of her tongue; it hung there for a breath, its fate in the balance; and then she released it, casually, when another second would have been too late.

"How is your work on the *Post* going?"

He wheeled as though she had struck him, and looked at her with a sudden odd hardening of the lower part of his face.

"The *Post* discharged me this morning."

"Oh—"

It was all that she could say, for she knew it very well. She had had it from Colonel Cowles two days before it happened, which was three days after the April meeting of the directors. Charles Gardiner West, who was to have raised his voice in behalf of Mr. Queed on that occasion, happened not to be present at all. Having effected the dissolution of Semple and West, he had gone to the country for a month's rest, in preparation for that mapping out of collegiate plans which was to precede his tour of Europe. Hence the directors, hearing no protests from intercessors, unanimously bestowed discretion upon the Colonel to replace the transcendental scientist with a juicier assistant at a larger salary.

"At least," the young man qualified, with a curious mixture of aggressiveness and intense mortification, "the *Post* will discharge me on the 15th day of May unless I show marked improvement. I believe that improvement was exactly the word the estimable Colonel employed."

"I'm awfully sorry," said Sharlee—"awfully! But after all, you want only some routine hack-work—any routine hack-work—to establish a little income. It will not be very hard to find something else, as good or even better."

"You do not appear to grasp the fact that, apart from any considerations of that sort, this is an unpleasant, a most offensive thing to have happen—"

"Oh, but that is just what it isn't, Mr. Queed," said Sharlee, who quite failed to appreciate his morbid tenderness for even the least of his intellectual offspring. "You have taken no pride in the newspaper work; you look down on it as altogether beneath you. You cannot mind this in any personal way—"

"I mind it," said he, "like the devil."

The word fell comically from his lips, but Sharlee, leaning against the shut door, looked at him with grave sympathy in her eyes.

"Mr. Queed, if you had tried to write nursery rhymes and—failed, would you have taken it to heart?"

"Never mind arguing it. In fact, I don't know that I could explain it to you in a thoroughly logical and convincing way. The central fact, the concrete thing, is that I do object most decidedly. I have spent too much time in equipping myself to express valuable ideas in discriminating language to be kicked out of a second-rate newspaper office like an incompetent office-boy. Of course I shall not submit to it."

"Do you care to tell me what you mean to do?"

"Do!" He hit the door-post a sudden blow with an unexpectedly large hand. "I shall have myself elected editor of the *Post*."

"But—but—but—" said the girl, taken aback by the largeness of this order—"But you don't expect to oust Colonel Cowles?"

"We are not necessarily speaking of to-morrow or next day. An actuary will tell you that I am likely to outlive Colonel Cowles. I mean, first, to have my dismissal recalled, and, second, to be made regular assistant editor at three times my present salary. That is my immediate reply to the directors of the Post. I am willing to let the editorship wait till old Cowles dies."

"Tell me," said Sharlee, "would you personally like to be editor of the *Post*?"

"*Like it!* I'll resign the day after they elect me. Call it sheer wounded vanity—anything you like! The name makes no difference. I know only that I will have the editorship for a day—and all for the worthless pleasure of pitching it in their faces." He looked past her out of the window, and his light gray eyes filled with an indescribable bitterness. "And to have the editorship," he thought out loud, "I must unlearn everything that I know about writing, and deliberately learn to write like a demagogic ass."

Sharlee tapped the calcimine with her pointed fingernails. He spoke, as ever, with overweening confidence, but she knew that he would never win any editorship in this spirit. He was going at the quest with a new burst of intellectual contempt, though it was this very intellectual contempt that had led to his downfall.

"But your own private work?"

"Don't speak of it, I beg!" He flinched uncontrollably; but of his own accord he added, in carefully repressed tones: "To qualify for the editorship of course means—a terrible interruption and delay. It means that *I must side-track My Book for two months or even longer!*"

Two months! It would take him five years and probably he would not be qualified then.

Sharlee hesitated. "Have you fully made up your mind to—to be editor?"

He turned upon her vehemently. "May I ask you never to waste my time with questions of that sort. I never—*never*—say anything until I have fully made up my mind about it. Good-morning."

"No, no, no! Don't go yet! Please—I want to speak to you a minute."

He stopped and turned, but did not retrace the three steps he had taken. Sharlee leaned against the door and looked away from him, out into the park.

The little Doctor was badly in need of a surgical operation. Somebody must perform it for him, or his whole life was a dusty waste. That he still had glimmerings, he had shown this very hour, in wanting to make a gift to his sick little fellow-lodger. His resentment over his dismissal from the *Post*, too, was an unexpectedly human touch in him. But in the same breath with these things the young man had showed himself at his worst: the glimmerings were so overlaid with an incredible snobbery of the mind, so encrusted with the rankest and grossest egotism, that soon they must flutter and die out, leaving him stone-blind against the sunshine and the morning. No scratch could penetrate that Achilles-armor of self-sufficiency. There must be a shock to break it apart, or a vicious stabbing to cut through it to such spark as was still alive.

Somebody must administer that shock or do that stabbing. Why not she? He would hate the sight of her forevermore, but ...

"Mr. Queed," said Sharlee, turning toward him, "you let me see, from what you are doing this morning, that you think of Fifi as your friend. I'd like to ask if you think of me in that way, too."

O Lord, *Lord!* Here was another one!

"No," he said positively. "Think of you as I do of Fifi! No, no! No, I do not."

"I don't mean to ask if you think of me as you do of Fifi. Of course I am sure you don't. I only mean—let me put it this way: Do you believe that I have your—interests at heart, and would like to do anything I could to help you?"

He thought this over warily. Doubtless doomed Smathers would have smiled to note the slowness with which his great rival's mind threshed out such a question as this.

"If you state your proposition in that way, I reply, tentatively, yes."

"Then can you spare me half an hour to-night after supper?"

"For what purpose?"

"For you and me," she smiled. "I'd like you to come and see me, at my house, where we could really have a little talk. You see, I know Colonel Cowles very well indeed, and I have read the *Post* for oh, many, many years! In this way I know something about the kind of articles people here like to read, and about—what is needed to write such articles. I think I might make a suggestion or two that—would help. Will you come?"

After somewhat too obvious a consideration, Queed consented. Sharlee thanked him.

"I'll put my address down on the back of that paper, shall I? And I think I'll put my name, too, for I don't believe you have the faintest idea what it is."

"Oh, yes. The name is Miss Charlie Weyland. It appears that you were named after a boy?"

"Oh, it's only a silly nickname. Here's your little directory back. I'll be very glad to see you—at half-past eight, shall we say? But, Mr. Queed—don't come unless you feel sure that I really want to help. For I'm afraid I'll have to say a good deal that will make you very mad."

He bowed and walked away. Sharlee went to the telephone and called Bartlett's, the florist. She told Mr. Bartlett that a young man would come in there in a few minutes—full description of the young man—asking for seventy-five cents' worth of red roses; Mr. Bartlett would please give him two dozen roses, and charge the difference to her, Miss Weyland; the entire transaction to be kept discreetly quiet.

However the transaction was not kept entirely quiet. The roses were delivered promptly, and became the chief topic of conversation at Mrs. Paynter's dinner-table. Through an enforced remark of Mr. Queed's, and the later discursive gossip of the boarders, it became disseminated over the town that Bartlett's was selling American Beauties at thirty-seven and a half cents a dozen, and the poor man had to buy ten inches, double column, in the *Post* next morning to get himself straightened out and reestablish Bartlett's familiar quotations.

CHAPTER XII

*More Consequences of the Plan about the Gift, and of how Mr.
Queed drinks his Medicine like a Man; Fifi on Men, and how they
do; Second Corruption of The Sacred Schedule.*

Queed's irrational impulse to make Fifi a small gift cost him the heart
of his morning. A call would have been cheaper, after all. Nor was the end
yet. In this world it never is, where one event invariably hangs by the tail of
another in ruthless concatenation. Starting out for Open-air Pedestrianism
at 4.45 that afternoon, the young man was waylaid in the hall by Mrs.
Paynter, at the very door of the big bedroom into which Fifi had long since
been moved. The landlady, backing Queed against the banisters, told him
how much her daughter had been pleased by his beautiful remembrance.
The child, she said, wanted particularly to thank him herself, and wouldn't
he please come in and see her just a moment?

As Mrs. Paynter threw open the door in the act of making the
extraordinary request, escape was impossible. Queed found himself inside
the room before he knew what he was doing. As for Mrs. Paynter, she
somewhat treacherously slipped away to consult with Laura as to what for
supper.

It was a mild sunny afternoon, with a light April wind idly kicking at
the curtains. Fifi sat over by the open window in a tilted-back Morris chair,
a sweet-faced little thing, all eyes and pallor. From her many covers she
extricated a fragile hand, frilled with the sleeve of a pretty flowered kimono.

"Look at them! Aren't they glorious!"

On a table at her elbow his roses nodded from a wide-lipped vase, a
gorgeous riot of flame and fragrance. Gazing at them, the young man
marvelled at his own princely prodigality.

"I don't know *how* to thank you for them, Mr. Queed, They are so, so
sweet, and I do love roses so!"

Indeed her joy in them was too obvious to require any words. Queed
decided to say nothing about the mitts.

"I'm glad that they please you," said he, pulling himself together for the ordeal of the call. "How are you getting along up here? Very well, I trust?"

"Fine. It's so quiet and nice.... And I don't mind about graduating a bit any more. Isn't that funny?"

"You must hurry up and get well and return to the dining-room again, F—F—Fifi—, and to the algebra lessons—"

"Don't," said Fifi. "I can't bear it."

But she whisked at her eyes with a tiny dab of a handkerchief, and when she looked at him she was smiling, quite clear and happy.

"Have you missed me since I stopped coming?"

"Missed you?" he echoed, exactly as he had done before.

But this time Fifi said, shamelessly, "I'll bet you have!—Haven't you?"

Come, Mr. Queed, be honest. You are supposed to have the scientist's passion for veracity. You mercilessly demand the truth from others. Now take some of your own medicine. Stand out like a man. Have you or have you not missed this girl since she stopped coming?

"Yes," said the little Doctor, rather hollowly, "I ... have missed you."

Fifi's smile became simply brazen. "Do you know what, Mr. Queed? You like me *lots* more than you will say you do."

The young man averted his eyes. But for some time there had been in his mind the subtle consciousness of something left undone, an occasion which he had failed to meet with the final word of justice. Since he had been in the room, a vague, unwelcome resolve had been forming in his mind, and at Fifi's bold words, it hardened into final shape. He drew a deep breath.

"You referred to me as your friend once, F—Fifi. And I said that I was not."

"I know."

"I was—mistaken"—so he drained his medicine to the dregs. "I ... am your friend."

Now the child's smile was the eternal motherly. "Lor', Mr. Queed, I knew it all the time."

Queed looked at the floor. The sight of Fifi affected him most curiously to-day. He felt strangely ill at ease with her, only the more so because she was so amazingly at home with him. She wore her reddish-brown hair not rounded up in front as of old, but parted smoothly in the middle, and this only emphasized the almost saintly purity of her wasted little face. Her buoyant serenity puzzled and disconcerted him.

Meantime Fifi was examining Queed carefully. "You've been doing something to yourself, Mr. Queed! What is it? Why, you look ten times better than even four weeks ago!"

"I think," he said drearily, "it must be Klinker's Exercises. I give them," broke from him, *"one hour and twenty minutes a day!"*

But he pulled himself together, conscientiously determined to take the cheery view with Fifi.

"It is an extraordinary thing, but I am feeling better, physically and mentally, than I ever felt before, and this though I never had a really sick day in my life. It must be the exercises, for that is the only change I have made in my habits. Yet I never supposed that exercise had any such practical value as that. However," he went on slowly, "I am beginning to believe that there are several things in this world that I do not understand."

Here, indeed, was a most humiliating, an epoch-making, confession to come from the little Doctor. It was accompanied with a vague smile, intended to be cheering and just the thing for a sick-room. But the dominant note in this smile was bewildered and depressed helplessness, and at it the maternal instinct sprang full-grown in Fifi's thin little bosom. A passionate wish to mother the little Doctor tugged at her heart.

"You know what you need, Mr. Queed? Friends—lots of good friends—"

He winced as from a blow. "I assure you—"

"Yes—you—DO!" said Fifi, with surprising emphasis for so weak a little voice. "You need first a good girl friend, one lots older and better than me—one just like Sharlee. O if only you and she *would* be friends!—she'd be the very best in the world! And then you need men friends, plenty of them, and to go around with them, and everything. You ought to like *men* more, Mr. Queed! You ought to learn to *be* like them, and—"

"Be like them!" he interrupted, "I am like them. Why," he conceded generously, "I am one of them."

Fifi dismissed this with a smile, but he immediately added: "Has it occurred to you that, apart from my greater concentration on my work, I am different from other men?"

"Why, Mr. Queed, you are no more like them than I am! You don't do any of the things they do. You don't—"

"Such as what? Now, Fifi, let us be definite as we go along. Suppose that it was my ambition to be, as you say, like other men. Just what things, in your opinion, should I do?"

"Well, smoke—that's one thing that all men do. And fool around more with people—laugh and joke, and tell funny stories and all. And then you could take an interest in your appearance—your clothes, you know; and be interested in all sorts of things going on around you, like politics and baseball. And go to see girls and take them out sometimes, like to the theatre. Some men that are popular drink, but of course I don't care for that."

Fifi, of course, had no idea that the little Doctor's world had been shattered to its axis that morning by three minutes' talk from Colonel Cowles. Therefore, though conscious that there never was a man who did not get a certain pleasure from talking himself over, she was secretly surprised at the patience, even the interest, with which he listened to her. She would have been still more surprised to know that his wonderful memory was nailing down every word with machine-like accuracy.

She expounded her little thesis in considerable detail, and at the end he said:—

"As I've told you, Fifi, my first duty is toward my book—to give it to the cause of civilization at the earliest possible moment. Therefore, the whole question is one of time, rather than of deliberate personal inclination. At present I literally cannot afford to give time to matters which, while doubtless pleasant enough in their fashion—"

"That's what you would have said about the exercise, two months ago. And now look, how it's helped you! And then, Mr. Queed—are you happy?"

Surprised and a little amused, he replied: "Really, I've never stopped to think. I should say, though, that I was perfectly content."

Fifi laughed and coughed. "There's a big difference—isn't there? Why, it's just like the exercise, Mr. Queed. Before you began it you were just *not sick*; now you are *very well*. That's the difference between content and happiness. Now I," she ran on, "am very, very happy. I wake up in the mornings *so* glad that I'm alive that sometimes I can hardly bear it, and all through the day it's like something singing away inside of me! Are you like that?"

No, Mr. Queed must confess that he was not like that. Indeed, few looking at his face at this moment would ever have suspected him of it. Fifi regarded him with a kind of wistful sadness, but he missed the glance, being engaged in consulting his great watch; after which he sprang noisily to his feet, horrified at himself.

"Good heavens—it's ten minutes past five! I must go immediately. Why, I'm twenty-five minutes behind My Schedule!"

Fifi smiled through her wistfulness. "Don't ask me to be sorry, Mr. Queed, because I don't think I can. You see, I haven't taken up a minute of your time for nearly a month, so I was entitled to some of it to-day."

You see! Hadn't he figured it exactly right from the beginning? Once give a human being a moment of your time, as a special and extraordinary kindness, and before you can turn around there that being is claiming it wholesale as a matter-of-course right!

"It was so sweet of you to send me these flowers, and then to come and see me, too.... Do you know, it's been the very best day I've had since I've been sick, and you've made it so!"

"It's all right. Well, good-bye, Fifi."

Fifi held out both her tiny hands, and he received them because, in the sudden emergency, he could think of no way of avoiding them.

"You'll remember what I said about friends, and *men*—won't you, Mr. Queed? Remember it begins with liking people, liking everybody. Then when you really like them you want to do things for them, and that is happiness."

He looked surprised at this definition of happiness, and then: "Oh—I see. That's your religion, isn't it?"

"No, it's just common sense."

"I'll remember. Well, Fifi, good-bye."

"Good-bye—and thank you for everything."

Into her eyes had sprung a tenderness which he was far from understanding. But he did not like the look of it in the least, and he extricated his hands from the gentle clasp with some abruptness.

From the safe distance of the door he looked back, and wondered why Fifi's great eyes were fixed so solemnly on him.

"Well—good-bye, again. Hurry up and get well—"

"Good-bye—oh, good-bye," said Fifi, and turned her head toward the open window with the blue skies beyond.

Did Fifi know? How many have vainly tortured themselves with that question, as they have watched dear ones slipping without a word down the slopes to the dark Valley! If this child knew that her name had been read out for the greater Graduation, she gave no sign. Sometimes in the mornings she cried a little, without knowing why. Sometimes she said a vague, sad little thing that brought her mother's heart, stone cold, to her mouth. But her talk was mostly very bright and hopeful. Ten minutes before Queed came in she had been telling Mrs. Paynter about something she would do in the fall. If sometimes you would swear that she knew there would never be another fall for her, her very next remark might confound you. So her little face turned easily to the great river with the shining farther shore, and, for her part, there would be no sadness of farewell when she embarked.

By marvelous work, Queed closed up the twenty-five minutes of time he had bestowed upon Fifi, and pulled into supper only three minutes behind running-time. Afterwards, he sat in the Scriptorium, his face like a carven image, the sacred Schedule in his hands. For it had come down to that. Either he must at any cost hew his way back to the fastness of his early days, or he must corrupt the Schedule yet again.

Every minute that he took away from his book meant just that much delay in giving the great work to the world. That fact was the eternal backbone of all his consciousness. On the other balance of his personal equation, there was Buck Klinker and there was Fifi Paynter.

Klinker evidently felt that all bars were down as to him. It would be a hard world indeed if a trainer was denied free access to his only pupil, and Klinker, though he had but the one, was always in as full blast as Muldoon's. He had acquired a habit of "dropping in" at all hours, especially late at night, which, to say the least, was highly wasteful of time. It was Queed's privilege to tell Klinker that he must keep away from the Scriptorium; but in that case Klinker might fairly retort that he would no longer give the Doc free physical culture. Did he care to bring that issue to the touch? No, he did not. In fact, he must admit that he had a distinct need of Buck, a distinct dependence upon him, for awhile yet at any rate. So he could make no elimination of the non-essential there.

Then there was Fifi. In a week, or possibly two weeks, Fifi would doubtless reappear in his dining-room, and if she had no lessons to trouble him with, she would at any rate feel herself free to talk to him whenever the whim moved her. Had she not let out this very day that she considered that she had a kind of title to his time? So it would be to the end of the chapter. It had been his privilege to tell Fifi that he could not spare her another minute of time till his work was finished.... Had been—but no longer was. Looking back now, he found it impossible to reconstruct the chain of impulse and circumstance which had trapped him into it, but the stark fact was that his own lips had authorized Fifi to profane at will his holy time. Not three hours before he had been betrayed into weakly telling her that he was her friend. He was a man of truth and honor. He could not possibly get back of that confession of friendship, or of the privileges it bestowed. So there was no elimination of the non-essential he could make there.

These were the short and ugly facts. And now he must take official cognizance of them.

With a leaden heart and the hands of lamentation, he took the Schedule to pieces and laboriously fitted it together again with a fire-new item in its midst. The item was Human Intercourse, and to it he allotted the sum of thirty minutes per diem.

It was a historic moment in his life, and, unlike most men at such partings of the ways, he was fully conscious of it. Nevertheless, he passed straight from it to another performance hardly less extraordinary. From his table drawer he produced a little memorandum book, and in it—just below a diagram of a new chest-developing exercise invented last night by Klinker—he jotted down the things that Fifi said a man must do to be like other men.

A clean half-hour remained before he must go and call on the young lady with the tom-boy name, Charles Weyland, who knew "what the public liked." He spent it, he, the indefatigable minute-shaver, sitting with the head that no longer ached clamped in his hand. It had been the most disturbing day of his life, but he was not thinking of that exactly. He was thinking what a mistake it had been to leave New York. There he had had but two friends with no possibility of getting any more. Here—it was impossible to blink the fact any longer—he already had two, with at least two more determinedly closing in on him. He had Fifi and he had Buck—yes, Buck; the young lady Charles Weyland had offered him her friendship this very day; and unless he looked alive he would wake up some morning to find that Nicolovius also had captured him as a friend.

He was far better off in New York, where days would go by in which he never saw Tim or Murphy Queed. And yet ... did he want to go back?

CHAPTER XIII

"Taking the Little Doctor Down a Peg or Two": as performed for the First and Only Time by Sharlee Weyland.

The Star that fought in its course for men through Sharlee Weyland was of the leal and resolute kind. It did not swerve at a squall. Sharlee had thought the whole thing out, and made up her mind. Gentle raillery, which would do everything necessary in most cases, would be wholly futile here. She must doff all gloves and give the little Doctor the dressing-down of his life. She must explode a mine under that enormously exaggerated self-esteem which swamped the young man's personality like a goitre. Sharlee did not want to do this. She liked Mr. Queed, in a peculiar sort of way, and yet she had to make it impossible for him ever to speak to her again. Her nature was to give pleasure, and therefore she was going to do her utmost to give him pain. She wanted him to like her, and consequently she was going to insult him past forgiveness. And she was not even sure that it was going to do him any good.

When her guest walked into her little back parlor that evening, Sharlee was feeling very self-sacrificing and noble. However, she merely looked uncommonly pretty and tremendously engrossed in herself. She was in evening dress. It was Easter Monday, and at nine, as it chanced, she was to go out under the escortage of Charles Gardiner West to some forgathering of youth and beauty. But her costume was so perfectly suited to the little curtain-raiser called Taking the Little Doctor Down a Peg or Two, that it might have been appointed by a clever stage-manager with that alone in mind. She was the haughty beauty, the courted princess, graciously bestowing a few minutes from her crowding fêtes upon some fourth-rate dependant. And indeed the little Doctor, with his prematurely old face and his shabby clothes, rather looked the part of the dependant. Sharlee's greeting was of the briefest.

"Ah, Mr. Queed.... Sit down."

Her negligent nod set him away at an immense distance; even he was aware that Charles Weyland had undergone some subtle but marked change since the morning. The colored maid who had shown him in was retained to button her mistress' long gloves. It proved to be a somewhat slow process. Over the mantel hung a gilt-framed mirror, as wide as the mantel itself. To this mirror, the gloves buttoned, Miss Weyland passed, and reviewed her appearance with slow attention, giving a pat here, making a minor readjustment there. But this survey did not suffice for details, it seemed; a more minute examination was needed; over the floor she trailed with leisurely grace, and rang the bell.

"Oh, Mary—my vanity-box, please. On the dressing-table."

Seating herself under the lamp, she produced from the contrivance the tiniest little mirror ever seen. As she raised it to let it perform its dainty function, her glance fell on Queed, sitting darkly in his rocking-chair. A look of mild surprise came into her eye: not that it was of any consequence, but plainly she had forgotten that he was there.

"Oh ... You don't mind waiting a few minutes?"

"I do m—"

"You promised half an hour I think? Never fear that I shall take longer—"

"I did not promise half an hour for such—"

"It was left to me to decide in what way the time should be employed, I believe. What I have to say can be said briefly, but to you, at least, it should prove immensely interesting." She stifled a small yawn with the gloved finger-tips of her left hand. "However, of course don't let me keep you if you are pressed for time."

The young man made no reply. Sharlee completed at her leisure her conference with the vanity-box; snapped the trinket shut; and, rising, rang the bell again. This time she required a glass of water for her good comfort. She drank it slowly, watching herself in the mantel mirror as she did so, and setting down the glass, took a new survey of her whole effect, this time in a long-distance view.

"Now, Mr. Queed!"

She sat down in a flowered arm-chair so large that it engulfed her, and fixed him with a studious, puckering gaze as much as to say: "Let's see. Now, what was his trouble?"

"Ah, yes!—the *Post*."

She glanced at the little clock on the mantel, appeared to gather in her thoughts from remote and brilliant places, and addressed the dingy youth briskly but not unkindly.

"Unfortunately, I have an engagement this evening and can give you very little time. You will not mind if I am brief. Here, then, is the case. A man employed in a minor position on a newspaper is notified that he is to be discharged for incompetence. He replies that, so far from being discharged, he will be promoted at the end of a month, and will eventually be made editor of the paper. Undoubtedly this is a magnificent boast, but to make it good means a complete transformation in the character of this man's work—namely, from entire incompetence to competence of an unusual sort, all within a month's time. You are the man who has made this extraordinary boast. To clear the ground before I begin to show you where your trouble is, please tell me how you propose to make it good."

Not every man feeling inside as the little Doctor felt at that moment would have answered with such admirable calm.

"I purpose," he corrected her, "to take the files of the *Post* for the past few years and read all of Colonel Cowles's amusing articles. He, I am informed, is the editorial mogul and paragon. I purpose to study those articles scientifically, to analyze them, to take them apart and see exactly how they are put together. I purpose to destroy my own style and build up another one precisely like the Colonel's—if anything, a shade more so. In short I purpose to learn to write like an ass, of asses, for asses."

"That is your whole programme?"

"It is more than enough, I think."

"Ah?" She paused a moment, looking at him with faint, distant amusement. "Now, as my aunt's business woman, I, of course, take an interest in the finances of her boarders. Therefore I had better begin at once looking about for a new place for you after May 15th. What other kinds of work do you think yourself qualified to do, besides editorial writing and the preparation of thesauruses?"

He looked at her darkly. "You imagine that the *Post* will discharge me on May 15th?"

"There is nothing in the world that seems to me so certain."

"And why?"

"Why will the Post discharge you? For exactly the same reason it promises to discharge you now. Incompetence."

"You agree with Colonel Cowles, then? You consider me incompetent to write editorials for the *Post*?"

"Oh, totally. And it goes a great deal deeper than style, I assure you. Mr. Queed, you're all wrong from the beginning."

Her eyes left his face; went first to the clock; glanced around the room. Sharlee's dress was blue, and her neck was as white as a wave's foamy tooth. Her manner was intended to convey to Mr. Queed that he was the smallest midge on all her crowded horizon. It did not, of course, have that effect, but it did arrest and pique his attention most successfully. It was in his mind that Charles Weyland had been of some assistance to him in first suggesting work on the *Post*; and again about the roses for Fifi. He was still ready to believe that she might have some profitable suggestion about his new problem. Was she not that "public" and that "average reader" which he himself so despised and detested? Yet he could not imagine where such a little pink and white chit found the hardihood to take this tone with one of the foremost scientists of modern times.

"You interest me. I am totally incompetent now; I will be totally incompetent on May 15th; this because I am all wrong from the beginning. Pray proceed."

Sharlee, her thoughts recalled, made a slight inclination of her head. "Forgive my absent-mindedness. First, then, as to why you are a failure as an editorial writer. You are quite mistaken in supposing that it is a mere question of style, though right in regarding your style as in itself a fatal handicap. However, the trouble has its root in your amusing attitude of superiority to the work. You think of editorial writing as small hack-work, entirely beneath the dignity of a man who has had one or two articles accepted by a prehistoric magazine which nobody reads. In reality, it is one of the greatest and most splendid of all professions, fit to call out the very best of a really big man. You chuckle and sneer at Colonel Cowles and think yourself vastly his superior as an editorial writer, when, in the opinion of everybody else, he is in every way your superior. I doubt if the *Post* has a single reader who would not prefer to read an article by him, on any subject, to reading an article by you. I doubt if there is a paper in the world that would not greatly prefer him as an editor to you—"

"You are absurdly mistaken," he interrupted coldly. "I might name various papers—"

"Yes, the *Political Science Quarterly* and the *Journal of the Anthropological Institute*." Sharlee smiled tolerantly, and immediately resumed: "When you sit down at the office to write an article, whom do you think you are writing for? A company of scientists? An institute of gray-bearded scholars? An academy of fossilized old doctors of laws? There are not a dozen people of that sort who read the *Post*. Has it never occurred to you to call up before your mind's eye the people you actually are writing for? You can see them any day as you walk along the street. Go into a street car at six o'clock any night and look around at the faces. There is your public, the readers of the *Post*—shop-clerks, stenographers, factory-hands, office-men, plumbers, teamsters, drummers, milliners. Look at them. Have you anything to say to interest them? Think. If they were to file in here now and ask you to make a few remarks, could you, for the life of you, say one single thing that would interest them?"

"I do not pretend, or aspire," said Mr. Queed, "to dispense frothy nothings tricked out to beguile the tired brick-layer. My duty is to give forth valuable information and ripened judgment couched in language—"

"No, your duty is to get yourself read; if you fail there you fail everywhere. Is it possible that you don't begin to grasp that point yet? I fancied that your mind was quicker. You appear to think that the duty of a newspaper is to back people up against a wall and ram helpful statistics into them with a force-pump. You are grotesquely mistaken. Your ideal newspaper would not keep a dozen readers in this city: that is to say, it would be a complete failure while it lasted and would bankrupt Mr. Morgan in six months. A dead newspaper is a useless one, the world over. At the same time, every living and good newspaper is a little better, spreads a little more sweetness and light, gives out a little more valuable information, ripened judgment, et cetera, than the vast majority of its readers want or will absorb. The *Post* is that sort of newspaper. It is constantly tugging its readers a little higher than they—I mean the majority, and not the cultured few—are willing to go. But the *Post* always recognizes that its first duty is to get itself read: if it does not succeed in that, it lacks the principle of life and dies. Perhaps the tired bricklayer you speak of, the middle-class, commonplace, average people who make up nearly all of the world, ought to be interested in John Stuart Mill's attitude toward the single-tax. But the fact is that they aren't. The *Post* wisely deals with the condition, and not a theory: it means to get itself read. It is your first duty, as a writer for it, to get yourself read. If you fail to get yourself read, you are worse than useless to the *Post*. Well, you have completely failed to do this, and that is why the *Post* is discharging you. Come, free yourself from exaggerated notions about your own importance and look at this simple point with the calm detachment of a scientist. The *Post* can save money, while preserving just the same effect, by discharging you and printing every morning a half-column from the Encyclopedia Britannica."

She rose quickly, as though her time was very precious, and passed over to the table, where a great bowl of violets stood. The room was pretty: it had reminded Queed, when he entered it, of Nicolovius's room, though there was a softer note in it, as the flowers, the work-bag on the table, the balled-up veil and gloves on the mantel-shelf. He had liked, too, the soft-shaded lamps; the vague resolve had come to him to install a lamp in the Scriptorium later on. But now, thinking of nothing like this, he sat in a thick silence gazing at her with unwinking sternness.

Sharlee carefully gathered the violets from the bowl, shook a small shower of water from their stems, dried them with a pocket handkerchief about the size of a silver dollar. Next she wrapped the stems with purple tinfoil, tied them with a silken cord and tassel and laid the gorgeous bunch upon a magazine back, to await her further pleasure. Then, coming back, she resumed her seat facing the shabby young man she was assisting to see himself as others saw him.

"I might," she said, "simply stop there. I might tell you that you are a failure as an editorial writer because you have nothing at all to say that is of the smallest interest to the great majority of the readers of editorials, and would not know how to say it if you had. That would be enough to satisfy most men, but I see that I must make things very plain and definite for you. Mr. Queed, you are a failure as an editorial writer because you are first a failure in a much more important direction. You're a failure as a human being—as a man."

She was watching his face lightly, but closely, and so she was on her feet as soon as he, and had her hand out before he had even thought of making this gesture.

"It is useless for this harangue to continue," he said, with a brow of storm. "Your conception of helpful advice ..."

But Sharlee's voice, which had begun as soon as his, drowned him out.... "Complimented you a little too far, I see. I shall be sure to remember after this," she said with such a sweet smile, "that, after all your talk, you are just the average man, and want to hear only what flatters your little vanity. *Good*-night. So nice to have seen you."

She nodded brightly, with faint amusement, and turning away, moved off toward the door at the back. Queed, of course, had no means of knowing that she was thinking, almost jubilantly: "I *knew* that mouth meant spirit!" He only knew that, whereas he had meant to terminate the interview with a grave yet stinging rebuke to her, she had given the effect of terminating the interview with a graceful yet stinging rebuke to him. This was not what he wanted in the least. Come to think of it, he doubted if he wanted the interview to end at all.

"Miss Weyland ..."

She turned on the threshold of the farther door. "I beg your pardon! I thought you'd gone! Your hat?—I think you left it in the hall, didn't you?"

"It is not my hat."

"Oh—what is it?"

"God knows," said the little Doctor, hoarsely.

He was standing in the middle of the floor, his hands jammed into his trousers pockets, his hair tousled over a troubled brow, his breast torn by emotions which were entirely new in his experience and which he didn't even know the names of. All the accumulation of his disruptive day was upon him. He felt both terrifically upset inside, and interested to the degree of physical pain in something or other, he had no idea what. Presently he started walking up and down the room, nervous as a caged lion, eyes fixed on space or on something within, while Sharlee stood in the doorway watching him casually and unsurprised, as though just this sort of thing took place in her little parlor regularly, seven nights a week.

"Go ahead! Go ahead!" he broke out abruptly, coming to a halt. "Pitch into me. Do it for all you're worth. I suppose you think it's what I need."

"Certainly," said Sharlee, pleasantly.

She stood beside her chair again, flushed with a secret sense of victory, liking him more for his temper and his control than she ever could have liked him for his learning. But it was not her idea that the little Doctor had got it anywhere near hard enough as yet.

"Won't you sit down, Mr. Queed?"

It appeared that Mr. Queed would.

"I am paying you the extraordinary compliment," said Sharlee, "of talking to you as others might talk about you behind your back—in fact, as everybody does talk about you behind your back. I do this on the theory that you are a serious and honest-minded man, sincerely interested in learning the truth about yourself and your failures, so that you may correct them. If you are interested only in having your vanity fed by flattering fictions, please say so right now. I have no time," she said, hardly able for her life to suppress a smile, "for butterflies and triflers."

Butterflies and triflers! Mr. Queed, proprietor of the famous Schedule, a butterfly and a trifler!

He said in a muffled voice: "Proceed."

"Since an editorial writer," said Sharlee, seating herself and beginning with a paragraph as neat as a public speaker's, "must be able, as his first qualification, to interest the common people, it is manifest that he must be interested in the common people. He must feel his bond of humanity with them, sympathize with them, like them, love them. This is the great secret of Colonel Cowles's success as an editor. A fine gentleman by birth, breeding, and tradition, he is yet always a human being among human beings. All his life he has been doing things with and for the people. He went all through the war, and you might have thought the whole world depended on him, the way he went up Cemetery Ridge on the 3rd of July, 1863. He was shot all to pieces, but they patched him together, and the next year there he was back in the fighting around Petersburg. After the war he was a leader against the carpet-baggers, and if this State is peaceful and prosperous and comfortable for you to live in now, it is because of what men like him and my father did a generation ago. When he took the *Post* he went on just the same, working and thinking and fighting for men and with men, and all in the service of the people. I suppose, of course, his views through all these years have not always been sound, but they have always been honest and honorable, sensible, manly, and sweet. And they have always had a practical relation with the life of the people. The result is that he has thousands and thousands of readers who feel that their day has been wanting in something unless they have read what he has to say. There is Colonel Cowles—Does this interest you, Mr. Queed? If not, I need not weary us both by continuing."

He again requested her, in the briefest possible way, to proceed.

"Well! There is Colonel Cowles, whom you presume to despise, because you know, or think you know, more political and social science than he does. Where you got your preposterously exaggerated idea of the value of text-book science I am at a loss to understand. The people you aspire to lead— for that is what an editorial writer must do—care nothing for it. That tired bricklayer whom you dismiss with such contempt of course cares nothing for it. But that bricklayer is the People, Mr. Queed. He is the very man that Colonel Cowles goes to, and puts his hand on his shoulder, and tries to help—help him to a better home, better education for his children, more and more wholesome pleasures, a higher and happier living. Colonel Cowles thinks of life as an opportunity to live with and serve the common, average, everyday people. You think of it as an opportunity to live by yourself and serve your own ambition. He writes to the hearts of the people. You write to the heads of scientists. Doubtless it will amaze you to be told that his paragraph on the death of Moses Page, the Byrds' old negro butler, was a far more useful article in every way than your long critique on the currency system of Germany which appeared in the same issue. Colonel Cowles is a big-hearted human being. You—you are a scientific formula. And the worst of it is that *you're proud of it!* The hopeless part of it is that you actually consider a few old fossils as bigger than the live people all around you! How can I show you your terrible mistake?... Why, Mr. Queed, the life and example of a little girl ..." she stopped, rather precipitately, stared hard at her hands, which were folded in her lap, and went resolutely on: "The life and example of a little girl like Fifi are worth more than all the text-books you will ever write."

A silence fell. In the soft lamplight of the pretty room, Queed sat still and silent as a marble man; and presently Sharlee, plucking herself together, resumed:—

"Perhaps you now begin to glimpse a wider difference between yourself and Colonel Cowles than mere unlikeness of literary style. If you continue to think this difference all in your own favor, I urge you to abandon any idea of writing editorials for the *Post*. If on the other hand, you seriously wish to make good your boast of this morning, I urge you to cease sneering at men like Colonel Cowles, and humbly begin to try to imitate them. I say that you are a failure as an editorial writer because you are a failure as a man, and I say that you are a failure as a man because you have no relation at all with man's life. You aspire to teach and lead human beings, and you have not the least idea what a human being is, and not the slightest wish to find out. All around you are men, live men of flesh and blood, who are moving the world, and you, whipping out your infinitesimal measuring-rod, dismiss them as inferior cattle who know nothing of text-book science. Here is a real and living world, and you roll through it like a billiard-ball. And all because you make the fatal error of mistaking a sorry handful of mummies for the universe."

"It is a curious coincidence," said Queed, with great but deceptive mildness, "that Fifi said much the same thing to me, though in quite a different way, this afternoon."

"She told me. But Fifi was not the first. You had the same advice from your father two months ago."

"My father?"

"You have not forgotten his letter that you showed me in your office one afternoon?"

It seemed that he had; but he had it in his pocket, as it chanced, and dug it out, soiled and frayed from long confinement. Stooping forward to introduce it into the penumbra of lamplight, he read over the detective-story message: "*Make friends: mingle with people and learn to like them. This is the earnest injunction of Your father.*"

"You complain of your father's treatment of you," said Sharlee, "but he offered you a liberal education there, and you declined to take it."

She glanced at the clock, turned about to the table and picked up her beautiful bouquet. A pair of long bodkins with lavender glass heads were waiting, it appeared; she proceeded to pin on her flowers, adjusting them with careful attention; and rising, again reviewed herself in the mantel-mirror. Then she sat down once more, and calmly said:

"As you are a failure as an editorial writer and as a man, so you are a failure as a sociologist ..."

It was the last straw, the crowning blasphemy. She hardly expected him to endure it, and he did not; she was glad to have it so. But the extreme mildness with which he interrupted her almost unnerved her, so confidently had she braced herself for violence.

"Do you mind if we omit that? I think I have heard enough about my failures for one night."

He had risen, but stood, for a wonder, irresolute. It was too evident that he did not know what to do next. Presently, having nowhere else to go, he walked over to the mantel-shelf and leant his elbow upon it, staring down at the floor. A considerable interval passed, broken only by the ticking of the clock before he said:—

"You may be an authority on editorial writing—even on manhood—life. But I can hardly recognize you in that capacity as regards sociology."

Sharlee made no reply. She had no idea that the young man's dismissal from the *Post* had been a crucifixion to him, an unendurable infamy upon his virginal pride of intellect. She had no conception of his powers of self-control, which happened to be far greater than her own, and she would have given worlds to know what he was thinking at that moment. For her part she was thinking of him, intensely, and in a personal way. Manners he had none, but where did he get his manner? Who had taught him to bow in that way? He had mentioned insults: where had he heard of insults, this stray who had raised himself in the house of a drunken policeman?

"Well," said Queed, with the utmost calmness, "you might tell me, in a word, why you think I am a failure as a sociologist."

"You are a failure as a sociologist," said Sharlee, immediately, "for the same reason as both your other failures: you are wholly out of relation with real life. Sociology is the science of human society. You know absolutely nothing about human society, except what other men have found out and written down in text-books. You say that you are an evolutionary sociologist.

Yet a wonderful demonstration in social evolution is going on all around you, and *you don't even know it*. You are standing here directly between two civilizations. On the one side there are Colonel Cowles and my old grandmother—mother of your landlady, plucky dear! On the other there are our splendid young men, men who, with traditions of leisure and cultured idleness in their blood, have pitched in with their hands and heads to make this State *hum*, and will soon be meeting and beating your Northern young men at every turn. On one side there is the old slaveholding aristocracy; on the other the finest Democracy in the world; and here and now human society is evolving from one thing to the other. A real sociologist would be absorbed in watching this marvelous process: social evolution actually surprised in her workshop. But you—I doubt if you even knew it was going on. A tremendous social drama is being acted out under your very window and you yawn and *pull down the blind*."

There was a brief silence. In the course of it the door-bell was heard to ring; soon the door opened; a masculine murmur; then the maid Mary's voice, clearly: "Yassuh, she's in.... Won't you rest your coat, Mr. West?"

Mary entered the little back parlor, a card upon a tray. "Please draw the folding doors," said Sharlee. "Say that I'll be in in a few minutes."

They were alone once more, she and the little Doctor; the silence enfolded them again; and she broke it by saying the last word she had to say.

"I have gone into detail because I wanted to make the unfavorable impression you produce upon your little world clear to you, for once. But I can sum up all that I have said in less than six words. If you remember anything at all that I have said, I wish you would remember this. Mr. Queed, you are afflicted with a fatal malady. Your cosmos is all Ego."

She started to rise, thought better of it, and sat still in her flowered chair full in the lamplight. The little Doctor stood at the mantel-shelf, his elbow upon it, and the silence lengthened. To do something, Sharlee pulled off her right long glove and slowly put it back again. Then she pulled off her left long glove, and about the time she was buttoning the last button he began speaking, in a curious, lifeless voice.

"I learned to read when I was four years old out of a copy of the New York *Evening Post*. It came to the house, I remember, distinctly, wrapped around two pork chops. That seemed to be all the reading matter we had in the house for a long time—I believe Tim was in hard luck in those days—and by the time I was six I had read that paper all through from beginning to end, five times. I have wondered since if that incident did not give a bent to my whole mind. If you are familiar with the *Evening Post*, you may appreciate what I mean.... It came out in me exactly like a duck's yearning for water; that deep instinct for the printed word. Of course Tim saw that I was different from him. He helped me a little in the early stages, and then he stood back, awed by my learning, and let me go my own gait. When I was about eight, I learned of the existence of public libraries. I daresay it would surprise you to know the books I was reading in this period of my life—and writing too: for in my eleventh year I was the author of a one-volume history of the world, besides several treatises. And I early began to think, too. What was the fundamental principle underlying the evolution of a higher and higher human type? How could this principle be unified through all branches of science and reduced to an operable law? Questions such as these kept me awake at night while I still wore short trousers. At fourteen I was boarding alone in a kind of tenement on the East Side. Of course I was quite different from all the people around me. Different. I don't remember that they showed any affectionate interest in me, and why on earth should they? As I say, I was different. There was nothing there to suggest a conception of that brotherhood of man you speak of. I was born with this impulse for isolation and work, and everything that happened to me only emphasized it. I never had a day's schooling in my life, and never a word of advice or admonition—never a scolding in all my life till now. Here is a point on which your Christian theory of living seems to me entirely too vague: how to reconcile individual responsibility with the forces of heredity and circumstance. From my point of view your talk would have been better rounded if you had touched on that. Still, it was striking and interesting as it was. I like to hear a clear statement of a point of view, and that your statement happens to riddle me, personally, of course does not affect the question in any way. If I regard human society and human life too much as the biologist regards his rabbit, which appears to be the gist of your criticism, I can at least cheerfully take my own turn on the operating table as occasion requires. There is, of course, a great deal that I might say in reply, but I do not understand that either of us desires a debate. I will simply assert that your fundamental conception of life, while novel and piquant, will not hold water for a moment. Your conception is, if I state it fairly, that a man's life, to be useful, to be a life of service, must be given immediately to his fellows. He must do visible and tangible things with other men. I think a little reflection will convince you that, on the contrary, much or most of the best work of the world has been done by men whose personal lives were not unlike my own. There was Palissy, to take a familiar minor instance. Of course his neighbors saw in him only a madman whose cosmos was all Ego. Yet people are grateful to Palissy to-day, and think little of the suffering of his wife and children. Newton was no genial leader of the people. Bacon could not even be loyal to his friends. The living world around Socrates put him to death.

The world's great wise men, inventors, scientists, philosophers, prophets, have not usually spent their days rubbing elbows with the bricklayer. Yet these men have served their race better than all the good-fellows that ever lived. To each his gifts. If I succeed in reducing the principle of human evolution to its eternal law, I need not fear the judgment of posterity upon my life. I shall, in fact, have performed the highest service to humankind that a finite mind can hope to compass. Nevertheless, I am impressed by much that you say. I daresay a good deal of it is valuable. All of it I engage to analyze and consider dispassionately at my leisure. Meantime, I thank you for your interest in the matter. Good-evening."

"Mr. Queed."

Sharlee rose hurriedly, since hurry was so evidently necessary. She felt profoundly stirred, she hardly knew why; all her airs of a haughty princess were fled; and she intercepted him with no remnant of her pretense that she was putting a shabby inferior in his place.

"I want to tell you," she said, somewhat nervously, "that I—I—admire very much the way you've taken this. No ordinary man would have listened with such—"

"I never pretended to be an ordinary man."

He moved, but she stood unmoving in front of him, the pretty portrait of a lady in blue, and the eyes that she fastened upon him reminded him vaguely of Fifi's.

"Perhaps I—should tell you," said Sharlee, "just why I—"

"Now don't," he said, smiling faintly at her with his old air of a grandfather—"don't spoil it all by saying that you didn't mean it."

Under his smile she colored a little, and, despite herself, looked confused. He took advantage of her embarrassment to pass her with another bow and go out, leaving her struggling desperately with the feeling that he had got the best of her after all.

But the door opened again a little way, almost at once, and the trim-cut, academic face, with the lamplight falling upon the round glasses and blotting them out in a yellow smudge, appeared in the crevice.

"By the way, you were wrong in saying that I pulled down my blind on the evolutionary process now going on in the South. I give four thousand words to it in my Historical Perspective, volume one."

CHAPTER XIV

In which Klinker quotes Scripture, and Queed has helped Fifi with her Lessons for the Last Time.

The tax-articles in the *Post* had ceased after the adjournment of the Legislature, which body gave no signs of ever having heard of them. Mr. Queed's new series dealt authoritatively with "Currency Systems of the World." He polished the systems off at the rate of three a week. But he had asked and obtained permission to submit, also, voluntary contributions on topics of his own choosing, and now for a fortnight these offerings had died daily in Colonel Cowles's waste-basket.

As for his book, Queed could not bear to think of it in these days. Deliberately he had put a winding-sheet about his heart's desire, and laid it away in a drawer, until such time as he had indisputably qualified himself to be editor of the *Post*. Having qualified, he could open that drawer again, with a rushing access of stifled ardor, and await the Colonel's demise; but to do this, he figured now, would take him not less than two months and a half. Two months and a half wrenched from the Schedule! That sacred bill of rights not merely corrupted, but for a space nullified and cancelled! Yes, it was the ultimate sacrifice that outraged pride of intellect had demanded; but the young man would not flinch. And there were moments when Trainer Klinker was startled by the close-shut misery of his face.

The Scriptorium had been degraded into a sickening school of journalism. Day after day, night after night, Queed sat at his tiny table poring over back files of the *Post*, examining Colonel Cowles's editorials as a geologist examines a Silurian deposit. He analyzed, classified, tabulated, computed averages, worked out underlying laws; and gradually, with great travail—for the journalese language was to him as Greek to another—he deduced from a thousand editorials a few broad principles, somewhat as follows:—

1. That the Colonel dealt with a very wide range of concrete topics, including many that appeared extremely trivial. (Whereas he, Queed, had dealt almost exclusively with abstract principles, rarely taking cognizance of any event that had happened later than 1850.)

2. That nearly all the Colonel's "best" articles—*i.e.*, best-liked, most popular: the kind that Major Brooke and Mr. Bylash, or even Miss Miller, were apt to talk about at the supper-table—dealt with topics of a purely local and ephemeral interest.

3. That the Colonel never went deeply or exhaustively into any group of facts, but that, taking one broad simple hypothesis as his text, he hammered that over and over, saying the same thing again and again in different ways, but always with a wealth of imagery and picturesque phrasing.

4. That the Colonel invariably got his humorous effects by a good-natured but sometimes sharp ridicule, the process of which was to exaggerate the argument or travesty the cause he was attacking until it became absurd.

5. That the Colonel, no matter what his theme, always wrote with vigor and heat and color: so that even if he were dealing with something on the other side of the world, you might suppose that he, personally, was intensely gratified or extremely indignant about it, as the case might be.

These principles Queed was endeavoring, with his peculiar faculty for patient effort, to apply practically in his daily offerings. It is enough to say that he found the task harder than Klinker's Exercises, and that the little article on the city's method of removing garbage, which failed to appear in this morning's *Post*, had stood him seven hours of time.

It was a warm rainy night in early May. Careful listening disclosed the fact that Buck Klinker, who had as usual walked up from the gymnasium with Queed, was changing his shoes in the next room, preparatory for supper. Otherwise the house was very still. Fifi had been steadily reported "not so well" for a long time and, for two days, very ill. Queed sitting before the table, his gas ablaze and his shade up, tilted back his chair and thought of her now. All at once, with no conscious volition on his part, he found himself saying over the startling little credo that Fifi had suggested for his taking, on the day he sent her the roses.

To like men and do the things that men do. To smoke. To laugh. To joke and tell funny stories. To take a ...

The door of the Scriptorium-editorium opened and Buck Klinker, entering without formalities, threw himself, according to his habit, upon the tiny bed. This time he came by invitation, to complete the decidedly interesting conversation upon which the two men had walked up town; but talk did not at once begin. A book rowelled the small of Klinker's back as he reclined upon the pillow, and plucking it from beneath him, he glanced at the back of it.

"*Vanity Fair.* Didn't know you ever read story-books, Doc."

The Doc did not answer. He was occupied with the thought that not one of the things that Fifi had urged upon him did he at present do. Smoking he could of course take up at any time. Buck Klinker worked in a tobacconist's shop; it might be a good idea to consult him as to what was the best way to begin. As for telling funny stories—did he for the life of him know one to tell? He racked his brain in vain. There were two books that he remembered having seen in the Astor Library, *The Percy Anecdotes*, and Mark Lemon's *Jest Book*; perhaps the State Library had them.... Stay! Did not Willoughby himself somewhere introduce an anecdote of a distinctly humorous nature?

"It ain't much," said Buck, dropping Thackeray to the floor. "I read the whole thing once.—No, I guess I'm thinkin' of *The County Fair*, a drammer that I saw at the Bee-jou. But I guess they're all the same, those Fairs."

"Say Doc," he went on presently, "I'm going to double you on Number Seven, beginning from to-morrow, hear?"

Number Seven was one of the stiffest of Klinker's Exercises for All Parts of the Body. Queed looked up absently.

"That's right," said his trainer, inexorably. "It's just what you need. I had a long talk with Smithy, last night."

"Buck," said the Doctor, clearing his throat, "have I ever—ahem—told you of the famous reply of Dr. Johnson to the Billingsgate fishwives?"

"Johnson? Who? Fat, sandy-haired man lives on Third Street?"

"No, Dr. Samuel Johnson, the well-known English author and—character. It is related that on one occasion Dr. Johnson approached the fishwives at Billingsgate to purchase of their wares. The exact details of the story are not altogether clear in my memory, but, as I recall it, something the good Doctor said angered these women, for they began showering him with profane and blasphemous names. At this style of language the fishwives are said to be extremely proficient. What do you fancy that Dr. Johnson called them in return? But you could hardly guess. He called them parallelopipedons. I am not entirely certain whether it was parallelopipedons or isosceles triangles. Possibly there are two versions of the story."

Buck stared at him, frankly and greatly bewildered, and noticed that the little Doctor was staring at him, with strong marks of anxiety on his face.

"I should perhaps say," added Queed, "that parallelopipedons and isosceles triangles are not profane or swearing words at all. They are, in fact, merely the designations applied to geometrical figures."

"Oh," said Klinker. "Oh."

There was a brief pause.

"Ah, well!... Go on with what you were telling me as we walked up, then!"

"Sure thing. But I don't catch the conversation. What was all that con you were giving me—?"

"Con?"

"About Johnson and the triangles."

"It simply occurred to me to tell you a funny story, of the sort that men are known to like, with the hope of amusing you—"

"Why, that wasn't a funny story, Doc."

"I assure you that it was."

"Don't see it," said Klinker.

"That is not my responsibility, in any sense."

Thus Doctor Queed, sitting stiffly on his hard little chair, and gazing with annoyance at Klinker through the iron bars at the foot of the bed.

"Blest if I pipe," said Buck, and scratched his head.

"I cannot both tell the stories and furnish the brains to appreciate them. Kindly proceed with what you were telling me."

So Buck, obliging but mystified, dropped back upon the bed and proceeded, tooth-pick energetically at work. His theme was a problem with which nearly every city is unhappily familiar. In Buck's terminology, it was identified as "The Centre Street mashers": those pimply, weak-faced, bad-eyed young men who congregate at prominent corners every afternoon, especially Saturdays, to smirk at the working-girls, and to pass, wherever they could, from their murmured, "Hello, Kiddo," and "Where you goin', baby?" to less innocent things.

Buck's air of leisureliness dropped from him as he talked; his orange-stick worked ever more and more furiously; his honest voice grew passionate as he described conditions as he knew them.

"... And some fool of a girl, no more than a child for knowing what she's doin', laughs and answers back—just for the fun of it, not looking for harm, and right there's where your trouble begins. Maybe that night after doin' the picture shows; maybe another night; but it's sure to come. Dammit, Doc, I'm no saint nor sam-singer and I've done things I hadn't ought like other men, and woke up shamed the next morning, too, but I've got a sister who's a decent good girl as there is anywhere, and by God, sir, I'd *kill* a man who just looked at her with the dirty eyes of them little soft-mouth blaggards!"

Queed, unaffectedly interested, asked the usual question—could not the girls be taught at home the dangers of such acquaintances?—and Buck pulverized it in the usual way.

"Who in blazes is goin' to teach 'em? Don't you know *anything* about what kind of homes they got? Why, man, they're *the sisters of the little blaggards!*"

He painted a dark picture of the home-life of many of these girls: its hard work and unrelenting poverty; its cheerlessness; the absence of any fun; the irresistible allurement of the flashily-dressed stranger who jingles money in his pocket and offers to "show a good time." Then he told a typical story, the story of a little girl he knew, who worked in a department store for three dollars and a half a week, and whose drunken father took over the last cent of that every Saturday night. This girl's name was Eva Bernheimer, and she was sixteen years old and "in trouble."

"You know what, Doc?" Buck ended. "You'd ought to take it up in the *Post*—that's what. There's a fine piece to be written, showin' up them little hunters."

It was characteristic of Doctor Queed that such an idea had not and would not have occurred to him: applying his new science of editorial writing to a practical problem dipped from the stream of everyday life was still rather beyond him. But it was also characteristic of him that, once the idea had been suggested to him, he instantly perceived its value. He looked at Buck admiringly through the iron bars.

"You are quite right. There is."

"You know they are trying to get up a reformatory—girls' home, some call it. That's all right, if you can't do better, but it don't get to the bottom of it. The right way with a thing like this is to *take it before it happens!*"

"You are quite right, Buck."

"Yes—but how're you goin' to do it? You sit up here all day and night with your books and studies, Doc—where's your cure for a sorry trouble like this?"

"That is a fair question. I cannot answer definitely until I have studied the situation out in a practical way. But I will say that the general problem is one of the most difficult with which social science has to deal."

"I know what had ought to be done. The blaggards ought to be shot. Damn every last one of them, I say."

Klinker conversed in his anger something like the ladies of Billingsgate, but Queed did not notice this. He sat back in his chair, absorbedly thinking that here, at all events, was a theme which had enough practical relation with life. He himself had seen a group of the odious "mashers" with his own eyes; Buck had pointed them out as they walked up. Never had a social problem come so close home to him as this: not a thing of text-book theories, but a burning issue working out around the corner on people that Klinker knew. And Klinker's question had been an acute one, challenging the immediate value of social science itself.

His thought veered, swept out of its channel by an unwonted wave of bitterness. Klinker had offered him this material, Klinker had advised him to write an editorial about it, Klinker had pointed out for him, in almost a superior way, just where the trouble lay. Nor was this all. Of late everybody seemed to be giving him advice. Only the other week it was Fifi; and that same day, the young lady Charles Weyland. What was there about him that invited this sort of thing?... And he was going to take Klinker's advice; he had seized upon it gratefully. Nor could he say that he was utterly insensate to Fifi's: he had caught himself saying over part of it not ten minutes ago. As for Charles Weyland's ripsaw criticisms, he had analyzed them dispassionately, as he had promised, and his reason rejected them in toto. Yet he could not exactly say that he had wholly purged them out of his mind. No ... the fact was that some of her phrases had managed to burn themselves into his brain.

Presently Klinker said another thing that his friend the little Doctor remembered for a long time.

"Do you know what's the finest line in Scripture, Doc? *But He spake of the temple of His body.* I heard a minister get that off in a church once, in a sermon, and I don't guess I'll ever forget it. A dandy, ain't it?... Exercise and live straight. Keep your temple strong and clean. If I was a parson, I tell you, I'd go right to Seventh and Centre next Saturday and give a talk to them blaggards on that. *But He spake of ...*"

Klinker stopped as though he had been shot. A sudden agonized scream from downstairs jerked him off the bed and to his feet in a second solemn as at the last trump. He stared at Queed wide-eyed, his honest red face suddenly white.

"God forgive me for talkin' so loud.... I'd ought to have known...."

"What is it? Who was that?" demanded Queed, startled more by Klinker's look than by that scream.

But Klinker only turned and slipped softly out of the door, tipping on his toes as though somebody near at hand were asleep.

Queed was left bewildered, and completely at a loss. Whatever the matter was, it clearly concerned Buck Klinker. Equally clearly, it did not concern him. People had a right to scream if they felt that way, without having a horde of boarders hurry out and call them to book.

However, his scientist's fondness for getting at the underlying causes — or as some call it, curiosity — presently obtained control of him, and he went downstairs.

There is no privacy of grief in the communism of a middle-class boarding-house. It is ordered that your neighbor shall gaze upon your woe and you shall stare at his anguish, when both are new and raw. That cry of pain had been instantly followed by a stir of movement; a little shiver ran through the house. Doors opened and shut; voices murmured; quick feet sounded on the stairs. Now the boarders were gathered in the parlor, very still and solemn, yet not to save their lives unaware that for them the humdrum round was to go on just the same. And here, of course, is no matter of a boarding-house: for queens must eat though kings lie high in state.

To Mrs. Paynter's parlor came a girl, white-faced and shadowy-eyed, but for those hours at least, calm and tearless and the mistress of herself. The boarders rose as she appeared in the door, and she saw that after all she had no need to tell them anything. They came and took her hand, one by one, which was the hardest to bear, and even Mr. Bylash seemed touched with a new dignity, and even Miss Miller's pompadour looked human and sorry. But two faces Miss Weyland did not see among the kind-eyed boarders: the old professor, who had locked himself in his room, and the little Doctor who was at that moment coming down the steps.

"Supper's very late," said she. "Emma and Laura ... have been much upset. I'll have it on the table in a minute."

She turned into the hall and saw Queed on the stairs. He halted his descent five steps from the bottom, and she came to the banisters and stood and looked up at him. And if any memory of their last meeting was with them then, neither of them gave any sign of it.

"You know — ?"

"No, I don't know," he replied, disturbed by her look, he did not know why, and involuntarily lowering his voice. "I came down expressly to find out."

"Fifi — She — "

"Is worse again?"

"She ... stopped breathing a few minutes ago."

"*Dead!*"

Sharlee winced visibly at the word, as the fresh stricken always will.

The little Doctor turned his head vaguely away. The house was so still that the creaking of the stairs as his weight shifted from one foot to another, sounded horribly loud; he noticed it, and regretted having moved. The idea of Fifi's dying had of course never occurred to him. Something put into his head the simple thought that he would never help the little girl with her algebra again, and at once he was conscious of an odd and decidedly unpleasant sensation, somewhere far away inside of him. He felt that he ought to say something, to sum up his attitude toward the unexpected event, but for once in his life he experienced a difficulty in formulating his thought in precise language. However, the pause was of the briefest.

"I think," said Sharlee, "the funeral will be Monday afternoon.... You will go, won't you?"

Queed turned upon her a clouded brow. The thought of taking personal part in such mummery as a funeral—"barbaric rites," he called them in the forthcoming Work—was entirely distasteful to him. "No," he said, hastily. "No, I could hardly do that—"

"Fifi—would like it. It is the last time you will have to do anything for her."

"Like it? It is hardly as if she would know—!"

"Mightn't you show your regard for a friend just the same, even if your friend was never to know about it?... Besides—I think of these things another way, and so did Fifi."

He peered down at her over the banisters, oddly disquieted. The flaring gas lamp beat mercilessly upon her face, and it occurred to him that she looked tired around her eyes.

"I think Fifi will know ... and be glad," said Sharlee. "She liked and admired you. Only day before yesterday she spoke of you. Now she ... has gone, and this is the one way left for any of us to show that we are sorry."

Long afterwards, Queed thought that if Charles Weyland's lashes had not glittered with sudden tears at that moment he would have refused her. But her lashes did so glitter, and he capitulated at once; and turning instantly went heavy-hearted up the stairs.

CHAPTER XV

In a Country Churchyard, and afterwards; of Friends: how they take your Time while they live, and then die, upsetting your Evening's Work; and what Buck Klinker saw in the Scriptorium at 2 a.m.

Queed was caught, like many another rationalist before him, by the stirring beauty of the burial service of the English church.

Fifi's funeral was in the country, at a little church set down in a beautiful grove which reminds all visitors of the saying about God's first temples. Near here Mrs. Paynter was born and spent her girlhood; here Fifi, before her last illness, had come every Sabbath morning to the Sunday-school; here lay the little strip of God's acre that the now childless widow called her own. You come by the new electric line, one of those high-speed suburban roads which, all over the country, are doing so much to persuade city people back to the land. The cars are steam-road size. Two of them had been provided for the mourners, and there was no room to spare; for the Paynter family connection was large, and it seemed that little Fifi had many friends.

From Stop 11, where the little station is, your course is by the woodland path; past the little springhouse, over the tiny rustic bridge, and so on up the shady slope to the cluster of ancient pines. In the grove stood carriages; buggy horses reined to the tall trees; even that abomination around a church, the motor of the vandals. In the walk through the woods, Queed found himself side by side with a fat, scarlet-faced man, who wore a vest with brass buttons and immediately began talking to him like a lifelong friend. He was a motorman on the suburban line, it seemed, and had known Fifi very well.

"No, sir, I wouldn't believe it when my wife seen it in the paper and called it out to me, an' I says there's some mistake, you can be sure, and she says no, here it is in the paper, you can read it for y'self. But I wouldn't believe it till I went by the house on the way to my run, and there was the crape on the door. An' I tell you, suh, I couldn't a felt worse if 'twas one o' my own kids. Why, it seems like only the other morning she skipped onto my car, laughin' and sayin', 'How are you to-day, Mr. Barnes?' Why she and me been buddies for nigh three years, and she took my 9.30 north car every Sunday morning, rain or shine, just as reg'lar, and was the only one I ever let stand out on *my* platform, bein' strictly agin all rules, and my old partner Hornheim was fired for allowin' it, it ain't six months since. But what could I do when she asked me, *please, Mr. Barnes*, with that sweet face o' hers, and her rememberin' me every Christmas that came along just like I was her Pa...."

The motorman talked too much, but he proved useful in finding seats up near the front, where, being fat, he took up considerably more than his share of room.

Unless Tim had taken him to the Cathedral once, twenty years ago, it was the first time that Queed had ever been inside a church. He had read Renan at fourteen, finally discarding all religious beliefs in the same year. Approximately Spencer's First Cause satisfied his reason, though he meant to buttress Spencer's contention in its weakest place and carry it deeper than Spencer did. But in fact, the exact limits he should assign to religious beliefs as an evolutionary function were still indeterminate in his system. He, like all cosmic philosophers, found this the most baffling and elusive of all his problems. Meantime, here in this little country church, he was to witness the supreme rite of the supreme religious belief. There was some compensation for his enforced attendance in that thought. He looked about him with genuine and candid interest. The hush, the dim light, the rows upon rows of sober-faced people, seemed to him properly impressive. He was struck by the wealth of flowers massed all over the chancel, and wondered if that was its regular state. The pulpit and the lectern; the altar, which he easily identified; the stained-glass windows with their obviously symbolic pictures; the bronze pipes of the little organ; the unvested choir, whose function he vaguely made out—over all these his intelligent eye swept, curiously; and lastly it went out of the open window and lost itself in the quiet sunny woods outside.

Strange and full of wonder. This incredible instinct for adoration—this invincible insistence in believing, in defiance of all reason, that man was not born to die as the flesh dies. What, after all, was the full significance of this unique phenomenon?

I am the resurrection and the life, saith the Lord; he that believeth in me, though he were dead, yet shall he live....

A loud resonant voice suddenly cut the hush with these words and immediately they were all standing. Queed was among the first to rise; the movement was like a reflex action. For there was something in the thrilling timbre of that voice that seemed to pull him to his feet regardless of his will; something, in fact, that impelled him to crane his neck around and peer down the dim aisle to discover immediately who was the author of it.

His eye fell on a young man advancing, clad in white robes the like of which he had never seen, and wearing the look of the morning upon his face. In his hands he bore an open book, but he did not glance at it. His head was thrown back; his eyes seemed fastened on something outside and beyond the church; and he rolled out the victorious words as though he would stake all that he held dearest in this world that their prophecy was true.

Whom I shall see for myself, and MINE *eyes shall behold, and not another....*

But behind the young man rolled a little stand on wheels, on which lay a long box banked in flowers; and though the little Doctor had never been at a funeral before, and never in the presence of death, he knew that here must lie the mortal remains of his little friend, Fifi. From this point onward Queed's interest in the service became, so to say, less purely scientific.

There was some antiphonal reciting, and then a long selection which the young man in robes read with the same voice of solemn triumph. It is doubtful if anybody in the church followed him with the fascinated attention of the young evolutionist. Soon the organ rumbled, and the little choir, standing, broke into song.

For all the Saints who from their labors rest....

Saints! Well, well, was it imaginable that they thought of Fifi that way *already*? Why, it was only three weeks ago that he had sent her the roses and she....

A black-gloved hand, holding an open book, descended out of the dim space behind him. It came to him, as by an inspiration, that the book was being offered for his use in some mysterious connection. He grasped it gingerly, and his friend the motorman, jabbing at the text with a scarlet hand, whispered raucously: "'S what they're singin'." But the singers had traveled far before the young man was able to find and follow them.

> And when the strife is fierce, the warfare long,
> Steals on the ear the distant triumph song,
> And hearts are brave again, and arms are strong.

The girls in the choir sang on, untroubled by a doubt:—

> But lo, there breaks a yet more glorious day;
> The saints triumphant rise in bright array;
> The King of glory passes on His way.

They marched outside following the flower-banked casket into the little cemetery, and Queed stood with bared head like the others, watching the committal of dust unto dust. In the forefront of the mournful gathering, nearest the grave's edge, there stood three women heavily swathed in black. Through all the rite now, suppressed sobbing ran like a motif. Soon fell upon all ears the saddest of all sounds, the pitiless thud of the first earth upon the stiff lid. On the other side of the irregular circle, Queed saw the coarse red motorman; tears were rolling down his fat cheeks; but never noticing them he was singing loudly, far off the key, from the book the black-gloved hand had given Queed. The hymn they were singing now also spoke surely and naturally of the saints. The same proud note, the young man observed, ran through the service from beginning to end. Hymn and prayer and reading all confidently assumed that Fifi was dead only to this mortal eye, but in another world, open to all those gathered about the grave for their seeking, she lived in some marvelously changed form—her body being made *like unto his own glorious body.*...

In the homeward-bound car, Queed fully recaptured his poise, and redirected his thoughts into rational channels.

The doctrine of the immortality of the soul had not a rational leg to stand on. The anima, or spirit, being merely the product of certain elements combined in life, was wiped out when those elements dissolved their union in death. It was the flame of a candle blown out. Yet with what unbelievable persistence this doctrine had survived through history. Science had annihilated it again and again, but these people resolutely stopped their ears to science. They could not answer science with argument, so they had answered her with the axe and the stake; and they were still capable of doing that whenever they thought it desirable. Strange spectacle! What was the "conflict between Religion and Science" but man's desperate struggle against his own reason? Benjamin Kidd had that right at any rate.

Yet did these people really believe their doctrine of the saved body and the saved soul? They said they did, but did they? If they believed it surely, as they believed that this night would be followed by a new day, if they believed it passionately as they believed that money is the great earthly good, then certainly the biggest of their worldly affairs would be less than a grain of sand by the sea against the everlasting glories that awaited them. Yet ... look at them all about him in the car, these people who told themselves that they had started Fifi on the way to be a saint, in which state they expected to remeet her. Did they so regard their worldly affairs? By to-morrow they would be at each other's throats, squabbling, cheating, slandering, lying, fighting desperately to gain some ephemeral advantage—all under the eye of the magnificent guerdon they pretended to believe in and knew they were jeopardizing by such acts. No, it was pure self-hypnosis. Weak man demanded offsets for his earthly woes, and he had concocted them in a world of his own imagining. That was the history of man's religions; the concoction of other-worldly offsets for worldly woes. In their heart of hearts, all knew that they were concoctions, and the haruspices laughed when they met each other.

Supper was early at Mrs. Paynter's, as though to atone for the tardiness of yesterday. The boarders dispatched it not without recurring cheerfulness, broken now and again by fits of decorous silence. You could see that by to-morrow, or it might be next day, the house would be back in its normal swing again.

Mr. Queed withdrew to his little chamber. He trod the steps softly for once, and perhaps this was why, as he passed Mrs. Paynter's room, his usually engrossed ear caught the sound of weeping, quiet but unrestrained, ceaseless, racking weeping, running on evermore, the weeping of Rachel for her children, who would not be comforted.

The little Doctor shut the door of the Scriptorium and lit the gas. So far, his custom; but here his whim and his wont parted. Instead of seating himself at his table, where the bound *Post* for January-March, 1902, awaited his exploration, he laid himself down on his tiny bed.

If he were to die to-night, who would weep for him like that?

The thought had come unbidden to his mind and stuck in his metaphysics like a burr. Now he remembered that the question was not entirely a new one. Fifi had once asked him who would be sorry if he died, and had answered herself by saying that she would. However, Fifi was dead, and therefore released from her promise.

Yes, Fifi was dead. He would never help her with her algebra again. The thought filled him with vague, unaccountable regrets. He felt that he would willingly take twenty minutes a night from the wrecked Schedule to have her come back, but unfortunately there was no way of arranging that now. He remembered the night he had sent Fifi out of the dining-room for coughing, and the remembrance made him distinctly uncomfortable. He rather wished that he had told Fifi he was sorry about that, but it was too late now. Still he had told her that he was her friend; he was glad to remember that. But here, from a new point of view, was the trouble about having friends. They took your time while they lived, and then they went off and died and upset your evening's work.

Clearly, Fifi left behind many sorrowful friends, as shown by her remarkable funeral. If he himself were to die, Tim and Murphy Queed would probably feel sorrowful, but they would hardly come to the funeral. For one thing, Tim could not come because of his duties on the force, and Murphy, for all he knew, was undergoing incarceration. About the only person he could think of as a probable attendant at his graveside was William Klinker. Yes, Buck would certainly be there, though it was asking a good deal to expect him to weep. A funeral consisting of only one person would look rather odd to those who were familiar with such crowded churches as that he had seen to-day. People passing by would nudge each other and say that the dead must have led an eccentric life, indeed, to be so alone at the end.... Come to think of it, though, there wouldn't be any funeral. He had nothing to do with those most interesting but clearly barbaric rites. Of course his body would be cremated by directions in the will. The operation would be private, attracting no attention from anybody. Buck would make the arrangements. He tried to picture Buck weeping near the incinerator, and failed.

Then there was his father, whom, in twenty-four years' sharing of the world together, he had never met. The man's behavior was odd, to say the least. From the world's point of view he had declined to own his son. For such an unusual breach of custom, there must be some adequate explanation, and the circumstances all pointed one way. This was that his mother (whom his boyhood had pictured as a woman of distinction who had eloped with somebody far beneath her) had failed to marry his father. The persistent mystery about his birth had always made him skeptical of Tim's statement that he had been present at the marriage. But he rarely thought of the matter at all now. The moral responsibility was none of his; and as for a name, Queed was as good as any other. X or Y was a good enough name for a real man, whose life could demonstrate his utter independence of the labels so carefully pasted upon him by environment and circumstance.

Still, if he were to die, he felt that his father, if yet alive, should come forward and weep for him, even as Mrs. Paynter was weeping for Fifi down in the Second Front. He should stand out like a man and take from Buck's hand the solemn ceremonies of cremation. He tried to picture his father weeping near the incinerator, and failed, partly owing to the mistiness surrounding that gentleman's bodily appearance. He felt that his father was dodging his just responsibilities. For the first time in his life he perceived that, under certain circumstances, it might be an advantage to have some definite individual to whom you can point and say: "There goes my father."

As it was, it all came down to him and Buck. He and Buck were alone in the world together. He rather clung to the thought of Buck, and instantly caught himself at it. Very well; let him take it that way then. Take Buck as a symbol of the world, of those friendships which played such certain havoc with a man's Schedule. Was he glad that he had Buck or was he not?

The little Doctor lay on his back in the glare thinking things out. The gas in his eyes was an annoyance, but he did not realize it, and so did not get up, as another man would have done, and put it out.

Certainly it was an extraordinary thing that the only critics he had ever had in his life had all three attacked his theory of living at precisely the same point. They had all three urged him to get in touch with his environment. He himself could unanswerably demonstrate that in such degree as he succeeded in isolating himself from his environment—at least until his great work was done—in just that degree would his life be successful. But these three seemed to declare, with the confidence of those who state an axiom, that in just that degree was his life a failure. Of course they could not demonstrate their contention as he could demonstrate his, but the absence of reasoning did not appear to shake their assurance in the smallest. Here then was another apparent conflict of instinct with reason: their instinct with his reason. Perhaps he might have dismissed the whole thing as merely their religion, but that his father, with that mysterious letter of counsel, was among them. He did not picture his father as a religious man. Besides, Fifi, asked point-blank if that was her religion, had denied, assuring him, singularly enough, that it was only common-sense.

And among them, among all the people that had touched him in this new life, there was no denying that he had had some curiously unsettling experiences.

He had been ready to turn the pages of the book of life for Fifi, an infant at his knee, and all at once Fifi had taken the book from his hands and read aloud, in a language which was quite new to him, a lecture on his own short-comings. There was no denying that her question about his notions on altruism had given him an odd, arresting glimpse of himself from a new peak. He had set out in his pride to punish Mr. Pat, and Mr. Pat had severely punished him, revealing him humiliatingly to himself as a physical incompetent. He had dismissed Buck Klinker as a faintly amusing brother to the ox, and now Buck Klinker was giving him valuable advice about his editorial work, to say nothing of jerking him by the ears toward physical competency. He had thought to honor the *Post* by contributing of his wisdom to it, and the *Post* had replied by contemptuously kicking him out. He had laughed at Colonel Cowles's editorials, and now he was staying out of bed of nights slavishly struggling to imitate them. He had meant to give Miss Weyland some expert advice some day about the running of her department, and suddenly she had turned about and stamped him as an all-around failure, meet not for reverence, but the laughter and pity of men.

So far as he knew, nobody in the world admired him. They might admire his work, but him personally they felt sorry for or despised. Few even admired his work. The *Post* had given him satisfactory proof of that. Conant, Willoughby, and Smathers would admire it—yes, wish to the Lord that they had written it. But would that fill his cup to overflowing? By the way, had not Fifi asked him that very question, too—whether he would consider a life of that sort a successful life? Well—would he? Or could it imaginably be said that Fifi, rather, had had a successful life, as evidenced by her profoundly interesting funeral?

Was it possible that a great authority on human society could make himself an even greater authority by personally assuming a part in the society which he theoretically administered? Was it possible that he was missing some factor of large importance by his addiction to isolation and a schedule?

In short, was it conceivable that he had it all wrong from the beginning, as the young lady Charles Weyland had said?

The little Doctor lay still on his bed and his precious minutes slipped into hours.... If he finished his book at twenty-seven, what would he do with the rest of his life? Besides defending it from possible criticism, besides expounding and amplifying it a little further as need seemed to be, there would be no more work for him to do. Supreme essence of philosophy, history, and all science as it was, it was the final word of human wisdom. You might say that with it the work of the world was done. How then should he spend the remaining thirty or forty years of his life? As matters stood now he had, so to say, twenty years start on himself. Through the peculiar circumstances of his life, he had reached a point in his reading and study at twenty-four which another man could not hope to reach before he was forty-five or fifty. Other men had done daily work for a livelihood, and had only their evenings for their heart's desire. Spencer was a civil engineer. Mill was a clerk in an India house. Comte taught mathematics. But he, in all his life, had not averaged an hour a week's enforced distraction: all had gone to his own work. You might say that he was entitled to a heavy arrears in this direction. If he liked, he could idle for ten years, twenty years, and still be more than abreast of his age.

And as it was, he could not pretend that he had kept the faith, that he was inviolably holding his Schedule unspotted from the world. No, he himself had outraged and deflowered the Schedule. Klinker's Exercises and the *Post* were deliberate impieties. And he could not say that they had the sanction of his reason. The exercises had only a partial sanction; the *Post* no sanction at all. Both were but sops to wounded pride. Here, then, was a pretty situation: he, the triumphant rationalist, the toy of utterly irrational impulses—of an utterly irrational instinct. And this new impulse tugging at his inside, driving him to heed the irrational advice of his critics—what could it be but part and parcel of the same mysterious but apparently deep-seated instinct? And what was the real significance of this instinct, and what in the name of Jerusalem was the matter with him anyway?

He was twenty-four years old, without upbringing, and utterly alone in the world. He had raised himself, body and soul, out of printed books, and about all the education he ever had was half an hour's biting talk from Charles Weyland. Of course he did not recognize his denied youth when it rose and fell upon him, but he did recognize that his assailant was doughty. He locked arms with it and together they fell into undreamed depths.

Buck Klinker, returning from some stag devilry at the hour of two A.M., and attracted to the Scriptorium by the light under the door, found the little Doctor pacing the floor in his stocking feet, with the gas blazing and the shade up as high as it would go. He halted in his marchings to stare at Buck with wild unrecognition, and his face looked so white and fierce that honest Buck, like the good friend he was, only said, "Well—good-night, Doc," and unobtrusively withdrew.

CHAPTER XVI

Triumphal Return of Charles Gardiner West from the Old World;
and of how the Other World had wagged in his Absence.

Many pictured post-cards and an occasional brief note reminded Miss Weyland during the summer that Charles Gardiner West was pursuing his studies in the Old World with peregrinative zest. By the trail of colored photographs she followed his triumphal march. Rome knew the president-elect in early June; Naples, Florence, Milan, Venice in the same period. He investigated, presumably, the public school systems of Geneva and Berlin; the higher education drew him through the château country of France; for three weeks the head-waiters of Paris (in the pedagogical district) were familiar with the clink of his coin; and August's first youth was gone before he was in London with the lake region a tramped road behind him.

From the latter neighborhood (picture: Rydal Mount) he wrote Sharlee as follows:

> Sailing on the 21st, after the most glorious trip in history.
> Never so full of energy and enthusiasm. Running over with
> the most beautiful plans.

The exact nature of these plans the writer did not indicate, but Sharlee's mother, who always got down to breakfast first and read all the postals as they came, explained that the reference was evidently to Blaines College. West, however, did not sail on the 21st, even though that date was some days behind his original intentions. The itinerary with which he had set out had him home again, in fact, on August 15. For in the stress and hurry of making ready for the journey, together with a little preliminary rest which he felt his health required, he had to let his advertising campaign and other schemes for the good of the college go over until the fall. But collegiate methods obtaining in London were too fascinating, apparently, to be dismissed with any cursory glance. He sailed on the 25th, arrived home on the 3rd of September, and on the 4th surprised Sharlee by dropping in upon her in her office.

He was browned from his passage, appeared a little stouter, was very well dressed and good to look at, and fairly exuded vitality and pleasant humor. Sharlee was delighted and quite excited over seeing him again, though it may be noted, as shedding a side-light upon her character, that she did not greet him with "Hello, Stranger!" However, her manner of salutation appeared perfectly satisfactory to West.

They had the little office to themselves and plenty to talk about.

"Doubtless you got my postals?" he asked.

"Oh, stacks of them. I spent all one Saturday afternoon pasting them in an album as big as this table. They made a perfect fireside grand tour for me. What did you like best in all your trip?"

"I think," said West, turning his handsome blue eyes full upon her, "that I like getting back."

Sharlee laughed. "It's done you a world of good; that's plain, anyway. You look ready to remove mountains."

"Why, I can eat them—bite their heads off! I feel like a fighting-cock who's been starved a shade too long for the good of the bystanders."

He laughed and waved his arms about to signify enormous vitality. Sharlee asked if he had been able to make a start yet with his new work.

"You might say," he replied, "that I dived head-first into it from the steamer."

He launched out into eager talk about his hopes for Blaines College. In all his wide circle of friends, he knew no one who made so sympathetic and intelligent a listener as she. He talked freely, lengthily, even egotistically it might have seemed, had they not been such good friends and he so sure of her interest. Difficulties, it seemed, had already cropped out. He was not sure of the temper of his trustees, whom he had called together for an informal meeting that morning. Starting to advertise the great improvements that had taken place in the college, he had collided with the simple fact that no improvements had taken place. Even if he privately regarded his own accession in that light, he humorously pointed out, he could hardly advertise it, with old Dr. Gilfillan, the retired president, living around the corner and reading the papers. Again, taking his pencil to make a list of the special advantages Blaines had to offer, he was rather forcibly struck with the fact that it had no special advantages. But upon these and other difficulties, he touched optimistically, as though confident that under the right treatment, namely his treatment, all would soon yield.

Sharlee, fired by his gay confidence, mused enthusiastically. "It's inspiring to think what can be done! Really, it is no empty dream that the number of students might be doubled—quadrupled—in five years."

"Do you know," said he, turning his glowing face upon her, "I'm not so eager for mere numbers now. That is one point on which my views have shifted during my studies this summer. My ideal is no longer a very large college—at least not necessarily large—but a college of the very highest standards. A distinguished faculty of recognized authorities in their several lines; an earnest student body, large if you can get them, but always made of picked men admitted on the strictest terms; degrees recognized all over the country as an unvarying badge of the highest scholarship—these are what I shall strive for. My ultimate ambition," said Charles Gardiner West, dreamily, "is to make of Blaines College an institution like the University of Paris."

He sprang up presently with great contrition, part real, part mock, over having absorbed so much of the honest tax-payer's property, the Departmental time. No, he could not be induced to appropriate a moment more; he was going to run on up the street and call on Colonel Cowles.

"How is the old gentleman, anyway?"

"His spirits," said Sharlee, "were never better, and he is working like a horse. But I'm afraid the dear is beginning to feel his years a little."

"He's nearly seventy, you know. By the bye, what ever became of that young helper you and I unloaded on him last year—the queer little man with the queer little name?"

Sharlee saw that President West had entirely forgotten their conversation six months before, when he had promised to protect this same young helper from Colonel Cowles and the *Post* directors. She smiled indulgently at this evidence of the absent-mindedness of the great.

"Became of him! Why, you're going to make him regular assistant editor at your directors' meeting next month."

"Are we, though! I had it in the back of my head that he was fired early in the summer."

"Well, you see, when he saw the axe descending, he pulled off a little revolution all by himself and all of a sudden learned to write. Make the Colonel tell you about it."

"I'm not surprised," said West. "I told you last winter, you know, that I believed in that boy. Great heavens! It's glorious to be back in this old town again!"

He went down the broad steps of the Capitol, and out the winding white walkway through the park. Nearly everybody he met stopped him with a friendly greeting and a welcome home. He walked the shady path with his light stick swinging, his eyes seeing, not an arch of tangible trees, but the shining vista which dreamers call the Future.... He stood upon a platform, fronting a vast white meadow of upturned faces. He was speaking to this meadow, his theme being "Education and the Rise of the Masses," and the people, displaying an enthusiasm rare at lectures upon such topics, roared their approval as he shot at them great terse truths, the essence of wide reading and profound wisdom put up in pellets of pungent epigram. He rose at a long dinner-table, so placed that as he stood his eye swept down rows upon rows of other long tables, where the diners had all pushed back their chairs to turn and look at him. His words were honeyed, of a magic compelling power, so that as he reached his peroration, aged magnates could not be restrained from producing fountain-pen and check-book; he saw them pushing aside coffee-cups to indite rows of o's of staggering length. Blaines College now tenanted a new home on a grassy knoll outside the city. The single ramshackle barn which had housed the institution prior to the coming of President West was replaced by a cluster of noble edifices of classic marble. The president sat in his handsome office, giving an audience to a delegation of world-famous professors from the University of Paris. They had been dispatched by the French nation to study his methods on the ground.

"Why, *hello*, Colonel! Bless your heart, I *am* glad to see you, sir...."

Colonel Cowles, looking up from his ancient seat, gave an exclamation of surprise and pleasure. He welcomed the young man affectionately. West sat down, and once more pen-sketched his travels and his plans for Blaines College. He was making a second, or miniature, grand tour that afternoon, regreeting all his friends, and was thus compelled to tell his story many times; but his own interest in it appeared ever fresh. For Blaines he asked and was promised the kindly offices of the Post.

The Colonel, in his turn, gave a brief account of his vacationless summer, of his daily work, of the progress of the *Post's* Policies.

"I hear," said West, "that that little scientist I made you a present of last year has made a ten-strike."

"Queed? An extraordinary thing," said the Colonel, relighting his cigar. "I was on the point of discharging him, you remember, with the hearty approval of the directors. His stuff was dismal, abysmal, and hopeless. One day he turned around and began handing in stuff of a totally different kind. First-rate, some of it. I thought at first that he must be hiring somebody to do it for him. Did you see the paper while you were away?"

"Very irregularly, I'm sorry to say."

"Quite on his own hook, the boy turned up one day with an article on the Centre Street 'mashers' that was a screamer. You know what that situation was—"

"Yes, yes."

"I had for some time had it in mind to tackle it myself. The fact was that we were developing a class of boy Don Juans that were a black disgrace to the city. It was a rather unpleasant subject, but this young man handled it with much tact, as well as with surprising vigor and ability. His improvement seemed to date from right there. I encouraged him to follow up his first effort, and he wrote a strong series which attracted attention all through the State, and has already brought about decided improvement."

"Splendid! You know," said West, "the first time I ever looked at that boy, I was sure he had the stuff in him."

"Then you are a far keener observer than I. However, the nature of the man seems to be undergoing some subtle change, a curious kind of expansion—I don't remember anything like it in my experience. A more indefatigable worker I never saw, and if he goes on this way.... Well, God moves in a mysterious way. It's a delight to see you again, Gardiner. Take supper with me at the club, won't you? I feel lonely and grown old, as the poet says."

West accepted, and presently departed on his happy round. The Colonel glanced at his watch; it was 3.30 o'clock, and he fell industriously to work again. On the stroke of four, as usual, the door of the adjoining office opened, and he heard his assistant enter and seat himself at the new desk recently provided for him. Another half-hour passed, and the Colonel, putting a double cross-mark at the bottom of his paper—that being how you write "Finis" on the press—raised his head.

"Mr. Queed."

"Yes."

The connecting door opened, and the young man walked in. His chief eyed him thoughtfully.

"Young man, you have picked up a complexion like a professional beauty's. What is your secret?"

"I daresay it is exercise. I have just walked out to Kern's Castle and back."

"H'm. Five miles if it's a step."

"And a half. I do it—twice a week—in an hour and seven minutes."

The Colonel thought of his own over-rubicund cheek and sighed. "Well, whom or what do you wish to crucify to-morrow?"

"I am at your orders there."

"Have you examined Deputy Clerk Folsom's reply to Councilman Hannigan's charge? What do you think of it?"

"I think it puts Hannigan in a very awkward position."

"I agree with you. Suppose you seek to show that to the city in half a column."

Queed bowed. "I may, perhaps, remind you, Colonel, of the meeting in New York to-morrow to prepare for the celebration of the Darwin centennial. If you desired I should be glad to prepare, apropos of this, a brief monograph telling in a light, popular way what Darwin did for the world."

"And what did Darwin do for the world?"

The grave young man made a large grave gesture which indicated the immensity of Darwin's doings for the world.

"Which topic do you prefer to handle—Folsom on Hannigan, or what Darwin did for the world?"

"I think," said Queed, "that I should prefer to handle both."

"Ten people will read Hannigan to one who reads Darwin."

"Don't you think that it is the *Post's* business to reduce that proportion?"

"Take them both," said the Colonel presently. "But always remember this: the great People are more interested in a cat-fight at the corner of Seventh and Centre Streets than they are in the greatest exploit of the greatest scientific theorist that ever lived."

"I will remember what you say, Colonel."

"I want you," resumed Colonel Cowles, "to take supper with me at the club. Not to-night—I'm engaged. Shall we say to-morrow night, at seven?"

Queed accepted without perceptible hesitation. Some time had passed since he became aware that the Colonel had somehow insinuated himself into that list of friends which had halted so long at Tim and Murphy Queed.

Besides, he had a genuine, unscientific desire to see what a real club looked like inside. So far, his knowledge of clubs was absolutely confined to the Mercury Athletic Association, B. Klinker, President.

The months of May, June, July, and August had risen and died since Queed, threshing out great questions through the still watches of the night, had resolved to give a modified scheme of life a tentative and experimental trial. He had kept this resolution, according to his wont. Probably his first liking for Colonel Cowles dated back to the very beginning of this period. It might be traced to the day when the precariously-placed assistant had submitted his initial article on the thesis his friend Buck had given him—the first article in all his life that the little Doctor had ever dipped warm out of human life. This momentous composition he had brought and laid upon the Colonel's desk, as usual; but he did not follow his ancient custom by instantly vanishing toward the Scriptorium. Instead he stuck fast in the sanctum, not pretending to look at an encyclopedia or out of the window as another man might have done, but standing rigid on the other side of the table, gaze glued upon the perusing Colonel. Presently the old editor looked up.

"Did you write this?"

"Yes. Why not?"

"It's about as much like your usual style as my style is like Henry James's."

"You don't consider it a good editorial, then?"

"You have not necessarily drawn the correct inference from my remark. I consider it an excellent editorial. In fact—I shall make it my leader to-morrow morning. But that has nothing to do with how you happen to be using a style exactly the reverse of your own."

Queed had heaved a great sigh. The article occupied three pages of copy-paper in a close handwriting, and represented sixteen hours' work. Its author had rewritten it eleven times, incessantly referring to his text-book, the files of the *Post*, and subjecting each phrase to the most gruelling examination before finally admitting it to the perfect structure. However, it seemed no use to bore one's employer with details such as these.

"I have been doing a little studying of late—"

"Under excellent masters, it seems. Now this phrase, 'the ultimate reproach and the final infamy"—the Colonel unconsciously smacked his lips over it—"why, sir, it sounds like one of my own."

Queed started.

"If you must know, it is one of your own. You used it on October 26, 1900, during, as you will recall, the closing days of the presidential campaign."

The Colonel stared at him, bewildered.

"I decided to learn editorial-writing—as the term is understood," Queed reluctantly explained. "Therefore, I have been sitting up till two o'clock in the mornings, studying the files of the *Post*, to see exactly how you did it."

The Colonel's gaze gradually softened. "You might have been worse employed; I compliment and congratulate you," said he; and then added: "Whether you have really caught the idea and mastered the technique or not, it is too soon to say. But I'll say frankly that this article is worth more to me than everything else that you've written for the *Post* put together."

"I am—ahem—gratified that you are pleased with it."

The Colonel, whose glance had gone out of the window, swung around in his chair and smote the table a testy blow.

"For the Lord's sake," he exploded, "get some heat in you! Squirt some color into your way of looking at things! Be kind and good-natured in your heart—just as I am at this moment—but for heaven's sake learn to write as if you were mad, and only kept from yelling by phenomenal will-power."

This was in early May. Many other talks upon the art of editorial writing did the two have, as the days went. The Colonel, mystified but pleased by revelations of actuality and life in his heretofore too-embalmed assistant, found an increasing interest in developing him. Here was a youth, with the qualities of potential great valuableness, and the wise editor, as soon as this appeared, gave him his chance by calling him off the fields of taxation and currency and assigning him to topics plucked alive from the day's news.

On the fatal 15th of May, the Colonel told Queed merely that the *Post* desired his work as long as it showed such promise as it now showed. That was all the talk about the dismissal that ever took place between them. The Colonel was no believer in fulsome praise for the young. But to others he talked more freely, and this was how it happened that the daughter of his old friend John Randolph Weyland knew that Mr. Queed was slated for an early march upstairs.

For Queed the summer had been a swift and immensely busy one. To write editorials that have a relation with everyday life, it gradually became clear to him that the writer must himself have some such relation. In June the Mercury Athletic Association had been thoroughly reorganized and rejuvenated, and regular meets were held every Saturday night. At Trainer Klinker's command, Queed had resolutely permitted himself to be inducted into the Mercury; moreover, he made it a point of honor to attend the Saturday night functions, where he had the ideal chance to match his physical competence against that of other men. Early in the sessions at the gymnasium, Buck had introduced his pupil to boxing-glove and punching-bag, his own special passions, and now his orders ran that the Doc should put on the gloves with any of the Mercuries that were willing. Most of the Mercuries were willing, and on these early Saturday nights, Stark's rocked with the falls of Dr. Queed. But under Klinker's stern discipline, he was already acquiring something like a form. By midsummer he had gained a small reputation for scientific precision buttressed by invincible inability to learn when he was licked, and autumn found many of the Mercuries decidedly less Barkis-like than of old.

Queed lived now in the glow of perfect physical health, a very different thing, as Fifi had once pointed out, from merely not feeling sick. In the remarkable development that his body was undergoing, he had found an unexpected pride. But the Mercury, though he hardly realized it at the time, was useful to him in a bigger way than bodily improvement.

Here he met young men who were most emphatically in touch with life. They treated him as an equal with reference to his waxing muscular efficiency, and with some respect as regards his journalistic connection. "Want you to shake hands with the editor of the *Post*," so kindly Buck would introduce him. After the bouts or the "exhibition" of a Saturday, there was always a smoker, and in the highly instructed and expert talk of his club-mates the Doctor learned many things that were to be of value to him later on. Some of the Mercuries, besides their picturesque general knowledge, knew much more about city politics than ever got into the papers. There was Jimmy Wattrous, for example, already rising into fame as Plonny Neal's most promising lieutenant. Jimmy bared his heart with the Mercuries, and was particularly friendly with the representative of the great power which moulds public opinion. Now and then, Neal himself looked in, Plonny, the great boss, who was said to hold the city in the hollow of his hand. Many an editorial that surprised and pleased Colonel Cowles was born in that square room back of Stark's.

And all these things took time ... took time.... And there were nights when Queed woke wide-eyed with cold sweat on his brow and the cold fear in his heart that he and posterity were being cheated, that he was making an irretrievable and ghastly blunder.

Desperate months were May, June, and July for the little Doctor. In all this time he never once put his own pencil to his own paper. Manuscript and Schedule lay locked together in a drawer, toward which he could never bear to glance. Thirteen hours a day he gave to the science of editorial writing; two hours a day to the science of physical culture; one hour a day (computed average) to the science of Human Intercourse; but to the Science of Sciences never an hour on never a day. The rest was food and sleep. Such was his life for three months; a life that would have been too horrible to contemplate, had it not been that in all of his new sciences he uncovered a growing personal interest which kept him constantly astonished at himself.

By the end of June he found it safe to give less and less time to the study of editorial paradigms, for he had the technique at his fingers' ends; and so he gave more and more time to the amassment of material. For he had made a magnificent boast, and he never had much idea of permitting it to turn out empty, for all his nights of torturing misgivings. He read enormously with expert facility and a beautifully trained memory; read history, biography, memoirs, war records, old newspapers, old speeches, councilmanic proceedings, departmental reports—everything he could lay his hands on that promised capital for an editorial writer in that city and that State. By the end of July he felt that he could slacken up here, too, having pretty well exhausted the field, and the first day of August—red-letter day in the annals of science—saw him unlock the sacred drawer with a close-set face. And now the Schedule, so long lapsed, was reinstated, with Four Hours a Day segregated to Magnum Opus. A pitiful little step at reconstruction, perhaps, but still a step. And henceforth every evening, between 9.30 and 1.30, Dr. Queed sat alone in his Scriptorium and embraced his love.

Insensibly summer faded into autumn, and still the science of Human Intercourse was faithfully practiced. The Paynter parlor knew Queed not infrequently in these days, where he could sometimes be discovered not merely suffering, but encouraging, Major Brooke to talk to him of his victories over the Republicans in 1870-75. Nor was he a stranger to Nicolovius's sitting-room, having made it an iron-clad rule with himself to accept one out of every two invitations to that charming cloister. After all, there might be something to learn from both the Major's fiery reminiscences and the old professor's cultured talk. He himself, he found, tended naturally toward silence. Listeners appeared to be needed in a world where the supply of talkers exceeded the demand. The telling of humorous anecdote he had definitely excided from his creed. It did not appear needed of him; and he was sure that the author of his creed would himself have authorized him to drop it. He never missed Fifi now, according to the way of this world, but he thought of her sometimes, which is all that anybody has a right to expect.

Miss Weyland he had not seen since the day Fifi died. Mrs. Paynter had been away all summer, a firm spinster cousin coming in from the country to run the boarders, and the landlady's agent came to the house no more. Buck Klinket he saw incessantly; he was the first person in the world, probably, that the little Doctor had ever really liked. It was Buck who suggested to his pupil, in October, a particularly novel experience for his soul's unfolding, which Queed, though failing to adopt it, sometimes dandled before his mind's eye with a kind of horrified fascination, viz: the taking of Miss Miller to the picture shows.

But the bulk of his time this autumn was still going to his work on the *Post*. With ever fresh wonderment, he faced the fact that this work, first taken up solely to finance the Scriptorium, and next enlarged to satisfy a most irrational instinct, was growing slowly but surely upon his personal interest. Certainly the application of a new science to a new set of practical conditions was stimulating to his intellect; the panorama of problems whipped out daily by the telegraph had a warmth and immediateness wanting to the abstractions of closet philosophy. Queed's articles lacked the Colonel's expert fluency, his loose but telling vividness, his faculty for broad satire which occasionally set the whole city laughing. On the other hand, they displayed an exact knowledge of fact, a breadth of study and outlook, and a habit of plumbing bottom on any and all subjects which critical minds found wanting in the Colonel's delightful discourses. And nowadays the young man's articles were constantly reaching a higher and higher level of readability. Not infrequently they attracted public comment, not only, indeed not oftenest, inside the State. Queed knew what it was to be quoted in that identical New York newspaper from whose pages, so popular for wrapping around pork chops, he had first picked out his letters.

Of these things the honorable *Post* directors were not unmindful. They met on October 10, and upon Colonel Cowles's cordial recommendation, named Mr. Queed assistant editor of the *Post* at a salary of fifteen hundred dollars per annum. And Mr. Queed accepted the appointment without a moment's hesitation.

So far, then, the magnificent boast had been made good. The event fell on a Saturday. The Sunday was sunny, windy, and crisp. Free for the day and regardful of the advantages of open-air pedestrianism, the new assistant editor put on his hat from the dinner-table and struck for the open country. He rambled far, over trails strange to him, and came up short, about 4.30 in the afternoon, in a grove of immemorial pines which he instantly remembered to have seen before.

CHAPTER XVII

*A Remeeting in a Cemetery: the Unglassed Queed who loafed on
Rustic Bridges; of the Consequences of failing to tell a Lady that
you hope to see her again soon.*

Fifi's grave had long since lost its first terrible look of bare newness.
Grass grew upon it in familiar ways. Rose-bushes that might have stood
a lifetime nodded over it by night and by day. Already "the minute grey
lichens, plate o'er plate," were "softening down the crisp-cut name and
date"; and the winds of winter and of summer blew over a little mound that
had made itself at home in the still city of the dead.

Green was the turf above Fifi, sweet the peacefulness of her little
churchyard. Her cousin Sharlee, who had loved her well, disposed
her flowers tenderly, and stood awhile in reverie of the sort which the
surroundings so irresistibly invited. But the schedules of even electric car-
lines are inexorable; and presently she saw from a glance at her watch that
she must turn her face back to the city of the living.

On the little rustic bridge a hundred yards away, a man was standing,
with rather the look of having stopped at just that minute. From a distance
Sharlee's glance swept him lightly; she saw that she did not know him; and
not fancying his frank stare, she drew near and stepped upon the bridge
with a splendid unconsciousness of his presence. But just when she was
safely by, her ears were astonished by his voice speaking her name.

"How do you do, Miss Weyland?"

She turned, surprised by a familiar note in the deep tones, looked,
and—yes, there could be no doubt of it—it was—

"Mr. Queed! Why, *how* do you do!"

They shook hands. He removed his hat for the process, doing it with a
certain painstaking precision which betrayed want of familiarity with the
engaging rite.

"I haven't seen you for a long time," said Sharlee brightly.

The dear, old remark—the moss-covered remark that hung in the well! How on earth could we live without it? In behalf of Sharlee, however, some excuses can be urged; for, remembering the way she had talked to Mr. Queed once on the general subject of failures, she found herself struggling against a most absurd sense of embarrassment.

"No," replied Queed, replacing his hat as though following from memory the diagram in a book of etiquette. He added, borrowing one of the Colonel's favorite expressions, "I hope you are very well."

"Yes, indeed.... I'm so glad you spoke to me, for to tell you the truth, I never, never should have known you if you hadn't."

"You think that I've changed? Well," said he, gravely, "I ought to have. You might say that I've given five months to it."

"You've changed enormously."

She examined with interest this new Mr. Queed who loafed on rustic bridges, five miles from a Sociology, and hailed passing ladies on his own motion. He appeared, indeed, decidedly altered.

In the first place, he looked decidedly bigger, and, to come at once to the fact, he was. For Klinker's marvelous exercises for all parts of the body had done more than add nineteen pounds to his weight, and deepen his chest, and broaden his shoulders. They had pulled and tugged at the undeveloped tissues until they had actually added a hard-won three-quarters of an inch to his height. The stoop was gone, and instead of appearing rather a small man, Mr. Queed now looked full middle-height or above. He wore a well-made suit of dark blue, topped by a correct derby. His hair was cut trim, his color was excellent, and, last miracle of all, he wore no spectacles. It was astonishing but true. The beautiful absence of these round disfigurements brought into new prominence a pair of grayish eyes which did not look so very professorial, after all.

But what Sharlee liked best about this unglassed and unscienced Mr. Queed was his entire absence of any self-consciousness in regard to her. When he told her that Easter Monday night that he cheerfully took his turn on the psychological operating-table, anæsthetics barred, and no mercy asked or given, it appeared that he, alone among men, really meant it.

Under the tiny bridge, a correspondingly tiny brook purled without surcease, its heart set upon somewhere finding the sea. Over their heads a glorious maple was taking off its coat of many colors in the wind. Sharlee put back a small hand into a large muff and said:—

"At church this morning I saw Colonel Cowles. He told me about you. I don't know how you look at it, but I think you're a subject for the heartiest congratulations. So here are mine."

"The men at the Mercury were pleased, too," mused Mr. Queed, looking out over the landscape. "Do you ever read my articles now?"

"For many years," said Sharlee, evasively, "I have always read the *Post* from cover to cover. It's been to me like those books you see in the advertisements and nowhere else. Grips the reader from the start, and she cannot lay it down till the last page is turned."

A brief smile appeared in the undisguised eyes. "Do you notice any distinctions now between me and the Encyclopedia Britannica?"

"Unless you happen to refer to Lombroso or Buckle or Aristotle or Plato," said Sharlee, not noticing the smile, "I never know whether it's your article or Colonel Cowles's. Do you mind walking on? It's nearly time for my car."

"A year ago," said he, "I certainly should not have liked that. I do now, since it means that I have succeeded in what I set out to do. I've thought a good deal about that tired bricklayer this summer," he went on, quite unembarrassed. "By the way, I know one personally now: Timrod Burns, of the Mercury. Only I can't say that I ever saw Timmy tired."

Down the woodland path they passed side by side, headed for the little station known as Stop 11. Sharlee was pleased that he had remembered about the bricklayer; she could have been persuaded that his remark was vaguely intended to convey some sort of thanks to her. But saying no more of this, she made it possible to introduce casually a reference to his vanished glasses.

"Yes," said he, "I knocked them off the bureau and broke them one day. So I just let them go. They were rather striking-looking glasses, I always thought. I don't believe I ever saw another pair quite like them."

"But," said Sharlee, puzzled, "do you find that you can see perfectly well without them?"

"Oh, yes; if anything, better." He paused, and added with entire seriousness: "You see those spectacles, striking-looking as they were, were only window-glass. I bought them at a ten-cent store on Sixth Avenue when I was twelve years old."

"Oh! What made you do that?"

"All the regulars at the Astor Library wore them. At the time it seemed to be the thing to do, and of course they soon became second nature to me. But I daresay no one ever had a sounder pair of eyes than I."

To Sharlee this seemed one of the most pathetic of all his confidences; she offered no comment.

"You were in the churchyard," stated Mr. Queed. "I was there just ahead of you. I was struck with that motto or text on the headstone, and shall look it up when I get home. I have been making a more careful study of your Bible this autumn and have found it exceptionally interesting. You, I suppose, subscribe to all the tenets of the Christian faith?"

Sharlee hesitated. "I'm not sure that I can answer that with a direct yes, and I *will* not answer it with any sort of no. So I'll say that I believe in them all, modified a little in places to satisfy my reason."

"Ah, they are subject to modification, then?"

"Certainly. Aren't you? Am not I? Whatever is alive is subject to modification. These doctrines," said she, "are evolving because they have the principle of life in them."

"So you are an evolutionist?"

"The expert in evolutionary sociology will hardly quarrel with me for that."

"The expert in evolutionary sociology deals with social organisms, nations, the human race. Your Bible deals with Smith, Brown, and Jones."

"Well, what are your organisms and nations but collections of my Smiths, Browns, and Joneses? My Bible deals with individuals because there is nothing else to deal with. The individual conscience is the beginning of everything."

"Ah! So you would found your evolution of humanity upon the increasing operation of what you call conscience?"

"Probably I would not give *all* the credit to what I call conscience. Probably I'd give some of it to what I call intellect."

"In that case you would almost certainly fall into a fatal error."

"Why, don't you consider that the higher the intellectual development the higher the type?"

"Suppose we go more slowly," said Mr. Queed, intently plucking a dead bough from an overhanging young oak.

"How do you go about measuring a type? When you speak of a high type, exactly what do you mean?"

"When I speak of a high type," said Sharlee, who really did not know exactly what she meant, "I will merely say that I mean a type that is high—lofty, you know—towering over other types."

She flaunted a gloved hand to suggest infinite altitude.

"You ought to mean," he said patiently, "a type which most successfully sketches the civilization of the future, a type best fitted to dominate and survive. Now you have only to glance at history to see that intellectual supremacy is no guarantee whatever of such a type."

"Oh, Mr. Queed, I don't know about that."

"Then I will convince you," said he. "Look at the French—the most brilliant nation intellectually among all the European peoples. Where are they in the race to-day? The evolutionist sees in them familiar symptoms of a retrogression which rarely ends but in one way. Look at the Greeks. Every schoolboy knows that the Greeks were vastly the intellectual superiors of any dominant people of to-day. An anthropologist of standing assures us that the intellectual interval separating the Greek of the Periclean age from the modern Anglo-Saxon is as great as the interval between the Anglo-Saxon and the African savage. Point to a man alive to-day who is the intellectual peer of Aristotle, Plato, or Socrates. Yet where are the Greeks? What did their exalted intellectual equipment do to save them in the desperate struggle for the survival of the fittest? The Greeks of to-day are selling fruit at corner stands; Plato's descendants shine the world's shoes. They live to warn away the most casual evolutionist from the theory that intellectual supremacy necessarily means supremacy of type. Where, then, you may ask, does lie the principle of triumphant evolution? Here we stand at the innermost heart of every social scheme. Let us glance a moment," said Mr. Queed, "at Man, as we see him first emerging from the dark hinterlands of history."

So, walking through the sweet autumn woods with the one girl he knew in all the world—barring only Miss Miller—Queed spoke heartily of the rise and fall of peoples and the destiny of man. Thus conversing, they came out of the woods and stood upon the platform of the rudimentary station.

The line ran here on an elevation, disappearing in the curve of a heavy cut two hundred yards further north. In front the ground fell sharply and rolled out in a vast green meadow, almost treeless and level as a mill-pond. Far off on the horizon rose the blue haze of a range of foothills, upon which the falling sun momentarily stood, like a gold-piece edge-up on a table. Nearer, to their right, was a strip of uncleared woods, a rainbow of reds and pinks. Through the meadow ran a little stream, such as a boy of ten could leap; for the instant it stood fire-red under the sun.

Sharlee, obtaining the floor for a moment, asked Queed how his own work had been going. He told her that in one sense it had not been going at all: not a chapter written from May to September.

"However," he said, with an unclouded face, "I am now giving six hours a day to it. And it is just as well to go slow. The smallest error of angle at the centre means a tremendous going astray at the circumference. I—ahem—do not feel that my summer has been wasted, by any means. You follow me? It is worth some delay to be doubly sure that I put down no plus signs as minuses."

"Yes, of course. How beautiful that is out there, isn't it?"

His eyes followed hers over the sunset spaces. "No, it is too quiet, too monotonous. If there must be scenery, let it have some originality and character. You yourself are very beautiful, I think."

Sharlee started, almost violently, and colored perceptibly. If a text-book in differential calculus, upon the turning of a page, had thrown problems to the winds and begun gibbering purple poems of passion, she could not have been more completely taken aback. However, there was no mistaking the utter and veracious impersonality of his tone.

"Oh, do you think so? I'm very glad, because I'm afraid not many people do...."

Mr. Queed remained silent. So far, so good; the conversation stood in a position eminently and scientifically correct; but Sharlee could not for the life of her forbear to add: "But I had no idea you ever noticed people's looks."

"So far as I remember, I never did before. I think it was the appearance of your eyes as you looked out over the plain that attracted my attention. Then, looking closer, I noticed that you are beautiful."

The compliment was so unique and perfect that another touch could only spoil it. Sharlee immediately changed the subject.

"Oh, Mr. Queed, has the Department you or Colonel Cowles to thank for the editorial about the reformatory this morning?"

"Both of us. He suggested it and I wrote it. So you really cannot tell us apart?"

She shook her head. "All this winter we shall work preparing the State's mind for this institution, convincing it so thoroughly that when the legislature meets again, it simply will not dare to refuse us. When I mention we and us, understand that I am speaking to you Departmentally. After that there are ten thousand other things that we want to do. But everything is so immortally slow! We are not allowed to raise our fingers without a hundred years' war first. Don't you ever wish for money—oceans and oceans of lovely money?"

"Good heavens, no!"

"I do. I'd pepper this State with institutions. Did you know," she said sweetly, "that I once had quite a little pot of money? When I was one month old."

"Yes," said Queed, "I knew. In fact, I had not been here a week before I heard of Henry G. Surface. Major Brooke speaks of him constantly, Colonel Cowles occasionally. Do you," he asked, "care much about that?"

"Well," said Sharlee, gently, "I'm glad my father never knew."

From half a mile away, behind the bellying woodland, a faint hoot served notice that the city-bound car was sweeping rapidly toward them. It was on the tip of Queed's tongue to remind Miss Weyland that, in the case of Fifi, she had taken the ground that the dead did know what was going on upon earth. But he did not do so. The proud way in which she spoke of *my father* threw another thought uppermost in his mind.

"Miss Weyland," he said abruptly, "I made a—confidence to you, of a personal nature, the first time I ever talked with you. I did not, it is true, ask you to regard it as a confidence, but—"

"I know," interrupted Sharlee, hurriedly. "But of course I *have* regarded it in that way, and have never spoken of it to anybody."

"Thank you. That was what I wished to say."

If Sharlee had wanted to measure now the difference that she saw in Mr. Queed, she could have done it by the shyness that they both felt in approaching a topic they had once handled with the easiest simplicity. She was glad of his sensitiveness; it became him better than his early callousness. Sharlee wore a suit of black-and-gray pin-checks, and it was very excellently tailored; for if she purchased but two suits a year, she invariably paid money to have them made by one who knew how. Her hat was of the kind that other girls study with cool diligence, while feigning engrossment in the conversation; and, repairing to their milliners, give orders for accurate copies of it. From it floated a silky-looking veil of gray-white, which gave her face that airy, cloud-like setting that photographers of the baser sort so passionately admire. The place was as windy as Troy; from far on the ringing plains the breeze raced and fell upon this veil, ceaselessly kicking it here and there, in a way that would have driven a strong man lunatic in seven minutes. Sharlee, though a slim girl and no stronger than another, remained entirely unconscious of the behavior of the veil; long familiarity had bred contempt for its boisterous play; and, with her eyes a thousand miles away, she was wishing with her whole heart that she dared ask Mr. Queed a question.

Whereupon, like her marionette that she worked by a string, he opened his mouth and gravely answered her.

"I have three theories about my father. One is that he is an eccentric psychologist with peculiar, not to say extraordinary, ideas about the bringing up of children. Another is that because of his own convenience or circumstances, he does not care to own me as I am now. The third is that because of my convenience or circumstances, he thinks that I may not care to own him as he is now. I have never heard of or from him since the letter I showed you, nearly nine months ago. I rather incline to the opinion," he said, "that my father is dead."

"If he isn't," said Sharlee, gently, as the great car whizzed up and stopped with a jerk, "I am very sure that you are to find him some day. If he hadn't meant that, he would never have asked you to come all the way from New York to settle here—do you think so?"

"Do you know," said Mr. Queed—so absorbedly as to leave her to clamber up the car steps without assistance—"if I subscribed to the tenets of your religion, I might believe that my father was merely a mythical instrument of Providence—a tradition created out of air *just to bring me down here.*"

"Why," said Sharlee, looking down from the tall platform, as the car whizzed and buzzed and slowly started, "aren't you *coming?*"

"No, I'm walking," said Mr. Queed, and remembered at the last moment to pluck off his glistening new derby.

Thus they parted, almost precipitately, and, for all of him, might never have met again in this world. Half a mile up the road, it came to the young man that their farewell had lacked that final word of ceremony to which he now aspired. To those who called at his office, to the men he met at the sign of the Mercury, even to Nicolovius when he betook himself from the lamp-lit sitting-room, it was his carefully attained habit to say: "I hope to see you again soon." He meant the hope, with these, only in the most general and perfunctory sense. Why, then, had he omitted this civil tag and postscript in his parting with Miss Weyland, to whom he could have said it—yes, certainly—with more than usual sincerity? Certainly; he really did hope to see her again soon. For she was an intelligent, sensible girl, and knew more about him than anybody in the world except Tim Queed.

Gradually it was borne in upon him that the reason he had failed to tell Miss Weyland that he hoped to see her again soon was exactly the fact that he did hope to see her again soon. Off his guard for this reason, he had fallen into a serious lapse. Looking with untrained eyes into the future, he saw no way in which a man who had failed to tell a lady that he hoped to see her again soon was ever to retrieve his error. It was good-by, Charles Weyland, for sure.

However, Miss Weyland herself resolved all these perplexities by appearing at Mrs. Paynter's supper-table before the month was out; and this exploit she repeated at least once, and maybe twice, during the swift winter that followed.

On January 14, or February 23, or it might have been March 2, Queed unexpectedly reentered the dining-room, toward eight o'clock, with the grave announcement that he had a piece of news. Sharlee was alone in the room, concluding the post-prandial chores with the laying of the Turkey-red cloth. She was in fickle vein this evening, as it chanced; and instead of respectfully inquiring the nature of his tidings, as was naturally and properly expected of her, she received the young man with a fire of breezy inconsequentialities which puzzled and annoyed him greatly.

She admitted, without pressure, that she had been hoping for his return; had in fact been dawdling over the duties of the dining-room on that very expectation. From there her fancy grew. Audaciously she urged his reluctant attention to the number of her comings to Mrs. Paynter's in recent months. With an exceedingly stagey counterfeit of a downcast eye, she hinted at gossip lately arising from public observation of these visits: gossip, namely, to the effect that Miss Weyland's ostensible suppings with her aunt were neither better nor worse than so many bold calls upon Mr. Queed. Her lip quivered alarmingly over such a confession; undoubtedly she looked enormously abashed.

Mr. Queed, for his part, looked highly displeased and more than a shade uncomfortable. He annihilated all such foolishness by a look and a phrase; observed, in a stately opening, that she would hardly trouble to deny empty rumor of this sort, since—

"I can't deny it, you see! Because," she interrupted, raising her eyes and turning upon him a sudden dazzling yet outrageous smile—"*it's true.*"

She skipped away, smiling to herself, happily putting things away and humming an air. Queed watched her in annoyed silence. His adamantine gravity inspired her with an irresistible impulse to levity; so the law of averages claimed its innings.

"While you are thinking up what to say," she rattled on, "might I ask your advice on a sociological problem that was just laid before me by Laura?"

"Well," he said impatiently, "who is Laura?"

"Laura is the loyal negress who cooks the food for Mrs. Paynter's bright young men. Her husband first deserted her, next had the misfortune to get caught while burgling, and is at present doing time, as the saying is. Now a young bright-skin negro desires to marry Laura, and speaks in urgent tones of the divorce court. Her attitude is more than willing, but she learns that a divorce, at the lowest conceivable price, will cost fifteen dollars, and she had rather put the money in a suit and bonnet. But a thought no larger than a man's hand has crossed her mind, and she said to me just now: 'I 'clare, Miss Sharly, it do look like, when you got a beau and he want to marry you, and all the time axin' and coaxin' an' beggin' you to get a div-o'ce, it do look like *he* ought to pay for the div-o'ce.' Now what answer has your old science to give to a real heart problem such as that?"

"May I ask that you will put the napkins away, or at the least remain stationary? It is impossible for me to talk with you while you flutter about in this way."

At last she came and sat down meekly at the table, her hands clasped before her in rather a devotional attitude, while he, standing, fixed her with his unwavering gaze.

"I speak to you," he began, uncompromisingly, "as to Mrs. Paynter's agent. Professor Nicolovius is going to move in the spring and take an apartment or small house. He has invited me to share such apartment or house with him."

"What! But you declined?"

"On the contrary, I accepted at once."

Mrs. Paynter's agent was much surprised and interested by this news, and said so. "But how in the world," she went on, puzzled, "did you make him like you so? I always supposed that he hated everybody—he does me, I know."

"I believe he does hate everybody but me."

"Strange—extraordinary!" said Sharlee, picturing the two scholars alone together in their flat, endeavoring to soft-boil eggs on one of those little fixtures over the gas.

"I can see nothing in the least extraordinary in the refusal of a cultured gentleman to hate me."

"I don't mean it that way at all—not at all! But Professor Nicolovius must know cultured gentlemen, congenial roomers, who are nearer his own age—"

"Oh, not necessarily," said Queed, and sat down in the chair by her, Major Brooke's chair. "He is a most unsocial sort of man,"—this from the little Doctor!—"and I doubt if he knows anybody better than he knows me. That he knows me so well is due solely to the fact that we have been forced on each other three times a day for over a year. For the first month or so after I came here, we remained entire strangers, I remember, and passed each other on the stairs without speaking. Gradually, however, he has come to take a great fancy to me."

"And is that why you are going off to a honeymoon cottage with him?"

"Hardly. I am going because it will be the best sort of arrangement for me."

"Oh!"

"I will pay, you see," said Queed, "no more than I am paying here; for that matter, I have no doubt that I could beat him down to five dollars a week, if I cared to do so. In return I shall have decidedly greater comforts and conveniences, far greater quiet and independence, and complete freedom from interruptions and intrusions. The arrangement will be a big gain in several ways for me."

"And have you taken a great fancy to Professor Nicolovius, too?"

"Oh, no!—not at all. But that has very little to do with it. At least he has the great gift of silence."

Sharlee looked at his absorbed face closely. She thought that his head in profile was very fine, though certainly his nose was too prominent for beauty. But what she was wondering was whether the little Doctor had really changed so much after all.

"Well," said she, slowly, "I'm sorry you're going."

"Sorry—why? It would appear to me that under the tenets of your religion you ought to be glad. You ought to compliment me for going."

"I don't find anything in the tenets of my religion that requires you to go off and room-keep with Professor Nicolovius."

"You do not? It is a tremendous kindness to him, I assure you. To have a place of his own has long been his dream, he tells me; but he cannot afford it without the financial assistance I would give. Again, even if he could finance it, he would not venture to try it alone, because of his health. It appears that he is subject to some kind of attacks—heart, I suppose—and does not want to be alone. I have heard him walking his floor at 3 o'clock in the morning. Do you know anything about his life?"

"No. Nothing."

"I know everything."

He paused for her to ask him questions, that he might have the pleasure of refusing her. But instead of prying, Sharlee said: "Still I'm sorry that you are going."

"Well? Why?"

"Because," said Sharlee.

"Proceed."

"Because I don't like his eyes."

"The question, from your point of view," said Mr. Queed, "is a moral—not an optic one. These acts which confer benefits on others," he continued, "so peculiarly commended by your religion, are conceived by it to work moral good to the doer. The *eyes* (which you use synecdochically to represent the *character*) of the person to whom they are done, have nothing—"

"Mr. Queed," said Sharlee, briskly interrupting his exegetical words, "I believe you are going off with Professor Nicolovius chiefly because—you think he needs you!"

He looked up sharply, much surprised and irritated. "That is absolutely foolish and absurd. I have nothing in the world to do with what Professor Nicolovius needs. You must always remember that I am not a subscriber to the tenets of your religion."

"It is not too late. I always remember that too."

"But I must say frankly that I am much surprised at the way you interpret those tenets. For if—"

"Oh, you should never have tested me on such a question! Don't you see that I'm the judge sitting in his or her own case? Two boarders gone at one swoop! How shall I break the news to Aunt Jennie?"

He thought this over in silence and then said impatiently; "I'm sorry, but I do not feel that I can consider that phase of the matter."

"Certainly not."

"The arrangement between us is a strictly business one, based on mutual advantage, and to be terminated at will as the interests of either party dictates."

"Exactly."

He turned a sharp glance on her, and rose. Having risen he stood a moment, irresolute, frowning, troubled by a thought. Then he said, in an annoyed, nervous voice:—

"Look here, will it be a serious thing for your aunt to lose me?"

The agent burst out laughing. He was surprised by her merriment; he could not guess that it covered her instantaneous discovery that she liked him more than she would ever have thought possible.

"While I'm on the other side—remember that," said she, "I'm obliged to tell you that we can let the rooms any day at an hour's notice. Not that the places of our two scholars can ever be filled, but the boarding-house business is booming these days. We are turning them away. Do you remember the night that you walked in here an hour late for supper, and I arose and collected twenty dollars from you?"

"Oh, yes.... By the way—I have never asked—whatever became of that extraordinary pleasure-dog of yours?"

"Thank you. He is bigger and more pleasurable than ever. I take him out every afternoon, and each day, just as the clock strikes five, he knocks over a strange young man for me. It is delightful sport. But he has never found any young man that he enjoyed as heartily as he did you."

Gravely he moved toward the door. "I must return to my work. You will tell your aunt I have given notice? Well—good-evening."

"*Good*-evening, Mr. Queed."

The door half shut upon him, but opened again to admit his head and shoulders.

"By the way, there was a curious happening yesterday which might be of interest to you. Did you see it in the *Post*—a small item headed 'The Two Queeds'?"

"Oh—no! About you and Tim?"

"About Tim, but not about me. His beat was changed the other day, it seems, and early yesterday morning a bank in his new district was broken into. Tim went in and arrested the burglar after a desperate fight in the dark. When other policemen came and turned on the lights, Tim discovered to his horror that he had captured his brother Murphy."

CHAPTER XVIII

Of President West of Old Blaines College, his Trustees and his Troubles; his Firmness in the Brown-Jones Hazing Incident so misconstrued by Malicious Asses; his Article for the Post, and why it was never printed: all ending in West's Profound Dissatisfaction with the Rewards of Patriotism.

The way of Blaines College was not wholly smooth that winter, and annoyances rose to fret the fine edge of President West's virgin enthusiasms. The opening had been somewhat disappointing. True, there were more students than last year, the exact increment being nine. But West had hoped for an increase of fifty, and had communicated his expectations to the trustees, who were correspondingly let down when the actual figures — total enrolment, 167 — were produced at the October meeting. The young president explained about the exasperating delays in getting out his advertising literature, but the trustees rather hemmed over the bills and said that that was a lot of money. And one of them bluntly called attention to the fact that the President had not assumed his duties till well along in September.

West, with charming humility and good humor, asked indulgence for his inexperience. His mistake, he said, in giving an excess of time to the study of the great collegiate systems of the old world, if it was a mistake, was one that could hardly be repeated. Next year ...

"Meantime," said the blunt trustee, "you've got a ten per cent increase in expenditures and but nine more stoodents."

"Let us not wholly forget," said West, with his disarming smile, "my hope to add substantially to the endowment."

But he marked this trustee as one likely to give trouble in the future, and hence to be handled with care. He was a forthright, upstanding, lantern-jawed man of the people, by the name of James E. Winter. A contractor by profession and a former member of the city council, he represented the city on the board of trustees. For the city appropriated seventy-five hundred dollars a year, for the use of the college, and in return for this munificence, reserved the right to name three members of the board.

Nor was Mr. Winter the only man of his kidney on that directorate. From his great friend among the trustees, Mr. Fyne, donator of the fifty thousand dollar endowment on which Blaines College partly subsisted, West learned that his election to the presidency had failed of being unanimous. In fact, the vote had stood seven to five, and the meeting at which he was chosen had at times approached violence. Of the five, two had voted against West because they thought that old Dr. Gilfillan's resignation did not have that purely spontaneous character so desirable under the circumstances; two because they did not think that West had the qualifications, or would have the right point of view, for a people's college; and one for all these reasons, or for any other reason, which is to say for personal reasons. This one, said Mr. Fyne, was James E. Winter.

"I know," said West. "He's never got over the poundings we used to give him in the *Post* when he trained with those grafters on the Council. He'd put poison in my tea on half a chance."

Unhappily, the sharp cleft made in the board at the time of the election survived and deepened. The trustees developed a way of dividing seven to five on almost all of West's recommendations which was anything but encouraging. An obstinate, but human, pride of opinion tended to keep the two factions facing each other intact, and matters very tiny in themselves served, as the weeks went by, to aggravate this feeling. Once, at least, before Christmas, it required all of West's tact and good-humor to restore the appearance of harmony to a meeting which was fast growing excited.

But the young president would not allow himself to become discouraged. He earnestly intended to show James E. Winter which of the two knew most about running a modern institution of the higher learning. Only the perfectest bloom of his ardor faded under the constant handling of rough fingers. The interval separating Blaines College and the University of Paris began to loom larger than it had seemed in the halcyon summer-time, and the classic group of noble piles receded further and further into the prophetic haze. But West's fine energy and optimism remained. And he continued to see in the college, unpromising though the outlook was in some respects, a real instrument for the uplift.

The president sat up late on those evenings when social diversions did not claim his time, going over and over his faculty list with a critical eye, and always with profound disapproval. There were only three Ph.D.'s among them, and as a whole the average of attainment was below, rather than above, the middle grade. They were, he was obliged to admit, a lot of cheap men for a cheap college. With such a staff, a distinguished standard was clearly not to be hoped for. But what to do about it? His general idea during the summer had been mercilessly to weed out the weak brothers in the faculty, a few at a time, and fill their places with men of the first standing. But now a great obstacle presented itself. Men of the first standing demanded salaries of the first standing. Blaines College was not at present in position to pay such salaries. Obviously one of two courses remained. Either the elevation of the faculty must proceed in a very modest form, or else Blaines College must get in position to pay larger salaries. West decided to move in both directions.

There was one man on the staff that West objected to from the first faculty meeting. This was a man named Harkly Young, a youngish, tobacco-chewing fellow of lowly origin and unlessoned manners, who was "assistant professor" of mathematics at a salary of one thousand dollars a year. Professor Young's bearing and address did anything but meet the president's idea of scholarliness; and West had no difficulty in convincing himself of the man's incompetence. Details came to his attention from time to time during the autumn which served to strengthen his snap-shot judgment, but he made the mistake, doubtless, of failing to communicate his dissatisfaction to Professor Young, and so giving him an inkling of impending disaster. West knew of just the man for this position, a brilliant young assistant superintendent of schools in another part of the state, who could be secured for the same salary. Eager to begin his house-cleaning and mark some definite progress, West hurled his bolt from the blue. About the middle of December he dispatched a letter to the doomed man notifying him that his services would not be required after the Christmas recess.

Instead of accepting his dismissal in a quiet and gentlemanly way, and making of himself a glad thank-offering on the altar of scholarship, Professor Young had the poor taste to create an uproar. After satisfying himself in a stirring personal interview that the president's letter was final, he departed in a fury, and brought suit against the college and Charles Gardiner West personally for his year's salary. He insisted that he had been engaged for the full college year. To the court he represented that he was a married man with six children, and absolutely dependent upon his position for his livelihood.

Professor Young happened to be very unpopular with both his colleagues and the students, and probably all felt that it was a case of good riddance, particularly as West's new man rode rapidly into general popularity. These facts hampered the Winterites on the board, but nevertheless they made the most of the incident, affecting to believe that Young had been harshly treated. The issue, they intimated, was one of the classes against the masses. The *Chronicle*, the penny evening paper which found it profitable business to stand for the under-dog and "the masses," scareheaded a jaundiced account of the affair, built up around an impassioned statement from

Professor Young. The same issue carried an editorial entitled, "The Kid Glove College." West laughed at the editorial, but he was a sensitive man to criticism and the sarcastic gibes wounded him. When the attorneys for the college advised a settlement out of court by paying the obstreperous Young three hundred dollars in cash, James Winter was outspoken in his remarks. A resolution restraining the president from making any changes in the faculty, without the previous consent and approval of the board, was defeated, after warm discussion, by the margin of seven votes to five.

"By the Lord, gentlemen," said Mr. Fyne, indignantly, "if you cannot put any confidence in the discretion of your president, you'd better get one whose discretion you can put confidence in."

"That's just what I say," rejoined James E. Winter, with instant significance.

Other changes in his faculty West decided to defer till the beginning of a new year. All his surplus energy should be concentrated, he decided, on raising an endowment fund which should put the college on a sound financial basis before that time came. But here again he collided with the thick wall of trustee bigotry.

In the city, despite his youth, he was already well known as a speaker, and was a favorite orator on agreeable occasions of a semi-public nature. This was a sort of prestige that was well worth cultivating. In the State, and even outside of it, he had many connections through various activities, and by deft correspondence he easily put himself in line for such honors as they had to offer. Invitations to speak came rolling in in the most gratifying way. His plan was to mount upon these to invitations of an even higher class. In December he made a much admired address before the Associated Progress Boards. The next month, through much subtle wire-pulling, he got himself put on the toast list at the annual banquet of the distinguished American Society for the Promotion of the Higher Education. There his name met on equal terms with names as yet far better known. He spoke for ten minutes and sat down with the thrill of having surpassed himself. A famous financier who sat with him at the speaker's table told him that his speech was the best of the evening, because the shortest, and asked several questions about Blaines College. The young President returned home in a fine glow, which the hostile trustees promptly subjected to a cold douche.

"I'd like to inquire," said James E. Winter, sombrely, at the January board meeting, "what is the point, if any, of the President of Blaines College trapesing all over the country to attend these here banquets."

They used unacademic as well as plain language in the Blaines board meeting by this time. West smiled at Trustee Winter's question. To him the man habitually seemed as malapropos as a spiteful old lady.

"The point is, Mr. Winter, to get in touch with the sources of endowment funds. Blaines College on its present foundation cannot hope to compete with enlightened modern colleges of from five to one hundred times its resources. If we mean to advance, we must do it by bringing Blaines favorably to the attention of philanthropists who—"

"No, *sir!*" roared Winter, bringing his contractor's fist down thuddingly upon the long table. "Such noo-fangled ideas are against the traditions of old Blaines College, I say! Old Blaines College is not asking for alms. Old Blaines College is not a whining beggar, whatever those Yankee colleges may be. I say, gentlemen, it's beneath the dignity of old Blaines College for its president to go about Noo York bowing and scraping and passing the hat to Rockyfeller, and such-like boocaneers."

To West's unfeigned surprise, this view of the matter met with solid backing. Reminiscences of the "tainted money" controversy appeared in the trustees' talk. "Subsidized education" was heard more than once. One spoke bitterly of Oil Colleges. No resolution was introduced, James E. Winter having inadvertently come unprepared, but the majority opinion was clearly that old Blaines College (founded 1894) should draw in her traditional skirts from the yellow flood then pouring over the country, and remain, small it may be, but superbly incorruptible.

For once, West left his trustees thoroughly disgusted and out of humor.

"Why, *why* are we doomed to this invincible hostility to a new idea?" he cried, in the bitterness of his soul. "Here is the spirit of progress not merely beckoning to us, but fairly springing into our laps, and because it speaks in accents that were unfamiliar to the slave patriarchy of a hundred years ago, we drag it outside the city and crucify it. I tell you these old Bourbons whom we call leaders are millstones around our necks, and we can never move an inch until we've laid the last one of them under the sod."

Sharlee Weyland, to whom he repeated this thought, though she was all sympathy with his difficulties, did not nevertheless think that this was quite fair. "Look," she said, "at the tremendous progress we've made in the last ten years."

"Yes," he flashed back at her, "and who can say that a state like Massachusetts, with the same incomparable opportunities, wouldn't have made ten times as much!"

But he was the best-natured man alive, and his vexation soon faded. In a week, he was once more busy planning out ways and means. He sought funds in the metropolis no more, and the famous financier spared him the mortification of having to refuse a donation by considerately not offering one. But he continued to make addresses in the State, and in the city he was in frequent demand. However, the endowment fund remained obstinately immovable. By February there had been no additions, unless we can count five hundred dollars promised by dashing young Beverley Byrd on the somewhat whimsical condition that his brother Stewart would give an equal amount.

"Moreover," said young Mr. Byrd, "I'll increase it to seven hundred and fifty dollars if your friend Winter will publicly denounce me as a boocaneer. It'll help me in my business to be lined up with Rockefeller and all those Ikes."

But this gift never materialized at all, for the reason that Stewart Byrd kindly but firmly refused to give anything. A rich vein of horse-sense underlay Byrd's philanthropic enthusiasms; and even the necessity for the continued existence of old Blaines College appeared to be by no means clear in his mind.

"If you had a free hand, Gardiner," said he, "that would be one thing, but you haven't. I've had my eye on Blaines for a long time, and frankly I don't think it is entitled to any assistance. You have an inferior plant and a lot of inferior men; a small college governed by small ideas and ridden by a close corporation of small trustees—"

"But heavens, man!" protested West, "your argument makes a perfect circle. You won't help Blaines because it's poorly equipped, and Blaines is poorly equipped because the yellow-rich—that's you—won't help it."

Stewart Byrd wiped his gold-rimmed glasses, laughing pleasantly. He was the oldest of the four brothers, a man of authority at forty; and West watched him with a secret admiration, not untouched by a flicker of envy.

"What's the answer? Blessed if I know! The fact is, old fellow, I think you've got an utterly hopeless job there, and if I were you, I believe I'd get ready to throw it over at the first opportunity."

West replied that it was only the hard things that were worth doing in this life. None the less, as winter drew to a close, he insensibly relaxed his efforts toward the immediate exaltation of old Blaines. As he looked more closely into the situation, he realized that his too impetuous desire for results had driven him to waste energy in hopeless directions. How could he ever do anything, with a lot of moss-backed trustees tying his hands and feet every time he tried to toddle a step forward—he and Blaines? Clearly the first step of all was to oust the fossils who stood like rocks in the path of progress, and fill their places with men who could at least recognize a progressive idea when they were beaten across the nose with it. He studied his trustee list now more purposefully than he had ever pored over his faculty line up. By the early spring, he was ready to set subtle influences going looking to the defeat of the insurgent five, including James E. Winter, whose term happily expired on the first of January following.

But the president's lines did not all fall in gloomy and prickly places in these days. His perennial faculty for enjoyment never deserted him even in his darkest hours. His big red automobile, acquired on the crest of Semple and West's prosperity, was constantly to be seen bowling down the street of an early-vernal afternoon, or dancing down far country lanes light with a load of two. The Thursday German had known him as of old, and many were the delightful dinners where he proved, by merit alone, the life of the party. Nor were his pleasures by any means all dissociated from Blaines College. The local prestige that the president acquired from his position was decidedly agreeable to him. Never an educational point arose in the life of the city or the nation but the *Post* carried a long interview giving Mr. West's views upon it. Corner-stone laying afforded him a sincere joy. Even discussions with parents about their young hopefuls was anything but irksome to his buoyant nature.

Best and pleasantest of all was his relation with the students. His notable gift for popularity, however futile it might be with embittered asses like James E. Winter, served him in good stead here. West could not conceal from himself that the boys idolized him. With secret delight he saw them copying his walk, his taste in waistcoats, the way he brushed back his hair. He had them in relays to his home to supper, skipping only those of too hopeless an uncouthness, and sent them home enchanted. He had introduced into the collegiate programme a five-minute prayer, held every morning at nine, at which he made brief addresses on some phase of college ideals every Tuesday and Friday. Attendance at these gatherings was optional, but it kept up in the most gratifying way, and sometimes on a Friday the little assembly-room would be quite filled with the frankly admiring lads. "Why should I mind the little annoyances," would flash into his mind as he rose to speak, "when I can look down into a lot of fine, loyal young faces like this. *Here* is what counts." His appearance at student gatherings was always attended by an ovation. He loved to hear the old Blaines cheer, with three ringing "Prexy's" tacked on the end. One Saturday in early April, Prexy took Miss Avery to a baseball game, somewhat against her will, solely that she might see how his students worshiped him. On the following Saturday, all with even-handed liberality, he took Miss Weyland to another baseball game, with the same delightful purpose.

The spring found West stronger and more contented with his lot as president of a jerkwater college, decidedly happier for the burning out of the fires of hot ambition which had consumed his soul six months earlier. He told himself that he was reconciled to a slow advance with fighting every inch of the way. But he saw the uselessness of fighting trustees who were doomed soon to fall, and resigned himself to a quiet, in fact a temporarily suspended, programme of progress. And then, just when everything seemed most comfortably serene, a new straw suddenly appeared in the wind, which quickly multiplied into a bundle and then a bale, and all at once the camel's back had more than it could bear. April was hardly dead before the college world was in a turmoil, by the side of which the Young affair was the mere buzzing of a gnat.

History is full of incidents of the kind: incidents which are trifling beyond mention in the beginning, but which malign circumstance distorts and magnifies till they set nations daggers-drawn at each other's throats. Two students lured a "freshman" to their room and there invited him to drink a marvelous compound the beginnings of which were fat pork and olive oil; this while standing on his head. The freshman did not feel in a position to deny their request. But his was a delicate stomach, and the result of his accommodating spirit was that he became violently, though not seriously, ill. Thus the matter came to the attention of his parents, and so to the college authorities. The sick lad stoutly declined to tell who were his persecutors, but West managed to track one of them down and summoned him to his office. We may call this student Brown; a pleasant-mannered youth of excellent family, whose sister West sometimes danced with at the Thursday German. Brown said that he had, indeed, been present during the sad affair, that he had, in fact, to his eternal humiliation and regret, aided and abetted it; but he delicately hinted that the prime responsibility rested on the shoulders of the other student. Rather unwisely, perhaps, West pressed him to disclose the name of his collaborator. (Brown afterwards, to square himself with the students, alleged "intimidation.") A youth whom we may describe as Jones was mentioned, and later, in the august private office, was invited to tell what he knew of the disorder. Henceforward accounts vary. Jones declared to the end that the president promised a light punishment for all concerned if he would make a clean breast. West asserted—and who would doubt his statement?—that he had made no promise, or even a suggestion of a promise, of any kind. Be that as it may, Jones proceeded, though declining to mention any other name than his own. He declared positively that the idea of hazing the freshman had not originated with him, but that he had taken a culpable part in it, for which he was heartily sorry. Asked whether he considered himself or his colleague principally responsible for the injury to the freshman's health, he said that he preferred not to answer. To West this seemed a damaging admission, though perhaps not everybody would have so viewed it. He sent Jones away with no intimation of what he proposed to do.

There was the situation, plain as a barn at noonday. All that was needed was tact, judgment, and a firm hand. The young president hesitated. Ordinarily he would have taken a quiet hour in the evening to think it all over carefully, but as it happened—like Lord George Germaine and the dispatch to Burgoyne—social engagements rushed forward to occupy his time. Next morning his mail brought several letters, urging him to set his foot ruthlessly on the serpent-head of hazing. His telephone rang with the same firm counsel. The *Post*, he saw, had a long leading article insisting that discipline must be maintained at all hazards. It was observed that this article thundered in the old Colonel's best style, and this was the more noteworthy in that the article in question happened to be written by a young man of the name of Queed.

West would have preferred to let the matter stand for a day or so, but he saw that prompt and decisive action was expected of him. Denying himself to callers, he shut himself in his office, to determine what was just and fair and right. The advice of his correspondents, and of the *Post*, tallied exactly with what the trustees had told him in the beginning about the traditions of old Blaines. Hazing was not to be tolerated under any circumstances. Therefore, somebody's head would now have to fall. There could hardly be any occasion for expelling nice young Brown. For a minor consideration, it would be decidedly awkward henceforward, to have to offer salt to Mrs. Brown at dinner, as he had done only last week, with the hand that had ruined her son's career. Much more important, it seemed clear enough to West that the boy had only been weak, and had been tempted into misbehavior by his older and more wilful comrade. West had never liked young Jones. He was a rawboned, unkempt sprig of the masses, who had not been included in any of the student suppers at the president's house. Jones's refusal to speak out fully on all the details of the affair pointed strongly, so West argued, to consciousness of damning guilt. The path of administrative duty appeared plain. West, to say truth, had not at first expected to apply the drastic penalty of expulsion at all, but it was clear that this was what the city expected of him. The universal cry was for unshrinking firmness. Well, he would show them that he was firm, and shrank from no unpleasantness where his duty was concerned. Brown he ordered before him for a severe reprimand, and Jones he summarily dismissed from old Blaines College.

These decrees went into effect at noon. At 4 o'clock in the afternoon the war-dogs broke their leashes. Four was the hour when the "night" edition of the *Evening Chronicle* came smoking hot from the presses. It appeared that young Jones was the son, not merely of a plumber, but of a plumber who was decidedly prominent in lodge circles and the smaller areas of politics. His case was therefore precisely the kind that the young men of the Chronicle loved to espouse. The three-column scare-head over their bitterly partisan "story" ran thus:

POOR BOY KICKED OUT
BY PRESIDENT WEST

Close beside this, lest the reader should fail to grasp the full meaning of the boldface, was a three-column cartoon, crudely drawn but adroit enough. It represented West, unpleasantly caricatured, garbed in a swallow-tail coat and enormous white gloves, with a gardenia in his buttonhole, engaged in booting a lad of singular nobility of countenance out of an open door. A tag around the lad's neck described him as "The Workingman's Son." Under the devilish drawing ran a line which said, succinctly, "His Policies." On page four was a double column, double-leaded editorial, liberal with capitals and entitled: "Justice in Silk Stockings."

But this was only a beginning. Next morning's *Post*, which West had counted on to come to his assistance with a ringing leader, so earnestly discussed rotation of crops and the approaching gubernatorial campaign, that it had not a line for the little disturbance at the college. If this was a disappointment to West, a greater blow awaited him. Not to try to gloss over the mortifying circumstance, he was hissed when he entered the morning assembly—he, the prince, idol, and darling of his students. Though the room was full, the hissing was of small proportions, but rather too big to be ignored. West, after debating with himself whether or not he should notice it, made a graceful and manly two-minute talk which, he flattered himself, effectually abashed the lads who had so far forgotten themselves. None the less the demonstration cut him to the quick. When four o'clock came he found himself waiting for the appearance of the *Chronicle* with an anxiety which he had never conceived possible with regard to that paper. A glance at its lurid front showed that the blatherskites had pounded him harder than ever. A black headline glared with the untruth that President West had been "Hissed by Entire Student Body." Editorially, the *Chronicle* passionately inquired whether the taxpayers enjoyed having the college which they so liberally supported (exact amount seventy-five hundred dollars a year) mismanaged in so gross a way.

West put a laughing face upon these calumnies, but to himself he owned that he was deeply hurt. Dropping in at the club that night, he found a group of men, all his friends, eagerly discussing the shindig, as they called it. Joining in with that perfect good-humor and lack of false pride which was characteristic of him, he gathered that all of them thought he had made a mistake. It seemed to be considered that Brown had put himself in a bad light by trying to throw the blame on Jones. Jones, they said, should not have been bounced without Brown, and probably the best thing would have been not to bounce either. The irritating thing about this latter view was that it was exactly what West had thought in the first place, before pressure was applied to him.

In the still watches of the night the young man was harried by uncertainties and tortured by stirring suspicions. Had he been fair to Jones, after all? Was his summary action in regard to that youth prompted in the faintest degree by personal dislike? Was he conceivably the kind of man who is capable of thinking one thing and doing another? The most afflicting of all doubts, doubt of himself, kept the young man tossing on his pillow for at least an hour.

But he woke with a clear-cut decision singing in his mind and gladdening his morning. He would take Jones back. He would generously reinstate the youth, on the ground that the public mortification already put upon him was a sufficient punishment for his sins and abundant warning for others like-minded. This would settle all difficulties at one stroke and definitely lay the ghost of a disagreeable occurrence. The solution was so simple that he marvelled that he had not thought of it before.

His morning's mail, containing one or two very unpleasant letters, only strengthened his determination. He lost no time in carrying it out. By special messenger he dispatched a carefully written and kindly letter to Jones, Senior. Jones, Senior, tore it across the middle and returned it by the same messenger. He then informed the *Chronicle* what he had done. The *Chronicle* that afternoon shrieked it under a five-column head, together with a ferocious statement from Jones, Senior, saying that he would rather see his son breaking rocks in the road than a student in such a college as Blaines was, under the present régime. The editor, instead of seeing in West's letter a spontaneous act of magnanimity in the interest of the academic uplift, maliciously twisted it into a grudging confession of error, "unrelieved by the grace of manly retraction and apology." So ran the editorial, which was offensively headed "West's Fatal Flop." Some of the State papers, it seemed from excerpts printed in another column, were foolishly following the *Chronicle's* lead; Republican cracker-box orators were trying somehow to make capital of the thing; and altogether there was a very unpleasant little mess, which showed signs of developing rapidly into what is known as an "issue."

That afternoon, when the tempest in the collegiate teapot was storming at its merriest, West, being downtown on private business, chanced to drop in at the Post office, according to his frequent habit. He found the sanctum under the guard of the young assistant editor. The Colonel, in fact, had been sick in bed for four days, and in his absence, Queed was acting-editor and sole contributor of the leaded minion. The two young men greeted each other pleasantly.

"I'm reading you every day," said West, presently, "and, flattery and all that aside, I've been both surprised and delighted at the character of the work you're doing. It's fully up to the best traditions of the *Post*, and that strikes me as quite a feat for a man of your years."

Because he was pleased at this tribute, Queed answered briefly, and at once changed the subject. But he did it maladroitly by expressing the hope that things were going well with Mr. West.

"Well, not hardly," said West, and gave his pleasant laugh. "You may possibly have noticed from our esteemed afternoon contemporary that I'm in a very pretty little pickle. But by the way," he added, with entire good humor, "the *Post* doesn't appear to have noticed it after all."

"No," said Queed, slowly, not pretending to misunderstand. He hesitated, a rare thing with him. "The fact is I could not write what you would naturally wish to have written, and therefore I haven't written anything at all."

West threw up his hands in mock horror. "Here's another one! Come on, fellers! Kick him!—he's got no friends! You know," he laughed, "I remind myself of the man who stuck his head in at the teller's window, wanting to have a check cashed. The teller didn't know him from Adam. 'Have you any friends here in the city?' asked he. 'Lord, no!' said the stranger; 'I'm the weather man.'"

Queed smiled.

"And I was only trying in my poor way," said West, mournfully, "to follow the advice that you, young man, roared at me for a column on the fatal morning."

"I've regretted that," said Queed. "Though, of course, I never looked for any such developments as this. I was merely trying to act on Colonel Cowles's advice about always playing up local topics. You are doubtless familiar with his dictum that the people are far more interested in a cat-fight at Seventh and Centre Streets than in the greatest exploits of science."

West laughed and rose to go. Then a good-natured thought struck him. "Look here," said he, "this must be a great load, with the Colonel away—doing all of three columns a day by yourself. How on earth do you manage it?"

"Well, I start work at eight o'clock in the morning."

"And what time does that get you through?"

"Usually in time to get to press with it."

"Oh, I say! That won't do at all. You'll break yourself down, playing both ends against the middle like that. Let me help you out, won't you? Let me do something for you right now?"

"If you really feel like it," said Queed, remembering how the Colonel welcomed Mr. West's occasional contributions to his columns, "of course I shall be glad to have something from you."

"Why, my dear fellow, certainly! Hand me some copy-paper there, and go right on with your work while I unbosom my pent-up Uticas."

He meditated a moment, wrote rapidly for half an hour, and rose with a hurried glance at his watch.

"Here's a little squib about the college that may serve as a space-filler. I must fly for an engagement. I'll try to come down to-morrow afternoon anyway, and if you need anything to-night, 'phone me. Delighted to help you out."

Queed picked up the scattered sheets and read them over carefully. He found that Director West had written a very able defense, and whole-hearted endorsement, of President West's position in the Blaines College hazing affair.

The acting editor sat for some time in deep thought. Eighteen months' increasing contact with Buck Klinker and other men of action had somewhat tamed his soaring self-sufficiency. He was not nearly so sure as he once was that he knew everything there was to know, and a little more besides. West, personally, whom he saw often, he had gradually come to admire with warmth. By slow degrees it came to him that the popular young president had many qualities of a very desirable sort which he himself lacked. West's opinion on a question of college discipline was likely to be at least as sound as his own. Moreover, West was one of the owners and managers of the *Post*.

Nevertheless, he, Queed, did not see how he could accept and print this article.

It was the old-school Colonel's fundamental axiom, drilled into and fully adopted by his assistant, that the editor must be personally responsible for every word that appeared in his columns. Those columns, to be kept pure, must represent nothing but the editor's personal views. Therefore, on more than one occasion, the Colonel had refused point-blank to prepare articles which his directors wished printed. He always accompanied these refusals with his resignation, which the directors invariably returned to him, thereby abandoning their point. Queed was for the moment editor in the Colonel's stead. Over the telephone, Colonel Cowles had instructed him, four days before, to assume full responsibility, communicating with him or with the directors if he was in doubt, but standing firmly on his own legs. As to where those legs now twitched to lead him, the young man could have no doubt. If he had a passion in his scientist's bosom, it was for exact and unflinching veracity. Even to keep the *Post* silent had been something of a strain upon his instinct for truth, for a voice within him had whispered that an honest journal *ought* to have some opinion to express on a matter so locally interesting as this. To publish this editorial would strain the instinct to the breaking point and beyond. For it would be equivalent to saying, whether anybody else but him knew it or not, that he, the present editor of the *Post* approved and endorsed West's position, when the truth was that he did nothing of the sort.

At eight o'clock that night, he succeeded, after prolonged search of the town on the part of the switchboard boy, in getting West to the telephone.

"Mr. West," said Queed, "I am very sorry, but I don't see how I can print your article."

"Oh, Lord!" came West's untroubled voice back over the wire. "And a man's enemies shall be those of his own household. What's wrong with it, Mr. Editor?"

Queed explained his reluctances. "If that is not satisfactory to you," he added, at the end, "as it hardly can be, I give you my resignation now, and you yourself can take charge immediately."

"Bless your heart, no! Put it in the waste-basket. It doesn't make a kopeck's worth of difference. Here's a thought, though. Do you approve of the tactics of those *Chronicle* fellows in the matter?"

"No, I do not."

"Well, why not show them up to-morrow?"

"I'll be glad to do it."

So Queed wrote a stinging little article of a couple of sticks' length, holding up to public scorn journalistic redshirts who curry-combed the masses, and preached class hatred for the money there was in it. It is doubtful if this article helped matters much. For the shameless *Chronicle* seized on it as showing that the *Post* had tried to defend the president, and utterly failed. "Even the West organ," so ran its brazen capitals, "does not dare endorse its darling. And no wonder, after the storm of indignation aroused by the *Chronicle's* fearless exposures."

West kept his good humor and self-control intact, but it was hardly to be expected that he enjoyed venomous misrepresentation of this sort. The solidest comfort he got in these days came from Sharlee Weyland, who did not read the *Chronicle,* and was most beautifully confident that whatever he had done was right. But after all, the counselings of Miss Avery, of whom he also saw much that spring, better suited his disgruntled humor.

"They are incapable of appreciating you," said she, a siren in the red motor. "You owe it to yourself to enter a larger field. And"—so ran the languorous voice—"to your friends."

The trustees met on Saturday, with the *Chronicle* still pounding away with deadly regularity. Its editorial of the afternoon before was entitled, "We Want A College President—Not A Class President," and had frankly urged the trustees of old Blaines to consider whether a change of administration was not advisable. This was advice which some of the trustees were only too ready to follow. James E. Winter, coming armed cap-à-pie to the meeting, suggested that Mr. West withdraw for a time, which Mr. West properly declined to do. The implacable insurgent thereupon launched into a bitter face-to-face denunciation of the president's conduct in the hazing affair, outpacing the *Chronicle* by intimating, too plainly for courtesy, that the president's conduct toward Jones was characterized by duplicity, if not wanting in consistent adherence to veracity. "I had a hard time to keep from hitting him," said West afterwards, "but I knew that would be the worst thing I could possibly do." "Maybe so," sighed Mr. Fyne, apparently not with full conviction. Winter went too far in moving that the president's continuance in office was prejudicial to the welfare of Blaines College, and was defeated 9 to 3. Nevertheless, West always looked back at this meeting as one of the most unpleasant incidents in his life. He flung out of it humiliated, angry, and thoroughly sick at heart.

West saw himself as a persecuted patriot, who had laid a costly oblation on the altar of public spirit only to see the base crowd jostle forward and spit upon it. He was poor in this world's goods. It had cost him five thousand a year to accept the presidency of Blaines College. And this was how they rewarded him. To him, as he sat long in his office brooding upon the darkness of life, there came a visitor, a tall, angular, twinkling-eyed, slow-speaking individual who perpetually chewed an unlighted cigar. He was Plonny Neal, no other, the reputed great chieftain of city politics. Once the *Post*, in an article inspired by West, had referred to Plonny as "this notorious grafter." Plonny could hardly have considered this courteous; but he was a man who never remembered a grudge, until ready to pay it back with compound interest. West's adolescent passion for the immediate reform of politics had long since softened, and nowadays when the whirligig of affairs threw the two men together, as it did not infrequently, they met on the easiest and friendliest terms. West liked Plonny, as everybody did, and of Plonny's sincere liking for him he never had the slightest doubt.

In fact, Mr. Neal's present call was to report that the manner in which a lady brushes a midge from her summering brow was no simpler than the wiping of James E. Winter off the board of Blaines College.

That topic being disposed of, West introduced another.

"Noticed the way the *Chronicle* is jumping on me with all four feet, Plonny?" he asked, with rather a forced laugh. "Why can't those fellows forget it and leave me alone?"

By a slow facial manoeuvre, Mr. Neal contrived to make his cigar look out upon the world with contemptuousness unbearable.

"Why, nobody pays no attention to them fellers' wind, Mr. West. You could buy them off for a hundred dollars, ten dollars down, and have them praising you three times a week for two hundred dollars, twenty-five dollars down. I only take the paper," said Mr. Neal, "because their Sunday is mighty convenient f'r packin' furniture f'r shipment."

The *Chronicle* was the only paper Mr. Neal ever thought of reading, and this was how he stabbed it in the back.

"I don't want to butt in, Mr. West," said he, rising, "and you can stop me if I am, but as a friend of yours—why are you botherin' yourself at all with this here kid's-size proposition?"

"What kid's-size proposition?"

"This little two-by-twice grammar school that tries to pass itself off for a college. And you ain't even boss of it at that! You got a gang of mossbacks sitting on your head who don't get a live idea among 'em wunst a year. Why, the archangel Gabriel wouldn't have a show with a lot of corpses like them! Of course it ain't my business to give advice to a man like you, and I'm probably offendin' you sayin' this, but someway you don't seem to see what's so plain to everybody else. It's your modesty keeps you blind, I guess. But here's what I don't see: why don't you come out of this little hole in the ground and get in line?"

"In line?"

"You're dead and buried here. Now you mention the *Evening Windbag* that nobody pays no more attention to than kids yelling in the street. How about having a paper of your own some day, to express your own ideas and get things done, big things, the way you want 'em?"

"You mean the *Post*?"

"Well, the editor of the *Post* certainly would be in line, whereas the president of Blaines Grammar School certainly ain't."

"What do you mean by in line, Plonny?"

Mr. Neal invested his cigar with an enigmatic significance. "I might mean one thing and I might mean another. I s'pose you never give a thought to poltix, did you?"

"Well, in a general way I have thought of it sometimes."

"Think of it some more," said Mr. Neal, from the door. "I see a kind of shake-up comin'. People say I've got infloonce in poltix, and sort of help to run things. Of course it ain't so. I've got no more infloonce than what my ballot gives me, and my takin' an intelligent public interest in what's goin' on. But it looks to an amatoor like the people are gettin' tired of this ring-rule they been givin' us, and 're goin' to rise in their majesty pretty soon, and fill the offices with young progressive men who never heeled f'r the organization."

He went away, leaving the young president of Blaines vastly cheered. Certainly no language could have made Neal's meaning any plainer. He had come to tell West that, if he would only consent to get in line, he, great Neal, desired to put him in high office—doubtless the Mayoralty, which in all human probability meant the Governorship four years later.

West sat long in rapt meditation. He marveled at himself for having ever accepted his present position. Its limitations were so narrow and so palpable, its possibilities were so restricted, its complacent provincialism so glaring, that the imaginative glories with which he had once enwrapped it seemed now simply grotesque. As long as he remained, he was an entombed nonentity. Beyond the college walls, out of the reach of the contemptible bigotry of the trustees of this world, the people were calling for him. He could be the new type of public servant, the clean, strong, fearless, idolized young Moses, predestined to lead a tired people into the promised land of political purity. Once more a white meadow of eager faces rolled out before the eye of his mind; and this time, from the buntinged hustings, he did not extol learning with classic periods, but excoriated political dishonesty in red-hot phrases which jerked the throngs to their feet, frenzied with ardor....

And it was while he was still in this vein of thought, as it happened, that Colonel Cowles, at eleven o'clock on the first night of June, dropped dead in his bathroom, and left the *Post* without an editor.

CHAPTER XIX

The Little House on Duke of Gloucester Street; and the Beginning of Various Feelings, Sensibilities, and Attitudes between two Lonely Men.

One instant thought the news of the Colonel's death struck from nearly everybody's mind: *He'll miss the Reunion.* For within a few days the city was to witness that yearly gathering of broken armies which, of all assemblages among men, the Colonel had loved most dearly. In thirty years, he had not missed one, till now. They buried the old warrior with pomp and circumstance, not to speak of many tears, and his young assistant in the sanctum came home from the graveside with a sense of having lost a valued counselor and friend. Only the home to which the assistant returned with this feeling was not the Third Hall Back of Mrs. Paynter's, sometimes known as the Scriptorium, but a whole suite of pleasant rooms, upstairs and down, in a nice little house on Duke of Gloucester Street. For Nicolovius had made his contemplated move on the first of May, and Queed had gone with him.

It was half-past six o'clock on a pretty summer's evening. Queed opened the house-door with a latch-key and went upstairs to the comfortable living-room, which faithfully reproduced the old professor's sitting-room at Mrs. Paynter's. Nicolovius, in his black silk cap, was sitting near the open window, reading and smoking a strong cigarette.

"Ah, here you are! I was just thinking that you were rather later than usual this evening."

"Yes, I went to Colonel Cowles's funeral. It was decidedly impressive."

"Ah!"

Queed dropped down into one of Nicolovius's agreeable chairs and let his eyes roam over the room. He was extremely comfortable in this house; a little too comfortable, he was beginning to think now, considering that he paid but seven dollars and fifty cents a week towards its support. He had a desk and lamp all his own in the living-room, a table and lamp in his bedroom, ease and independence over two floors. An old negro man looked after the two gentlemen and gave them excellent things to eat. The house was an old one, and small; it was in an unfashionable part of town, and having stood empty for some time, could be had for thirty-five dollars a month. However, Nicolovius had wiped out any economy here by spending his money freely to repair and beautify. He had had workmen in the house for a month, papering, painting, plumbing, and altering.

"Dozens of people could not get in the church," said Queed. "They stood outside in the street till the service was over."

Nicolovius was looking out of the window, and answered casually. "I daresay he was an excellent man according to his lights."

"Coming to know him very well in the past year, I found that his lights stood high."

"As high, I am sure, as the environment in which he was born and raised made possible."

"You have a low opinion, then, of ante-bellum civilization in the South?"

"Who that knows his history could have otherwise?"

"You know history, I admit," said Queed, lightly falling upon the side issue, "surprisingly, indeed, considering that you have not read it for so many years."

"A man is not likely to forget truths burned into him when he is young."

"Everything depends," said Queed, returning to his muttons, "upon how you are going to appraise a civilization. If the only true measure is economic efficiency, no one can question that the old Southern system was one of the worst ever conceived."

"Can you, expert upon organized society as you are, admit any doubts upon that point?"

"I am admitting doubts upon a good many points these days."

Nicolovius resumed his cigarette. Talk languished. Both men enjoyed a good silence. Many a supper they ate through without a word. The old man's attitude toward the young one was charming. He had sloughed off some of the too polished blandness of his manner, and now offered a simpler meeting ground of naturalness and kindliness. They had shared the Duke of Gloucester Street roof-tree for a month, but Queed did not yet accept it as a matter of course. He was decidedly more prone to be analytical than he had been a year ago. Yet whatever could be urged against it, the little house was in one way making a subtle tug upon his regard: it was the nearest thing to a home that he had ever had in his life, or was ever likely to have.

"And when will the *Post* directors meet to choose his successor?"

"I haven't heard. Very soon, I should think."

"It is certain, I suppose," said Nicolovius, "that they will name you?"

"Oh, not at all—by no means! I am merely receptive, that is all."

Queed glanced at his watch and rose. "There is half an hour before supper, I see. I think I must turn it to account."

Nicolovius looked regretful. "Why not allow yourself this minute's rest, and me the pleasure of your society?"

Queed hesitated. "No—I think my duty is to my work."

He passed into the adjoining room, which was his bedroom, and shut the door. Here at his table, he passed all of the hours that he spent in the house, except after supper, when he did his work in the sitting-room with Nicolovius. He felt that, in honor, he owed some companionship, of the body at least, to the old man in exchange for the run of the house, and his evenings were his conscientious concession to his social duty. But sometimes he felt the surprising and wholly irrational impulse to concede more, to give the old man a larger measure of society than he was, so to say, paying for. He felt it now as he seated himself methodically and opened his table drawer.

From a purely selfish point of view, which was the only point of view from which such a compact need be considered, he could hardly think that his new domestic arrangement was a success. Greater comforts he had, of course, but it is not upon comforts that the world's work hangs. The important facts were that he was paying as much as he had paid at Mrs. Paynter's, and was enjoying rather less privacy. He and Nicolovius were friends of convenience only. Yet somehow the old professor managed to obtrude himself perpetually upon his consciousness. The young man began to feel an annoying sense of personal responsibility toward him, an impulse which his reason rejected utterly.

He was aware that, personally, he wished himself back at Mrs. Paynter's and the Scriptorium. A free man, in possession of this knowledge, would immediately pack up and return. But that was just the trouble. He who had always, hitherto, been the freest man in the world, appeared no longer to be free. He was aware that he would find it very difficult to walk into the sitting-room at this moment, and tell Nicolovius that he was going to leave. The old man would probably make a scene. The irritating thing about it was that Nicolovius, being as solitary in the great world as he himself, actually *minded* his isolation, and was apparently coming to depend upon *him*.

But after all, he was contented here, and his work was prospering largely. The days of his preparation for his *Post* labors were definitely over. He no longer had to read or study; he stood upon his feet, and carried his editorial qualifications under his hat. His duties as assistant editor occupied him but four or five hours a day; some three hours a day—the allotment was inexact, for the Schedule had lost its first rigid precision—to the Sciences of Physical Culture and Human Intercourse; all the rest to the Science of Sciences. Glorious mornings, and hardly less glorious nights, he gave, day after day, week after week, to the great book; and because of his astonishingly enhanced vitality, he made one hour tell now as an hour and a half had told in the period of the establishment of the Scriptorium.

And now, without warning and prematurely, the jade Fortune had pitched a bomb at this new Revised Schedule of his, leaving him to decide whether he would patch up the pieces or not. And he had decided that he would not patch them up. Colonel Cowles was dead. The directors of the *Post* might choose him to succeed the Colonel, or they might not. But if they did choose him, he had finally made up his mind that he would accept the election.

In his attitude toward the newspaper, Queed was something like those eminent fellow-scientists of his who have set out to "expose" spiritualism and "the occult," and have ended as the most gullible customers of the most dubious of "mediums." The idea of being editor for its own sake, which he had once jeered and flouted, he had gradually come to consider with large respect. The work drew him amazingly; it was applied science of a peculiarly fascinating sort. And in the six days of the Colonel's illness in May, when he had full charge of the editorial page—and again now—he had an exhilarating consciousness of personal power which lured him, oddly, more than any sensation he had ever had in his life.

No inducements of this sort, alone, could ever have drawn him from his love. However, his love was safe, in any case. If they made him editor, they would give him an assistant. He would keep his mornings for himself—four hours a day. In the long vigil last night, he had threshed the whole thing out. On a four-hour schedule he could finish his book in four years and a half more:—an unprecedentedly early age to have completed so monumental a work. And who could say that in thus making haste slowly, he would not have acquired a breadth of outlook, and closer knowledge of the practical conditions of life, which would be advantageously reflected in the Magnum Opus itself?

The young man sat at his table, the sheaf of yellow sheets which made up the chapter he was now working on ready under his hand. Around him were his reference books, his note-books, his pencils and erasers, all the neat paraphernalia of his trade. Everything was in order; yet he touched none of them. Presently his eyes fell upon his open watch, and his mind went off into new channels, or rather into old channels which he thought he had abandoned for this half-hour at any rate. In five minutes more, he put away his manuscript, picked up his watch, and strolled back into the sitting-room.

Nicolovius was sitting where he had left him, except that now he was not reading but merely staring out of the window. He glanced around with a look of pleased surprise and welcome.

"Ah-h! Did genius fail to burn?" he asked, employing a bromidic phrase which Queed particularly detested.

"That is one way of putting it, I suppose."

"Or did you take pity on my solitariness? You must not let me become a drag upon you."

Queed, dropping into a chair, rather out of humor, made no reply. Nicolovius continued to look out of the window.

"I see in the *Post*," he presently began again, "that Colonel Cowles, after getting quite well, broke himself down again in preparing for the so-called Reunion. It seems rather hard to have to give one's life for such a rabble of beggars."

"That is how you regard the veterans, is it?"

"Have you ever seen the outfit?"

"Never."

"I have lived here long enough to learn something of them. Look at them for yourself next week. Mix with them. Talk with them. You will find them worth a study—and worth nothing else under the sun."

"I have been looking forward to doing something of that sort," said Queed, introspectively.

Had not Miss Weyland, the last time he had seen her—namely, one evening about two months before,—expressly invited him to come and witness the Reunion parade from her piazza?

"You will see," said Nicolovius, in his purring voice, "a lot of shabby old men, outside and in, who never did an honest day's work in their lives."

He paused, finished his cigarette and suavely resumed:

"They went to war as young men, because it promised to be more exciting than pushing a plow over a worn-out hillside. Or because there was nothing else to do. Or because they were conscripted and kicked into it. They came out of the war the most invincible grafters in history. The shiftless boor of a stable-boy found himself transformed into a shining hero, and he meant to lie back and live on it for the rest of his days. Be assured that he understood very well the cash value of his old uniform. If he had a peg-leg or an empty sleeve, so much the more impudently could he pass around his property cap. For forty years, he and his mendicant band have been a cursed albatross hung around the necks of their honest fellows. Able-bodied men, they have lolled back and eaten up millions of dollars, belonging to a State which they pretend to love and which, as they well know, has needed every penny for the desperate struggle of existence. Since the political party which dominates this State is too cowardly to tell them to go to work or go to the devil, it will be a God's mercy when the last one of them is in his grave. You may take my word for that."

But Queed, being a scientist by passion, never took anybody's word for anything. He always went to the original sources of information, and found out for himself. It was a year now since he had begun saturating himself in the annals of the State and the South, and he had scoured the field so effectually that Colonel Cowles himself had been known to appeal to him on a point of history, though the Colonel had forty years' start on him, and had himself helped to make that history.

Therefore Queed knew that Nicolovius, by taking the case of one soldier in ten, perhaps, or twenty or fifty, and offering it as typical of the whole, was bitterly caricaturing history; and he wondered why in the world the old man cared to do it.

"My own reading of the recent history of the South," said Queed, "can hardly sustain such a view."

"You have only to read further to be convinced."

"But I thought you yourself never read recent history."

Nicolovius flung him a sharp look, which the young man, staring thoughtfully at the floor, missed. The old professor laughed.

"My dear boy! I read it on the lips of Major Brooke, I read it daily in the newspapers, I read it in such articles as your Colonel Cowles wrote about this very Reunion. I cannot get away from history in the making, if I would. Ah, there is the supper bell—I'm quite ready for it, too. Let us go down."

They went down arm in arm. On the stairs Nicolovius said: "These Southern manifestations interest me because, though extreme, they are after all so absurdly typical of human nature. I have even seen the same sort of thing in my own land."

Queed, though he knew the history of Ireland very well, could not recall any parallel to the United Confederate Veterans in the annals of that country. Still, a man capable of distorting history as Nicolovius distorted it could always find a parallel to anything anywhere.

When the meal was about half over, Queed said:—

"You slept badly last night, didn't you?"

"Yes—my old enemy. The attack soon passed. However, you may be sure that it is a comfort at such times to know that I am not alone."

"If you should need any—ahem—assistance, I assume that you will call me," said Queed, after a pause.

"Thank you. You can hardly realize what your presence here, your companionship and, I hope I may say, your friendship, mean to me."

Queed glanced at him over the table, and hastily turned his glance away. He had surprised Nicolovius looking at him with a curiously tender look in his black diamond eyes.

The young man went to the office that night, worried by two highly irritating ideas. One was that Nicolovius was most unjustifiably permitting himself to become dependent upon him. The other was that it was very peculiar that a Fenian refugee should care to express slanderous views of the soldiers of a Lost Cause. Both thoughts, once introduced into the young man's mind, obstinately stuck there.

CHAPTER XX

Meeting of the Post Directors to elect a Successor to Colonel Cowles; Charles Gardiner West's Sensible Remarks on Mr. Queed; Mr. West's Resignation from Old Blaines College, and New Consecration to the Uplift.

The *Post* directors gathered in special meeting on Monday. Their first act was to adopt some beautiful resolutions, prepared by Charles Gardiner West, in memory of the editor who had served the paper so long and so well. Next they changed the organization of the staff, splitting the late Colonel's heavy duties in two, by creating the separate position of managing editor; this official to have complete authority over the news department of the paper, as the editor had over its editorial page. The directors named Evan Montague, the able city editor of the Post, to fill the new position, while promoting the strongest of the reporters to fill the city desk.

The chairman, Stewart Byrd, then announced that he was ready to receive nominations for, or hear discussion about, the editorship.

One of the directors, Mr. Hopkins, observed that, as he viewed it, the directors should not feel restricted to local timber in the choice of a successor to the Colonel. He said that the growing importance of the *Post* entitled it to an editor of the first ability, and that the directors should find such a one, whether in New York, or Boston, or San Francisco.

Another director, Mr. Boggs, remarked that it did not necessarily follow that a thoroughly suitable man must be a New York, Boston, or San Francisco man. Unless he was greatly deceived, there was an eminently suitable man, not merely in the city, but in the office of the *Post*, where, since Colonel Cowles's death, he was doing fourteen hours of excellent work per day for the sum of fifteen hundred dollars per annum.

"Mr. Boggs's point," said Mr. Hickok, a third director, who looked something like James E. Winter, "is exceedingly well taken. A United States Senator from a Northern State is a guest in my house for Reunion week. The Senator reads the editorials in the *Post* with marked attention, has asked me the name of the writer, and has commended some of his utterances most highly. The Senator tells me that he never reads the editorials in his own paper—a Boston paper, Mr. Hopkins, by the bye—his reason being that they are never worth reading."

Mr. Shorter and Mr. Porter, fourth and fifth directors, were much struck with Mr. Hickok's statement. They averred that they had made a point of reading the *Post* editorials during the Colonel's absence, with a view to sizing up the assistant, and had been highly pleased with the character of his work.

Mr. Wilmerding, a sixth director, declared that the Colonel had, in recent months, more than once remarked to him that the young man was entirely qualified to be his successor. In fact, the Colonel had once said that he meant to retire before a great while, and, of course with the directors' approval, turn over the editorial helm to the assistant. Therefore, he, Mr. Wilmerding, had pleasure in nominating Mr. Queed for the position of editor of the *Post*.

Mr. Shorter and Mr. Porter said that they had pleasure in seconding this nomination.

Mr. Charles Gardiner West, a seventh director, was recognized for a few remarks. Mr. West expressed his intense gratification over what had been said in eulogy of Mr. Queed. This gratification, some might argue, was not wholly disinterested, since it was Mr. West who had discovered Mr. Queed and sent him to the *Post*. To praise the able editor was therefore to praise the alert, watchful, and discriminating director. (Smiles.) Seriously, Mr. Queed's work, especially during the last few months, had been of the highest order, and Mr. West, having worked beside him more than once, ventured to say that he appreciated his valuable qualities better than any other director. If the Colonel had but lived a year or two longer, there could not, in his opinion, be the smallest question as to what step the honorable directors should now take. But as it was, Mr. West, as Mr. Queed's original sponsor on the *Post*, felt it his duty to call attention to two things. The first was the young man's extreme youth. The second was the fact that he was a stranger to the State, having lived there less than two years. At his present rate of progress, it was of course patent to any observer that he was a potential editor of the *Post*, and a great one. But might it not be, on the whole, desirable—Mr. West merely suggested the idea in the most tentative way, and wholly out of his sense of sponsorship for Mr. Queed—to give him a little longer chance to grow and broaden and learn, before throwing the highest responsibility and the final honors upon him?

Mr. West's graceful and sensible remarks made a distinct impression upon the directors, and Mr. Hopkins took occasion to say that it was precisely such thoughts as these that had led him to suggest looking abroad for a man. Mr. Shorter and Mr. Porter asserted that they would deprecate doing anything that Mr. West, with his closer knowledge of actual conditions, thought premature. Mr. Boggs admitted that the ability to write editorials of the first order was not all that should be required of the editor of the *Post*. It might be doubtful, thought he, whether so young a man could represent the *Post* properly on occasions of a semi-public nature, or in emergency situations such as occasionally arose in an editorial office.

Mr. Wilmerding inquired the young man's age, and upon being told that he was under twenty-six, remarked that only very exceptional abilities could counteract such youth as that.

"That," said Mr. Hickok, glancing cursorily at Charles Gardiner West, "is exactly the sort of abilities Mr. Queed possesses."

Discussion flagged. The chairman asked if they were ready for a vote upon Mr. Queed.

"No, no—let's take our time," said Mr. Wilmerding.

"Perhaps somebody has other nominations to offer."

No one seemed to have other nominations to offer. Some minutes were consumed by random suggestions and unprogressive recommendations. Busy directors began to look at their watches.

"Look here, Gard—I mean Mr. West," suddenly said young Theodore Fyne, the baby of the board. "Why couldn't we persuade *you* to take the editorship?... Resign from the college, you know?"

"Now you *have* said something!" cried Mr. Hopkins, enthusiastically.

Mr. West, by a word and a gesture, indicated that the suggestion was preposterous and the conversation highly unwelcome.

But it was obvious that young Mr. Fyne's suggestion had caught the directors at sight. Mr. Shorter and Mr. Porter affirmed that they had not ventured to hope, etc., etc., but that if Mr. West could be induced to consider the position, no choice would appear to them so eminently—etc., etc. So said Mr. Boggs. So said Messrs. Hopkins, Fyne, and Wilmerding.

Mr. Hickok, the director who resembled James E. Winter, looked out of the window.

Mr. West, obviously restive under these tributes, was constrained to state his position more fully. For more than one reason which should be evident, he said, the mention of his name in this connection was most embarrassing and distasteful to him. While thanking the directors heartily for their evidences of good-will, he therefore begged them to desist, and proceed with the discussion of other candidates.

"In that case," said Mr. Hickok, "it appears to be the reluctant duty of the nominator to withdraw Mr. West's name."

But the brilliant young man's name, once thrown into the arena, could no more be withdrawn than the fisherman of legend could restore the genie to the bottle, or Pandora get her pretty gifts back into the box again. There was the idea, fairly out and vastly alluring. The kindly directors pressed it home. No doubt they, as well as Plonny Neal, appreciated that Blaines College did not give the young man a fair field for his talents; and certainly they knew with admiration the articles with which he sometimes adorned the columns of their paper. Of all the directors, they now pointed out, he had stood closest to Colonel Cowles, and was most familiar with the traditions and policies of the *Post*. Their urgings increased in force and persistence; perhaps they felt encouraged by a certain want of finality in the young man's tone; and at length West was compelled to make yet another statement.

He was, he explained, utterly disconcerted at the turn the discussion had taken, and found the situation so embarrassing that he must ask his friends, the directors, to extricate him from it at once. The editorship of the *Post* was an office which he, personally, had never aspired to, but it would be presumption for him to deny that he regarded it as a post which would reflect honor upon any one. He was willing to admit, in this confidential circle, moreover, that he had taken up college work chiefly with the ambition of assisting Blaines over a critical year or two in its history, and that, to put it only generally, he was not indefinitely bound to his present position. But under the present circumstances, as he said, he could not consent to any discussion of his name; and unless the directors would agree to drop him from further consideration, which he earnestly preferred, he must reluctantly suggest adjournment.

"An interregnum," said Mr. Hickok, looking out of the window, "is an unsatisfactory, not to say a dangerous thing. Would it not be better, since we are gathered for that purpose, to take decisive action to-day?"

"What is your pleasure, gentlemen?" inquired Chairman Byrd.

Mr. Hickok was easily overruled. The directors seized eagerly on Mr. West's suggestion. On motion of Mr. Hopkins, seconded by Mr. Shorter and Mr. Porter, the meeting stood adjourned to the third day following at noon.

On the second day following the *Post* carried the interesting announcement that Mr. West had resigned from the presidency of Blaines College, a bit of news which his friends read with sincere pleasure. The account of the occurrence gave one to understand that all Mr. West's well-known persuasiveness had been needed to force the trustees to accept his resignation. And when James E. Winter read this part of it, at his suburban breakfast, he first laughed, and then swore. The same issue of the *Post* carried an editorial, mentioning in rather a sketchy way the benefits Mr. West had conferred upon Blaines College, and paying a high and confident tribute to his qualities as a citizen. The young acting-editor, who never wrote what he did not think, had taken much pains with this editorial, especially the sketchy part. Of course the pestiferous *Chronicle* took an entirely different view of the situation. "The *Chronicle* has won its great fight," so it nervily said, "against classism in Blaines College." And it had the vicious taste to add: "Nothing in Mr. West's presidential life became him like the leaving of it."

On the third day the directors met again. With characteristic delicacy of feeling, West remained away from the meeting. However, Mr. Hopkins, who seemed to know what he was talking about, at once expressed his conviction that they might safely proceed to the business which had brought them together.

"Perceiving clearly that I represent a minority view," said Mr. Hickok, "I request the director who nominated Mr. Queed to withdraw his name. I think it proper that our action should be unanimous. But I will say, frankly, that if Mr. Queed's name remains before the board, I shall vote for him, since I consider him from every point of view the man for the position."

Mr. Queed's name having been duly withdrawn, the directors unanimously elected Charles Gardiner West to the editorship of the *Post*. By a special resolution introduced by Mr. Hopkins, they thanked Mr. Queed for his able conduct of the editorial page in the absence of the editor, and voted him an increased honorarium of eighteen hundred dollars a year.

The directors adjourned, and Mr. Hickok stalked out, looking more like James E. Winter than ever. The other directors, however, looked highly gratified at themselves. They went out heartily congratulating each other. By clever work they had secured for their paper the services of one of the ablest, most gifted, most polished and popular young men in the State. Nevertheless, though they never knew it, their action was decidedly displeasing to at least one faithful reader of the *Post*, to wit, Miss Charlotte

Lee Weyland, of the Department of Charities. Sharlee felt strongly that Mr. Queed should have had the editorship, then and there. It might be said that she had trained him up for exactly that position. Of course, Mr. West, her very good friend, would make an editor of the first order. But, with all the flocks that roamed upon his horizon, ought he to have reached out and plucked the one ewe lamb of the poor assistant? Besides, she thought that Mr. West ought to have remained at Blaines College.

But how could she maintain this attitude of criticism when the new editor himself, bursting in upon her little parlor in a golden nimbus of optimism, radiant good humor and success, showed up the shallowness and the injustice of it?

"To have that college off my neck—Whew! I'm as happy, my friend, as a schoolboy on the first day of vacation. I haven't talked much about it to you," continued Mr. West, "for it's a bore to listen to other people's troubles—but that college had become a perfect old man of the sea! The relief is glorious! I'm bursting with energy and enthusiasm and big plans for the *Post*."

"And Mr. Queed?" said Sharlee. "Was he much disappointed?"

West was a little surprised at the question, but he gathered from her tone that she thought Mr. Queed had some right to be.

"Why, I think not," he answered, decisively. "Why in the world should he be? Of course it means only a delay of a year or two for him, at the most. I betray no confidence when I tell you that I do not expect to remain editor of the *Post* forever."

Sharlee appeared struck by this summary of the situation, which, to tell the truth, had never occurred to her. Therefore, West went on to sketch it more in detail to her.

"The last thing in the world that I would do," said he, "is to stand in that boy's light. My one wish is to push him to the front just as fast as he can stride. Why, I discovered Queed—you and I did, that is—and I think I may claim to have done something toward training him. To speak quite frankly, the situation was this: In spite of his great abilities, he is still very young and inexperienced. Give him a couple of years in which to grow and broaden and get his bearings more fully, and he will be the very best man in sight for the place. On the other hand, if he were thrust prematurely into great responsibility, he would be almost certain to make some serious error, some fatal break, which would impair his usefulness, and perhaps ruin it forever. Do you see my point? As his sponsor on the *Post*, it seemed to me unwise and unfair to expose him to the risks of forcing his pace. That's the whole story. I'm not the king at all. I'm only the regent during the king's minority."

Sharlee now saw how unjust she had been, to listen to the small whisper of doubt of West's entire magnanimity.

"You are much wiser and farther-sighted than I."

"Perish the thought!"

"I'm glad my little Doctor—only he isn't either little or very much of a doctor any more—has such a good friend at court."

"Nonsense. It was only what anybody who stopped to think a moment would have done."

"Not everybody who stops to think is so generous...."

This thought, too, Mr. West abolished by a word.

"But you will like the work, won't you!" continued Sharlee, still self-reproachful. "I do hope you will."

"I shall like it immensely," said West, above pretending, as some regents would have done, that he was martyring himself for his friend, the king. "Where can you find any bigger or nobler work? At Blaines College of blessed memory, the best I could hope for was to reach and influence a handful of lumpish boys. How tremendously broader is the opportunity on the *Post!* Think of having a following of a hundred thousand readers a day! (You allow three or four readers to a copy, you know.) Think of talking every morning to such an audience as that, preaching progress and high ideals, courage and honesty and kindness and faith—moulding their opinions and beliefs, their ambitions, their very habits of thought, as I think they ought to be moulded ..."

He talked in about this vein till eleven o'clock, and Sharlee listened with sincere admiration. Nevertheless, he left her still troubled by a faint doubt as to how Mr. Queed himself felt about what had been done for his larger good. But when she next saw Queed, only a few days later, this doubt instantly dissolved and vanished. She had never seen him less inclined to indict the world and his fortune.

CHAPTER XXI

*Queed sits on the Steps with Sharlee, and sees Some Old Soldiers
go marching by.*

Far as the eye could see, either way, the street was two parallels of
packed humanity. Both sidewalks, up and down, were loaded to capacity
and spilling off surplus down the side-streets. Navigation was next to
impossible; as for crossing you were a madman to think of such a thing.
At the sidewalks' edge policemen patrolled up and down in the street with
their incessant cry of "Back there!" —pausing now and then to dislodge small
boys from trees, whither they had climbed at enormous peril to themselves
and innocent by-standers. Bunting, flags, streamers were everywhere; now
and then a floral arch bearing words of welcome spanned the roadway;
circus day in a small town was not a dot upon the atmosphere of thrilled
expectancy so all-pervasive here. It was, in fact, the crowning occasion of
the Confederate Reunion, and the fading remnants of Lee's armies were
about to pass in annual parade and review.

Mrs. Weyland's house stood full on the line of march. It was the house
she had come to as a bride; she owned it; and because it could not easily
be converted over her head into negotiable funds, it had escaped the
predacious clutches of Henry G. Surface. After the crash, it would doubtless
have been sensible to sell it and take something cheaper; but sentiment made
her cling to this house, and her daughter, in time, went to work to uphold
sentiment's hands. It was not a large house, or a fine one, but it did have a
very comfortable little porch. To-day this porch was beautifully decorated,
like the whole town, with the colors of two countries, one living and one
dead; and the decorations for the dead were three times greater than the
decorations for the living. And why not? Yet, at that, Sharlee was liberal-
minded and a thorough-going nationalist. On some houses, the decorations
for the dead were five times greater, like Benjamin's mess; on others, ten
times; on yet others, no colors at all floated but the beloved Stars and Bars.

Upon the steps of Mrs. Weyland's porch sat Mr. Queed, come by special
invitation of Mrs. Weyland's daughter to witness the parade.

The porch, being so convenient for seeing things, was hospitably taxed to its limits. New people kept turning in at the gate, mostly ladies, mostly white-haired ladies wearing black, and Sharlee was incessantly springing up to greet them. However, Queed, feeling that the proceedings might be instructive to him, had had the foresight to come early, before the sidewalks solidified with spectators; and at first, and spasmodically thereafter, he had some talk with Sharlee.

"So you didn't forget?" she said, in greeting him.

He eyed her reflectively. "When I was seven years old," he began, "Tim once asked me to attend to something for him while he went out for a minute. It was to mind some bacon that he had put on to broil for supper. I became absorbed in a book I was reading, and Tim came back to find the bacon a crisp. I believe I have never forgotten anything from that day to this. You have a holiday at the Department?"

"Why, do you suppose we'd work to-day!" said Sharlee, and introduced him to her mother, who, having attentively overheard his story of Tim and the bacon, proceeded to look him over with some care.

Sharlee left them for a moment, and came back bearing a flag about the size of a man's visiting card.

"You are one of us, aren't you? I have brought you," she said, "your colors."

Queed looked and recognized the flag that was everywhere in predominance that day. "And what will it mean if I wear it?"

"Only," said Sharlee, "that you love the South."

Vaguely Queed saw in her blue-spar eyes the same kind of softness that he noticed in people's voices this afternoon, a softness which somehow reminded him of a funeral, Fifi's or Colonel Cowles's.

"Oh, very well, if you like."

Sharlee put the flag in his buttonhole under her mother's watchful gaze. Then she got cushions and straw-mats, and explained their uses in connection with steps. Next, she gave a practical demonstration of the same by seating the young man, and sitting down beside him.

"One thing I have noticed about loving the South. Everybody does it, who takes the trouble to know us. Look at the people!—millions and millions...."

"Colonel Cowles would have liked this."

"Yes—dear old man." Sharlee paused a moment, and then went on. "He was in the parade last year—on the beautifullest black horse—You never saw anything so handsome as he looked that day. It was in Savannah, and I went. I was a maid of honor, but my real duties were to keep him from marching around in the hot sun all day. And now this year ... You see, that is what makes it so sad. When these old men go tramping by, everybody is thinking: 'Hundreds of them won't be here next year, and hundreds more the next year, and soon will come a year when there won't be any parade at all.'"

She sprang up to welcome a new arrival, whom she greeted as either Aunt Mary or Cousin Maria, we really cannot undertake to say which.

Queed glanced over the group on the porch, to most of whom he had been introduced, superfluously, as it seemed to him. There must have been twenty or twenty-five of them; some seated, some standing at the rail, some sitting near him on the steps; but all, regardless of age and sex, wearing the Confederate colors. He noticed particularly the white-haired old ladies, and somehow their faces, also, put him in mind of Fifi's or Colonel Cowles's funeral.

Sharlee came and sat down by him again. "Mr. Queed," said she, "I don't know whether you expect sympathy about what the *Post* directors did, or congratulations."

"Oh, congratulations," he answered at once. "Considering that they wanted to discharge me a year ago, I should say that the testimonial they gave me represented a rather large change of front."

"Personally, I think it is splendid. But the important thing is: does it satisfy *you?*"

"Oh, quite." He added: "If they had gone outside for a man, I might have felt slighted. It is very different with a man like West. I am perfectly willing to wait. You may remember that I did not promise to be editor in any particular year."

"I know. And when they do elect you—you see I say when, and not if—shall you pitch it in their faces, as you said?"

"No—I have decided to keep it—for a time at any rate."

Sharlee smiled, but it was an inward smile and he never knew anything about it. "Have you gotten really interested in the work—personally interested, I mean?"

He hesitated. "I hardly like to say how much."

"The more you become interested in it—and I believe it will be progressive—the less you will mind saying so."

"It is a strange interest—utterly unlike me—"

"How do you know it isn't more like you than anything you ever did in your life?"

That struck him to silence; he gave her a quick inquiring glance, and looked away at once; and Sharlee, for the moment entirely oblivious of the noise and the throng all about her, went on.

"I called that a magnificent boast once—about your being editor of the *Post*. Do you remember? Isn't it time I was confessing that you have got the better of me?"

"I think it is too soon," he answered, in his quietest voice, "to say whether I have got the better of you, or you have got the better of me."

Sharlee looked off down the street. "But you certainly will be editor of the *Post* some day."

"As I recall it, we did not speak only of editorial writing that night."

"Oh, listen ...!"

From far away floated the strains of "Dixie," crashed out by forty bands. The crowd on the sidewalks stirred; prolonged shouts went up; and now all those who were seated on the porch arose at one motion and came forward.

Sharlee had to spring up to greet still another relative. She came back in a moment, sincerely hoping that Mr. Queed would resume the conversation which her exclamation had interrupted. But he spoke of quite a different matter, a faint cloud on his intelligent brow.

"You should hear Professor Nicolovius on these veterans of yours."

"What does he say about them? Something hateful, I'm sure."

"Among other things, that they are a lot of professional beggars who have lived for forty years on their gray uniforms, and can best serve their country by dying with all possible speed. Do you know," he mused, "if you could hear him, I believe you would be tempted to guess that he is a former Union officer—who got into trouble, perhaps, and was cashiered."

"But of course you know all about him?"

"No," said he, honest, but looking rather annoyed at having given her such an opening, "I know only what he told me."

"Sharlee," came her mother's voice from the rear, "are you sitting on the cold stone?"

"No, mother. Two mats and a cushion."

"Well, he is not a Union officer," said Sharlee to Queed, "for if he were, he would not be bitter. All the bitterness nowadays comes from the non-combatants, the camp-followers, the sutlers, and the cowards. Look, Mr. Queed! *Look!*"

The street had become a tumult, the shouting grew into a roar. Two squares away the head of the parade swept into view, and drew steadily nearer. Mr. Queed looked, and felt a thrill in despite of himself.

At the head of the column came the escort, with the three regimental bands, mounted and bicycle police, city officials, visiting military, sons of veterans, and the militia, including the resplendent Light Infantry Blues of Richmond, a crack drill regiment with an honorable history dating from 1789, and the handsomest uniforms ever seen. Behind the escort rode the honored commander-in-chief of the veterans, and staff, the grand marshal and staff, and a detachment of mounted veterans. The general commanding rode a dashing white horse, which he sat superbly despite his years, and received an ovation all along the line. An even greater ovation went to two festooned carriages which rolled behind the general staff: they contained four black-clad women, no longer young, who bore names that had been dear to the hearts of the Confederacy. After these came the veterans afoot, stepping like youngsters, for that was their pride, in faded equipments which contrasted sharply with the shining trappings of the militia. They marched by state divisions, each division marshaled into brigades, each brigade subdivided again into camps. At the head of each division rode the major-general and staff, and behind each staff came a carriage containing the state's sponsor and maids of honor. And everywhere there were bands, bands playing "Dixie," and the effect would have been even more glorious, if only any two of them had played the same part of it at the same time.

Everybody was standing. It is doubtful if in all the city there was anybody sitting now, save those restrained by physical disabilities. Conversation on the Weyland piazza became exceedingly disjointed. Everybody was excitedly calling everybody else's attention to things that seemed particularly important in the passing spectacle. To Queed the amount these people appeared to know about it all was amazing. All during the afternoon he heard Sharlee identifying fragments of regiments with a sureness of knowledge that he, an authority on knowledge, marveled at.

The escort passed, and the officers and staffs drew on. The fine-figured old commander-in-chief, when he came abreast, turned and looked full at the Weyland piazza, seemed to search it for a face, and swept his plumed hat to his stirrup in a profound bow. The salute was greeted on the porch with a burst of hand-clapping and a great waving of flags.

"That was for my grandmother. He was in love with her in 1850," said Sharlee to Queed, and immediately whisked away to tell something else to somebody else.

One of the first groups of veterans in the line, heading the Virginia Division, was the popular R.E. Lee Camp of Richmond. All afternoon they trod to the continual accompaniment of cheers. No exclusive "show" company ever marched in better time than these septuagenarians, and this was everywhere the subject of comment. A Grand Army man stood in the press on the sidewalk, and, struck by the gallant step of the old fellows, yelled out good-naturedly:—

"You boys been drillin' to learn to march like that, haven't you?"

Instantly a white-beard in the ranks called back: "No, sir! *We never have forgot!*"

Other camps were not so rhythmic in their tread. Some of the lines were very dragging and straggly; the old feet shuffled and faltered in a way which showed that their march was nearly over. Not fifty yards away from Queed, one veteran pitched out of the ranks; he was lifted up and received into the house opposite which he fell. Sadder than the men were the old battle-flags, soiled wisps that the aged hands held aloft with the most solicitous care. The flag-poles were heavy and the men's arms weaker than once they were; sometimes two or even three men acted jointly as standard-bearer.

These old flags, mere unrecognizable fragments as many of them were, were popular with the onlookers. Each as it marched by, was hailed with a new roar. Of course there were many tears. There was hardly anybody in all that crowd, over fifty years old, in whom the sight of these fast dwindling ranks did not stir memories of some personal bereavement. The old ladies on the porch no longer used their handkerchiefs chiefly for waving. Queed saw one of them wave hers frantically toward a drooping little knot of passing gray-coats, and then fall back into a chair, the same handkerchief at her eyes. Sharlee, who was explaining everything that anybody wanted to know, happened to be standing near him; she followed his glance and whispered gently:—

"Her husband and two of her brothers were killed at Gettysburg. Her husband was in Pickett's Division. Those were Pickett's men that just passed—about all there are left now."

A little while afterwards, she added: "It is not so gay as one of your Grand Army Days, is it? You see ... it all comes home very close to us. Those old men that can't be with us much longer are our mothers' brothers, and sweethearts, and uncles, and fathers. They went out so young—so brave and full of hope—they poured out by hundreds of thousands. Down this very street they marched, no more than boys, and our mothers stood here where we are standing, to bid them godspeed. And now look at what is left of them, straggling by. There is nobody on this porch—but you—who did not lose somebody that was dear to them. And then there was our pride ... for we were proud. So that is why our old ladies cry to-day."

"And why your young ladies cry, too?"

"Oh, ... I am not crying."

"Don't you suppose I know when people are crying and when they aren't?—Why do you do it?"

Sharlee lowered her eyes. "Well ... it's all pretty sad, you know ... pretty sad."

She turned away, leaving him to his own devices. From his place on the top step, Queed turned and let his frank glance run over the ladies on the porch. The sadness of face that he had noticed earlier had dissolved and precipitated now: there was hardly a dry eye on that porch but his own. What were they all crying for? Miss Weyland's explanation did not seem very convincing. The war had ended a generation ago. The whole thing had been over and done with many years before she was born.

He turned again, and looked out with unseeing eyes over the thick street, with the thin strip of parade moving down the middle of it. He guessed that these ladies on the porch were not crying for definite brothers, or fathers, or sweethearts they had lost. People didn't do that after forty years; here was Fifi only dead a year, and he never saw anybody crying for her. No, they were weeping over an idea; it was sentiment, and a vague, misty, unreasonable sentiment at that. And yet he could not say that Miss Weyland appeared simply foolish with those tears in her eyes. No, the girl somehow managed to give the effect of seeing farther into things than he himself.... Her tears evidently were in the nature of a tribute: she was paying them to an idea. Doubtless there was a certain largeness about that. But obviously the paying of such a tribute could do no possible good—unless—to the payer. Was there anything in that?—in the theory....

Unusual bursts of cheering broke their way into his consciousness, and he recalled himself to see a squad of negro soldiers, all very old men, hobbling by. These were of the faithful, whom no number of proclamations could shake from allegiance to Old Marster. One of them declared himself to be Stonewall Jackson's cook. Very likely Stonewall Jackson's cooks are as numerous as once were ladies who had been kissed by LaFayette, but at any rate this old negro was the object of lively interest all along the line. He was covered with reunion badges, and carried two live chickens under his arm.

Queed went down to the bottom step, the better to hear the comments of the onlookers, for this was what interested him most. He found himself standing next to an exceptionally clean-cut young fellow of about his own age. This youth appeared a fine specimen of the sane, wholesome, successful young American business man. Yet he was behaving like a madman, yelling like Bedlam, wildly flaunting his hat—a splendid-looking Panama—now and then savagely brandishing his fists at an unseen foe. Queed heard him saying fiercely, apparently to the world at large: "They couldn't lick us now. By the Lord, they couldn't lick us now!"

Queed said to him: "You were badly outnumbered when they licked you."

Flaunting his hat passionately at the thin columns, the young man shouted into space: "Outnumbered—outarmed—outequipped—outrationed—but not outgeneraled, sir, not outsoldiered, not outmanned!"

"You seem a little excited about it. Yet you've had forty years to get used to it."

"Ah," brandished the young man at the soldiers, a glad battlenote breaking into his voice, "I'm being addressed by a Yankee, am I?"

"No," said Queed, "you are being addressed by an American."

"That's a fair reply," said the young man; and consented to take his eyes from the parade a second to glance at the author of it. "Hello! You're Doc—Mr. Queed, aren't you?"

Queed, surprised, admitted his identity.

"Ye-a-a-a!" said the young man, in a mighty voice. This time he shouted it directly at a tall old gentleman whose horse was just then dancing by. The gentleman smiled, and waved his hand at the flaunted Panama.

"A fine-looking man," said Queed.

"My father," said the young man. "God bless his heart!"

"Was your father in the war?"

"Was he in the war? My dear sir, you might say that he was the war. But you could scrape this town with a fine-tooth comb without finding anybody of his age that wasn't in the war."

The necessity for a new demonstration checked his speech for a moment.

Queed said: "Who are these veterans? What sort of people are they?"

"The finest fellows in the world," said the young man. "An occasional dead-beat among them, of course, but it's amazing how high an average of character they strike, considering that they came out of four years of war—war's demoralizing, you know!—with only their shirts to their backs, and often those were only borrowed. You'll find some mighty solid business men in the ranks out there, and then on down to the humblest occupations. Look! See that little one-legged man with the beard that everybody's cheering! That's Corporal Henkel of Petersburg, commended I don't know how many times for bravery, and they would have given him the town for a keepsake when it was all over, if he had wanted it. Well, Henkel's a cobbler—been one since '65—and let me tell you he's a blamed good one, and if you're ever in Petersburg and want any half-soling done, let me tell you—Yea-a-a! See that trim-looking one with the little mustache—saluting now? He tried to save Stonewall Jackson's life on the 2d of May, 1863,—threw himself in front of him and got badly potted. He's a D.D. now. Yea-a-a-a!"

A victoria containing two lovely young girls, sponsor and maid of honor for South Carolina, dressed just alike, with parasols and enormous hats, rolled by. The girls smiled kindly at the young man, and he went through a very proper salute.

"Watch the people!" he dashed on eagerly. "Wonderful how they love these old soldiers, isn't it?—they'd give 'em anything! And what a fine thing that is for them!—for the people, not the soldiers, I mean. I tell you we all give too much time to practical things—business—making money—taking things away from each other. It's a fine thing to have a day now and then which appeals to just the other side of us—a regular sentimental spree. Do you see what I mean? Maybe I'm talking like an ass.... But when you talk about Americans, Mr. Queed—let me tell you that there isn't a State in the country that is raising better Americans than we are raising right here in this city. We're as solid for the Union as Boston. But that isn't saying that we have forgotten all about the biggest happening in our history—the thing that threw over our civilization, wiped out our property, and turned our State into a graveyard. If we forgot that, we wouldn't be Americans, because we wouldn't be men."

He went on fragmentarily, ever and anon interrupting himself to give individual ovations to his heroes and his gods:—

"Through the North and West you may have one old soldier to a village; here we have one to a house. For you it was a foreign war, which meant only dispatches in the newspapers. For us it was a war on our own front lawns, and the way we followed it was by the hearses backing up to the door. You can hardly walk a mile in any direction out of this city without stumbling upon an old breastworks. And in the city—well, you know all the great old landmarks, all around us as we stand here now. On this porch behind us sits a lady who knew Lee well. Many's the talk she had with him after the war. My mother, a bride then, sat in the pew behind Davis that Sunday he got the message which meant that the war was over. History! Why this old town drips with it. Do you think we should forget our heroes, Mr. Queed? Up there in Massachusetts, if you have a place where John Samuel Quincy Adams once stopped for a cup of tea, you fence it off, put a brass plate on the front door, and charge a nickel to go in. Which will history say is the greater man, Sam Adams or Robert F. Lee? If these were Washington's armies going by, you would probably feel a little excited, though you have had a hundred and twenty years to get used to Yorktown and the Philadelphia Congress. Well, Washington is no more to the nation than Lee is to the South.

"But don't let anybody get concerned about our patriotism. We're better Americans, not worse, because of days like these, the reason being, as I say, that we are better men. And if your old Uncle Sammy gets into trouble some day, never fear but we'll be on hand to pull him out, with the best troops that ever stepped, and another Lee to lead them."

Somewhere during the afternoon there had returned to Queed the words in which Sharlee Weyland had pointed out to him—quite unnecessarily— that he was standing here between two civilizations. On the porch now sat Miss Weyland's grandmother, representative of the dead aristocracy. By his side stood, clearly, a representative of the rising democracy—one of those "splendid young men" who, the girl thought, would soon be beating the young men of the North at every turn. It was valuable professionally to catch the point of view of these new democrats; and now he had grasped the fact that whatever the changes in outward form, it had an unbroken sentimental continuity with the type which it was replacing.

"Did you ever hear Ben Hill's tribute to Lee?" inquired the young man presently.

Queed happened to know it very well. However, the other could not be restrained from reciting it for his own satisfaction.

"It is good—a good piece of writing and a fine tribute," said Queed. "However, I read a shorter and in some ways an even better one in *Harper's Weekly* the other day."

"*Harper's Weekly!* Good Heavens! They'll find out that William Lloyd Garrison was for us next. What'd it say?"

"It was in answer to some correspondents who called Lee a traitor. The editor wrote five lines to say that, while it would be exceedingly difficult ever to make 'traitor' a word of honorable distinction, it would be done if people kept on applying it to Lee. In that case, he said, we should have to find a new word to mean what traitor means now."

The young man thought this over until its full meaning sank into him. "I don't know how you could say anything finer of a man," he remarked presently, "than that applying a disgraceful epithet to him left him entirely untouched, but changed the whole meaning of the epithet. By George, that's pretty fine!"

"My only criticism on the character, or rather on the greatness, of Lee," said Queed, introspectively, "is that, so far as I have ever read, he never got angry. One feels that a hero should be a man of terrible passions, so strong that once or twice in his life they get away from him. Washington always seems a bigger man because of his blast at Charles Lee."

The young man seemed interested by this point of view. He said that he would ask Mrs. Beauregard about it.

Not much later he said with a sigh: "Well!—It's about over. And now I must pay for my fun—duck back to the office for a special night session."

Queed had taken a vague fancy to this youth, whose enviably pleasant manners reminded him somehow of Charles Gardiner West. "I supposed that it was only in newspaper offices that work went on without regard to holidays."

The young man laughed, and held out his hand. "I'm very industrious, if you please. I'm delighted to have met you, Mr. Queed—I've known of you for a long time. My name's Byrd—Beverley Byrd—and I wish you'd come and see me some time. Good-by. I hope I haven't bored you with all my war-talk. I lost a grandfather and three uncles in it, and I can't help being interested."

The last of the parade went by; the dense crowd broke and overran the street; and Queed stood upon the bottom step taking his leave of Miss Weyland. Much interested, he had lingered till the other guests were gone; and now there was nobody upon the porch but Miss Weyland's mother and grandmother, who sat at the further end of it, the eyes of both, did Mr. Queed but know it, upon him.

"Why don't you come to see me sometimes?" the daughter and granddaughter was saying sweetly. "I think you will have to come now, for this was a party, and a party calls for a party-call. Oh, can you make as clever a pun as that?"

"Thank you—but I never pay calls."

"Oh, but you are beginning to do a good many things that you never did before."

"Yes," he answered with curious depression. "I am."

"Well, don't look so glum about it. You mustn't think that any change in your ways of doing is necessarily for the worse!"

He refused to take up the cudgels; an uncanny thing from him. "Well! I am obliged to you for inviting me here to-day. It has been interesting and—instructive."

"And now you have got us all neatly docketed on your sociological operating table, I suppose?"

"I am inclined to think," he said slowly, "that it is you who have got me on the operating table again."

He gave her a quick glance, at once the unhappiest and the most human look that she had ever seen upon his face.

"No," said she, gently,—"if you are on the table, you have put yourself there this time."

"Well, good-by—"

"And are you coming to see me—to pay your party-call?"

"Why should I? What is the point of these conventions—these little rules—?"

"Don't you *like* being with me? Don't you get a *great deal* of pleasure from my society?"

"I have never asked myself such a question."

He was gazing at her for a third time; and a startled look sprang suddenly into his eyes. It was plain that he was asking himself such a question now. A curious change passed over his face; a kind of dawning consciousness which, it was obvious, embarrassed him to the point of torture, while he resolutely declined to flinch at it.

"Yes—I get pleasure from your society."

The admission turned him rather white, but he saved himself by instantly flinging at her: "However, *I am no hedonist.*"

Sharlee retired to look up hedonist in the dictionary.

Later that evening, Mrs. Weyland and her daughter being together upstairs, the former said:—

"Sharlee, who is this Mr. Queed that you paid so much attention to on the porch this evening?"

"Why, don't you know, mother? He is the assistant editor of the *Post*, and is going to be editor just the minute Mr. West retires. For you see, mother, everybody says that he writes the most wonderful articles, although I assure you, a year ago—"

"Yes, but who is he? Where does he come from? Who are his people?"

"Oh, I see. That is what you mean. Well, he comes from New York, where he led the most interesting literary sort of life, studying all the time, except when he was doing articles for the great reviews, or helping a lady up there to write a thesaurus. You see, he was fitting himself to compose a great work—"

"Who are his people?"

"Oh, that!" said Sharlee. "Well, that question is not so easy to answer as you might think. It opens up a peculiar situation: to begin with, he is a sort of an orphan, and—"

"How do you mean, a sort of an orphan?"

"You see, that is just where the peculiar part comes in. There is the heart of the whole mystery, and yet right there is the place where I must be reticent with you, mother, for though I know all about it, it was told to me confidentially—professionally, as my aunt's agent—and therefore—"

"Do you mean that you know nothing about his people?"

"I suppose it might be stated, crudely, in that way, but—"

"And knowing nothing about who or what he was, you simply picked him up at the boarding-house, and admitted him to your friendship?"

"Picking-up is not the word that the most careful mothers employ, in reference to their daughters' attitude toward young men. Mother, don't you understand? I'm a democrat."

"It is not a thing," said Mrs. Weyland, with some asperity, "for a lady to be."

Sharlee, fixing her hair in the back before the mirror, laughed long and merrily. "Do you dare—do you *dare* look your own daughter in the eye and say she is no lady?"

"Do you like this young man?" Mrs. Weyland continued.

"He interests me, heaps and heaps."

Mrs. Weyland sighed. "I can only say," she observed, sinking into a chair and picking up her book, "that such goings on were never heard of in my day."

CHAPTER XXII

In which Professor Nicolovius drops a Letter on the Floor, and Queed conjectures that Happiness sometimes comes to Men wearing a Strange Face.

Queed sat alone in the sitting-room of the Duke of Gloucester Street house. His afternoon's experiences had interested him largely. By subtle and occult processes which defied his analysis, what he had seen and heard had proved mysteriously disturbing—all this outpouring of irrational sentiment in which he had no share. So had his conversation with the girl disturbed him. He was in a condition of mental unrest, undefined but acute; odds and ends of curious thought kicked about within him, challenging him to follow them down to unexplored depths. But he was paying no attention to them now.

He sat in the sitting-room, wondering how Nicolovius had ever happened to think of that story about the Fenian refugee.

For Queed had been gradually driven to that unpleasant point. While living in the old man's house, he was, despite his conscientious efforts, virtually spying upon him.

The Fenian story had always had its questionable points; but so long as the two men were merely chance fellow-boarders, it did as well as any other. Now that they lived together, however, the multiplying suggestions that the old professor was something far other than he pretended became rather important. The young man could not help being aware that Nicolovius neither looked nor talked in the slightest degree like an Irishman. He could not help being certain that an Irishman who had fled to escape punishment for a political crime, in 1882, could have safely returned to his country long ago; and would undoubtedly have kept up relations with his friends overseas in the meantime. Nor could he help being struck with such facts as that Nicolovius, while apparently little interested in the occasional cables about Irish affairs, had become seemingly absorbed in the three days' doings of the United Confederate Veterans.

Now it was entirely all right for the old man to have a secret, and keep it. There was not the smallest quarrel on that score. But it was not in the least all right for one man to live with another, pretending to believe in him, when in reality he was doubting and questioning him at every move. The want of candor involved in his present relations with Nicolovius continually fretted Queed's conscience. Ought he not in common honesty to tell the old man that he could not believe the Irish biography, leaving it to him to decide what he wanted to do about it?

Nicolovius, tramping in only a few minutes behind Queed, greeted his young friend as blandly as ever. Physically, he seemed tired; much dust of city streets clung to his commonly spotless boots; but his eyes were so extraordinarily brilliant that Queed at first wondered if he could have been drinking. However, this thought died almost as soon as it was born.

The professor walked over to the window and stood looking out, hat on head. Presently he said: "You saw the grand parade, I suppose? For indeed there was no escaping it."

Queed said that he had seen it.

"You had a good place to see it from, I hope?"

Excellent; Miss Weyland's porch.

"Ah!" said Nicolovius, with rather an emphasis, and permitted a pause to fall. "A most charming young lady—charming," he went on, with his note of velvet irony which the young man peculiarly disliked. "I hear she is to marry your Mr. West. An eminently suitable match in every way. Yet I shall not soon forget how that delightful young man defrauded you of the editorship."

Silence from Mr. Queed, the question of the editorship having already been thoroughly threshed out between them.

"I, too, saw the gallant proceedings," resumed Nicolovius, retracing his thought. "What an outfit! What an outfit!"

He dropped down into his easy chair by the table, removed his straw hat with traces of a rare irritation in his manner, put on his black skull cap, and presently purred his thoughts aloud:—

"No writer has yet done anything like justice to the old soldier cult in the post-bellum South. Doubtless it may lie out of the province of you historians, but what a theme for a new Thackeray! With such a fetish your priestcraft of the Middle Ages is not to be compared for a moment. There is no parallel among civilized nations; to find one you must go to the Voodooism of the savage black. For more than a generation all the intelligence of the South has been asked, nay compelled, to come and bow down before these alms-begging loblollies. To refuse to make obeisance was treason. The entire public thought of a vast section of the country has revolved around the figure of a worthless old grafter in a tattered gray shirt. Every question is settled when some moth-eaten ne'er-do-well lets out what is known as a 'rebel yell.' The most polished and profound speech conceivable is answered when a jackass mounts the platform and brays out something about the gallant boys in gray. The cry for progress, for material advancement, for moral and social betterment, is stifled, that everybody may have breath to shout for a flapping trouser's leg worn by a degraded old sot. All that your Southern statesmen have had to give a people who were stripped to the bone is fulsome rhetoric about the Wounded Warrior of Wahoo, or some other inflated nonentity, whereupon the mesmerized population have loyally fallen on their faces and shouted, 'Praise the Lord.' And all the while they were going through this wretched mummery, they were hungry and thirsty and naked—destitute in a smiling land of plenty. Do you wonder that I think old-soldierism is the meanest profession the Lord ever suffered to thrive? I tell you Baal and Moloch never took such toll of their idolaters as these shabby old gods of the gray shirt."

"Professor Nicolovius," said Queed, with a slow smile, "where on earth do you exhume your ideas of Southern history?"

"Observation, my dear boy! God bless us, haven't I had three years of this city to use my eyes and ears in? And I had a peculiar training in my youth," he added, retrospectively, "to fit me to see straight and generalize accurately."

... Couldn't the man see that no persecuted Irishman ever talked in such a way since the world began? If he had a part to play, why in the name of common sense couldn't he play it respectably?

Queed got up, and began strolling about the floor. In his mind was what Sharlee Weyland had said to him two hours before: "All the bitterness nowadays comes from the non-combatants, the camp-followers, the sutlers, and the cowards." Under which of these heads did his friend, the old professor, fall?... Why had he ever thought of Nicolovius as, perhaps, a broken Union officer? A broken Union officer would feel bitter, if at all, against the Union. A man who felt so bitter against the South—

A resolution was rapidly hardening in the young man's mind. He felt this attitude of doubt and suspicion, these thoughts that he was now thinking about the man whose roof he shared, as an unclean spot upon his chaste passion for truth. He could not feel honest again until he had wiped it off.... And, after all, what did he owe to Nicolovius?

"But I must not leave you under the impression," said Nicolovius, almost testily for him, "that my ideas are unique and extraordinary. They are shared, in fact, by Southern historians of repute and—"

Queed turned on him. "But you never read Southern historians."

Nicolovius had a smile for that, though his expression seemed subtly to shift. "I must make confession to you. Three days ago, I broke the habits of quarter of a century. At the second-hand shop on Centre Street I bought, actually, a little volume of history. It is surprising how these Southern manifestations have interested me."

Queed was an undesirable person for any man to live with who had a secret to keep. His mind was relentlessly constructive; it would build you up the whole dinosaur from the single left great digitus. For apparently no reason at all, there had popped into his head a chance remark of Major Brooke's a year ago, which he had never thought of from that day to this: "I can't get over thinking that I've seen that man before a long time ago, when he looked entirely different, and yet somehow the same too."

"I will show you my purchase," added Nicolovius, after a moment of seeming irresolution.

He disappeared down the hall to his bedroom, a retreat in which Queed had never set foot, and returned promptly carrying a dingy duodecimo in worn brown leather. As he entered the room, he absently raised the volume to his lips and blew along the edges.

Queed's mental processes were beyond his own control. "Three days old," flashed into his mind, "and he blows dust from it."

"What is the book?" he asked.

"A very able little history of the Reconstruction era in this State. I have a mind to read you a passage and convert you."

Nicolovius sat down, and began turning the pages. Queed stood a step away, watching him intently. The old man fluttered the leaves vaguely for a moment; then his expression shifted and, straightening up, he suddenly closed the book.

"I don't appear to find," he said easily, "the little passage that so impressed me the day before yesterday. And after all, what would be the use of reading it to you? You impetuous young men will never listen to the wisdom of your elders."

Smiling blandly, the subject closed, it might have been forever, Nicolovius reached out toward the table to flick the ash from his cigarette. In so doing, as luck had it, he struck the book and knocked it from his knees. Something shook from its pages as it dropped, and fell almost at Queed's feet. Mechanically he stooped to pick it up.

It was a letter, at any rate an envelope, and it had fallen face up, full in the light of the open window. The envelope bore an address, in faded ink, but written in a bold legible hand. Not to save his soul could Queed have avoided seeing it:

Henry G. Surface, Esq.,
36 Washington Street.

There was a dead silence: a silence that from matter-of-fact suddenly became unendurable.

Queed handed the envelope to Nicolovius. Nicolovius glanced at it, while pretending not to, and his eyelash flickered; his face was about the color of cigar ashes. Queed walked away, waiting.

He expected that the old man would immediately demand whether he had seen that name and address, or at least would immediately say something. But he did nothing of the sort. When Queed turned at the end of the room, Nicolovius was fluttering the pages of his book again, apparently absorbed in it, apparently quite forgetting that he had just laid it aside. Then Queed understood. Nicolovius did not mean to say or do anything. He meant to pass over the little incident altogether.

However, the pretense had now reached a point when Queed could no longer endure it.

"Perhaps, after all," said Nicolovius, in his studiously bland voice, "I am a little sweeping—"

Queed stood in front of him, interrupting, suddenly not at ease. "Professor Nicolovius."

"Yes?"

"I must say something that will offend you, I'm afraid. For some time I have found myself unable to believe the—story of your life you were once good enough to give me."

"Ah, well," said Nicolovius, engrossed in his book, "it is not required of you to believe it. We need have no quarrel about that."

Suddenly Queed found that he hated to give the stab, but he did not falter.

"I must be frank with you, professor. I saw whom that envelope was addressed to just now."

"Nor need we quarrel about that."

But Queed's steady gaze upon him presently grew unbearable, and at last the old man raised his head.

"Well? Whom was it addressed to?"

Queed felt disturbingly sorry for him, and, in the same thought, admired his iron control. The old professor's face was gray; his very lips were colorless; but his eyes were steady, and his voice was the voice of every day.

"I think," said Queed, quietly, "that it is addressed to you."

There was a lengthening silence while the two men, motionless, looked into each other's eyes. The level gaze of each held just the same look of faint horror, horror subdued and controlled, but still there. Their stare became fascinated; it ran on as though nothing could ever happen to break it off. To Queed it seemed as if everything in the world had dropped away but those brilliant eyes, frightened yet unafraid, boring into his.

Nicolovius broke the silence. The triumph of his intelligence over his emotions showed in the fact that he attempted no denial.

"Well?" he said somewhat thickly. "Well?—Well?"

Under the look of the younger man, he was beginning to break. Into the old eyes had sprung a deadly terror, a look as though his immortal soul might hang on what the young man was going to say next. To answer this look, a blind impulse in Queed bade him strike out, to say or do something; and his reason, which was always detached and impersonal, was amazed to hear his voice saying:—

"It's all right, professor. Not a thing is going to happen."

The old man licked his lips. "You ... will stay on here?"

And Queed's voice answered: "As long as you want me."

Nicolovius, who had been born Surface, suffered a moment of collapse. He fell back in his chair, and covered his face with his hands.

The dying efforts of the June sun still showed in the pretty sitting-room, though the town clocks were striking seven. From without floated in the voices of merry passers; eddies of the day's celebration broke even into this quiet street. Queed sat down in a big-armed rocker, and looked out the window into the pink west.

So, in a minute's time and by a wholly chance happening, the mystery was out at last. Professor Nicolovius, the bland recluse of Mrs. Paynter's, and Henry G. Surface, political arch-traitor, ex-convict, and falsest of false friends, were one and the same man.

The truth had been instantly plain to Queed when the name had blazed up at him from the envelope on the floor. It was as though Fate herself had tossed that envelope under his eyes, as the answer to all his questionings. Not an instant's doubt had troubled him; and now a score of memories were marshaling themselves before him to show that his first flashing certainty had been sound. As for the book, it was clearly from the library of the old man's youth, kept and hidden away for some reason, when nearly everything else had been destroyed. Between the musty pages the accusing letter had lain forgotten for thirty years, waiting for this moment.

He turned and glanced once at the silent figure, huddled back in the chair with covered eyes; the unhappy old man whom nobody had ever trusted without regretting it. *Henry G. Surface*—whose name was a synonym for those traits and things which honest men of all peoples and climes have always hated most, treachery, perfidy, base betrayal of trust, shameful dishonesty—who had crowded the word *infamy* from the popular lexicon of politics with the keener, more biting epithet, *Surfaceism*. And here—wonder of wonders—sat Surface before him, drawn back to the scene of his fall like a murderer to the body and the scarlet stain upon the floor, caught, trapped, the careful mask of many years plucked from him at a sudden word, leaving him no covering upon earth but his smooth white hands. And he, Queed, was this man's closest, his only friend, chosen out of all the world to live with him and minister to his declining years....

"It's true!" now broke through the concealing hands. "I am that man.... God help me!"

Queed looked unseeingly out of the window, where the sun was couching in a bed of copper flame stippled over with brightest azure. Why had he done it? What crazy prompting had struck from him that promise to yoke his destiny forever with this terrible old man? If Nicolovius, the Fenian refugee, had never won his liking, Surface, the Satan apostate, was detestable to him. What devil of impulse had trapped from him the mad offer to spend his days in the company of such a creature, and in the shadow of so odious an ill-fame?

As on the day when Fifi had asked him her innocent question about altruism, a sudden tide swept the young man's thoughts inward. And after them, this time, groped the blundering feet of his spirit.

Here was he, a mature man, who, in point of work, in all practical and demonstrable ways, was the millionth man. He was a great editorial writer, which was a minor but genuine activity. He was a yet greater writer on social science, which was one of the supreme activities. On this side, then, certainly the chief side, there could be no question about the successfulness of his life. His working life was, or would be before he was through, brilliantly successful. But it had for some time been plain to him that he stopped short there. He was a great workman, but that was all. He was a superb rationalist; but after that he did not exist.

Through the science of Human Intercourse, he saw much more of people now than he had ever done before, and thus it had become driven home upon him that most people had two lives, their outer or practical lives, and their inner or personal lives. But he himself had but one life. He was a machine; a machine which turned out matchless work for the enlightenment of the world, but after all a machine. He was intellect. He was Pure Reason. Yet he himself had said, and written, that intellectual supremacy was not the true badge of supremacy of type. There was nothing sure of races that was not equally sure of the individuals which make up those races. Yet intellect was all he was. Vast areas of thought, feeling, and conduct, in which the people around him spent so much of their time, were entirely closed to him. He had no personal life at all. That part of him had atrophied from lack of use, like the eyes of the mole and of those sightless fishes men take from the waters of caverns.

And now this part of him, which had for some time been stirring uneasily, had risen suddenly without bidding of his and in defiance of his reason, and laid hold of something in his environment. In doing so, it appeared to have thrust upon him an inner, or personal, life from this time forward. That life lay in being of use to the old man before him: he who had never been of personal use to anybody so far, and the miserable old man who had no comfort anywhere but in him.

He knew the scientific name of this kind of behavior very well. It was altruism, the irrational force that had put a new face upon the world. Fifi, he remembered well, had assured him that in altruism he would find that fiercer happiness which was as much better than content as being well was better than not being sick. But ... could this be happiness, this whirling confusion that put him to such straits to keep a calm face above the tumult of his breast? If this was happiness, then it came to him for their first meeting wearing a strange face....

"You know the story?"

Queed moved in his chair. "Yes. I—have heard it."

"Of course," said Nicolovius. "It is as well known as Iscariot's. By God, how they've hounded me!"

Evidently he was recovering fast. There was bitterness, rather than shame, in his voice. He took his hands from his eyes, adjusted his cap, stiffened up in his chair. The sallow tints were coming back into his face; his lips took on color; his eye and hand were steady. Not every man could have passed through such a cataclysm and emerged so little marked. He picked up his cigarette from the table; it was still going. This fact was symbolic: the great shock had come and passed within the smoking of an inch of cigarette. The pretty room was as it was before. Pale sunshine still flickered on the swelling curtain. The leather desk-clock gayly ticked the passing seconds. The young man's clean-cut face looked as quiet as ever.

Upon Queed the old man fastened his fearless black eyes.

"I meant to tell you all this some day," he said, in quite a natural voice. "Now the day has come a little sooner than I had meant—that is all. I know that my confidence is safe with you—till I die."

"I think you have nothing to fear by trusting me," said Queed, and added at once: "But you need tell me nothing unless you prefer."

A kind of softness shone for a moment in Surface's eyes. "Nobody could look at your face," he said gently, "and ever be afraid to trust you."

The telephone rang, and Queed could answer it by merely putting out his hand. It was West, from the office, asking that he report for work that night, as he himself was compelled to be away.

Presently Surface began talking; talking in snatches, more to himself than to his young friend, rambling backward over his broken life in passionate reminiscence. He talked a long time thus, while the daylight faded and dusk crept into the room, and then night; and Queed listened, giving him all the rein he wanted and saying never a word himself.

"... Pray your gods," said Surface, "that you never have such reason to hate your fellow-men as I have had, my boy. For that has been the keynote of my unhappy life. God, how I hated them all, and how I do yet!... Not least Weyland, with his ostentatious virtue, his holier-than-thou kindness, his self-righteous magnanimity tossed even to me ... the broken-kneed idol whom others passed with averted face, and there was none so poor to do me reverence...."

So this, mused Queed, was the meaning of the old professor's invincible dislike for Miss Weyland, which he had made so obvious in the boarding-house that even Mr. Bylash commented on it. He had never been able to forgive her father's generosity, which he had so terribly betrayed; her name and her blood rankled and festered eternally in the heart of the faithless friend and the striped trustee.

Henderson, the ancient African who attended the two men, knocked upon the shut door with the deprecatory announcement that he had twice rung the supper-bell.

"Take the things back to the kitchen, Henderson," said Queed. "I'll ring when we are ready."

The breeze was freshening, blowing full upon Surface, who did not appear to notice it. Queed got up and lowered the window. The old man's neglected cigarette burned his fingers; he lit another; it, too, burned itself down to the cork-tip without receiving the attention of a puff.

Presently he went on talking:

"I was of a high-spirited line. Thank God, I never learned to fawn on the hand that lashed me. Insult I would not brook. I struck back, and when I struck, I struck to kill.—Did I not? So hard that the State reeled.... So hard that if I had had something better than mean negroes and worse whites for my tools, fifth-rate scavengers, buzzards of politics ... this hand would have written the history of the State in these forty years.

"That was the way I struck, and how did they answer me?—Ostracism ... Coventry ... The weapons of mean old women, and dogs.... The dogs! That is what they were....

"Well, other arms were ready to receive me. Others were fairer-minded than the cowardly bigots who could blow hot or cold as their selfish interests and prostituted leaders whispered. I was not a man to be kept down. Oh, my new friends were legion, and I was king again. But it was never the same. In that way, they beat me. I give them that.... Not they, though. It was deep calling to deep. My blood—heritage—tradition—education—all that I was ... this was what tortured me with what was gone, and kept calling.

"Wicked injustice and a lost birthright.... Oh, memory was there to crucify me, by day and by night. And yet.... Why, it was a thing that is done every day by men these people say their prayers to.... Oh, yes—I wanted to punish—*him* for his smug condescension, his patronizing playing of the good Samaritan. And through him all these others ... show them that their old idol wore claws on those feet of clay. But not in that way. No, a much cleverer way than that. Perhaps there would be no money when they asked for it, but I was to smile blandly and go on about my business. They were never to reach *me*. But the Surfaces were never skilled at juggling dirty money....

"They took me off my guard. The most technical fault—a trifle.... Another day or two and everything would have been all right. They had my word for it—and you know how they replied.... The infamous tyranny of the majority. The greatest judicial crime in a decade, and they laughed.

"So now I lie awake in the long nights with nine years of *that* to look back on.

"Let my life be a lesson to you teaching you—if nothing else—that it is of no use to fight society. They have a hopeless advantage, the contemptible advantage of numbers, and they are not ashamed to use it.... But my spirit would not let me lie quiet under injury and insult. I was ever a fighter, born to die with my spurs on. And when I die at last, they will find that I go with a Parthian shot ... and after all have the last word.

"So I came out into a bright world again, an old man before my time, ruined forever, marked with a scarlet mark to wear to my grave....

"And then in time, as of course it would, the resolve came to me to come straight back here to die. A man wants to die among his own people. They were all that ever meant anything to me—they have that to boast of.... I loved this city once. To die anywhere else ... why, it was meaningless, a burlesque on death. I looked at my face in the glass; my own mother would not have known me. And so I came straight to Jennie Paynter's, such was my whim ... whom I held on my knee fifty years ago.

"... Oh, it's been funny ... so funny ... to sit at that intolerable table, and hear poor old Brooke on Reconstruction.

"And I've wondered what little Jennie Paynter would do, if I had risen on one of these occasions and spoken my name to the table. How I've hated her—hated the look and sight of her—and all the while embracing it for dear life. She has told me much that she never knew I listened to—many a bit about old friends ... forty years since I'd heard their names. And Brooke has told me much, the doting old ass.

"But the life grew unbearable to a man of my temper. I could afford the decency of privacy in my old age. For I had worked hard and saved since....

"And then you came ... a scholar and a gentleman."

It was quite dark in the room. Surface's voice had suddenly changed. The bitterness faded out of it; it became gentler than Queed had ever heard it.

"I did not find you out at once. My life had made me unsocial—and out of the Nazareth of that house I never looked for any good to come. But when once I took note of you, each day I saw you clearer and truer. I saw you fighting, and asking no odds—for elbow-room to do your own work, for your way up on the newspaper, for bodily strength and health—everywhere I saw you, you were fighting indomitably. I have always loved a fighter. You were young and a stranger, alone like me; you stirred no memories of a past that now, in my age, I would forget; your face was the face of honor and truth. I thought: What a blessing if I could make a friend of this young man for the little while that is left me!... And you have been a blessing and a joy—more than you can dream. And now you will not cast me off, like the others.... I do not know the words with which to try to thank you...."

"Oh, don't," came Queed's voice hastily out of the dark. "There is no question of thanks here."

He got up, lit the lamps, pulled down the shade. The old man lay back in his chair, his hands gripping its arms, the lamplight full upon him. Never had Queed seen him look less inspiring to affection. His black cap had gotten pushed to one side, which both revealed a considerable area of hairless head, and imparted to the whole face an odd and rakish air; the Italian eyes did not wholly match with the softness of his voice; the thin-lipped mouth under the long auburn mustache looked neither sorrowful nor kind. It was Queed's lifelong habit never to look back with vain regrets; and he needed all of his resolution now.

He stood in front of the man whose terrible secret he had surprised, and outwardly he was as calm as ever.

"Professor Nicolovius," he said, with a faint emphasis upon the name, "all this is as though it had never passed between us. And now let's go and get some supper."

Surface rose to his height and took Queed's hand in a grip like iron. His eyes glistened with sudden moisture.

"God bless you, boy! You're a *man!*"

It had been a memorable conversation in the life of both men, opening up obvious after-lines of more or less momentous thought. Yet each of them, as it happened, neglected these lines for a corollary detail of apparently much less seriousness, and pretty nearly the same detail at that. For Surface sat long that evening, meditating how he might most surely break up the friendship between his young friend and Sharlee Weyland; while Queed, all during his busy hours at the office, found his thoughts of Nicolovius dominated by speculations as to what Miss Weyland would say, if she knew that he had formed a lifelong compact with the man who had betrayed her father's friendship and looted her own fortune.

CHAPTER XXIII

Of the Bill for the Reformatory, and its Critical Situation; of West's Second Disappointment with the Rewards of Patriotism; of the Consolation he found in the most Charming Resolve in the World.

In January the legislature met again. All autumn and early winter the *Post* had been pounding without surcease upon two great issues: first, the reform of the tax-laws, and, second, the establishment of a reformatory institution for women. It was palpably the resolve of the paper that the legislature should not overlook these two measures through lack of being shown where its duty lay.

To the assistant editor had been assigned both campaigns, and he had developed his argument with a deadly persistence. A legislature could no more ignore him than you could ignore a man who is pounding you over the head with a bed-slat. Queed had proved his cases in a dozen ways, historically and analogically, politically, morally, and scientifically, socially and sociologically. Then, for luck, he proceeded to run through the whole list again a time or two; and now faithful readers of the *Post* cried aloud for mercy, asking each other what under the sun had got into the paper that it thus massacred and mutilated the thrice-slain.

But the *Post*, aided by the press of the State which had been captivated by its ringing logic, continued its merciless fire, and, as it proved, not insanely. For when the legislature came together, it turned out to be one of those "economy" sessions, periodically thrust down the throats of even the wiliest politicians. Not "progress" was its watchword, but "wise retrenchment." Every observer of events, especially in states where one party has been long in control, is familiar with these recurrent manifestations. There is a long period of systematic reduplication of the offices, multiplying generosity to the faithful, and enormous geometrical progression of the public payroll. Some mishap, one day, focuses attention upon the princely totalities of the law-making spenders, and a howl goes up from the "sovereigns," who, as has been wisely observed, never have any power until they are mad. The party managers, always respectful to an angry electorate, thereupon announce that, owing to the wonderful period of progress and expansion brought about by their management, the State can afford to slow up for a brief period, hold down expenses and enjoy its (party-made) prosperity. This strikes the "keynote" for the next legislature, which pulls a long face, makes a tremendous noise about "economy," and possibly refrains from increasing expenses, or even shades them down about a dollar and a half. Flushed with their victory, the innocent sovereigns return, Cincinnatus-wise, to their plows, and the next session of the legislature, relieved of that suspicionful scrutiny so galling to men of spirit, proceeds to cut the purse-strings loose with a whoop.

Such a brief spasm had now seized the State. Expenses had doubled and redoubled with a velocity which caused even hardened prodigals to view with alarm. The number of commissions, boards, assistant inspectors, and third deputy clerks was enormous, far larger than anybody realized. If you could have taken a biological cross-section through the seat of State Government, you would doubtless have discovered a most amazing number of unobtrusive gentlemen with queer little titles and odd little duties, sitting silent and sleek under their cover; their hungry little mouths affixed last year to the public breast, or two years ago, or twenty, and ready to open in fearful wailing if anybody sought to pluck them off. In an aggregate way, attention had been called to them during the gubernatorial campaign of the summer. Attacks from the rival stump had, of course, been successfully "answered" by the loyal leaders and party press. But the bare statement of the annual expenditures, as compared with the annual expenditures of ten years ago, necessarily stood, and in cold type it looked bad. Therefore the legislature met now for an "economy session." The public was given to understand that every penny would have to give a strict account of itself before it would receive a pass from the treasury, and that public institutions, asking for increased support, could consider themselves lucky if they did not find their appropriations scaled down by a fourth or so.

The *Post's* tax reform scheme went through with a bang. Out of loose odds and ends of vague discontent, Queed had succeeded in creating a body of public sentiment that became invincible. Moreover, this scheme cost nothing. On the contrary, by a rearrangement of items and a stricter system of assessment, it promised, as the *Post* frequently remarked, to put hundreds of thousands into the treasury. But the reformatory was a horse of a totally different color. Here was a proposal, for a mere supposititious moral gain, evanescent as air, to take a hundred thousand dollars of hard money out of the crib, and saddle the State with an annual obligation, to boot. An excellent thing in itself, but a most unreasonable request of an economy session, said the organization leaders. In fact, this hundred thousand dollars happened to be precisely the hundred thousand dollars they needed to lubricate "the organization," and discharge, by some choice new positions, a few honorable obligations incurred during the campaign.

Now it was written in the recesses of the assistant editor's being, those parts of him which he never thought of mentioning to anybody, that the reformatory bill must pass. Various feelings had gradually stiffened an early general approval into a rock-ribbed resolve. It was on a closely allied theme that he had first won his editorial spurs—the theme of Klinker's "blaggards," who made reformatories necessary. That was one thing: a kind of professional sentiment which the sternest scientist need not be ashamed to acknowledge. And then, beyond that, his many talks with Klinker had invested the campaign for the reformatory with a warmth of meaning which was without precedent in his experience. This was, in fact, his first personal contact with the suffering and sin of the world, his first grapple with a social problem in the raw. Two years before, when he had offered to write an article on this topic for the Assistant Secretary of Charities, his interest in a reformatory had been only the scientific interest which the trained sociologist feels in all the enginery of social reform. But now this institution had become indissolubly connected in Queed's mind with the case of Eva Bernheimer, whom Buck Klinker knew, Eva Bernheimer who was "in trouble" at sixteen, and had now "dropped out." A reformatory had become in his thought a living instrument to catch the Eva Bernheimers of this world, and effectually prevent them from dropping out.

And apart from all this, here was the first chance he had ever had to do a service for Sharlee Weyland.

However, the bill stuck obstinately in committee. Now the session was more than half over, February was nearly gone, and there it still stuck. And when it finally came out, it was evidently going to be a toss of a coin whether it would be passed by half a dozen votes, or beaten by an equal number. But there was not the slightest doubt that the great majority of the voters, so far as they were interested in it at all, wanted it passed, and the tireless *Post* was prodding the committee every other day, observing that now was the time, etc., and demanding in a hundred forceful ways, how about it?

With cheerfulness and confidence had West intrusted these important matters to his young assistant. Not only was Queed an acknowledged authority on both taxation and penological science, but he had enjoyed the advantage of writing articles on both themes under Colonel Cowles's personal direction. The Colonel's bones were dust, his pen was rust, his soul was with the saints, we trust; but his gallant spirit went marching on. He towered out of memory a demigod, and what he said and did in his lifetime had become as the law of the Medes and Persians now.

But there was never any dispute about the division of editorial honors on the *Post*, anyway. The two young men, in fact, were so different in every way that their relations were a model of mutual satisfaction. Never once did Queed's popular chief seek to ride over his valued helper, or deny him his full share of opportunity in the department. If anything, indeed, he leaned quite the other way. For West lacked the plodder's faculty for indefatigable application. Like some rare and splendid bird, if he was kept too closely in captivity, his spirit sickened and died.

It is time to admit frankly that West, upon closer contact with newspaper work, had been somewhat disillusioned, and who that knows, will be surprised at that? To begin with, he had been used to much freedom, and his new duties were extremely confining. They began soon after breakfast, and no man could say at what hour they would end. The night work, in especial, he abhorred. It interfered with much more amusing things that had hitherto beguiled his evenings, and it also conflicted with sleep, of which he required a good deal. There was, too, a great amount of necessary but most irksome drudgery connected with his editorial labors. Because the *Post* was a leader of public thought in the State, and as such enjoyed a national standing, West found it necessary to read a vast number of papers, to keep up with what was going on. He was also forced to write many perfunctory articles on subjects which did not interest him in the least, and about which, to tell the truth, he knew very little. There were also a great many letters either to be answered, or to be prepared for publication in the People's Forum column, and these letters were commonly written by dull asses who had no idea what they were talking about. Prosy people were always coming in with requests or complaints, usually the latter. First and last there was a quantity of grinding detail which, like the embittered old fogeyism of the Blaines College trustees, had not appeared on his rosy prospect in the Maytime preceding.

With everything else favorable, West would cheerfully have accepted these things, as being inextricably embedded in the nature of the work. But unfortunately, everything else was not favorable. Deeper than the grind of the routine detail, was the constant opposition and adverse criticism to which his newspaper, like every other one, was incessantly subjected. It has long been a trite observation that no reader of any newspaper is so humble as not to be outspokenly confident that he could run that paper a great deal better than those who actually are running it. Every upstanding man who pays a cent for a daily journal considers that he buys the right to abuse it, nay incurs the manly duty of abusing it. Every editor knows that the highest praise he can expect is silence. If his readers are pleased with his remarks, they nobly refrain from comment. But if they disagree with one jot or tittle of his high-speed dissertations, he must be prepared to have quarts of ink squirted at him forthwith.

Now this was exactly the reverse of Editor West's preferences. He liked criticism of him to be silent, and praise of him to be shouted in the market-place. For all his good-humor and poise, the steady fire of hostile criticism fretted him intensely. He did not like to run through his exchanges and find his esteemed contemporaries combatting his positions, sometimes bitterly or contemptuously, and always, so it seemed to him, unreasonably and unfairly. He did not like to have friends stop him on the street to ask why in the name of so-and-so he had said such-and-such; or, more trying still, have them pass him with an icy nod, simply because he, in some defense of truth and exploitation of the uplift, had fearlessly trod upon their precious little toes. He did not like to have his telephone ring with an angry protest, or to get a curt letter from a railroad president (supposedly a good friend of the paper's) desiring to know by return mail whether the clipping therewith inclosed represented the *Post's* attitude toward the railroads. A steady procession of things like these wears on the nerves of a sensitive man, and West, for all his confident exterior, was a sensitive man. A heavy offset in the form of large and constant public eulogies was needed to balance these annoyances, and such an offset was not forthcoming.

West was older now, a little less ready in his enthusiasms, a shade less pleased with the world, a thought less sure of the eternal merits of the life of uplift. In fact he was thirty-three years old, and he had moments, now and then, when he wondered if he were going forward as rapidly and surely as he had a right to expect. This was the third position he had had since he left college, and it was his general expectation to graduate into a fourth before a great while. Semple frequently urged him to return to the brokerage business; he had made an unquestioned success there at any rate. As to Blaines College, he could not be so confident. The college had opened this year with an increased enrollment of twenty-five; and though West privately felt certain that his successor was only reaping where he himself had sown, you could not be certain that the low world would so see it. As for the *Post*, it was a mere stop-gap, a momentary halting-place where he preened for a far higher flight. There were many times that winter when West wondered if Plonny Neal, whom he rarely or never saw, could possibly have failed to notice how prominently he was in line.

But these doubts and dissatisfactions left little mark upon the handsome face and buoyant manner. Changes in West, if there were any, were of the slightest. Certainly his best friends, like those two charming young women, Miss Weyland and Miss Avery, found him as delightful as ever.

In these days, West's mother desired him to marry. After the cunning habit of women, she put the thought before him daily, under many an alluring guise, by a thousand engaging approaches. West himself warmed to the idea. He had drunk freely of the pleasures of single blessedness, under the most favorable conditions; was now becoming somewhat jaded with them; and looked with approval upon the prospect of a little nest, or indeed one not so little, duly equipped with the usual faithful helpmeet who should share his sorrows, joys, etc. The nest he could feather decently enough himself; the sole problem, a critical one in its way, was to decide upon the helpmeet. West was neither college boy nor sailor. His heart was no harem of beautiful faces. Long since, he had faced the knowledge that there were but two girls in the world for him. Since, however, the church and the law allowed him but one, he must more drastically monogamize his heart and this he found enormously difficult. It was the poet's triangle with the two dear charmers over again.

One blowy night in late February, West passed by the brown stone palace which Miss Avery's open-handed papa, from Mauch Chunk, occupied on a three years' lease with privilege of buying; and repaired to the more modest establishment where dwelt Miss Weyland and her mother. The reformatory issue was then at the touch. The bill had come out of committee with a six-and-six vote; rumor had it that it would be called up in the House within the week; and it now appeared as though a push of a feather's weight might settle its fate either way. Sharlee and West spoke first of this. She was eagerly interested, and praised him warmly for the interest and valuable help of the *Post*. Her confidence was unshaken that the bill would go through, though by a narrow margin.

"The opposition is of the deadliest sort," she admitted, "because it is silent. It is silent because it knows that its only argument—all this economy talk—is utterly insincere. But Mr. Dayne knows where the opposition is—and the way he goes after it! Never believe any more that ministers can't lobby!"

"Probably the root of the whole matter," offered West, easing himself back into his chair, "is that the machine fellows want this particular hundred thousand dollars in their business."

"Isn't it horrid that men can be so utterly selfish? You don't think they will really venture to do that?"

"I honestly don't know. You see I have turned it all over to Queed, and I confess I haven't studied it with anything like the care he has."

Sharlee, who was never too engrossed in mere subjects to notice people's tones, said at once: "Oh, I am sure they won't dare do it," and immediately changed the subject. "You are going to the German, of course?"

"Oh, surely, unless the office pinches me."

"You mustn't let it pinch you—the last of the year, heigho! Did you hear about Robert Byrd and Miss—no, I won't give you her name—and the visiting girl?"

"Never a word."

"She's a thoroughly nice girl, but—well, not pretty, I should say, and I don't think she has had much fun here. Beverley and Robert Byrd were here the other night. Why *will* they hunt in pairs, do you know? I told Beverley that he positively must take this girl to the German. He quarreled and complained a good deal at first, but finally yielded like a dear boy. Then he seemed to enter in the nicest way into the spirit of our altruistic design. He said that after he had asked the girl, it would be very nice if Robert should ask her too. He would be refused, of course, but the girl would have the pleasant feeling of getting a rush, and Robert would boost his standing as a philanthropist, all without cost to anybody. Robert was good-natured, and fell in with the plan. Three days later he telephoned me, simply furious. He had asked the girl—you know he hasn't been to a German for five years—and she accepted at once with tears of gratitude."

"But how—?"

"Of course Beverley never asked her. He simply trapped Robert, which he would rather do than anything else in the world."

West shouted. "Speaking of Germans," he said presently, "I am making up my list for next year—the early bird, you know. How many will you give me?"

"Six."

"Will you kindly sign up the papers to-night?"

"No—my mother won't let me. I might sign up for one if you want me to."

"What possible use has your mother for the other five that is better than giving them all to me?"

"Perhaps she doesn't want to spoil other men for me."

West leaned forward, interest fully awakened on his charming face, and Sharlee watched him, pleased with herself.

It had occurred to her, in fact, that Mr. West was tired; and this was the solemn truth. He was a man of large responsibilities, with a day's work behind him and a night's work ahead of him. His personal conception of the way to occupy the precious interval did not include the conscientious talking of shop. Jaded and brain-fagged, what he desired was to be amused, beguiled, soothed, fascinated, even flattered a bit, mayhap. Sharlee's theory of hospitality was that a guest was entitled to any type of conversation he had a mind to. Having dismissed her own troubles, she now proceeded to make herself as agreeable as she knew how; and he has read these pages to little purpose who does not know that that was very agreeable indeed.

West, at least, appeared to think so. He lingered, charmed, until quarter past eleven o'clock, at which hour Mrs. Weyland, in the room above, began to let the tongs and poker fall about with unmistakable significance; and went out into the starlit night radiant with the certainty that his heart, after long wandering, had found its true mate at last.

CHAPTER XXIV

Sharlee's Parlor on Another Evening; how One Caller outsat Two, and why; also, how Sharlee looked in her Mirror for a Long Time, and why.

On the very night after West made his happy discovery, namely on the evening of February 24, at about twenty minutes of nine, Sharlee Weyland's door-bell rang, and Mr. Queed was shown into her parlor.

His advent was a complete surprise to Sharlee. For these nine months, her suggestion that he should call upon her had lain utterly neglected. Since the Reunion she had seen him but four times, twice on the street, and once at each of their offices, when the business of the reformatory had happened to draw them together. The last of these meetings, which had been the briefest, was already six weeks old. In all of her acquaintance with him, extending now over two years and a half, this was the first time that he had ever sought her out with intentions that were, presumably, deliberately social.

The event, Sharlee felt in greeting him, could not have happened, more unfortunately. Queed found the parlor occupied, and the lady's attention engaged, by two young men before him. One of them was Beverley Byrd, who saluted him somewhat moodily. The other was a Mr. Miller—no relation to Miss Miller of Mrs. Paynter's, though a faint something in his *ensemble* lent plausibility to that conjecture—a newcomer to the city who, having been introduced to Miss Weyland somewhere, had taken the liberty of calling without invitation or permission. It was impossible for Sharlee to be rude to anybody under her own roof, but it is equally impossible to describe her manner to Mr. Miller as exactly cordial. He himself was a cordial man, mustached and anecdotal, who assumed rather more confidence than he actually felt. Beverley Byrd, who did not always hunt in pairs, had taken an unwonted dislike to him at sight. He did not consider him a suitable person to be calling on Sharlee, and he had been doing his best, with considerable deftness and success, to deter him from feeling too much at home.

Byrd wore a beautiful dinner jacket. So did Mr. Miller, with a gray tie, and a gray, brass-buttoned vest, to boot. Queed wore his day clothes of blue, which were not so new as they were the day Sharlee first saw them, on the rustic bridge near the little cemetery. He had, of course, taken it for granted that he would find Miss Weyland alone. Nevertheless, he did not appear disconcerted by the sudden discovery of his mistake, or even by Mr. Miller's glorious waistcoat; he was as grave as ever, but showed no signs of embarrassment. Sharlee caught herself observing him closely, as he shook hands with the two men and selected a chair for himself; she concluded that constant contact with the graces of Charles Gardiner West had not been without its effect upon him. He appeared decidedly more at his ease than Mr. Miller, for instance, and he had another valuable possession which that personage lacked, namely, the face of a gentleman.

But it was too evident that he felt little sense of responsibility for the maintenance of the conversation. He sat back in a chair of exceptionable comfortableness, and allowed Beverley Byrd to discourse with him; a privilege which Byrd exercised fitfully, for his heart was in the talk that Sharlee was dutifully supporting with Mr. Miller. Into this talk he resolutely declined to be drawn, but his ear was alert for opportunities—which came not infrequently—to thrust in a polished oar to the discomfiture of the intruder.

Not that he would necessarily care to do it, but the runner could read Mr. Miller, without a glass, at one hundred paces' distance. He was of the climber type, a self-made man in the earlier and less inspiring stages of the making. Culture had a dangerous fascination for him. He adored to talk of books; a rash worship, it seemed, since his but bowing acquaintance with them trapped him frequently into mistaken identities over which Sharlee with difficulty kept a straight face, while Byrd palpably rejoiced.

"You know *Thanatopsis*, of course," he would ask, with a rapt and glowing eye—"Lord Byron's beautiful poem on the philosophy of life? Now that is my idea of what poetry ought to be, Miss Weyland...."

And Beverley Byrd, breaking his remark to Queed off short in the middle, would turn to Sharlee with a face of studious calm and say:—

"Will you ever forget, Sharlee, the first time you read the other *Thanatopsis*—the one by William Cullen Bryant? Don't you remember how it looked—with the picture of Bryant—in the old Fifth Reader?"

Mr. Miller proved that he could turn brick-red, but he learned nothing from experience.

In time, the talk between the two young men, which had begun so desultorily, warmed up. Byrd had read something besides the Fifth Reader, and Queed had discovered before to-night that he had ideas to express. Their conversation progressed with waxing interest, from the President's message to the causes of the fall of Rome, and thence by wholly logical transitions to the French Revolution and Woman's Suffrage. Byrd gradually became so absorbed that he almost, but not quite, neglected to keep Mr. Miller in his place. As for Queed, he spoke in defense of the "revolt of woman" for five minutes without interruption, and his masterly sentences finally drew the silence and attention of Mr. Miller himself.

"Who is that fellow?" he asked in an undertone. "I didn't catch his name."

Sharlee told him.

"He's got a fine face," observed Mr. Miller. "I've made quite a study of faces, and I never saw one just like his—so absolutely on one note, if you know what I mean."

"What note is that?" asked Sharlee, interested by him for the only time so long as they both did live.

"Well, it's not always easy to put a name to it, but I'd call it ... *honesty.—If* you know what I mean."

Mr. Miller stayed until half-past ten. The door had hardly shut upon him when Byrd, too, rose.

"Oh, don't go, Beverley!" protested Sharlee. "I've hardly spoken to you."

"Duty calls," said Byrd. "I'm going to walk home with Mr. Miller."

"Beverley—don't! You were quite horrid enough while he was here." "But you spoiled it all by being so unnecessarily agreeable! It is my business, as your friend and well-wisher, to see that he doesn't carry away too jolly a memory of his visit. Take lunch downtown with me to-morrow, won't you, Mr. Queed—at the Business Men's Club? I want to finish our talk about the Catholic nations, and why they're decadent."

Queed said that he would, and Byrd hurried away to overtake Mr. Miller. Or, perhaps that gentleman was only a pretext, and the young man's experienced eye had read that any attempt to outsit the learned assistant editor was foredoomed to failure.

"I'm so glad you stayed," said Sharlee, as Queed reseated himself. "I shouldn't have liked not to exchange a word with you on your first visit here."

"Oh! This is not my first visit, you may remember."

"Your first voluntary visit, perhaps I should have said."

He let his eyes run over the room, and she could see that he was thinking, half-unconsciously, of the last time when he and she had sat here.

"I had no idea of going," he said absently, "till I had the opportunity of speaking to you."

A brief silence followed, which clearly did not embarrass him, at any rate. Sharlee, feeling the necessity of breaking it, still puzzling herself with speculations as to what had put it into his head to come, said at random:—

"Oh, do tell me—how is old Père Goriot?"

"Père Goriot? I never heard of him."

"Oh, forgive me! It is a name we used to have, long ago, for Professor Nicolovius."

A shadow crossed his brow. "He is extremely well, I believe."

"You are still glad that you ran off with him to live *tête-à-tête* in a bridal cottage?"

"Oh, I suppose so. Yes, certainly!"

His frank face betrayed that the topic was unwelcome to him. For he hated all secrets, and this secret, from this girl, was particularly obnoxious to him. And beyond all that part of it, how could he analyze for anybody his periods of strong revolt against his association with Henry G. Surface, followed by longer and stranger periods when, quite apart from the fact that his word was given and regrets were vain, his consciousness embraced it as having a certain positive value?

He rose restlessly, and in rising his eye fell upon the little clock on the mantel.

"Good heavens!" broke from him. "I had no idea it was so late! I must go directly. Directly."

"Oh, no, you mustn't think of it. Your visit to me has just begun—all this time you have been calling on Beverley Byrd."

"Why do you think I came here to-night?" he asked abruptly.

Sharlee, from her large chair, smiled. "*I* think to see me."

"Oh!—Yes, naturally, but—"

"Well, I think this is the call plainly due me from my Reunion party last year."

"No! Not at all! At the same time, it has been since that day that I have had you on my mind so much."

He said this in a perfectly matter-of-fact voice, but a certain nervousness had broken through into his manner. He took a turn up and down the room, and returned suddenly to his seat.

"Oh, have you had me on your mind?"

"Do you remember my saying that day," he began, resolutely, "that I was not sure whether I had got the better of you or you had got the better of me?"

"I remember very well."

"Well, I have come to tell you that—you have won."

He had plucked a pencil from the arsenal of them in his breast-pocket, and with it was beating a noiseless tattoo on his open left palm. With an effort he met her eyes.

"I say you were right," came from him nervously. "Don't you hear?"

"Was I? Won't you tell me just what you mean?"

"Don't you know?"

"Really I don't think I do. You see, when I used that expression that day, I was speaking only of the editorship—"

"But I was speaking of a theory of life. After all, the two things seem to have been bound together rather closely—just as you said."

He restored his pencil to his pocket, palpably pulled himself together, and proceeded:

"Oh, my theory was wholly rational—far more rational than yours; rationally it was perfect. It was a wholly logical recoil from the idleness, the lack of purpose, the slipshod self-indulgence under many names that I saw, and see, everywhere about me. I have work to do—serious work of large importance—and it seemed to me my duty to carry it through at all hazards. I need not add that it still seems so. Yet it was a life's work, already well along, and there was no need for me to pay an excessive price for mere speed. I elected to let everything go but intellect; I felt that I must do so; and in consequence, by the simplest sort of natural law, all the rest of me was shriveling up—had shriveled up, you will say. Yet I knew very well that my intellect was not the biggest part of me. I have always understood that.... Still, it seems that I required you to rediscover it for me in terms of everyday life...."

"No, no!" she interrupted, "I didn't do that. Most of it you did yourself. The start, the first push—don't you know?—it came from Fifi."

"Well," he said slowly, "what was Fifi but you again in miniature?"

"A great deal else," said Sharlee.

Her gaze fell. She sunk her chin upon her hand, and a silence followed, while before the mind's eye of each rose a vision of Fifi, with her wasted cheeks and great eyes.

"As I say, I sacrificed everything to reason," continued Queed, obviously struggling against embarrassment, "and yet pure reason was never my ideal. I have impressed you as a thoroughly selfish person—you have told me that—and so far as my immediate environment is concerned, I have been, and am. So it may surprise you to be told that a life of service has been from the beginning my ambition and my star. Of course I have always interpreted service in the broadest sense, in terms of the world; that was why I deliberately excluded all purely personal applications of it. Yet it is from a proper combination of reason with—the sociologist's 'consciousness of kind'—fellow-feeling, sympathy, if you prefer, that is derived a life of fullest efficiency. I have always understood the truth of this formula as applied to peoples. It seems that I—rather missed its force as to individuals. I—I am ready to admit that an individual life can draw an added meaning—and richness from a service, not of the future, but of the present—not of the race but ... well, of the unfortunate on the doorstep. Do you understand," he asked abruptly, "what I am trying to tell you?"

She assured him that she understood perfectly.

A slow painful color came into his face.

"Then you appreciate the nature and the size of the debt I owe you."

"Oh, no, no, no! If I have done anything at all to help you," said Sharlee, considerably moved, "then I am very glad and proud. But as for what you speak of ... no, no, people always do these things for themselves. The help comes from within—"

"Oh, *don't* talk like that!" broke from him. "You throw out the idea somehow that I consider that I have undergone some remarkable conversion and transformation. I haven't done anything of the sort. I am just the same as I always was. Just the same.... Only now I am willing to admit, as a scientific truth, that time given to things not in themselves directly productive, can be made to pay a good dividend. If what I said led you to think that I meant more than that, then I have, for once, expressed myself badly. I tell you this," he went on hurriedly, "simply because you once interested yourself in trying to convince me of the truth of these views. Some of the things you said that night managed to stick. They managed to stick. Oh, I give you that. I suppose you might say that they gradually became like mottoes or texts—

not scientific, of course ... personal. Therefore, I thought it only fair to tell you that while my cosmos is still mostly Ego—I suppose everybody's is in one way or another—I have—made changes, so that I am no longer wholly out of relation with life."

"I am glad you wanted to tell me," said Sharlee, "but I have known it for—oh, the longest time."

"In a certain sense," he hurried on—"quite a different sense—I should say that your talk—the only one of the kind I ever had—did for me the sort of thing ... that most men's mothers do for them when they are young."

She made no reply.

"Perhaps," he said, almost defiantly, "you don't like my saying that?"

"Oh, yes! I like it very much."

"And yet," he said, "I don't think of you as I fancy a man would think of his mother, or even of his sister. It is rather extraordinary. It has become clear to me that you have obtained a unique place in my thought—in my regard. Well, good-night."

She looked up at him, without, however, quite meeting his eyes.

"Oh! Do you think you must go?"

"Well—yes. I have said everything that I came to say. Did you want me to stay particularly?"

"Not if you feel that you shouldn't. You've been very good to give me a whole evening, as it is."

"I'll tell you one more thing before I go."

He took another turn up and down the room, and halted frowning in front of her.

"I am thinking of making an experiment in practical social work next year. What would be your opinion of a free night-school for working boys?"

Sharlee, greatly surprised by the question, said that the field was a splendid one.

He went on at once: "Technical training, of course, would be the nominal basis of it. I could throw in, also, boxing and physical culture. Buck Klinker would be delighted to help there. By the way, you must know Klinker: he has some first-rate ideas about what to do for the working population. Needless to say, both the technical and physical training would be only baits to draw attendance, though both could be made very valuable. My main plan is along a new line. I want to teach what no other school attempts—only one thing, but that to be hammered in so that it can never be forgotten."

Queed A Novel | 249

"What is that?"

"You might sum it all up as the doctrine of individual responsibility."

She echoed his term inquiringly, and he made a very large gesture.

"I want to see if I can teach boys that they are not individuals—not unrelated atoms in a random universe. Teach them that they live in a world of law—of evolution by law—that they are links, every one of them, in a splendid chain that has been running since life began, and will run on to the end of time. Knock into their heads that no chain is stronger than its weakest link, and that *this means them*. Don't you see what a powerful socializing force there is in the sense of personal responsibility, if cultivated in the right direction? A boy may be willing to take his chances on going to the bad— economically and socially, as well as morally—if he thinks that it is only his own personal concern. But he will hesitate when you once impress upon him that, in doing so, he is blocking the whole magnificent procession. My plan would be to develop these boys' social efficiency by stamping upon them the knowledge that the very humblest of them holds a trusteeship of cosmic importance."

"I understand.... How splendid—not to practice sociology on them, but to teach it to them—"

"But could we get the boys?"

She felt that the unconsciousness with which he took her into partnership was one of the finest compliments that had ever been paid her.

"Oh, I think so! The Department has all sorts of connections, as well as lots of data which would be useful in that way. How Mr. Dayne will welcome you as an ally! And I, too. I think it is fine of you, Mr. Queed, so generous and kind, to—"

"Not at all! Not in the least! I beg you," he interrupted, irritably, "not to go on misunderstanding me. I propose this simply as an adjunct to my own work. It is simply in the nature of a laboratory exercise. In five years the experiment might enable me to check up some of my own conclusions, and so prove very valuable to me."

"In the meantime the experiment will have done a great deal for a certain number of poor boys—unfortunates on your doorstep...."

"That," he said shortly, "is as it may be. But—"

"Mr. Queed," said Sharlee, "why are you honest in every way but one? Why won't you admit that you have thought of this school because you would like to do something to help in the life of this town?"

"Because I am not doing anything of the sort! Why will you harp on that one string? Good heavens! Aren't you yourself the author of the sentiment that a sociologist ought to have some first-hand knowledge of the problems of society?"

Standing, he gazed down at her, frowning insistently, bent upon staring her out of countenance; and she looked up at him with a Didymus smile which slowly grew. Presently his eyes fell.

"I cannot undertake," he said, in his stiffest way, "to analyze all my motives at all times for your satisfaction. They have nothing whatever to do with the present matter. The sole point up for discussion is the practical question of getting such a school started. Keep it in mind, will you? Give some thought as to ways and means. Your experience with the Department should be helpful to me in getting the plan launched."

"Certainly I will. If you don't object, I'll talk with Mr. Dayne about it, too. He—"

"All right. I don't object. Well, good-night."

Sharlee rose and held out her hand. His expression, as he took and shook it, suddenly changed.

"I suppose you think I have acquired the habit," he said, with an abrupt recurrence of his embarrassment, "of coming to you for counsel and assistance?"

"Well, why shouldn't you?" she answered seriously. "I have had the opportunity and the time to learn some things—"

"You can't dismiss your kindness so easily as that."

"Oh, I don't think I have been particularly kind."

"Yes, you have. I admit that. You have."

He took the conversation with such painful seriousness that she was glad to lighten it with a smile.

"If you persist in thinking so, you might feel like rewarding me by coming to see me soon again."

"Yes, yes! I shall come to see you soon again. Certainly. Of course," he added hastily, "it is desirable that I should talk with you more at length about my school."

He was staring at her with a conflict of expressions in which, curiously enough, pained bewilderment seemed uppermost. Sharlee laughed, not quite at her ease.

"Do you know, I am still hoping that some day you will come to see me, not to talk about anything definite—just to talk."

"As to that," he replied, "I cannot say. Good-night."

Forgetting that he had already shaken hands, he now went through with it again. This time the ceremony had unexpected results. For now at the first touch of her hand, a sensation closely resembling chain-lightning sprang up his arm, and tingled violently down through all his person. It was as if his arm had not merely fallen suddenly asleep, but was singing uproariously in its slumbers.

"I'm so glad you came," said Sharlee.

He retired in a confusion which he was too untrained to hide. At the door he wheeled abruptly, and cleared himself, with a white face, of evasions that were torturing his conscience.

"I will not say that a probable benefit to the boys *never* entered into my thoughts about the school. Nor do I say that my next visit will be *wholly* to talk about definite things, as you put it. For part of the time, I daresay I should like—just to talk."

Sharlee went upstairs, and stood for a long time gazing at herself in the mirror. Vainly she tried to glean from it the answer to a most interesting conundrum: Did Mr. Queed still think her very beautiful?

CHAPTER XXV

Recording a Discussion about the Reformatory between Editor West and his Dog-like Admirer, the City Boss; and a Briefer Conversation between West and Prof. Nicolovius's Boarder.

About one o'clock the telephone rang sharply, and Queed, just arrived for the afternoon work and alone in the office, answered it. It was the Rev. Mr. Dayne, Secretary of the Department of Charities; he had learned that the reformatory bill was to be called up in the house next day. The double-faced politicians of the machine, said Mr. Dayne, with their pretended zeal for economy, were desperately afraid of the Post. Would Mr. Queed be kind enough to hit a final ringing blow for the right in to-morrow's paper?

"That our position to-day is as strong as it is," said the kind, firm voice, "is due largely to your splendid work, Mr. Queed. I say this gladly, and advisedly. If you will put your shoulder to the wheel just once more, I am confident that you will push us through. I shall be eternally grateful, and so will the State. For it is a question of genuine moral importance to us all."

Mr. Dayne received assurance that Mr. Queed would do all that he could for him. He left the telephone rather wishing that the assistant editor could sometimes be inspired into verbal enthusiasm. But of his abilities the Secretary did not entertain the smallest doubt, and he felt that day that his long fight for the reformatory was as good as won.

Hanging up the receiver, Queed leaned back in his swivel chair and thoughtfully filled a pipe, which he smoked nowadays with an experienced and ripened pleasure. At once he relapsed into absorbed thought. Though he answered Mr. Dayne calmly and briefly according to his wont, the young man's heart was beating faster with the knowledge that he stood at the crisis of his longest and dearest editorial fight. He expected to win it. The whole subject, from every conceivable point of view, was at his fingers' ends. He knew exactly what to say; his one problem was how to say it in the most irresistible way possible.

Yet Queed, tilted back in his chair, and staring out over the wet roofs, was not thinking of the reformatory. He was thinking, not of public matters at all, but of the circumstances of his curious life with Henry G. Surface; and his thoughts were not agreeable in the least.

Not that he and the "old professor" did not get along well together. It was really surprising how well they did get along. Their dynamic interview of last June had at once been buried out of sight, and since then their days had flowed along with unbroken smoothness. If there had been times when the young man's thought recoiled from the compact and the intimacy, his manner never betrayed any sign of it. On the contrary, he found himself mysteriously answering the growing dependence of the old man with a growing sense of responsibility toward him, and discovering in the process a curious and subtle kind of compensation.

What troubled Queed about Nicolovius—as the world called him—was his money. He, Queed, was in part living on this money, eating it, drinking it, sleeping on it. Of late the old man had been spending it with increasing freedom, constantly enlarging the comforts of the joint ménage. He had reached, in fact, a scale of living which constantly thrust itself on Queed's consciousness as quite beyond the savings of a poor old school teacher. And if this appearance were true, where did the surplus come from?

The question had knocked unpleasantly at the young man's mind before now. This morning he faced it, and pondered deeply. A way occurred to him by which, possibly, he might turn a little light upon this problem. He did not care to take it; he shrank from doing anything that might seem like spying upon the man whose bread he broke thrice daily. Yet it seemed to him that a point had now been reached where he owed his first duty to himself.

"Come in," he said, looking around in response to a brisk knock upon his shut door; and there entered Plonny Neal, whom Queed, through the Mercury, knew very well now.

"Hi there, Doc! Playin' you was Horace Greeley?"

Mr. Neal opened the connecting door into West's office, glanced through, found it empty, and shut the door again. Whether he was pleased or the reverse over this discovery, his immobile countenance gave no hint; but the fact was that he had called particularly to see West on a matter of urgent private business.

"I was on the floor and thought I'd say howdy," he remarked pleasantly. "Say, Doc, I been readin' them reformatory drools of yours. Me and all the boys."

"I'm glad to hear it. They are certain to do you good."

Queed smiled. He had a genuine liking for Mr. Neal, which was not affected by the fact that their views differed diametrically on almost every subject under the sun.

Mr. Neal smiled, too, more enigmatically, and made a large gesture with his unlighted cigar.

"I ain't had such good laughs since Tommy Walker, him that was going to chase me out of the city f'r the tall timber, up and died. But all the same, I hate to see a likely young feller sittin' up nights tryin' to make a laughin' stock of himself."

"The last laughs are always the best, Mr. Neal. Did you ever try any of them?"

"You're beat to a pappyer mash, and whistlin' to keep your courage."

"Listen to my whistle day after to-morrow—"

But the door had shut on Mr. Neal, who had doubtless read somewhere that the proper moment to terminate a call is on some telling speech of one's own.

"I wonder what he's up to," mused Queed.

He brought his chair to horizontal and addressed himself to his reformatory article. He sharpened his pencil; tangled his great hand into his hair; and presently put down an opening sentence that fully satisfied him, his own sternest critic. Then a memory of his visitor returned to his mind, and he thought pleasurably:

"Plonny knows he is beaten. That's what's the matter with him."

Close observers had often noted, however, that that was very seldom the matter with Plonny, and bets as to his being beaten were always to be placed with diffidence and at very long odds. Plonny had no idea whatever of being beaten on the reformatory measure: on the contrary, it was the reformatory measure which was to be beaten. Possibly Mr. Neal was a white-souled patriot chafing under threatened extravagance in an economy year. Possibly he was impelled by more machine-like exigencies, such as the need of just that hundred thousand dollars to create a few nice new berths for the "organization." The man's motives are an immaterial detail. The sole point worth remembering is that Plonny Neal had got it firmly in his head that there should be no reformatory legislation that year.

It was Mr. Neal's business to know men, and he was esteemed a fine business man. Leaving the assistant editor, he sallied forth to find the editor. It might have taken Queed an hour to put his hand on West just then. Plonny did it in less than six minutes.

West was at Semple's (formerly Semple & West's), where he looked in once a day just to see what the market was doing. This was necessary, as he sometimes explained, in order that the *Post's* financial articles might have that authoritativeness which the paper's position demanded. West enjoyed the good man-talk at Semple's; the atmosphere of frank, cheery commercialism made a pleasant relief from the rarer altitudes of the uplift. He stood chatting gayly with a group of habitués, including some of the best known men of the town. All greeted Plonny pleasantly, West cordially. None of our foreign critics can write that the American man is a moral prude. On two occasions, Plonny had been vindicated before the grand jury by the narrow margin of one vote. Yet he was much liked as a human sinner who had no pretenses about him, and who told a good story surpassingly well.

Ten minutes later Mr. Neal and Mr. West met in a private room at Berringer's, having arrived thither by different routes. Over a table, the door shut against all-comers, Mr. Neal went at once to the point, apologizing diffidently for a "butting in" which Mr. West might resent, but which he, Mr. West's friend, could no longer be restrained from. The *Post*, he continued, had been going along splendidly—"better'n under Cowles even—everybody says so—" and then, to the sorrow and disappointment of the new editor's admirers, up had come this dashed old reformatory business and spoiled everything.

West, whose thoughts had unconsciously run back to his last private talk with Plonny—the talk about getting in line—good-naturedly asked his friend if he was really lined up with the wire-pulling moss-backs who were fighting the reformatory bill.

"You just watch me and see," said Plonny, with humorous reproachfulness. "No charge f'r lookin', and rain checks given in case of wet grounds."

"Then for once in your life, anyhow, you've called the turn wrong, Plonny. This institution is absolutely necessary for the moral and social upbuilding of the State. It would be necessary if it cost five times one hundred thousand dollars, and it's as sure to come as judgment day."

"Ain't it funny!" mused Plonny. "Take a man like you, with fine high ideas and all, and let anything come up and pass itself off f'r a maw'l question and he'll go off half-cocked ten times out of ten."

"Half-cocked!" laughed West. "We've been studying this question three years."

"Yes, and began your studies with your minds all made up."

Plonny fastened upon the young man a gaze in which superior wisdom struggled unsuccessfully with overwhelming affection. "You know what it is, Mr. West? You've been took in, you've bit on a con game like a hungry pike. Excuse my speaking so plain, but I told you a long time ago I was mightily interested in you."

"Speak as plain as you like, Plonny. In fact, my only request at the moment is that you will speak plainer still. Who is it that has taken me in, and who is working this little con game you mention?"

"Rev. George Dayne of the Charities," said Plonny at once. "You mentioned wire-pulling just now. Lemme tell you that in the Rev. George you got the champeen wire-puller of the lot, the king politician of them all—the only one in this town, I do believe, could have thrown a bag as neat over *your* head, Mr. West."

"Why, Plonny! Much learning has made you mad! I know Dayne like a book, and he's as straightforward a fellow as ever lived."

Mr. Neal let his eyes fall to the table-top and indulged in a slow smile, which appeared to be struggling courteously, but without hope, to suppress.

"O' course you got a right to your opinion, Mr. West."

A brief silence ensued, during which a tiny imp of memory whispered into West's ear that Miss Weyland herself had commented on the Rev. Mr. Dayne's marvelous gifts as a lobbyist.

"I'm a older man than you," resumed Neal, with precarious smilelessness, "and mebbe I've seen more of practical poltix. It would be a strange thing, you might say, if at my time of life, I didn't know a politician when I passed him in the road. Still, don't you take my word for it. I'm only repeating what others say when I tell you that Parson Dayne wants to be Governor of this State some day. That surprises you a little, hey? You was kind of thinking that 'Rev.' changed the nature of a man, and that ambition never thought of keeping open f'r business under a high-cut vest, now wasn't you? Well, I've seen funny things in my time. I'd say that the parson wants this reformatory some f'r the good of the State, and mostly f'r the good of Mr. Dayne. Give it to him, with the power of appointing employees—add this to what he's already got—and in a year he'll have the prettiest little private machine ever you did see. I don't ask you to believe me. All I ask is f'r you to stick a pin in what I say, and see 'f it don't come true."

West mused, impressed against his will. "You're wrong, Plonny, in my opinion, and if you were ten times right, what of it? You seem to think that the *Post* is advocating this reformatory because Dayne has asked for it. The *Post* is doing nothing of the sort. It is advocating the reformatory because it has studied this question to the bottom for itself, because it knows—"

"Right! Good f'r you!" exclaimed Mr. Neal, much gratified. "That's just what I tell the boys when they say you're playin' poltix with the little dominie. And that," said he, briskly, "is just why I'm *for* the reformatory, in spite of Rev. Dayne's little games."

"You're for it! You said just now that you were opposed to it."

"Not to the reformatory, Mr. West. Not at all. I'm only opposed to spending a hundred thousand dollars for it in a poverty year."

"Oh! You want the reformatory, but you don't want it now. That's where you stand, is it?"

"Yes, and everybody else that understands just what the situation is. I believe in this reformatory—the *Post* converted me, that's a fact—and if you'll only let her stand two years, take my word for it, she'll go through with a whoop. But if you're going to hurry the thing—"

"What's your idea of hurry exactly? The war has been over forty years—"

"And look how splendid we've got along these forty years without the reformatory! Will you care to say, Mr. West, that we couldn't make it forty-two without bringing great danger to the State?"

"No, certainly not. But the point is—"

"The point is that if we spend all this money now, the people will kick the party out at the next election. I wouldn't admit this to many, 'cause I'm ashamed of it, but it's gospel truth. Mr. West," said Plonny, earnestly, "I *know* you want the *Post* to stand for the welfare of the party—"

"Certainly. And it has been my idea that evidence of sane interest in public morals was a pretty good card for—"

"So it would be at any ordinary time. But it's mighty different when the people from one end of the State to the other are howling economy and saying that all expenses must go to bed-rock or they'll know the reason why. There's the practical side of it—look at it f'r a minute. The legislature was elected by these people on a platform promising strictest economy. They're tryin' to carry out their promise faithfully. They turn down and postpone some mighty good plans to advance the progress of the State. They rejuice salaries in various departments"—(one was the exact number)—"heelers come up lookin' f'r jobs, and they send 'em away empty-handed and sore. Old-established institutions, that have been doin' grand work upbuildin' the State f'r years, are told that they must do with a half or three quarters of their appropriations f'r the next two years. You've seen all this happen, Mr. West?"

West admitted that he had.

"Well, now when everything is goin' smooth and promisin', you come along and tell 'em they got to shell out a *hundred thousand dollars* right away f'r a brand-new institution, with an annual appropriation to keep it up. Now s'pose they do what you tell 'em. What happens? You think there's no poltix at all in this reformatory business, but I can tell you the Republicans won't take such a view as that. They'll say that the party spent a hundred thousand dollars of the people's money in a hard times year, just to make a few more jobs f'r favorites. They'll throw that up at us from every stump in the State. And when our leaders explain that it was done for the maw'l good of the State, they'll give us the laugh—same as they did when we established the Foundling Hospital in '98. Now I tell you the party can't stand any talk of that kind this year. We're on shaky ground right now f'r the same reason that we're all so proud of—spendin' money f'r the maw'l uplift of the State. We either got to slow up f'r awhile or take a licking. That's what all the talk comes down to—one simple question: Will we hold off this big expense f'r just two years, or will we send the old party down to defeat?"

West laughed, not quite comfortably.

In all this dialogue, Mr. Neal had over him the enormous advantage of exact and superior knowledge. To tell the truth, West knew very little about the reformatory situation, and considered it, among the dozens of matters in which he was interested, rather a small issue. Having turned the campaign over to his assistant, he had dismissed it from his mind; and beyond his general conviction that the reformatory would be a good thing for the State, he had only the sketchiest acquaintance with the arguments that were being used pro and con. Therefore Plonny Neal's passionate earnestness surprised him, and Plonny's reasoning, which he knew to be the reasoning of the thoroughly informed State leaders, impressed him very decidedly. Of the boss's sincerity he never entertained a doubt; to question that candid eye was impossible. That Plonny had long been watching him with interest and admiration, West knew very well. It began to look to him very much as though Queed, through excess of sociological zeal, had allowed himself to be misled, and that the paper's advanced position was founded on theory without reference to existing practical conditions.

West keenly felt the responsibility of his post. To safeguard and promote the welfare of the Democratic party had long been a cardinal principle of the paper whose utterances he now controlled. Still, it must be true that Neal was painting the situation in colors altogether too black.

"You're a pretty good stump performer yourself, Plonny. Don't you know that exactly the same argument will be urged two years from now?"

"I know it won't," said Plonny with the calmness of absolute conviction. "A fat legislature *always* follows a lean one. They come in strips, same as a shoulder of bacon."

"Well! I wouldn't think much of a party whose legs were so weak that a little step forward—everybody knows *it's* forward—would tumble it over in a heap."

"The party! I ain't thinking of the *party*, Mr. West. I'm thinking," said Neal, the indignation in his voice giving way to a sudden apologetic softness, "of *you*."

"Me? What on earth have I got to do with it?" asked West, rather touched by the look of dog-like affection in the other's eyes.

"Everything. If the party gets let in for this extravagance, you'll be the man who did it."

There was a silence, and then West said, rather nobly:

"Well, I suppose I will have to stand that. I must do what I think is right, you know, and take the consequences."

"Two years from now," said Mr. Neal, gently, "there wouldn't be no consequences."

"Possibly not," said West, in a firm voice.

"While the consequences now," continued Mr. Neal, still more gently, "would be to put you in very bad with the party leaders. Fine men they are, but they never forgive a man who puts a crimp into the party. You'd be a marked man to the longest day you lived!"

"Well, Plonny! I'm not asking anything of the party leaders—"

"But suppose some of your friends wanted to ask something for *you*?"

Suddenly Plonny leaned over the table, and began speaking rapidly and earnestly.

"Listen here, Mr. West. I understand your feelings and your position just like they was print, and I was reading them over your shoulder. You're walking with y'r eyes on the skies, and you don't like to look at the ground to see that you don't break nothing as you go forward. Your mind's full of the maw'l idea and desire to uplift the people, and it's kind of painful to you to stop and look at the plain practical way by which things get done. But I tell you that everybody who ever got anything big done in this world, got it done in a practical way. All the big men that you and I admire—all the public leaders and governors and reform mayors and so on—got where they have by doing practical good in a practical way. Now, you don't like me to say that if you do so-and-so, you'll be in bad with the State leaders, f'r that looks to you as if I thought you could be infloonced by what would be your personal advantage. And I honor you f'r them feelin's which is just what I knew you'd had, or I wouldn't be here talkin' to you now. But you mustn't blame others if they ain't as partic'lar, mebbe, as to how things might *look*. You mustn't blame y'r friends—and you've got a sight more of them than you have any idea of—if they feel all broke up to see you get in bad, both for your own sake and f'r the sake of the party."

Plonny's voice trembled with earnestness; West had had no idea that the man admired him so much.

"You want to serve the people, Mr. West? How could you do it better than in public orf'ce. Lemme talk to you straight f'r once—will you? Or am I only offendin' you by buttin' in this way, without having ever been asked?"

West gave his admirer the needed assurance.

"I'm glad of it, f'r I can hardly keep it in my system any longer. Listen here, Mr. West. As you may have heard, there's to be a primary f'r city orf'cers in June. Secret ballot or no secret ballot, the organization's going to win. You know that. Now, who'll the organization put up f'r Mayor? From what I hear, they dassen't put up any old machine hack, same's they been doin' f'r years. They might want to do it, but they're a-scared the people won't stand f'r it. From what little I hear, the feelin's strong that they *got* to put up some young progressive public-spirited man of the reformer type. Now s'posin' the friends of a certain fine young man, sittin' not a hundred miles from this table, had it in their minds to bring *him* forward f'r the nomination. This young man might say he wasn't seekin' the orf'ce and didn't want it, but I say public orf'ce is a duty, and no man that wants to serve the people can refuse it, partic'larly when he may be needed to save the party. And now I ask you this, Mr. West: What show would the friends of this young man have, if he had a bad spot on his record? What chance'd there be of namin' to lead the party in the city the *man who had knifed the party in the State*?"

West's chin rested upon his hand; his gaze fell dreamily upon the table-top. Before his mind's eye there had unrolled a favorite vision—a white meadow of faces focussed breathlessly upon a great orator. He recalled himself with a start, a stretch, and a laugh.

"Aren't you wandering rather carelessly into the future, Plonny?"

"If I am," said Mr. Neal, solemnly, "it's because you stand at the crossroads to-day."

West found the office deserted, his assistant being gone for lunch. He finished two short articles begun earlier in the day, and himself departed with an eye to food. Later, he had to attend a couple of board meetings, which ran off into protracted by-talk, and the rainy twilight had fallen before his office knew him again.

Not long after, Queed, already hatted and overcoated to go, pushed open the connecting door and entered. The two chatted a moment of the make-up of next day's "page." Presently West said: "By the bye, written anything about the reformatory?"

"Anything!" echoed Queed, with a faint smile. "You might say that I've written everything about it—the best article I ever wrote, I should say. It's our last chance, you know."

Queed thought of Eva Bernheimer, and a light crept into his ordinarily impassive eye. At the same time, West's ordinarily buoyant face fell a little.

"That so? Let me see how you've handled it, will you?"

"Certainly," said Queed, showing no surprise, though it was many a day since any composition of his had undergone supervision in that office.

It was on the tip of West's tongue to add, "I rather think we've been pressing that matter too hard," but he checked himself. Why should he make any explanation to his assistant? Was it not the fact that he had trusted the young man too far already?

Queed brought his article and laid it on West's desk, his face very thoughtful now. "If there is any information I can give you about the subject, I'll wait."

West hardly repressed a smile. "Thank you, I think I understand the situation pretty well."

Still Queed lingered and hesitated, most unlike himself. Presently he strolled over to the window and looked down unseeingly into the lamp-lit wetness of Centre Street. In fact, he was the poorest actor in the world, and never pretended anything, actively or passively, without being unhappy.

"It's raining like the mischief," he offered uncomfortably.

"Cats and dogs," said West, his fingers twiddling with Queed's copy.

"By the way," said Queed, turning with a poorly done air of casualness, "what is commonly supposed to have become of Henry G. Surface? Do people generally believe that he is dead?"

"Bless your heart, no!" said West, looking up in some surprise at the question. "That kind never die. They invariably live to a green old age—green like the bay-tree."

"I—have gotten very much interested in his story," said Queed, which was certainly true enough. "Where do people think that he is now?"

"Oh, in the West somewhere, living like a fat hog off Miss Weyland's money."

Queed's heart lost a beat. An instinct, swift as a reflex, turned him to the window again; he feared that his face might commit treason. A curious contraction and hardening seemed to be going on inside of him, a chilling petrifaction, and this sensation remained; but in the next instant he felt himself under perfect control, and was calmly saying:—

"Why, I thought the courts took all the money he had."

"They took all they could find. If you've studied high finance you'll appreciate the distinction." Amiably West tapped the table-top with the long point of his pencil, and wished that Queed would restore him his privacy. "Everybody thought at the time, you know, that he had a hundred thousand or so put away where the courts never got hold of it. The general impression was that he'd somehow smuggled it over to the woman he'd been living with—his wife", he said. "She died, I believe, but probably our friend Surface, when he got out, hadn't the slightest trouble in putting his hands on the money."

"No, I suppose not. An interesting story, isn't it? You'll telephone if you need anything to-night?"

"Oh, I shan't need anything. The page is shaping up very satisfactorily, I think. Good-night, my dear fellow."

Left alone, West picked up Queed's closely-written sheets, and leaning back in his chair read them with the closest attention. Involuntarily, his intellect paid a tribute to the writer as he read. The article was masterly. The argument was close and swift, the language impassioned, the style piquant. "Where did he learn to write like that!" wondered West. Here was the whole subject compressed into half a column, and so luminous a half column that the dullest could not fail to understand and admire. Two sarcastic little paragraphs were devoted to stripping the tatters from the nakedness of the economy argument, and these Mr. Queed's chief perused twice.

"The talk of a doctrinaire," mused he presently. "The closet philosopher's ideas. How far afield from the real situation ..."

It was a most fortunate thing, he reflected, that he himself had means of getting exact and accurate information at first hand. Suppose that he had not, that, like some editors, he had simply passed this article in without examination and correction. It would have made the *Post* ridiculous, and decidedly impaired its reputation for common sense and fair play. Whatever should or should not be said, this was certainly no way to talk of honest men, who were trying to conserve the party and who differed from the *Post* only on an unimportant question of detail.

West leaned back in his chair and stared at the farther wall.... For that was exactly what it was—an unimportant detail. The important thing, the one thing that he himself had insisted on, was that the State should have a reformatory. Whether the State had it now or two years from now, made relatively little difference, except to those who, like his editorial assistant, had sunk themselves in the question till their sense of proportion had deserted them. Was not that a fair statement of the case? Whatever he did, he must not let his views be colored by probable effects upon his own future.... Surely, to wait two brief years for the institution, with the positive assurance of it then, could be no hardship to a State which had got along very well without it for all the years of its lifetime. Surely not. Plonny Neal, whose sharp horse sense he would back against any man in the State, was absolutely sound there.

He tried to consider the question with chill judiciality, and believed that he was doing so. But the fervor which Plonny had imparted to it, and the respect which he had for Plonny's knowledge of practical conditions, stood by him, unconsciously guiding his thoughts along the line of least resistance.... Though nobody dared admit it publicly, the party was facing a great crisis; and it was in his hand to save or to wreck it. All eyes were anxiously on the *Post*, which wielded the decisive power. The people had risen with the unreasonable demand that progress be checked for a time, because of the cost of it. The leaders had responded to the best of their ability, but necessary expenses were so great that it was going to be a narrow shave at best—so narrow that another hundred thousand spent would land the whole kettle of fish in the fire. The grand old party would go crashing down the precipice. Was not that a criminal price to pay for getting a reformatory institution two years before the people were ready to pay for it? There was the whole question in a nutshell.

The one unpleasant aspect of this view was Sharlee Weyland, the dearest girl in the world. She would be much disappointed, and, for the first moment, would possibly be somewhat piqued with him personally. He knew that women were extremely unreasonable about these things; they looked at affairs from the emotional point of view, from the point of view of the loose, large "effect." But Sharlee Weyland was highly intelligent and sensible, and he had not the smallest doubt of his ability to make her understand what the unfortunate situation was. He could not tell her everything—Plonny had cautioned secrecy about the real gravity of the crisis—but he would tell her enough to show her how he had acted, with keen regrets, from his sternest sense of public duty. It was a cruel stroke of fate's that his must be the hand to bring disappointment to the girl he loved, but after all, would she not be the first to say that he must never put his regard for her preferences above the larger good of City and State? He could not love her, dear, so well, loved he not honor more.

He picked up Queed's article and glanced again at the astonishing words, words which, invested with the *Post's* enormous prestige, simply kicked and cuffed the party to its ruin. A wave of resentment against his assistant swept through the editor's mind. This was what came of trusting anything to anybody else. If you wanted to be sure that things were done right, do them yourself. Because he had allowed Queed a little rope, that young man had industriously gathered in almost enough to hang, not himself, for he was nothing, but the *Post* and its editor. However, there was no use crying over spilt milk. What was done was done. Fortunately, the *Post's* general position was sound; had not the editor himself dictated it? If the expression of that position in cold type had been gradually carried by a subordinate to a more and more violent extreme, to an intemperance of utterance which closely approached insanity, what was it the editor's duty to do? Obviously to take charge himself and swing the position back to a safe and sane mean, exactly where he had placed it to begin with. That was all that was asked of him—to shift back the paper's position to where he had placed it in the beginning, and by so doing to save the party from wreck. Could a sensible man hesitate an instant? And in return....

West's gaze wandered out of the window, and far on into the beyond.... His friends were watching him, silently but fearfully. Who and what these friends were his swift thought did not stay to ask. His glamorous fancy saw them as a great anxious throng, dominant men, yet respectful, who were trembling lest he should make a fatal step—to answer for it with his political life. Public life—he rejected the term political life—was of all things what he was preeminently fitted for. How else could a man so fully serve his fellows?—how so surely and strongly promote the uplift? And Plonny Neal had served notice on him that he stood to-day on the crossroads to large public usefulness. The czar of them all, the great Warwick who made and unmade kings by the lifting of his finger, had told him, as plain as language could speak, that he, West, was his imperial choice for the mayoralty, with all that that foreshadowed.... Truly, he had served his apprenticeship, and was meet for his opportunity. For eight long months he had stood in line, doing his duty quietly and well, asking no favor of anybody. And now at last Warwick had beckoned him and set the mystic star upon his forehead....

Iridescent visionry enwrapped the young man, and he swam in it goldenly. In time his spirit returned to his body, and he found himself leaning back in a very matter-of-fact chair, facing a very plain question. How could the shifting back, the rationalizing, of the paper's position be accomplished with the minimum of shock? How could he rescue the party with the least possible damage to the *Post's* consistency?

West went to a filing cabinet in the corner of the room, pulled out a large folder marked, *Reformatory*, and, returning to his seat, ran hurriedly through the *Post's* editorials on this subject during the past twelvemonth. Over some of the phrases he ground his teeth. They floated irritatingly in his head as he once more leaned back in his chair and frowned at the opposite wall.

Gradually there took form in his mind a line of reasoning which would appear to grow with some degree of naturalness out of what had gone before, harmonizing the basic continuity of the *Post's* attitude, and minimizing the change in present angle or point of view. His fertile mind played about it, strengthening it, building it up, polishing and perfecting; and in time he began to write, at first slowly, but soon with fluent ease.

CHAPTER XXVI

In which Queed forces the Old Professor's Hand, and the Old Professor takes to his Bed.

Raincoat buttoned to his throat, Queed set his face against the steady downpour. It was a mild, windless night near the end of February, foreshadowing the early spring already nearly due. He had no umbrella, or wish for one: the cool rain in his face was a refreshment and a vivifier.

So the worst had come to the worst, and he had been living for nearly a year on Sharlee Weyland's money, stolen from her by her father's false friend. Wormwood and gall were the fruits that altruism had borne him. Two casual questions had brought out the shameful truth, and these questions could have been asked as easily a year ago as now.

Bitterly did the young man reproach himself now, for his criminal carelessness in regard to the sources of Surface's luxurious income. For the better part of a year he had known the old man for an ex-convict whose embezzlings had run high into six figures. Yet he had gone on fatuously swallowing the story that the money of which the old rogue was so free represented nothing but the savings of a thrifty schoolteacher. A dozen things came back to him now to give the lie to that tale. He thought of the costly books that Surface was constantly buying; the expensive repairs he had made in his rented house; the wine that stood on the dinner-table every night; the casual statement from the old man that he meant to retire from the school at the end of the present session. Was there ever a teacher who could live like this after a dozen years' roving work? And the probability was that Surface had never worked at all until, returning to his own city, he had needed a position as a cover and a blind.

Mathematical computations danced through the young man's brain. He figured that their present scale of living must run anywhere from $3500 to $5000 a year. Surface's income from the school was known to be $900 a year. His income from his lodger was $390 a year. This difference between, say $4000 and $1290, was $2710 a year, or 4 per cent on some $70,000. And this tidy sum was being filched from the purse of Charlotte Lee Weyland, who worked for her living at an honorarium of $75 a month.

Queed walked with his head lowered, bent less against the rain than his own stinging thoughts. At the corner of Seventh Street a knot of young men, waiting under a dripping awning for a car that would not come, cried out gayly to the Doc; they were Mercuries; but the Doc failed to respond to their greetings, or even to hear them. He crossed the humming street, northerly, with an experienced sureness acquired since his exploit with the dog Behemoth; and so came into his own section of the town.

He was an apostle of law who of all things loved harmony. Already his mind was busily at work seeking to restore order out of the ruins of his house. Obviously the first thing to do, the one thing that could not wait an hour, was to get his sense of honesty somehow back again. He must compel Surface to hand over to Miss Weyland immediately every cent of money that he had. The delivery could be arranged easily enough, without any sensational revelations. The letter to Miss Weyland could come from a lawyer in the West; in Australia, if the old man liked; that didn't matter. The one thing that did matter was that he should immediately make restitution as fully as lay within the power of them both.

Surface, of course, would desperately resist such a suggestion. Queed knew of but one club which could drive him to agree to it, one goad which could rowel him to the height. This was his own continued companionship. He could compel Surface to disgorgement only at the price of a new offering of himself to the odious old man who had played false with him as with everybody else. Queed did not hesitate. At the moment every cost seemed small to clear his dearest belonging, which was his personal honesty, of this stain. As for Surface, nothing could make him more detestable in a moral sense than he had been all along. He had been a thief and a liar from the beginning. Once the cleansing storm was over, their unhappy domestic union could go on much as it had done before.

For his part, he must at once set about restoring his half of the joint living expenses consumed during the past nine months. This money could be passed in through the lawyer with the rest, so that she would never know. Obviously, he would have to make more money than he was making now, which meant that he would have to take still more time from his book. There were his original tax articles in the *Post*, which a publisher had asked him at the time to work over into a primer for college use. There might be a few hundreds to be made there. He could certainly place some articles in the reviews. If for the next twelve months he ruthlessly eliminated everything from his life that did not bring in money, he could perhaps push his earnings for the next year to three thousand dollars, which would be enough to see him through....

And busy with thoughts like these, he came home to Surface's pleasant little house, and was greeted by the old man with kindness and good cheer.

It was dinner-time—for they dined at night now, in some state—and they sat down to four dainty courses, cooked and served by the capable Henderson. The table was a round one, so small that the two men could have shaken hands across it without the smallest exertion. By old Surface's plate stood a gold-topped bottle, containing, not the ruddy burgundy which had become customary of late, but sparkling champagne. Surface referred to it, gracefully, as his medicine; doctors, he said, were apparently under the delusion that schoolmasters had bottomless purses. To this pleasantry Queed made no reply. He was, indeed, spare with his remarks that evening, and his want of appetite grieved old Henderson sorely.

The servant brought the coffee and retired. He would not be back again till he was rung for: that was the iron rule. The kitchen was separated from the dining-room by a pantry and two doors. Thus the diners were as private as they were ever likely to be in this world, and in the breast of one of them was something that would brook no more delay.

"Professor," said this one, with a face which gave no sign of inner turmoil, "I find myself obliged to refer once more to—an unwelcome subject."

Surface was reaching for his coffee cup; he was destined never to pick it up. His hand fell; found the edge of the table; his long fingers gripped and closed over it.

"Ah?" he said easily, not pretending to doubt what subject was meant. "I'm sorry. I thought that we had laid the old ghosts for good."

"I thought so, too. I was mistaken, it seems."

Across the table, the two men looked at each other. To Surface, the subject must indeed have been the most unwelcome imaginable, especially when forced upon him with so ominous a directness. Yet his manner was the usual bland mask; his face, rather like a bad Roman senator's in the days of the decline, had undergone no perceptible change.

"When I came here to live with you," said Queed, "I understood, of course, that you would be contributing several times as much toward our joint expenses as I. To a certain degree, you would be supporting me. Naturally, I did not altogether like that. But you constantly assured me, you may remember, that you would rather put your savings into a home than anything else, that you could not manage it without my assistance, and that you considered my companionship as fully offsetting the difference in the money we paid. So I became satisfied that the arrangement was honorable to us both."

Surface spoke with fine courtesy. "All this is so true, your contribution toward making our house a home has been so much greater than my own, that I feel certain nothing can have happened to disturb your satisfaction."

"Yes," said Queed. "I have assumed all the time that the money you were spending here was your own."

There was a silence. Queed looked at the table-cloth. He had just become aware that his task was hateful to him. The one thing to do was to get it over as swiftly and decisively as possible.

"I am at a loss," said the old man, dryly, "to understand where the assumption comes in, in view of the fact that I have stated, more than once—"

"I am forced to tell you that I cannot accept these statements."

For a moment the brilliant eyes looked dangerous. "Are you aware that your language is exceedingly offensive?"

"Yes. I'm very sorry. Nevertheless, this tooth must come out. It has suddenly become apparent to me that you must be spending here the income on hardly less than seventy-five thousand dollars. Do you seriously ask me to believe, now that I directly bring up the matter, that you amassed this by a few years of school-teaching?"

Surface lit a cigarette, and, taking a slow puff, looked unwinkingly into the young man's eyes, which looked as steadily back into his own. "You are mistaken in assuming," he said sternly, "that, in giving you my affection, I have given you any right to cross-examine me in—"

"Yes, you gave it to me when you invited me to your house as, in part, your guest—"

"I am behind the times, indeed, if it is esteemed the privilege of a guest to spy upon his host."

"That," said Queed, quietly, "is altogether unjust. You must know that I am not capable of spying on you. I have, on the contrary, been culpably short-sighted. Never once have I doubted anything you told me until you yourself insisted on rubbing doubts repeatedly into my eyes. Professor," he went on rapidly, "are you aware that those familiar with your story say that, when you—that, after your misfortune, you started life again with a bank account of between one and two hundred thousand dollars?"

The black eyes lit up like two shoe-buttons in the sunlight. "That is a wicked falsehood, invented at the time by a lying reporter—"

"Do you assert that everything you have now has been earned since your misfortune?"

"Precisely that."

The voice was indignantly firm, but Queed, looking into the old man's face, read there as plain as day that he was lying.

"Think a moment," he said sorrowfully. "This is pretty serious, you see. Are you absolutely sure that you carried over nothing at all?"

"In the sight of God, I did not. But let me tell you, my friend—"

A chair-leg scraped on the carpeted floor, and Queed was standing, playing his trump card with a grim face.

"We must say good-by, Professor—now. I'll send for my things in the morning."

"What do you mean, you—"

"That you and I part company to-night. Good-by."

"Stop!" cried Surface. He rose, greatly excited and leaned over the table. A faint flush drove the yellow from his cheek; his eyes were blazing. He shook a menacing finger at close range in Queed's face, which remained entirely unmoved by the demonstration.

"So this is the reward of my kindness and affection! I won't endure it, do you understand? I won't be kicked into the gutter like an old shoe, do you hear? Sit down in that chair. I forbid you to leave the house."

Queed's gaze was more formidable than his own. "Mr. Surface," he said, in a peculiarly quiet voice, "you forget yourself strangely. You are in no position to speak to me like this."

Surface appeared suddenly to agree with him. He fell back into his chair and dropped his face into his hands.

Queed, standing where he was, watched him across the tiny dinner-table and, against his reason, felt very sorry. How humiliating this ripping up of old dishonor was to the proud old man, rogue though he was, he understood well enough. From nobody in the world but him, he knew, would Surface ever have suffered it to proceed as far as this, and this knowledge made him want to handle the knife with as little roughness as possible.

"I—was wrong," said the muffled voice. "I ask your forgiveness for my outbreak."

"You have it."

Surface straightened himself up, and, by an obvious effort, managed to recapture something like his usual smoothness of voice and manner.

"Will you be good enough to sit down? I will tell you what you wish."

"Certainly. Thank you."

Queed resumed his seat. His face was a little pale, but otherwise just as usual. Inwardly, after the moment of critical uncertainty, he was shaken by a tempest of fierce exultation. His club, after all, was going to be strong enough; the old man would give up the money rather than give up him.

Surface picked up his cigarette. All his storm signals had disappeared as by magic.

"I did manage," began the old man, flicking off his ash with an admirable effect of calm, "to save a small nest-egg from the wreck, to keep me from the poorhouse in my old age. I did not wish to tell you this because, with your lack of acquaintance with business methods, the details would only confuse, and possibly mislead, you. I had, too, another reason for wishing to keep it a surprise. You have forced me, against my preferences, to tell you. As to this small pittance," he said, without the flicker of an eye-lash, "any court in the country would tell you that it is fairly and honorably mine."

"Thank you. I appreciate your telling me this." Queed leaned over the table, and began speaking in a quiet, brisk voice. "Now, then, here is the situation. You have a certain sum of money put away somewhere, estimated to be not less than a hundred thousand dollars—"

"Nothing of the sort! Far less than that! A few beggarly thousands, which—"

"Very well—a few thousands. Of course your books will readily show the exact figures. This money was withheld at the time your affairs were settled, and therefore was not applied to reducing the—the loss on the trustee account. Of course, if its existence had been known, it would have been so applied. In other words, the Weyland estate has been deprived to the exact extent of the sum withheld. Fortunately, it is never too late to correct an error of this sort. My idea is that we should make the restitution without the loss of an unnecessary day."

Doubtless the old man had seen it coming; he heard the galling proposal with a face which showed nothing stronger than profound surprise. "Restitution! My dear boy, I owe no restitution to any one."

"You hardly take the position that you have acquired a title to the Weyland trustee funds?"

"Ah, there it is!" purred Surface, making a melancholy gesture. "You see why I did not wish to open up this complicated subject. Your ignorance, if you will pardon me, of modern business procedure, makes it very difficult for you to grasp the matter in its proper bearings. Without going into too much detail, let me try to explain it to you. This settlement of my affairs that you speak of was forcibly done by the courts, in the interest of others, and to my great injury. The rascals set out to cut my throat—was it required of me to whet the knife for them? They set out to strip me of the last penny I had, and they had every advantage, despotic powers, with complete access to all my private papers. If the robbers overlooked something that I had, a bagatelle I needed for the days of my adversity, was it my business to pluck them by the sleeve and turn traitor to myself? Why, the law itself gave me what they passed over. I was declared a bankrupt. Don't you know what that means? It means that the courts assumed responsibility for my affairs, paid off my creditors, and, as a small compensation for having robbed me, wiped the slate clean and declared me free of all claims. And this was twenty-five years ago. My dear boy! Read the Bankruptcy Act. Ask a lawyer, any lawyer—"

"Let us not speak of lawyers—now," interrupted Queed, stirring in his chair. "Let their opinion wait as a last alternative, which, I earnestly hope, need never be used at all. I am not bringing up this point to you now as a legal question, but as a moral one."

"Ah! You do not find that the morals provided by the law are good enough for you, then?"

"If your reading of the law is correct—of which I am not so certain as you are, I fear—it appears that they are not. But—"

"It is my misfortune," interrupted the old man, his hand tightening on the table-edge, "that your sympathies are not with me in the matter. Mistaken sentiment, youthful Quixotism, lead you to take an absurdly distorted view of what—"

"No, I'm afraid not. You see, when stripped of all unnecessary language, the repulsive fact is just this: we are living here on money that was unlawfully abstracted from the Weyland estate. No matter what the law may say, we know that this money morally belongs to its original owners. Now I ask you—"

"Let me put it another way. I can show you exactly where your misapprehension is—"

Queed stopped him short by a gesture. "My mind is so clear on this point that discussion only wastes our time."

The young man's burst of exultation was all but stillborn; already despair plucked chilly at his heart-strings. For the first time the depth of his feeling broke through into his voice: "Say, if you like that I am unreasonable, ignorant, unfair. Put it all down to besotted prejudice.... Can't you restore this money because I ask it? Won't you do it as a favor to me?"

Surface's face became agitated. "I believe there is nothing else in the world—that I wouldn't do for you—a thousand times over—but—"

Then Queed threw the last thing that he had to offer into the scales, namely himself. He leaned over the table and fixed the old man with imploring eyes.

"I'd do my best to make it up to you. I'll—I'll live with you till one or the other of us dies. You'll have somebody to take care of you when you are old, and there will never be any talk of the poorhouse between you and me. It can all be arranged quietly through a lawyer, Professor—and nobody will guess your secret. You and I will find quiet lodgings somewhere, and live together—as friends—live cleanly, honorably, honestly—"

"For God's sake, stop!" said Surface, in a broken-voice. "This is more than I can bear."

So Queed knew that it was hopeless, and that the old man meant to cling to his dishonored money, and let his friend go. He sank back in his chair, sick at heart, and a painful silence fell.

"If I refuse," Surface took up the theme, "it is for your sake as well as mine. My boy, you don't know what you ask. It is charity, mere mad charity to people whom I have no love for, who—"

"Then," said Queed, "two things must happen. First, I must lay the facts before Miss Weyland."

Surface's manner changed; his eyes became unpleasant.

"You are not serious. You can hardly mean to repeat to anybody what I have told you in sacred confidence."

Queed smiled sadly. "No, you have not told me anything in confidence. You have never told me anything until I first found it out for myself, and then only because denial was useless."

"When I told you my story last June, you assured me—"

"However, you have just admitted that what you told me last June was not the truth."

Again their eyes clashed, and Surface, whose face was slowly losing all its color, even the sallowness, found no sign of yielding in those of the younger man.

Queed resumed: "However, I do not mean that I shall tell her who you are, unless you yourself compel me to. I shall simply let her know that you are known to be alive, within reach of the courts, and in possession of a certain sum of money withheld from the trustee funds. This will enable her to take the matter up with her lawyers and, as I believe, bring it before the courts. If her claim is sustained, she would doubtless give you the opportunity to make restitution through intermediaries, and thus sensational disclosures might be avoided. However, I make you no promises about that."

Surface drew a breath; he permitted his face to show signs of relief. "Since my argument and knowledge carry so little weight with you," he said with a fine air of dignity, "I am willing to let the courts convince you, if you insist. But I do beg—"

Queed cut him short; he felt that he could not bear one of the old man's grandiloquent speeches now. "There is one other thing that must be mentioned," he said in a tired voice. "You understand, of course, that I can live here no longer."

"My God! Don't say that! Aren't you satisfied with what you've done to me without that!"

"I haven't done anything to you. Whatever has been done, you have deliberately done to yourself. I have no desire to hurt or injure you. But— what are you thinking about, to imagine that I could continue to live here— on this money?"

"You contradict yourself twice in the same breath! You just said that you would let the courts settle that question—"

"As to the Weyland estate's claim, yes. But I do not let the courts regulate my own sense of honor."

Surface, elbows on the table, buried his face in his hands. Queed slowly rose, a heart of lead in his breast. He had failed. He had offered all that he had, and it had been unhesitatingly kicked aside. And, unless long litigation was started, and unless it ultimately succeeded, Henry G. Surface would keep his loot.

He glanced about the pleasant little dining-room, symbol of the only home he had ever known, where, after all, he had done great work, and been not unhappy. Personally, he was glad to leave it, glad to stand out from the shadow of the ruin of Henry G. Surface. Nevertheless it was a real parting, the end of an epoch in his life, and there was sadness in that. Sadness, too, he saw, deeper than his repugnance and anger, in the bowed figure before him, the lost old man whom he was to leave solitary henceforward. Saddest of all was the consciousness of his own terrible failure.

He began speaking in a controlled voice.

"This interview is painful to us both. It is useless to prolong it. I—have much to thank you for—kindness which I do not forget now and shall not forget. If you ever reconsider your decision—if you should ever need me for anything—I shall be within call. And now I must leave you ... sorrier than I can say that our parting must be like this." He paused: his gaze rested on the bent head, and he offered, without hope, the final chance. "Your mind is quite made up? You are sure that—this—is the way you wish the matter settled?"

Surface took his face from his hands and looked up. His expression was a complete surprise. It was neither savage nor anguished, but ingratiating, complacent, full of suppressed excitement. Into his eyes had sprung an indescribable look of cunning, the look of a broken-down diplomat about to outwit his adversary with a last unsuspected card.

"No, no! Of course I'll not let you leave me like this," he said, with a kind of trembling eagerness, and gave a rather painful laugh. "You force my hand. I had not meant to tell you my secret so soon. You can't guess the real reason why I refuse to give my money to Miss Weyland, even when you ask it, now can you? You can't guess, now can you?"

"I think I can. You had rather have the money than have me."

"Not a bit of it. Nothing of the kind! Personally I care nothing for the money. I am keeping it," said the old man, lowering his voice to a chuckling whisper, "*for you!*" He leaned over the table, fixing Queed with a gaze of triumphant cunning. "I'm going to make you *my heir!* Leave everything I have in the world *to you!*"

A wave of sick disgust swept through the young man, momentarily engulfing his power of speech. Never had the old man's face looked so loathsome to him, never the man himself appeared so utterly detestable.

Surface had risen, whispering and chuckling. "Come up to the sitting-room, my dear boy. I have some papers up there that may open your eyes. You need never work—"

"Stop!" said Queed, and the old man stopped in his tracks. "Can't I make you understand?" he went on, fighting hard for calmness. "Isn't it clear to you that *nothing* could induce me to touch another penny of this money?"

"Ah!" said Surface, in his softest voice. "Ah! And might I inquire the reason for this heroic self-restraint?"

"You choose your words badly. It is no restraint to honest men to decline to take other people's money."

"Ah, I see. I see. I see," said Surface, nodding his shining hairless head up and down.

"Good-by."

"No, no," said the old man, in an odd thick voice. "Not quite yet, if you please. There is still something that I want to say to you."

He came slowly around the tiny table, and Queed watched his coming with bursts of fierce repugnance which set his hard-won muscles to twitching. An elemental satisfaction there might be in throwing the old man through the window. Yet, in a truer sense, he felt that the necessity of manhandling him would be the final touch in this degrading interview.

"You value your society too high, my dear boy," said Surface with a face of chalk. "You want too big a price. I must fork over every penny I have, to a young trollop who happens to have caught your fancy—"

"Stand away from me!" cried Queed, with a face suddenly whiter than his own. "You will tempt me to do what I shall be sorry for afterwards."

But Surface did not budge, and to strike, after all, was hardly possible; it would be no better than murder. The two men stood, white face to white face, the two pairs of fearless eyes scarcely a foot apart. And beyond all the obvious dissimilarity, there appeared a curious resemblance in the two faces at that moment: in each the same habit of unfaltering gaze, the same high forehead, the same clean-cut chin, the same straight, thin-lipped mouth.

"Oh, I see through you clearly enough," said Surface. "You're in love with her! You think it is a pretty thing to sacrifice me to her, especially as the sacrifice costs you nothing—"

"Stop! Will you force me in the name of common decency—"

"But I'll not permit you to do it, do you hear?" continued Surface, his face ablaze, his lower lip trembling and twitching, as it does sometimes with the very old. "You need some discipline, my boy. Need some discipline—and you shall have it. You will continue to live with me exactly as you have heretofore, only henceforward I shall direct your movements and endeavor to improve your manners."

He swayed slightly where he stood, and Queed's tenseness suddenly relaxed. Pity rose in his heart above furious resentment; he put out his hand and touched the old man's arm.

"Control yourself," he said in an iron voice. "Come—I will help you to bed before I go."

Surface shook himself free, and laughed unpleasantly. "Go! Didn't you hear me tell you that you were not going? Who do you think I am that you can flout and browbeat and threaten—"

"Come! Let us go up to bed—"

"Who do you think I am!" repeated Surface, bringing his twitching face nearer, his voice breaking to sudden shrillness. "Who do you think I am, I say?"

Queed thought the old man had gone off his head, and indeed he looked it. He began soothingly: "You are—"

"I'm your father! Your *father*, do you hear!" cried Surface. "*You're my son—Henry G. Surface, Jr.!*"

This time, Queed, looking with a wild sudden terror into the flaming eyes, knew that he heard the truth from Surface at last. The revelation broke upon him in a stunning flash. He sprang away from the old man with a movement of loathing unspeakable.

"Father!" he said, in a dull curious whisper. "*O God! Father!*"

Surface gazed at him, his upper lip drawn up into his old purring sneer.

"So that is how you feel about it, my son?" he inquired suavely, and suddenly crumpled down upon the floor.

The young man shook him by the shoulder, but he did not stir. Henderson came running at the sound of the fall, and together they bore the old man, breathing, but inert as the dead, to his room. In an hour, the doctor had come and gone. In two hours, a trained nurse was sitting by the bed as though she had been there always. The doctor called it a "stroke," superinduced by a "shock." He said that Professor Nicolovius might live for a week, or a year, but was hardly likely to speak again on this side the dark river that runs round the world.

CHAPTER XXVII

Sharlee Weyland reads the Morning Post; of Rev. Mr. Dayne's Fight at Ephesus and the Telephone Message that never came; of the Editor's Comment upon the Assistant Editor's Resignation, which perhaps lacked Clarity; and of how Eight Men elect a Mayor.

Next morning, in the first moment she had, Sharlee Weyland read the Post's editorial on the reformatory. And as she read she felt as though the skies had fallen, and the friendly earth suddenly risen up and smitten her.

It was a rainy morning, the steady downpour of the night before turned into a fine drizzle; and Sharlee, who nearly always walked, took the car downtown. She was late this morning; there had been but flying minutes she could give to breakfast; not a second to give to anything else; and therefore she took the Post with her to read on the ride to "the" office. And, seating herself, she turned immediately to the editorial page, in which the State Department of Charities felt an especial interest this morning.

Both the name and the position of the editorial were immediately disappointing to her. It was not in the leading place, and its caption was simply "As to the Reformatory," which seemed to her too colorless and weak. Subconsciously, she passed the same judgment upon the opening sentences of the text, which somehow failed to ring out that challenge to the obstructionists she had confidently expected. As she read further, her vague disappointment gave way to a sudden breathless incredulity; that to a heartsick rigidity of attention; and when she went back, and began to read the whole article over, slowly and carefully, from the beginning, her face was about the color of the pretty white collar she wore. For what she was looking on at was, so it seemed to her, not simply the killing of the chief ambition of her two years' work, but the treacherous murder of it in the house of its friends.

As she reread "As to the Reformatory," she became impressed by its audacious cleverness. It would have been impossible to manage a tremendous shift in position with more consummate dexterity. Indeed, she was almost ready to take the *Post's* word for it that no shift at all had been made. From beginning to end the paper's unshakable loyalty to the reformatory was everywhere insisted upon; that was the strong keynote; the ruinous qualifications were slipped in, as it were, reluctantly, hard-wrung concessions to indisputable and overwhelming evidence. But there they were, scarcely noticeable to the casual reader, perhaps, but to passionate partisans sticking up like palm-trees on a plain. In a backhanded, sinuous but unmistakable way, the *Post* was telling the legislature that it had better postpone the reformatory for another two years. It was difficult to say just what phrase or phrases finally pushed the odious idea out into the light; but Sharlee lingered longest on a passage which, after referring to the "list of inescapable expenditures published elsewhere," said:

> Immediacy, of course, was never the great question; but it was a question; and the *Post* has therefore watched with keen regret the rolling up of absolutely unavoidable expenses to the point where the spending of another dollar for any cause, however meritorious in itself, must be regarded as of dubious wisdom.

That sentence was enough. It would be as good as a volume to the powerful opposition in the House, hardly repressed heretofore by the *Post's* thunders. The reformatory, which they had labored for so long, was dead.

The thought was bitter to the young assistant secretary. But from the first, her mind had jumped beyond it, to fasten on another and, to her, far worse one, a burning personal question by the side of which the loss of the reformatory seemed for the moment an unimportant detail.

Which of the two men had done it?

Rev. Mr. Dayne was sitting bowed over his desk, his strong head clamped in his hands, the morning Post crumpled on the floor beside him. He did not look up when his assistant entered the office; his response to her "Good-morning" was of the briefest. Sharlee understood. It was only the corporeal husk of her friend that was seated at the desk. All the rest of him was down at Ephesus fighting with the beasts, and grimly resolved to give no sign from the arena till he had set his foot upon their necks for the glory of God and the honor of his cloth.

Sharlee herself did not feel conversational. In silence she took off her things, and, going over to her own desk, began opening the mail. In an hour, maybe more, maybe less, the Secretary stood at her side, his kind face calm as ever.

"Well," he said quietly, "how do you explain it?"

Sharlee's eyes offered him bay-leaves for his victory.

"There is a suggestion about it," said she, still rather white, "of thirty pieces of silver."

"Oh! We can hardly say that. Let us give him the benefit of the doubt, as long as there can be any doubt. Let us view it for the present as a death-bed repentance."

Him? Which did he mean?

"No," said Sharlee, "it is not possible to view it that way. The *Post* has been as familiar with the arguments all along, from beginning to end, as you or I. It could not be honestly converted any more than you could. This," said she, struggling to speak calmly, "is treachery."

"Appearances, I am sorry to say, are much that way. Still—I think we should not condemn the paper unheard."

"Then why not have the hearing at once? An explanation is—"

"I shall seek none," interrupted Mr. Dayne, quietly. "The *Post* must volunteer it, if it has any to offer. Of course," he went on, "we know nothing of the history of that editorial now. Of one thing, however, I feel absolutely certain; that is, that it was published without the knowledge of Mr. West. Developments may follow.... As for instance a shake-up in the staff."

That settled it. This good man whom she admired so much had not entertained a doubt that the editorial was from the brain and pen of Mr. Queed.

She said painfully: "As to the effect upon the—the reformatory—"

"It is killed," said Mr. Dayne, and went away to his desk.

Sharlee turned in her desk-chair and looked out of the rain-blurred windows.

Through and beyond the trees of the park, over ridges of roofs and away to the west and north, she saw the weatherbeaten *Post* building, its distant gray tower cutting mistily out of the dreary sky. From where she sat she could just pick out, as she had so often noticed before, the tops of the fifth-floor row of windows, the windows from which the *Post's* editorial department looked out upon a world with which it could not keep faith. Behind one of those windows at this moment, in all likelihood, sat the false friend who had cut down the reformatory from behind.

Which was it? Oh, was not Mr. Dayne right, as he always was? Where was there any room for doubt?

Long before Sharlee knew Charles Gardiner West personally, when she was a little girl and he just out of college, she had known him by report as a young man of fine ideals, exalted character, the very pattern of stainless honor. Her later intimate knowledge of him, she told herself, had fully borne out the common reputation. Wherever she had touched him, she had found him generous and sound and sweet. That he was capable of what seemed to her the baldest and basest treachery was simply unthinkable. And what reason was there ever to drag his name into her thought of the affair at all? Was it not Mr. Queed who had written all the reformatory articles since Colonel Cowles's death—Mr. Queed who had promised only twenty-four hours ago to do his utmost for the cause at the critical moment to-day?

And yet ... and yet ... her mind clung desperately to the thought that possibly the assistant editor had not done this thing, after all. The memory of his visit to her, less than a week ago, was very vivid in her mind. What sort of world was it that a man with a face of such shining honesty could stoop to such shabby dishonesty?—that a man who had looked at her as he had looked at her that night, could turn again and strike her such a blow? That Queed should have done this seemed as inconceivable as that West should have done it. There was the wild hundredth chance that neither had done it, that the article had been written by somebody else and published by mistake.

But the hope hardly fluttered its wings before her reason struck it dead. No, there was no way out there. The fact was too plain that one of her two good friends, under what pressure she could not guess, had consented to commit dishonor and, by the same stroke, to wound her so deeply. For no honest explanation was possible; there was no argument in the case to-day that was not equally potent a month ago. It was all a story of cajolery or intimidation from the formidable opposition, and of mean yielding in the places of responsibility. And—yes—She felt it as bad for one of her two friends to be so stained as another. It had come to that. At last she must admit that they stood upon level ground in her imagination, the nameless little Doctor of two years back side by side with the beau ideal of all her girlhood. One's honor was as dear to her as another's; one's friendship as sweet; and now one of them was her friend no more.

And it was not West whom she must cast out. There was no peg anywhere to hang even the smallest suspicion of him upon. She scourged her mind for seeking one. It was Queed who, at the pinch, had broken down and betrayed them with a kiss: Queed, of the obscure parentage, dubious inheritance, and omitted upbringing; Queed, whom she had first stood upon his feet and started forward in a world of men, had helped and counseled and guided, had admitted to her acquaintance, her friendship—for this.

But because Sharlee had known Queed well as a man who loved truth, because the very thing that she had seen and most admired in him from the beginning was an unflinching honesty of intellect and character, because of the remembrance of his face as she had last seen it: a tiny corner of her mind, in defiance of all reason, revolted against this condemnation and refused to shut tight against him. All morning she sat at her work, torn by anxiety, hoping every moment that her telephone might ring with some unthought-of explanation, which would leave her with nothing worse upon her mind than the dead reformatory. But though the telephone rang often, it was never for this.

Sitting in a corner of the House gallery, about noon, Mr. Dayne saw the reformatory bill, which he himself had written, called up out of order and snowed under. The only speech was made by the Solon who had the bill called up, a familiar organization wheelhorse, named Meachy T. Bangor, who quoted with unconcealed triumph from the morning's *Post*, wholly ignoring all the careful safeguards and tearing out of the context only such portions as suited his humor and his need. Mr. Bangor pointed out that, inasmuch as the "acknowledged organ" of the State Department of Charities now at length "confessed" that the reformatory had better wait two years, there were no longer two sides to the question. Many of the gentleman's hearers appeared to agree with him. They rose and fell upon the bill, and massacred it by a vote of 54 to 32.

From "Sis" Hopkins, legislative reporter of the *Post*, the news went skipping over the telephone wire to the editorial rooms, where the assistant editor, who received it, remarked that he was sorry to hear it. That done, the assistant hung up the receiver, and resumed work upon an article entitled "A Constitution for Turkey?" He had hardly added a sentence to this composition before West came in and, with a cheery word of greeting, passed into his own office.

The assistant editor went on with his writing. He looked worn this morning, Henry Surface's son, and not without reason. Half the night he had shared the nurse's vigil at the bedside of Surface, who lay in unbroken stupor. Half the night he had maintained an individual vigil in his own room, lying flat on his back and staring wide-eyed into the darkness. And on the heels of the day, there had come new trouble for him, real trouble, though in the general cataclysm its full bearings and farther reaches did not at once come home to him. Running professionally through the *Post* at breakfast-time, his eye, like Miss Weyland's, had been suddenly riveted by that paper's remarks upon the reformatory.... What was the meaning of the staggering performance he had no idea, and need not inquire. Its immediate effect upon his own career was at least too plain for argument. His editorship and his reformatory had gone down together.

Yet he was in no hurry now about following West into his sanctum. Of all things Queed, as people called him, despised heroics and abhorred a "scene." Nothing could be gained by a quarrel now; very earnestly he desired the interview to be as matter-of-fact as possible. In half an hour, when he had come to a convenient stopping-place, he opened the door and stood uncomfortably before the young man he had so long admired.

West, sitting behind his long table, skimming busily through the paper with blue pencil and scissors, looked up with his agreeable smile.

"Well! What do you see that looks likely for—What's the matter? Are you sick to-day?"

"No, I am quite well, thank you. I find very little in the news, though. You notice that a digest of the railroad bill is given out?"

"Yes. You don't look a bit well, old fellow. You must take a holiday after the legislature goes. Yes, I'm going to take the hide off that bill. Or better yet—you. Don't you feel like shooting off some big guns at it?"

"Certainly, if you want me to. There is the farmers' convention, too. And by the way, I'd like to leave as soon as you can fill my place."

West dropped scissors, pencil, and paper and stared at him with dismayed amazement. "*Leave!* Why, you are never thinking of *leaving* me!"

"Yes. I'd—like to leave. I thought I ought to tell you this morning, so that you can at once make your plans as to my successor."

"But my dear fellow! I can't let you *leave me!* You've no idea how I value your assistance, how I've come to lean and depend upon you at every point. I never dreamed you were thinking of this. What's the matter? What have you got on your mind?"

"I think," said Queed, unhappily, "that I should be better satisfied off the paper than on it."

"Why, confound you—it's the money!" said West, with a sudden relieved laugh. "Why didn't you tell me, old fellow? You're worth five times what they're paying you—five times as much as I am for that matter—and I can make the directors see it. Trust me to make them raise you to my salary at the next meeting."

"Thank you—but no, my salary is quite satisfactory."

West frowned off into space, looking utterly bewildered. "Of course," he said in a troubled voice, "you have a perfect right to resign without saying a word. I haven't the smallest right to press you for an explanation against your will. But—good Lord! Here we've worked together side by side, day after day, for nearly a year, pretty good friends, as I thought, and—well, it hurts a little to have you put on your hat and walk out without a word. I wish you would tell me what's wrong. There's nothing I wouldn't do, if I could, to fix it and keep you."

The eyes of the two men met across the table, and it was Queed's that faltered and fell.

"Well," he said, obviously embarrassed, "I find that I am out of sympathy with the policy of the paper."

"Oh-h-ho!" said West, slowly and dubiously. "Do you mean my article on the reformatory?"

"Yes—I do."

"Why, my dear fellow!"

West paused, his handsome eyes clouded, considering how best he might put the matter to overcome most surely the singular scruples of his assistant.

"Let's take it this way, old fellow. Suppose that my standpoint in that article was diametrically wrong. I am sure I could convince you that it was not, but admit, for argument's sake, that it was. Do you feel that the appearance in the paper of an article with which you don't agree makes it necessary for you, in honor, to resign?"

"No, certainly not—"

"Is it that you don't like my turning down one of your articles and printing one of my own instead? I didn't know you objected to that, old fellow. You see—while your judgment is probably a hanged sight better than mine, after all I am the man who is held responsible, and I am paid a salary to see that my opinions become the opinions of the *Post*."

"It is entirely right that your opinions—"

"Then wherein have I offended? Be frank with me, like a good fellow, I beg you!"

Queed eyed him strangely. Was the editor's inner vision really so curiously astigmatic?

"I look at it this way," he said, in a slow, controlled voice. "The *Post* has said again and again that *this* legislature must establish a reformatory. That was the burden of a long series of editorials, running back over a year, which, as I thought, had your entire approval. Now, at the critical moment, when it was only necessary to say once more what had been said a hundred times before, the *Post* suddenly turns about and, in effect, authorizes this legislature not to establish the reformatory. The House killed the bill just now. Bangor quoted from the *Post* editorial. There can be no doubt, of course, that it turned a number of votes—enough to have safely carried the bill."

West looked disturbed and unhappy.

"But if we find out that this legislature is so drained by inescapable expenses that it simply cannot provide the money? Suppose the State had been swept by a plague? Suppose there was a war and a million of unexpected expenses had suddenly dropped on us from the clouds? Wouldn't you agree that circumstances altered cases, and that, under such circumstances, everything that was not indispensable to the State's existence would have to go over?"

Queed felt like answering West's pepper-fire of casuistry by throwing Eva Bernheimer at his head. Despite his determination to avoid a "scene," he felt his bottled-up indignation rising. A light showed in his stone-gray eyes.

"Can't you really see that these circumstances are not in the least like those? Did you do me the courtesy to read what I wrote about this so-called 'economy argument' last night?"

"Certainly," said West, surprised by the other's tone. "But clever as it was, it was not based, in my opinion, on a clear understanding of the facts as they actually exist. You and I stay so close inside of four walls here that we are apt to get out of touch with practical conditions. Yesterday, I was fortunate enough to get new facts, from a confidential and highly authoritative source. In the light of these—I wish I could explain them more fully to you, but I was pledged to secrecy—I am obliged to tell you that what you had written seemed to me altogether out of focus, unfair, and extreme."

"Did you get these facts, as you call them, from Plonny Neal?"

"As to that, I am at liberty to say nothing."

Queed, looking at him, saw that he had. He began to feel sorry for West.

"I would give four hundred and fifty dollars," he said slowly—"all the money that I happen to have—if you had told me last night that you meant to do this."

"I am awfully sorry," said West, with a touch of dignity, "that you take it so hard. But I assure you—"

"I know Plonny Neal even better than you do," continued Queed, "for I have known him as his social equal. He is laughing at you to-day."

West, of course, knew better than that. The remark confirmed his belief that Queed had brooded over the reformatory till he saw everything about it distorted and magnified.

"Well, old fellow," he said, without a trace of ill-humor in his voice or his manner, "then it is I he is laughing at—not you. That brings us right back to my point. If you feel, as I understand it, that the *Post* is in the position of having deserted its own cause, I alone am the deserter. Don't you see that? Not only am I the editor of the paper, and so responsible for all that it says; but I wrote the article, on my own best information and judgment. Whatever consequences there are," said West, his thoughts on the consequences most likely to accrue to the saviour of the party, "I assume them all."

"A few people," said Queed, slowly, "know that I have been conducting this fight for the *Post*. They may not understand that I was suddenly superseded this morning. But of course it isn't that. It is simply a matter—"

"Believe me, it can all be made right. I shall take the greatest pleasure in explaining to your friends that I alone am responsible. I shall call to-day—right now—at—"

"I'm sorry," said Queed, abruptly, "but it is entirely impossible for me to remain."

West looked, and felt, genuinely distressed. "I wish," he said, "the old reformatory had never been born"; and he went on in a resigned voice: "Of course I can't keep you with a padlock and chain, but—for the life of me, I can't catch your point of view. To my mind it appears the honorable and courageous thing to correct a mistake, even at the last moment, rather than stand by it for appearance's sake."

"You see I don't regard our principles as a mistake."

But he went back to his office marveling at himself for the ease with which West had put him in the wrong.

For friendship's sake, West had meant to call at the Charities Department that day, and explain to his two friends there how his sense of responsibility to the larger good had made it necessary for him to inflict a momentary disappointment upon them. But this disturbing interview with his assistant left him not so sure that an immediate call would be desirable, after all. At the moment, both Dayne and the dearest girl in the world would naturally be feeling vexed over the failure of their plan; wouldn't it be the sensible and considerate thing to give them a little time to conquer their pique and compose themselves to see facts as they were?

The *Chronicle* that afternoon finally convinced him that this would be the considerate thing. That offensive little busybody, which pretended to have been a champion of "this people's institution" came out with a nasty editorial, entitled "The *Post's* Latest Flop." "Flop" appeared to be an intensely popular word in the *Chronicle* office. The article boldly taxed "our more or less esteemed contemporary" with the murder of the reformatory, and showed unpleasant freedom in employing such phrases as "instantaneous conversion," "treacherous friendship," "disgusting somersaulting," and the like. Next day, grown still more audacious, it had the hardihood to refer to the *Post* as "The Plonny Neal organ."

Now, of course, the reformatory had not been in any sense a burning public "issue." Measures like this, being solid and really important, seldom interest the people. There was not the smallest popular excitement over the legislature's conduct, or the *Post's*. The *Chronicle's* venomous remarks were dismissed as the usual "newspaper scrap." All this West understood perfectly. Still, it was plain that a few enthusiasts, reformatory fanatics, were taking the first flush of disappointment rather hard. For himself, West reflected, he cared nothing about their clamor. Conscious of having performed an unparalleled service to his party, and thus to his State, he was willing to stand for a time the indignation of the ignorant, the obloquy of the malicious, even revolt and disloyalty among his own lieutenants. One day the truth about his disinterested patriotism would become known. For the present he would sit silent, calmly waiting at least until unjust resentment subsided and reason reasserted her sway.

Many days passed, as it happened, before West and the Secretary of Charities met; six days before West and the Assistant Secretary met. On the sixth night, about half-past seven in the evening, he came unexpectedly face to face with Sharlee Weyland in the vestibule of Mrs. Byrd, Senior's, handsome house. In the days intervening, Sharlee's state of mind had remained very much where it was on the first morning: only now the tiny open corner of her mind had shrunk to imperceptible dimensions. Of West she entertained not the smallest doubt; and she greeted him like the excellent friend she knew him to be.

There was a little dinner-dance at Mrs. Byrd's, for the season's *débutantes*. It became remembered as one of the most charming of all her charming parties. To the buds were added a sprinkling of older girls who had survived as the fittest, while among the swains a splendid catholicity as to age prevailed. A retinue of imported men, Caucasian at that, served dinner at six small tables, six at a table; the viands were fashioned to tickle tired epicures; there was vintage champagne such as kings quaff to pledge the comity of nations; Wissner's little band of artists, known to command its own price, divinely mingled melody with the rose-sweetness of the air. West, having dined beautifully, and lingered over coffee in the smoking-room among the last, emerged to find the polished floors crowded with an influx of new guests, come to enliven the dance. His was, as ever, a Roman progress; he stopped and was stopped everywhere; like a happy opportunist, he plucked the flowers as they came under his hand, and gayly whirled from one measure to another. So the glorious evening was half spent before, in an intermission, he found himself facing Sharlee Weyland, who was uncommonly well attended, imploring her hand for the approaching waltz.

Without the smallest hesitation, Sharlee drew her ornamental pencil through the next name on her list, and ordered her flowers and fan transferred from the hands of Mr. Beverley Byrd to those of Mr. Charles Gardiner West.

"Only," said she, thinking of her partners, "you'll have to hide me somewhere."

With a masterful grace which others imitated, indeed, but could not copy, West extricated his lady from her gallants, and led her away to a pretty haven; not indeed, to a conservatory, since there was none, but to a bewitching nook under the wide stairway, all banked about with palm and fern and pretty flowering shrub. There they sat them down, unseeing and unseen, near yet utterly remote, while in the blood of West beat the intoxicating strains of Straus, not to mention the vintage champagne, to which he had taken a very particular fancy.

All night, while the roses heard the flute, violin, bassoon, none in all the gay company had been gayer than Sharlee. Past many heads in the dining-room, West had watched her, laughing, radiant, sparkling as the wine itself, a pretty little lady of a joyous sweetness that never knew a care. In the dance, for he had watched her there, too, wondering, as she circled laughing by, whether she felt any lingering traces of pique with him, she had been the same: no girl ever wore a merrier heart. But a sudden change came now. In the friendly freedom of the green-banked alcove, Sharlee's gayety dropped from her like a painted mask, which, having amused the children, has done its full part. Against the back of the cushioned settle where they sat she leaned a weary head, and frankly let her fringed lids droop.

At another time West might have been pleased by such candid evidences of confidence and intimacy, but not to-night. He felt that Sharlee, having advertised a delightful gayety by her manner, should now proceed to deliver it: it certainly was not for tired sweetness and disconcerting silences that he had sought this *tête-à-tête*. But at last his failure to arouse her on indifferent topics became too marked to be passed over; and then he said in a gentle voice:—

"Confess, Miss Weyland. You're as tired as you can be."

She turned her head, and smiled a little into his eyes. "Yes—you don't mind, do you?"

"Indeed I do, though! You're going altogether too hard—working like a Trojan all day and dancing like a dryad all night. You'll break yourself down—indeed you will!"

Hardly conscious of it herself, Sharlee had been waiting with a tense anxiety of which her face began to give signs, for him to speak. And now she understood that he would not speak; and she knew why.... How her heart warmed to him for his honorable silence in defense of his unworthy friend.

But she herself was under no such restraint. "It isn't that," she said quickly. "It's the reformatory—I've worried myself sick over it."

West averted his gaze; he saw that it had come, and in a peculiarly aggravated form. He recognized at once how impossible it would be to talk the matter over, in a calm and rational way, under such conditions as these. This little girl had brooded over it till the incident had assumed grotesque and fantastic proportions in her mind. She was seeing visions, having nightmares. In a soothing, sympathetic voice, he began consoling her with the thought that a postponement for two brief years was really not so serious, and that—

"It isn't that!" she corrected him again, in the same voice. "That was pretty bad, but—what I have minded so much was M—— was the *Post's* desertion."

West's troubled eyes fell. But some hovering imp of darkness instantly popped it into his head to ask: "Have you seen Queed?"

"No," said Sharlee, colorlessly. "Not since—"

"You—didn't know, then, that he has left the *Post*?"

"Left the *Post!*" she echoed, with a face suddenly rigid. "No! Did he? Won't you tell me—?"

West looked unhappily at the floor. "Well—I'd much rather not go into this now. But the fact is that he left because ... well, we had a difference of opinion as to that reformatory article."

Sharlee turned hastily away, pretending to look for her fan. The sudden shutting of that tiny door had shot her through with unexpected pain. The last doubt fell now; all was plain. Mr. Queed had been discharged for writing an article which outraged his chief's sense of honor, that knightly young chief who still would not betray him by a word. The little door clicked; Sharlee turned the key upon it and threw away the key. And then she turned upon West a face so luminous with pure trust that it all but unsteadied him.

To do West justice, it was not until his words had started caroming down the eternal halls of time, that their possible implication dawned upon him. His vague idea had been merely to give a non-committal summary of the situation to ease the present moment; this to be followed, at a more suitable time, by the calm and rational explanation he had always intended. But the magical effect of his chance words, entirely unexpected by him, was quite too delightful to be wiped out. To erase that look from the tired little lady's face by labored exposition and tedious statistic would be the height of clumsy unkindness. She had been unhappy; he had made her happy; that was all that was vital just now. At a later time, when she had stopped brooding over the thing and could see and discuss it intelligently, he would take her quietly and straighten the whole matter out for her.

For this present, there was a look in her eyes which made a trip-hammer of his heart. Never had her face—less of the mere pretty young girl's than he had ever seen it, somewhat worn beneath its color, a little wistful under her smile—seemed to him so immeasurably sweet. In his blood Straus and the famous Verzenay plied their dizzying vocations. Suddenly he leaned forward, seeing nothing but two wonderful blue eyes, and his hand fell upon hers, with a grip which claimed her out of all the world.

"Sharlee" he said hoarsely. "Don't you know that—"

But he was, alas, summarily checked. At just that minute, outraged partners of Miss Weyland's espied and descended upon them with loud reproachful cries, and Charles Gardiner West's moment of superb impetuosity had flowered in nothing.

At a little earlier hour on the same evening, in a dining-room a mile away, eight men met "without political significance" to elect a new set of officers for the city. A bit of red-tape legislation permitted the people to ratify the choices at a "primary," to be held some months later; but the election came now. Unanimously, and with little or no discussion, the eight men elected one of their own number, Mr. Meachy T. Bangor by name, to the office of Mayor of the City.

One of them then referred humorously to Mr. Bangor as just the sort of progressive young reformer that suited *him*. Another suggested, more seriously, that they might have to allow for the genuine article some day. Plonny Neal, who sat at the head of the table, as being the wisest of them, said that the organization certainly must expect to knuckle to reform some day; perhaps in eight years, perhaps in twelve years, perhaps in sixteen.

"Got your young feller all picked out, Plonny?" queried the Mayor elect, Mr. Bangor, with a wink around the room.

Plonny denied that he had any candidate. Under pressure, however, he admitted having his eye on a certain youth, a "dark horse" who was little known at present, but who, in his humble judgment, was a coming man. Plonny said that this man was very young just now, but would be plenty old enough before they would have need of him.

Mr. Bangor once more winked at the six. "Why, Plonny, I thought you were rooting for Charles Gardenia West."

"Then there's two of ye," said Plonny, dryly, "he being the other one."

He removed his unlighted cigar, and spat loudly into a tall brass cuspidor, which he had taken the precaution to place for just such emergencies.

"Meachy," said Plonny, slowly, "I wouldn't give the job of dog-catcher to a man you couldn't trust to stand by his friends."

CHAPTER XXVIII

*How Words can be like Blows, and Blue Eyes stab deep; how Queed
sits by a Bedside and reviews his Life; and how a Thought leaps at
him and will not down.*

In the first crushing burst of revelation, Queed had had a wild impulse
to wash his hands of everything, and fly. He would pack Surface off to a
hospital; dispose of the house; escape back to Mrs. Paynter's; forget his
terrible knowledge, and finally bury it with Surface. His reason fortified the
impulse at every point. He owed less than nothing to his father; he had not
the slightest responsibility either toward him or for him; to acknowledge
the relation between them would do no conceivable good to anybody. He
would go back to the Scriptorium, and all would be as it had been before.

But when the moment came either to go or to stay, another and
deeper impulse rose against this one, and beat it down. Within him a voice
whispered that though he might go back to the Scriptorium, he would never
be as he had been before. Whether he acknowledged the relation or not, it
was still there. And, in time, his reason brought forth material to fortify this
impulse, too: it came out in brief, grim sentences which burned themselves
into his mind. Surface was his father. To deny the primal blood-tie was not
honorable. The sins of the fathers descended to the children. To suppress
Truth was the crowning blasphemy.

Queed did not go. He stayed, resolved, after a violent struggle—it was
all over in the first hour of his discovery—to bear his burden, shouldering
everything that his sonship involved.

By day and by night the little house stood very quiet. Its secret remained
inviolate; the young man was still Mr. Queed, the old one still Professor
Nicolovius, who had suffered the last of his troublesome "strokes." Inside
the darkened windows, life moved on silent heels. The doctor came, did
nothing, and went. The nurse did nothing but stayed. Queed would have
dismissed her at once, except that that would have been bad economy; he
must keep his own more valuable time free for the earning of every possible
penny. To run the house, he had, for the present, his four hundred and fifty

dollars in bank, saved out of his salary. This, he figured, would last nine weeks. Possibly Surface would last longer than that: that remained to be seen.

Late on a March afternoon, Queed finished a review article—his second since he had left the newspaper, four days before—and took it himself to the post-office. He wanted to catch the night mail for the North; and besides his body, jaded by two days' confinement, cried aloud for a little exercise. His fervent desire was to rush out all the articles that were in him, and get money for them back with all possible speed. But he knew that the market for this work was limited. He must find other work immediately; he did not care greatly what kind it was, provided only that it was profitable. Thoughts of ways and means, mostly hard thoughts, occupied his mind all the way downtown. And always it grew plainer to him how much he was going to miss, now of all times, his eighteen hundred a year from the *Post*.

In the narrowest corridor of the post-office—like West in the Byrds' vestibule—he came suddenly face to face with Sharlee Weyland.

The meeting was unwelcome to them both, and both their faces showed it. Sharlee had told herself, a thousand times in a week, that she never wanted to see Mr. Queed again. Queed had known, without telling himself at all, that he did not want to see Miss Weyland, not, at least, till he had more time to think. But Queed's dread of seeing the girl had nothing to do with what was uppermost in her mind—the *Post's* treacherous editorial. Of course, West had long since made that right as he had promised, as he would have done with no promising. But—ought he to tell her now, or to wait?... And what would she say when she knew the whole shameful truth about him—knew that for nearly a year Surface Senior and Surface Junior, shifty father and hoodwinked son, had been living fatly on the salvage of her own plundered fortune?

She would have passed him with a bow, but Queed, more awkward than she, involuntarily halted. The dingy gas-light, which happened to be behind him, fell full upon her face, and he said at once:—

"How do you do?—not very well, I fear. You look quite used up—not well at all."

Pride raised a red flag in her cheek. She lifted a great muff to her lips, and gave a little laugh.

"Thank you. I am quite well."

Continuing to gaze at her, he went ahead with customary directness: "Then I am afraid you have been taking—the reformatory too hard."

"No, not the reformatory. It is something worse than that. I had a friend once," said Sharlee, muff to her lips, and her level eyes, upon him, "and he was not worthy."

To follow out that thought was impossible, but Queed felt very sorry for West when he saw how she said it.

"I'm sorry that you should have had this—to distress you. However—"

"Isn't it rather late to think of that now? As to saying it—I should have thought that you would tell me of your sorrow immediately—or not at all."

A long look passed between them. Down the corridor, on both sides of them, flowed a stream of people bent upon mails; but these two were alone in the world.

"Have you seen West?" asked Queed, in a voice unlike his own.

She made a little movement of irrepressible distaste.

"Yes.... But you must not think that he told me. He is too kind, too honorable to betray his friend."

He stared at her, reft of the power of speech.

From under the wide hat, the blue eyes seemed to leap out and stab him; they lingered, turning the knife, while their owner appeared to be waiting for him to speak; and then with a final twist, they were pulled away, and Queed found himself alone in the corridor.

He dropped his long envelope in the slot labeled *North*, and turned his footsteps toward Duke of Gloucester Street again.

Within him understanding had broken painfully into flame. Miss Weyland believed that he was the author of the unforgivable editorial— *he*, who had so gladly given, first the best abilities he had, and then his position itself, to the cause of Eva Bernheimer. West had seen her, and either through deliberate falseness or his characteristic fondness for shying off from disagreeable subjects—Queed felt pretty sure it was the latter—had failed to reveal the truth. West's motives did not matter in the least. The terrible situation in which he himself had been placed was all that mattered, and that he must straighten out at once. What dumbness had seized his tongue just now he could not imagine. But it was plain that, however much he would have preferred not to see the girl at all, this meeting had made another one immediately necessary: he must see her at once, to-night, and clear himself wholly of this cruel suspicion. And yet ... he could never clear himself of her *having* suspected him; he understood that, and it seemed to him a terrible thing. No matter how humble her contrition, how abject her apologies, nothing could ever get back of what was written, or change the fact that she had believed him capable of that.

The young man pursued his thoughts over three miles of city streets, and returned to the house of Surface.

The hour was 6.30. He took the nurse's seat by the bedside of his father and sent her away to her dinner.

There was a single gas-light in the sick-room, turned just high enough for the nurse to read her novels. The old man lay like a log, though breathing heavily; under the flickering light, his face looked ghastly. It had gone all to pieces; advanced old age had taken possession of it in a night. Moreover the truth about the auburn mustaches and goatee was coming out in snowy splotches; the fading dye showed a mottle of red and white not agreeable to the eye. Here was not merely senility, but ignoble and repulsive senility.

His father!... his *father!* O God! How much better to have sprung, as he once believed, from the honest loins of Tim Queed!

The young man averted his eyes from the detestable face of his father, and let his thoughts turn inward upon himself. For the first time in all his years, he found himself able to trace his own life back to its source, as other men do. A flying trip to New York, and two hours with Tim Queed, had answered all questions, cleared up all doubts. First of all, it had satisfied him that there was no stain upon his birth. Surface's second marriage had been clandestine, but it was genuine; in Newark the young man found the old clergyman who had officiated at the ceremony. His mother, it seemed, had been Miss Floretta May Earle, a "handsome young opery singer," of a group, so Tim said, to which the gentleman, his father, had been very fond of giving his "riskay little bacheldore parties."

Tim's story, in fact, was comprehensive at all points. He had been Mr. Surface's coachman and favorite servant in the heyday of the Southern apostate's metropolitan glories. About a year before the final catastrophe, Surface's affairs being then in a shaky condition, the servants had been dismissed, the handsome house sold, and the financier, in a desperate effort to save himself, had moved off somewhere to modest quarters in a side street. That was the last Tim heard of his old patron, till the papers printed the staggering news of his arrest. A few weeks later, Tim one day received a message bidding him come to see his former master in the Tombs.

The disgraced capitalist's trial was then in its early stages, but he entertained not the smallest hope of acquittal. Broken and embittered, he confided to his faithful servant that, soon after the break-up of his establishment, he had quietly married a wife; that some weeks earlier she had presented him with a son; and that she now lay at the point of death with but remote chances of recovery. To supply her with money was impossible, for his creditors, he said, had not only swooped down like buzzards upon the remnant of his fortune, but were now watching his every move under the suspicion that he had managed to keep something back. All his friends had deserted him as though he were a leper, for his had been the unpardonable sin of being found out. In all the world there was no equal of whom he was not too proud to ask a favor.

In short, he was about to depart for a long sojourn in prison, leaving behind a motherless, friendless, and penniless infant son. Would Tim take him and raise him as his own?

While Tim hesitated over this amazing request, Surface leaned forward and whispered a few words in his ear. He *had* contrived to secrete a little sum of money, a very small sum, but one which, well invested as it was, would provide just enough for the boy's keep. Tim was to receive twenty-five dollars monthly for his trouble and expense; Surface pledged his honor as a gentleman that he would find a way to smuggle this sum to him on the first of every month. Tim, being in straits at the time, accepted with alacrity. No, he could not say that Mr. Surface had exhibited any sorrow over the impending decease of his wife, or any affectionate interest in his son. In fact the ruined man seemed to regard the arrival of the little stranger—"the brat," as he called him—with peculiar exasperation. Tim gathered that he never expected or desired to see his son, whatever the future held, and that, having arranged for food and shelter, he meant to wash his hands of the whole transaction. The honest guardian's sole instructions were to keep mum as the grave; to provide the necessaries of life as long as the boy was dependent upon him; not to interfere with him in any way; but if he left, always to keep an eye on him, and stand ready to produce him on demand. To these things, and particularly to absolute secrecy, Tim was sworn by the most awful of oaths; and so he and his master parted. A week later a carriage was driven up to Tim's residence in the dead of the night, and a small bundle of caterwauling humankind was transferred from the one to the other. Such was the beginning of the life of young Queed. The woman, his mother, had died a day or two before, and where she had been buried Tim had no idea.

So the years passed, while the Queeds watched with amazement the subtly expanding verification of the adage that blood will tell. For Mr. Surface, said Tim, had been a great scholard, and used to sit up to all hours reading books that Thomason, the butler, couldn't make head nor tail of; and so with Surface's boy. He was the strange duckling among chickens who, with no guidance, straightway plumed himself for the seas of printed knowledge. Time rolled on. When Surface was released from prison, as the papers announced, there occurred not the smallest change in the status of affairs; except that the monthly remittances now bore the name of Nicolovius, and came from Chicago or some other city in the west. More years passed; and at last, one day, after a lapse of nearly a quarter of a century, the unexpected happened, as it really will sometimes. Tim got a letter in a handwriting he knew well, instructing him to call next day at such-and-such a time and place.

Tim was not disobedient to the summons. He called; and found, instead of the dashing young master he had once known, a soft and savage old man whom he at first utterly failed to recognize. Surface paced the floor and spoke his mind. It seemed that an irresistible impulse had led him back to his old home city; that he had settled and taken work there; and there meant to end his days. Under these circumstances, some deep-hidden instinct—a whim, the old man called it—had put it into his head to consider the claiming and final acknowledgment of his son. After all the Ishmaelitish years of bitterness and wandering, Surface's blood, it seemed, yearned for his blood. But under no circumstances, he told Tim, would he acknowledge his son before his death, since that would involve the surrender of his incognito; and not even then, so the old man swore, unless he happened to be pleased with the youth—the son of his body whom he had so utterly neglected through all these years. Therefore, his plan was to have the boy where they would meet as strangers; where he could have an opportunity to watch, weigh, and come to know him in the most casual way; and thereafter to act as he saw fit.

So there, in the shabby lodging-house, the little scheme was hatched out. Surface undertook by his own means to draw his son, as the magnet the particle of steel, to his city. Tim, to whom the matter was sure to be broached, was to encourage the young man to go. But more than this: it was to be Tim's diplomatic task to steer him to the house where Surface, as Nicolovius, resided. Surface himself had suggested the device by which this was to be done; merely that Tim, mentioning the difficulties of the boarding-house question in a strange city, was to recall that through the lucky chance of having a cousin in this particular city, he knew of just the place: a house where accommodations were of the best, particularly for those who liked quiet for studious work, and prices ridiculously low. The little stratagem worked admirably. The address which Tim gave young Surface was the address of Mrs. Paynter's, where Surface Senior had lived for nearly three years. And so the young man had gone to his father, straight as a homing pigeon.

How strange, how strange to look back on all this now!

Half reclining in the nurse's chair, unseeing eyes on the shaded and shuttered window, for the fiftieth time Queed let his mind go back over his days at Mrs. Paynter's, reading them all anew in the light of his staggering knowledge. With three communications of the most fragmentary sort, his father had had his full will of his son. With six typewritten lines, he had drawn the young man to his side at his own good pleasure. Boarding-house gossip made it known that the son was in peril of ejectment for non-payment of board, and a twenty-dollar bill had been promptly transmitted—at some risk of discovery—to ease his stringency. Last came the mysterious counsel to make friends and to like people, the particular friends and people intended being consolidated, he could understand now, in the person of old Nicolovius. And that message out of the unknown had had its effect: Queed could see that now, at any rate. His father clearly had been satisfied with the result; he appeared as his father no more. Thenceforward he stalked his prey as Nicolovius—with what consummate skill and success!

Oh, but did he not have a clever father, a stealthy, cunning, merciless father, soft-winged, foul-eyed, hungry-taloned, flitting noiselessly in circles, that grew ever and ever narrower, sure, and unfaltering to the final triumphant swoop! Or no—Rather a coiled and quiescent father, horrible-eyed, lying in slimy rings at the foot of the tree, basilisk gaze fixed upward, while the enthralled bird fluttered hopelessly down, twig by twig, ever nearer and nearer.

But no—his metaphors were very bad; he was sentimentalizing, rhetorizing, a thing that he particularly abhorred. Not in any sense was he the pitiful prey of his father, the hawk or the snake. Rather was he glad that, after long doubt and perplexity, at last he knew. For that was the passion of all his chaste life: to know the truth and to face it without fear.

Surface stirred slightly in his bed, and Queed, turning his eyes, let them rest briefly on that repulsive face. *His father!*... And he must wear that name and shoulder that infamy forevermore!

The nurse came back and relieved him of his vigil. He descended the stairs to his solitary dinner. And as he went, and while he lingered over food which he did not eat, his thoughts withdrew from his terrible inheritance to centre anew on the fact that, within an hour, he was to see Miss Weyland again.

The prospect drew him while it even more strongly repelled.

For a week he had hesitated, unable to convince himself that he was justified in telling Miss Weyland at once the whole truth about himself, his father, and her money. There was much on the side of delay. Surface might die at any moment, and this would relieve his son from the smallest reproach of betraying a confidence: the old man himself had said that everything was to be made known when he died. On the other hand Surface might get well, and if he did, he ought to be given a final chance to make the restitution himself. Besides this, there was the great uncertainty about the money. Queed had no idea how much it was, or where it was, or whether or not, upon Surface's death, he himself was to get it by bequest. But all through these doubts, passionately protesting against them, had run his own insistent feeling that it was not right to conceal the truth, even under such confused conditions—not, at least, from the one person who was so clearly entitled to know it. This feeling had reached a climax even before he met the girl this afternoon. Somehow that meeting had served to precipitate his decision. After all, Surface had had both his chance and his warning.

That his sonship would make him detestable in Miss Weyland's sight was highly probable, but he could not let the fear of that keep him silent. His determination to tell her the essential facts had come now, at last, as a kind of corollary to his instant necessity of straightening out the reformatory situation. This latter necessity had dominated his thought ever since the chance meeting in the post-office. And as his mind explored the subject, it ramified, and grew more complicated and oppressive with every step of the way.

It gradually became plain to him that, in clearing himself of responsibility for the *Post's* editorial, he would have to put West in a very unpleasant position. He would have to convict him, not only of having written the perfidious article, but of having left another man under the reproach of having written it. But no; it could not be said that he was putting West in this position. West had put himself there. It was he who had written the article, and it was he who had kept silent about it. Every man must accept the responsibility for his own acts, or the world would soon be at sixes and sevens. In telling Miss Weyland the truth about the matter, as far as that went, he would be putting himself in an unpleasant position. Nobody liked to see one man "telling on" another. He did not like it himself, as he remembered, for instance, in the case of young Brown in the Blaines College hazing affair.

Queed sat alone in the candle-lit dining-room, thinking things out. A brilliant idea came to him. He would telephone to West, explain the situation to him, and ask him to set it right immediately. West, of course, would do so.

At the worst, he had only temporized with the issue—perhaps had lost sight of it altogether—and he would be shocked to learn of the consequences of his procrastination. He himself could postpone his call on Miss Weyland till to-morrow, leaving West to go to-night. Of course, however, nothing his former chief could do now would change the fact that Miss Weyland herself had doubted him.

Undoubtedly, the interview would be a painful one for West. How serious an offense the girl considered the editorial had been plain in his own brief conversation with her. And West would have to acknowledge, further, that he had kept quiet about it for a week. Miss Weyland would forgive West, of course, but he could never be the same to her again. He would always have that spot. Queed himself felt that way about it. He had admired West more than any man he ever knew, more even than Colonel Cowles, but now he could never think very much of him again. He was quite sure that Miss Weyland was like that, too. Thus the matter began to grow very serious. For old Surface, who was always right about people, had said that West was the man that Miss Weyland meant to marry.

Very gradually, for the young man was still a slow analyst where people were concerned, an irresistible conclusion was forced upon him.

Miss Weyland would rather think that he had written the editorial than to know that West had written it.

The thought, when he finally reached it, leapt up at him, but he pushed it away. However, it returned. It became like one of those swinging logs which hunters hang in trees to catch bears: the harder he pushed it away, the harder it swung back at him.

He fully understood the persistence of this idea. It was the heart and soul of the whole question. He himself was simply Miss Weyland's friend, the least among many. If belief in his dishonesty had brought her pain— and he had her word for that—it was a hurt that would quickly pass. False friends are soon forgotten. But to West belonged the shining pedestal in the innermost temple of her heart. It would go hard with the little lady to find at the last moment this stain upon her lover's honor.

He had only to sit still and say nothing to make her happy. That was plain. So the whole issue was shifted. It was not, as it had first seemed, merely a matter between West and himself. The real issue was between Miss Weyland and himself—between her happiness and his ... no, not his happiness—his self-respect, his sense of justice, his honor, his chaste passion for Truth, his ... yes, his happiness.

Did he think most of Miss Weyland or of himself? That was what it all came down to. Here was the new demand that his acknowledgment of a personal life was making upon him, the supreme demand, it seemed, that any man's personal life could ever make upon him. For if, on the day when Nicolovius had suddenly revealed himself as Surface, he had been asked to give himself bodily, he was now asked to give himself spiritually—to give all that made him the man he was.

From the stark alternative, once raised, there was no escape. Queed closed with it, and together they went down into deep waters.

CHAPTER XXIX

In which Queed's Shoulders can bear One Man's Roguery and Another's Dishonor, and of what these Fardels cost him: how for the Second Time in his Life he stays out of Bed to think.

Sharlee, sitting upstairs, took the card from the tray and, seeing the name upon it, imperceptibly hesitated. But even while hesitating, she rose and turned to her dressing-table mirror.

"Very well. Say that I'll be down in a minute."

She felt nervous, she did not know why; chilled at her hands and cold within; she rubbed her cheeks vigorously with a handkerchief to restore to them some of the color which had fled. There was a slightly pinched look at the corners of her mouth, and she smiled at her reflection in the glass, somewhat artificially and elaborately, until she had chased it away. Undoubtedly she had been working too hard by day, and going too hard by night; she must let up, stop burning the candle at both ends. But she must see Mr. Queed, of course, to show him finally that no explanation could explain now. It came into her mind that this was but the third time he had ever been inside her house—the third, and it was the last.

He had been shown into the front parlor, the stiffer and less friendly of the two rooms, and its effect of formality matched well with the temper of their greeting. By the obvious stratagem of coming down with book in one hand and some pretense at fancy-work in the other, Sharlee avoided shaking hands with him. Having served their purpose, the small burdens were laid aside upon the table. He had been standing, awaiting her, in the shadows near the mantel; the chair that he chanced to drop into stood almost under one of the yellow lamps; and when she saw his face, she hardly repressed a start. For he seemed to have aged ten years since he last sat in her parlor, and if she had thought his face long ago as grave as a face could be, she now perceived her mistake.

The moment they were seated he began, in his usual voice, and with rather the air of having thought out in advance exactly what he was to say.

"I have come again, after all, to talk only of definite things. In fact, I have something of much importance to tell you. May I ask that you will consider it as confidential for the present?"

At the very beginning she was disquieted by the discovery that his gaze was steadier than her own. She was annoyingly conscious of looking away from him, as she said:—

"I think you have no right to ask that of me."

Surface's son smiled sadly. "It is not about—anything that you could possibly guess. I have made a discovery of—a business nature, which concerns you vitally."

"A discovery?"

"Yes. The circumstances are such that I do not feel that anybody should know of it just yet, but you. However—"

"I think you must leave me to decide, after hearing you—"

"I believe I will. I am not in the least afraid to do so. Miss Weyland, Henry G. Surface is alive."

Her face showed how completely taken back she was by the introduction of this topic, so utterly remote from the subject she had expected of him.

"Not only that," continued Queed, evenly—"he is within reach. Both he—and some property which he has—are within reach of the courts."

"Oh! How do you know?... Where is he?"

"For the present I am not free to answer those questions."

There was a brief silence. Sharlee looked at the fire, the stirrings of painful memories betrayed in her eyes.

"We knew, of course, that he might be still alive," she said slowly. "I—hope he is well and happy. But—we have no interest in him now. That is all closed and done with. As for the courts—I am sure that he has been punished already more than enough."

"It is not a question of punishing him any more. You fail to catch my meaning, it seems. It has come to my knowledge that he has some money, a good deal of it—"

"But you cannot have imagined that I would want his money?"

"His money? He has none. It is all yours. That is why I am telling you about it."

"Oh, but that can't be possible. I don't understand."

Sitting upright in his chair, as businesslike as an attorney, Queed explained how Surface had managed to secrete part of the embezzled trustee funds, and had been snugly living on it ever since his release from prison.

"The exact amount is, at present, mere guesswork. But I think it will hardly fall below fifty thousand dollars, and it may run as high as a hundred thousand. I learn that Mr. Surface thinks, or pretends to think, that this money belongs to him. He is, needless to say, wholly mistaken. I have taken the liberty of consulting a lawyer about it, of course laying it before him as a hypothetical case. I am advised that when Mr. Surface was put through bankruptcy, he must have made a false statement in order to withhold this money. Therefore, that settlement counts for nothing, except to make him punishable for perjury now. The money is yours whenever you apply for it. That—"

"Oh—but I shall not apply for it. I don't want it, you see."

"It is not a question of whether you want it or not. It is yours—in just the way that the furniture in this room is yours. You simply have no right to evade it."

Through all the agitation she felt in the sudden dragging out of this long-buried subject, his air of dictatorial authority brought the blood to her cheek.

"I have a right to evade it, in the first place, and in the second, I am not evading it at all. He took it; I let him keep it. That is the whole situation. I don't want it—I couldn't touch it—"

"Well, don't decide that now. There would be no harm, I suppose, in your talking with your mother about it—even with some man in whose judgment you have confidence. You will feel differently when you have had time to think it over. Probably it—"

"Thinking it over will make not the slightest difference in the way I feel—"

"Perhaps it would if you stopped thinking about it from a purely selfish point of view. Other—"

"*What?*"

"I say," he repeated dryly, "that you should stop thinking of the matter from a purely selfish point of view. Don't you know that that is what you are doing? You are thinking only whether or not you, personally, desire this money. Well, other people have an interest in the question besides you. There is your mother, for example. Why not consider it from her standpoint? Why not consider it from—well, from the standpoint of Mr. Surface?"

"Of Mr. Surface?"

"Certainly. Suppose that in his old age he has become penitent, and wants to do what he can to right the old wrong. Would you refuse him absolution by declining to accept your own money?"

"I think it will be time enough to decide that when Mr. Surface asks me for absolution."

"Undoubtedly. I have particularly asked, you remember, that you do not make up your mind to anything now."

"But you," said she, looking at him steadily enough now—"I don't understand how you happen to be here apparently both as my counselor and Mr. Surface's agent."

"I have a right to both capacities, I assure you."

"Or—have you a habit of being—?"

She left her sentence unended, and he finished it for her in a colorless voice.

"Of being on two sides of a fence, perhaps you were about to say?"

She made no reply.

"That is what you were going to say, isn't it?"

"Yes, I started to say that," she answered, "and then I thought better of it."

She spoke calmly; but she was oddly disquieted by his fixed gaze, and angry with herself for feeling it.

"I will tell you," said he, "how I happen to be acting in both capacities."

The marks of his internal struggle broke through upon his face. For the first time, it occurred to Sharlee, as she looked at the new markings about his straight-cut mouth, that this old young man whom she had commonly seen so matter-of-fact and self-contained, might be a person of stronger emotions than her own. After all, what did she really know about him?

As if to answer her, his controlled voice spoke.

"Mr. Surface is my father. I am his son."

She smothered a little cry. "*Your father!*"

"My name," he said, with a face of stone, "is Henry G. Surface, Jr."

"Your father!" she echoed lifelessly.

Shocked and stunned, she turned her head hurriedly away; her elbow rested on the broad chair-arm, and her chin sank into her hand. Surface's son looked at her. It was many months since he had learned to look at her as at a woman, and that is knowledge that is not unlearned. His eyes rested upon her piled-up mass of crinkly brown hair; upon the dark curtain of lashes lying on her cheek; upon the firm line of the cheek, which swept so smoothly into the white neck; upon the rounded bosom, now rising and falling so fast; upon the whole pretty little person which could so stir him now to undreamed depths of his being.... No altruism here, Fifi; no self-denial to want to make *her* happy.

He began speaking quietly.

"I can't tell you now how I found out all this. It is a long story; you will hear it all some day. But the facts are all clear. I have been to New York and seen Tim Queed. It is—strange, is it not? Do you remember that afternoon in my office, when I showed you the letters from him? We little thought—"

"Oh me!" said Sharlee. "Oh me!"

She rose hastily and walked away from him, unable to bear the look on his face. For a pretense of doing something, she went to the fire and poked aimlessly at the glowing coals.

As on the afternoon of which he spoke, waves of pity for the little Doctor's worse than fatherlessness swept through her; only these waves were a thousand times bigger and stormier than those. How hardly he himself had taken his sonship she read in the strange sadness of his face. She dared not let him see how desperately sorry for him she felt; the most perfunctory phrase might betray her. Her knowledge of his falseness stood between them like a wall; blindly she struggled to keep it staunch, not letting her rushing pity undermine and crumble it. He had been false to her, like his father. Father and son, they had deceived and betrayed her; honor and truth were not in them.

"So you see," the son was saying, "I have a close personal interest in this question of the money. Naturally it—means a good deal to me to—have as much of it as possible restored. Of course there is a great deal which—he took, and which—we are not in position to restore at present. I will explain later what is to be done about that—"

"Oh, don't!" she begged. "I never want to see or hear of it again."

Suddenly she turned upon him, aware that her self-control was going, but unable for her life to repress the sympathy for him which welled up overwhelmingly from her heart.

"Won't you tell me something more about it? Please do! Where is he? Have you seen him—?"

"I cannot tell you—"

"Oh, I will keep your confidence. You asked me if I would. I will—won't you tell me? Is he here—in the city—?"

"You must not ask me these questions," he said with some evidence of agitation.

But even as he spoke, he saw knowledge dawn painfully on her face. His shelter, after all, was too small; once her glance turned that way, once her mind started upon conjectures, discovery had been inevitable.

"Oh!" she cried, in a choked voice.... "It is Professor Nicolovius!"

He looked at her steadily; no change passed over his face. When all was said, he was glad to have the whole truth out; and he knew the secret to be as safe with her as with himself.

"No one must know," he said sadly, "until his death. That is not far away, I think."

She dropped into a chair, and suddenly buried her face in her hands.

Surface's son had risen with her, but he did not resume his seat. He stood looking down at her bowed head, and the expression in his eyes, if she had looked up and captured it, might have taken her completely by surprise.

His chance, indeed, had summoned him, though not for the perfect sacrifice. Circumstance had crushed out most of the joy of giving. For, first, she had suspected him, which nothing could ever blot out; and now, when she knew the truth about him, there could hardly be much left for him to give. It needed no treacherous editorial to make her hate the son of his father; their friendship was over in any case.

Still, it was his opportunity to do for her something genuine and large; to pay in part the debt he owed her—the personal and living debt, which was so much greater than the dead thing of principal and interest.

No, no. It was not endurable that this proud little lady, who kept her head so high, should find at the last moment, this stain upon her lover's honor.

She dropped her hands and lifted a white face.

"And you—" she began unsteadily, but checked herself and went on in a calmer voice. "And you—after what he has done to you, too—you are going to stand by him—take his name—accept that inheritance—be his son?"

"What else is there for me to do?"

Their eyes met, and hers were hurriedly averted.

"Don't you think," he said, "that that is the only thing to do?"

Again she found it impossible to endure the knowledge of his fixed gaze. She rose once more and stood at the mantel, her forehead leaned against her hand upon it, staring unseeingly down into the fire.

"How can I tell you how fine a thing you are doing—how big—and splendid—when—"

A dark red color flooded his face from neck to forehead; it receded almost violently leaving him whiter than before.

"Not at all! Not in the least!" he said, with all his old impatience. "I could not escape if I would."

She seemed not to hear him. "How can I tell you that—and about how sorry I am—when all the time it seems that I can think only of—something else!"

"You are speaking of the reformatory," he said, with bracing directness.

There followed a strained silence.

"Oh," broke from her—"how could you bear to do it?"

"Don't you see that we cannot possibly discuss it? It is a question of one's honor—isn't it? It is impossible that such a thing could be argued about."

"But—surely you have something to say—some explanation to make! Tell me. You will not find me—a hard judge."

"I'm sorry," he said brusquely, "but I can make no explanation."

She was conscious that he stood beside her on the hearth-rug. Though her face was lowered and turned from him, the eye of her mind held perfectly the presentment of his face, and she knew that more than age had gone over it since she had seen it last. Had any other man in the world but West been in the balance, she felt that, despite his own words, she could no longer believe him guilty. And even as it was—how could that conceivably be the face of a man who—

"Won't you shake hands?"

Turning, she gave him briefly the tips of fingers cold as ice. As their hands touched, a sudden tragic sense overwhelmed him that here was a farewell indeed. The light contact set him shaking; and for a moment his iron self-control, which covered torments she never guessed at, almost forsook him.

"Good-by. And may that God of yours who loves all that is beautiful and sweet be good to you—now and always."

She made no reply; he wheeled, abruptly, and left her. But on the threshold he was checked by the sound of her voice.

The interview, from the beginning, had profoundly affected her; these last words, so utterly unlike his usual manner of speech, had shaken her through and through. For some moments she had been miserably aware that, if he would but tell her everything and throw himself on her mercy, she would instantly forgive him. And now, when she saw that she could not make him do that, she felt that tiny door, which she had thought double-locked forever, creaking open, and heard herself saying in a small, desperate voice:—

"You did write it, didn't you?"

But he paused only long enough to look at her and say, quite convincingly:—

"You need hardly ask that—now—need you?"

He went home, to his own bedroom, lit his small student-lamp, and sat down at his table to begin a new article. The debt of money which was his patrimony required of him that he should make every minute tell now.

In old newspaper files at the State Library, he had found the facts of his father's defalcations. The total embezzlement from the Weyland estate, allowing for $14,000 recovered in the enforced settlement of Surface's affairs, stood at $203,000. But that was twenty-seven years ago, and in all this time interest had been doubling and redoubling: simple interest, at 4%, brought it to $420,000; compound interest to something like $500,000, due at the present moment. Against this could be credited only his father's "nest-egg"—provided always that he could find it—estimated at not less than $50,000. That left his father's son staring at a debt of $450,000, due and payable now. It was of course, utterly hopeless. The interest on that sum alone was $18,000 a year, and he could not earn $5000 a year to save his immortal soul.

So the son knew that, however desperately he might strive, he would go to his grave more deeply in debt to Sharlee Weyland than he stood at this moment. But of course it was the trying that chiefly counted. The fifty thousand dollars, which he would turn over to her as soon as he got it—how he was counting on a sum as big as that!—would be a help; so would the three or four thousand a year which he counted on paying toward keeping down the interest. This money in itself would be a good. But much better than that, it would stand as a gage that the son acknowledged and desired to atone for his father's dishonor.

His book must stand aside now—it might be forever. Henceforward he must count his success upon a cash-register. But to-night his pencil labored and dragged. What he wrote he saw was not good. He could do harder things than force himself to sit at a table and put writing upon paper; but over the subtler processes of his mind, which alone yields the rich fruit, no man is master. In an hour he put out his lamp, undressed in the dark, and went to bed.

He lay on his back in the blackness, and in all the world he could find nothing to think about but Sharlee Weyland.

Of all that she had done for him, in a personal way, he had at least tried to give her some idea; he was glad to remember that now. And now at the last, when he was nearer worthy than ever before, she had turned him out because she believed that he had stooped to dishonor. She would have forgiven his sonship; he had been mistaken about that. She had felt sympathy and sorrow for Henry Surface's son, and not repulsion, for he had read it in her face. But she could not forgive him a personal dishonor. And he was glad that, so believing, she would do as she had done; it was the perfect thing to do; to demand honor without a blemish, or to cancel all. Never had she stood so high in his fancy as now when she had ordered him out of her life. His heart leapt with the knowledge that, though she would never know it, he was her true mate there, in their pure passion for Truth.

Whatever else might or might not have been, the knowledge remained with him that she herself had suspected and convicted him. In all that mattered their friendship had ended there. Distrust was unbearable between friends. It was a flaw in his little lady that she could believe him capable of baseness.... But not an unforgivable flaw, it would seem, since every hour that he had spent in her presence had become roses and music in his memory, and the thought that he would see her no more stabbed ceaselessly at his heart.

Yes, Surface's son knew very well what was the matter with him now. The knowledge pulled him from his bed to a seat by the open window; dragged him from his chair to send him pacing on bare feet up and down his little bedroom, up and down, up and down; threw him later, much later, into his chair again, to gaze out, quiet and exhausted, over the sleeping city.

He had written something of love in his time. In his perfect scheme of human society, he had diagnosed with scientific precision the instinct of sex attraction implanted in man's being for the most obvious and grossly practical of reasons: an illusive candle-glow easily lit, quickly extinguished when its uses were fulfilled. And lo, here was love tearing him by the throat till he choked; an exquisite torture, a rampant passion, a devastating flame, that most glorified when it burned most deeply, aroar and ablaze forevermore.

He sat by the window and looked out over the sleeping city.

By slow degrees, he had allowed himself to be drawn from his academic hermitry into contact with the visible life around him. And everywhere that he had touched life, it had turned about and smitten him. He had meant to be a great editor of the *Post* some day, and the *Post* had turned him out with a brand of dishonor upon his forehead. He had tried to befriend a friendless old man, and he had acquired a father whose bequest was a rogue's debt, and his name a byword and a hissing. He had let himself be befriended by a slim little girl with a passion for Truth and enough blue eyes for two, and the price of that contact was this pain in his heart which would not be still ... which would not be still.

Yet he would not have had anything different, would not have changed anything if he could. He was no longer the pure scientist in the observatory, but a bigger and better thing, a man ... A man down in the thick of the hurly-burly which we call This Life, and which, when all is said, is all that we certainly know. Not by pen alone, but also by body and mind and heart and spirit, he had taken his man's place in Society. And as for this unimagined pain that strung his whole being upon the thumb-screw, it was nothing but the measure of the life he had now, and had it more abundantly. Oh, all was for the best, all as it should be. He knew the truth about living at last, and it is the truth that makes men free.

CHAPTER XXX

Death of the Old Professor, and how Queed finds that his List of Friends has grown; a Last Will and Testament; Exchange of Letters among Prominent Attorneys, which unhappily proves futile.

On the merriest, maddest day in March, Henry G. Surface, who had bitterly complained of earthly justice, slipped away to join the invisible procession which somewhere winds into the presence of the Incorruptible Judge. He went with his lips locked. At the last moment there had been faint signs of recurring consciousness; the doctor had said that there was one chance in a hundred that the dying man might have a normal moment at the end. On this chance his son had said to the nurse, alone with him in the room:—

"Will you kindly leave me with him a moment? If he should be conscious there is a private question of importance that I must ask him."

She left him. The young man knelt down by the bedside, and put his lips close to the old man's ear. Vainly he tried to drive his voice into that stilled consciousness, and drag from his father the secret of the hiding-place of his loot.

"Father!" he said, over and over. "Father! *Where is the money?*"

There was no doubt that the old man stirred a little. In the dim light of the room it seemed to his son that his right eye half opened, leaving the other closed in a ghastly parody of a wink, while the upper lip drew away from the strong teeth like an evil imitation of the old bland sneer. But that was all.

So Surface died, and was gathered to his fathers. The embargo of secrecy was lifted; and the very first step toward righting the ancient wrong was to let the full facts be known. Henry G. Surface, Jr., took this step, in person, by at once telephoning all that was salient to the *Post*. Brower Williams, the *Post's* city editor, at the other end of the wire, called the name of his God in holy awe at the dimensions of the scoop thus dropped down upon him as from heaven; and implored the Doc, for old time's sake, by all that he held most sacred and most dear, to say not a word till the evening papers were out, thus insuring the sensation for the *Post*.

Mr. Williams's professional appraisement of the scoop proved not extravagant. The *Post's* five columns next morning threw the city into something like an uproar. It is doubtful if you would not have to go back to the '60's to find a newspaper story which eclipsed this one in effect. For a generation, the biography of Henry G. Surface had had, in that city and State, a quality of undying interest, and the sudden denouement, more thrilling than any fiction, captured the imagination of the dullest. Nothing else was mentioned at any breakfast-table where a morning paper was taken that day; hardly anything for many breakfasts to follow. In homes containing boys who had actually studied Greek under the mysterious Professor Nicolovius at Mimer's School, discussion grew almost hectic; while at Mrs. Paynter's, where everybody was virtually a leading actor in the moving drama, the excitement closely approached delirium.

Henry G. Surface, Jr., was up betimes on the morning after his father's death—in fact, as will appear, he had not found time to go to bed at all—and the sensational effects of the *Post's* story were not lost upon him. As early as seven o'clock, a knot of people had gathered in front of the little house on Duke of Gloucester Street, staring curiously at the shut blinds, and telling each other, doubtless, how well they had known the dead man. When young Surface came out of the front door, an awed hush fell upon them; he was aware of their nudges, and their curious but oddly respectful stare. And this, at the very beginning, was typical of the whole day; wherever he went, he found himself an object of the frankest public curiosity. But all of this interest, he early discovered, was neither cool nor impersonal.

To begin with, there was the *Post's* story itself. As he hurried through it very early in the morning, the young man was struck again and again with the delicacy of the phrasing. And gradually it came to him that the young men of the *Post* had made very special efforts to avoid hurting the feelings of their old associate and friend the Doc. This little discovery had touched him unbelievably. And it was only part with other kindness that came to him to soften that first long day of his acknowledged sonship. Probably the sympathy extended to him from various sources was not really so abundant, but to him, having looked for nothing, it was simply overwhelming. All day, it seemed to him, his door-bell and telephone rang, all day unexpected people of all sorts and conditions stopped him on the street—only to tell him, in many ways and sometimes without saying a word about it, that they were sorry.

The very first of them to come was Charles Gardiner West, stopping on his way to the office, troubled, concerned, truly sympathetic, to express, in a beautiful and perfect way, his lasting interest in his one-time assistant. Not far behind him had come Mr. Hickok, the director who looked like James

E. Winter, who had often chatted with the assistant editor in times gone by, and who spoke confidently of the day when he would come back to the *Post*. Beverley Byrd had come, too, manly and friendly; Plonny Neal, ill at ease for once in his life; Evan Montague, of the *Post*, had asked to be allowed to make the arrangements for the funeral; Buck Klinker had actually made those arrangements. Better than most of these, perhaps, were the young men of the Mercury, raw, embarrassed, genuine young men, who, stopping him on the street, did not seem to know why they stopped him, who, lacking West's verbal felicity, could do nothing but take his hand, hot with the fear that they might be betrayed into expressing any feeling, and stammer out: "Doc, if you want anything—why dammit, Doc—you call on *me*, hear?"

Best of all had been Buck Klinker—Buck, who had made him physically, who had dragged him into contact with life over his own protests, who had given him the first editorial he ever wrote that was worth reading—Buck, the first real friend he had ever had. It was to Buck that he had telephoned an hour after his father's death, for he needed help of a practical sort at once, and his one-time trainer was the man of all men to give it to him. Buck had come, constrained and silent; he was obviously awed by the Doc's sudden emergence into stunning notoriety. To be Surface's son was, to him, like being the son of Iscariot and Lucrezia Borgia. On the other hand, he was aware that, of Klinkers and Queeds, a Surface might proudly say: "There are no such people." So he had greeted his friend stiffly as Mr. Surface, and was amazed at the agitation with which that usually impassive young man had put a hand upon his shoulder and said: "I'm the same Doc always to you, Buck, only now I'm Doc Surface instead of Doc Queed." After that everything had been all right. Buck had answered very much after the fashion of the young men of the Mercury, and then rushed off to arrange for the interment, and also to find for Doc Surface lodgings somewhere which heavily undercut Mrs. Paynter's modest prices.

The sudden discovery that he was not alone in the world, that he had friends in it, real friends who believed in him and whom nothing could ever take away, shook the young man to the depths of his being. Was not this compensation for everything? Never had he imagined that people could be so kind; never had he dreamed that people's kindness could mean so much to him. In the light of this new knowledge, it seemed to him that the last scales fell from his eyes ... Were not these friendships, after all, the best work of a man's life? Did he place a higher value even on his book itself, which, it seemed, he might never finish now?

And now there returned to him something that the dead old Colonel had told him long ago, and to-day he saw it for truth. However his father had wronged him, he would always have this, at least, to bless his memory for. For it was his father who had called him to live in this city where dwelt, as the strong voice that was now still had said, the kindest and sweetest people in the world.

Henry G. Surface died at half-past two o'clock on the afternoon of March 24. At one o'clock that night, while the *Post's* startling story was yet in process of the making, his son stood at the mantel in Surface's sitting-room, and looked over the wreck that his hands had made. That his father's treasures were hidden somewhere here he had hardly entertained a doubt. Yet he had pulled the place all to pieces without finding a trace of them.

The once pretty sitting-room looked, indeed, as if a tornado had struck it. The fireplace was a litter of broken brick and mortar; half the floor was ripped up and the boards flung back anyhow; table drawers and bookcases had been ransacked, and looked it; books rifled in vain were heaped in disorderly hummocks wherever there was room for them; everywhere a vandal hand had been, leaving behind a train of devastation and ruin.

And it had all been fruitless. He had been working without pause since half-past six o'clock, and not the smallest clue had rewarded him.

It was one of those interludes when early spring demonstrates that she could play August convincingly had she a mind to. The night was stifling. That the windows had to be shut tight, to deaden the noise of loosening brick and ripping board, made matters so much the worse. Surface was stripped to the waist, and it needed no second glance at him, as he stood now, to see that he was physically competent. There was no one-sided over-development here; Klinker's exercises, it will be remembered, were for all parts of the body. Shoulders stalwart, but not too broad, rounded beautifully into the upper arm; the chest swelled like a full sail; many a woman in that town had a larger waist. Never he moved but muscle flowed and rippled under the shining skin; he raised his right hand to scratch his left ear, and the hard blue biceps leaped out like a live thing. In fact, it had been some months since the young man had first entertained the suspicion that he could administer that thrashing to Mr. Pat whenever he felt inclined. Only it happened that he and Mr. Pat had become pretty good friends now, and it was the proof-reader's boast that he had never once made a bull in "Mr. Queed's copy" since the day of the famous fleas.

In the quiet night the young man stood resting from his labors, and taking depressed thought. He was covered with grime and streaked with sweat; a ragged red stripe on his cheek, where a board had bounced up and struck him, detracted nothing from the sombreness of his appearance. Somewhere, valuable papers waited to be found; bank-books, certainly; very likely stock or bonds or certificates of deposit; please God, a will.

Somewhere—but where? From his father's significant remark during their last conversation, he would have staked his life that all these things were here, in easy reach. And yet—

Standing precariously on the loose-piled bricks of the fireplace, he looked over the ravaged room. He felt profoundly discouraged. Success in this search meant more to him than he liked to think about, and now his chance of success had shrunk to the vanishing point. The bowels of the room lay open before his eye, and there was no hiding-place in them. He knew of nowhere else to look. The cold fear seized him that the money and the papers were hidden beyond his finding—that they lay tucked away in some safety-deposit vault in New York, where his eye would never hunt them out.

Surface's son leaned against the elaborate mantel, illimitably weary. He shifted his position ever so little; and thereupon luck did for him what reason would never have done. The brick on which his right foot rested turned under his weight and he lost his foothold. To save himself, he caught the mantel-top with both hands, and the next moment pitched heavily backward to the floor.

The mantel, in fact, had come off in his hands. It pitched to the floor with him, speeding his fall, thumping upon his chest like a vigorous adversary. But the violence of his descent only made him the more sharply aware that this strange mantel had left its moorings as though on greased rollers.

His heart playing a sudden drum-beat, he threw the carven timber from him and bounded to his feet. The first flying glance showed him the strange truth: his blundering feet had marvelously stumbled into his father's arcana. For he looked, not at an unsightly mass of splintered laths and torn wall-paper and shattered plaster, but into as neat a little cupboard as a man could wish.

The cupboard was as wide as the mantel itself; lined and ceiled with a dark red wood which beautifully threw back the glare of the dancing gas-jet. It was half-full of things, old books, letters, bundles of papers held together with rubber bands, canvas bags—all grouped and piled in the most orderly way about a large tin dispatch-box. This box drew the young man's gaze like a sudden shout; he was hardly on his feet before he had sprung forward and jerked it out. Instantly the treacherous bricks threw him again; sprawled on the floor he seized one of them and smashed through the hasp at a blow.

Bit by bit the illuminating truth came out. In all his own calculations, close and exact as he had thought them, he had lost sight of one simple but vital fact. In the years that he had been in prison, his father had spent no money beyond the twenty-five dollars a month to Tim Queed; and comparatively little in the years of his wanderings. In all this time the interest upon his "nest-egg" had been steadily accumulating. Five per cent railroad bonds, and certificates of deposit in four different banks, were the forms in which the money had been tucked away, by what devilish cleverness could only be imagined. But the simple fact was that his father had died worth not less than two hundred thousand dollars and probably more. And this did not include the house, which, it appeared, his father had bought, and not leased as he said; nor did it include four thousand four hundred dollars in gold and banknotes which he found in the canvas sacks after his first flying calculation was made.

Early in the morning, when the newsboys were already crying the *Post* upon the streets, young Henry Surface came at last upon the will. It was very brief, but entirely clear and to the point. His father had left to him without conditions, everything of which he died possessed. The will was dated in June of the previous summer—he recalled a two days' absence of his father's at that time—and was witnessed, in a villainous hand, by Timothy Queed.

There were many formalities to be complied with, and some of them would take time. But within a week matters were on a solid enough footing to warrant a first step; and about this time Sharlee Weyland read, at her breakfast-table one morning, a long letter which surprised and disturbed her very much.

The letter came from a well-known firm of attorneys. At great length it rehearsed the misfortunes that had befallen the Weyland estate, through the misappropriations of the late Henry G. Surface. But the gist of this letter, briefly put, was that the late Henry G. Surface had died possessed of a property estimated to be worth two hundred thousand dollars, either more or less; that this property was believed to be merely the late trustee's appropriations from the Weyland estate, with accrued interest; that "our client Mr. Henry G. Surface, Jr., heir by will to his father's ostensible property," therefore purposed to pay over this sum to the Weyland estate, as soon as necessary formalities could be complied with; and that, further, our client, Mr. Henry G. Surface, Jr., assumed personal responsibility "for the residue due to your late father's estate, amounting to one hundred and seventeen thousand dollars, either more or less, with interest since 1881; and this debt, he instructs us to say, he will discharge from time to time, as his own resources will permit."

So wrote Messrs. Blair and Jamieson to Miss Charlotte Lee Weyland, congratulating her, "in conclusion, upon the strange circumstances which have brought you, after so long an interval, justice and restitution," and begging to remain very respectfully hers. To which letter after four days' interval, they received the following reply:

Messrs. Blair & Jamieson,
Commonwealth Building,
City.

DEAR SIRS:—

Our client, Miss C.L. Weyland, of this city, instructs us to advise you, in reply to your letter of the 4th inst., directed to her, that, while thanking you for the expression of intention therein contained anent the property left by the late Henry G. Surface, and very cordially appreciating the spirit actuating Mr. Henry G. Surface, Jr., in the matter, she nevertheless feels herself without title or claim to said property, and therefore positively declines to accept it, in whole or in any part.

Respectfully yours,

AMPERSAND, BOLLING AND BYRD.

A more argumentative and insistent letter from Messrs. Blair and Jamieson was answered with the same brief positiveness by Messrs. Ampersand, Bolling and Byrd. Thereafter, no more communications were exchanged by the attorneys. But a day or two after her second refusal, Sharlee Weyland received another letter about the matter of dispute, this time a more personal one. The envelope was directed in a small neat hand which she knew very well; she had first seen it on sheets of yellow paper in Mrs. Paynter's dining-room. The letter said:

DEAR Miss WEYLAND:—

Your refusal to allow my father's estate to restore to you, so far as it can, the money which it took from you, and thus to right, in part, a grave wrong, is to me a great surprise and disappointment. I had not thought it possible that you, upon due reflection, could take a position the one obvious effect of which is to keep a son permanently under the shadow of his father's dishonor.

Do not, of course, misunderstand me. I have known you too well to believe for a moment that you can be swayed by ungenerous motives. I am very sure that you are taking now the part which you believe most generous. But that view is, I assure you, so far from the real facts that I can only conclude that you have refused to learn what these facts are. Both legally and morally the money is yours. No one else on earth has a shadow of claim to it. I most earnestly beg that, in fairness to me, you will at least give my attorneys the chance to convince yours that what I write here is true and unanswerable.

Should you adhere to your present position, the money will, of course, be trusteed for your benefit, nor will a penny of it be touched until it is accepted, if not by you, then by your heirs or assigns. But I cannot believe that you will continue to find magnanimity in shirking your just responsibilities, and denying to me my right to wipe out this stain.

Very truly yours,

HENRY G. SURFACE, Jr.

No answer ever came to this letter, and there the matter rested through March and into the sultry April.

CHAPTER XXXI

God moves in a Mysterious Way: how the Finished Miss Avery appears as the Instrument of Providence; how Sharlee sees her Idol of Many Years go toppling in the Dust, and how it is her Turn to meditate in the Still Watches.

The print danced before his outraged eyes; his chest heaved at the revolting evidence of man's duplicity; and Charles Gardiner West laid down his morning's *Post* with a hand that shook.

Meachy T. Bangor announces his candidacy for the nomination for Mayor, subject to the Democratic primary.

For West had not a moment's uncertainty as to what this announcement meant. Meachy T. Bangor spoke, nay invented, the language of the tribe. He was elect of the elect; what the silent powers that were thought was his thought; their ways were his ways, their people his people. When Meachy T. Bangor announced that he was a candidate for the nomination for Mayor, it meant that the all-powerful machine had already nominated him for Mayor, and whom the organization nominated it elected. Meachy T. Bangor! Plonny Neal's young, progressive candidate of the reformer type!

Bitterness flooded West's soul when he thought of Plonny. Had the boss been grossly deceived or grossly deceiving? Could that honest and affectionate eye, whose look of frank admiration had been almost embarrassing, have covered base and deliberate treachery? Was it possible that he, West, who had always been confident that he could see as far into a millstone as another, had been a cheap trickster's easy meat?

Day by day, since the appearance of the reformatory article, West had waited for some sign of appreciation and understanding from those on the inside. None had come. Not a soul except himself, and Plonny, had appeared aware that he, by a masterly compromise, had averted disaster from the party, and clearly revealed himself as the young man of destiny. On the contrary, the House spokesmen, apparently utterly blind to any impending crisis, had, in the closing hours of the session, voted away some eighty thousand dollars of the hundred thousand rescued by West from the reformatory, in a multiplication of offices which it was difficult to regard as absolutely indispensable in a hard times year. This action, tallying so closely with what his former assistant had predicted, had bewildered and unsettled West; the continuing silence of the leaders—"the other leaders," he had found himself saying—had led him into anxious speculations; and now, in a staggering burst, the disgraceful truth was revealed to him. They had used him, tricked and used him like a smooth tool, and having used him, had deliberately passed him, standing fine and patient in the line, to throw the mantle over the corrupt and unspeakable Bangor.

By heavens, it was not to be endured. Was it for this that he had left Blaines College, where a career of honorable usefulness lay before him; that he had sacrificed personal wishes and ambitions to the insistent statement that his City and State had need of him; that he had stood ten months in the line without a murmur; and that at last, confronted with the necessity of choosing between the wishes of his personal intimates and the larger good, he had courageously chosen the latter and suffered in silence the suspicion of having played false with the best friends he had in the world? Was it for this that he had lost his valuable assistant, whose place he could never hope to fill?—for this that he was referred to habitually by an evening contemporary as the Plonny Neal organ?

He was thoroughly disgusted with newspaper work this morning, disgusted with the line, disgusted with hopeful efforts to uplift the people. What did his *Post* work really amount to?—unremitting toil, the ceaseless forcing up of immature and insincere opinions, no thanks or appreciation anywhere, and at the end the designation of the Plonny Neal organ. What did the uplift amount to? Could progress really ever be forced a single inch? And why should he wear out his life in the selfless service of those who, it seemed, acknowledged no obligation to him? As for public life, if this was a sample, the less he saw of it the better. He would take anything in the world sooner than a career of hypocrisy, double-dealing and treachery, of dirty looting in the name of the public good, of degrading traffic with a crew of liars and confidence men.

But through all the young man's indignation and resentment there ran an unsteadying doubt, a miserable doubt of himself. Had his motives in the reformatory matter been as absolutely spotless as he had charmed himself into believing?... What manner of man was he? Did he really have any permanent convictions about anything?... Was it possible, was it thinkable or conceivable, that he was a complaisant invertebrate whom the last strong man that had his ear could play upon like a flute?

West passed a most unhappy morning. But at lunch, at the club, it was his portion to have his buoyant good-humor completely restored to him. He fell in with ancient boon companions; they made much of him; involved him in gay talk; smoothed him down, patted him on the head, found his self-esteem for him, and handed it over in its pristine vigor. Before he had sat half an hour at the merry table, he could look back at his profound depression of the morning with smiling wonder. Where in the world had he gotten his terrible grouch? Not a thing in the world had happened, except that the mayoralty was not going to be handed to him on a large silver platter. Was that such a fearful loss after all? On the contrary, was it not rather a good riddance? Being Mayor, in all human probability, would be a horrible bore.

It was a mild, azure, zephyrous day; spring at her brightest and best. West, descending the club steps, sniffed the fragrant air affectionately, and was hanged if he would go near the office on such an afternoon. Let the *Post* readers plod along to-morrow with an editorial page both skimpy and inferior; anything he gave them would still be too good for them, middle-class drabs and dullards that they were.

The big red automobile was old now, and needed paint, but it still ran staunch and true; and Miss Avery had a face, a form, and a sinuous graceful manner, had veils and hats and sinuous graceful coats, that would have glorified a far less worthy vehicle. And she drove divinely. By invitation she took the wheel that afternoon, and with sure, clever hands whipped the docile leviathan over the hills and far away.

The world knows how fate uses her own instruments in her own way, frequently selecting far stranger ones than the delightful and wealthy Miss Avery. Now for more than a year this accomplished girl had been thinking that if Charles Gardiner West had anything to say to her, it was high time that he should say it. If she had not set herself to find out what was hobbling the tongue of the man she wanted, she would have been less than a woman; and Miss Avery was a good deal more. Hence, when she had seen West with Sharlee Weyland, and in particular on the last two or three times she had seen West with Sharlee Weyland, she had watched his manner toward that lady with profound misgivings, of the sort which starts every true woman to fighting for her own.

Now Miss Avery had a weapon, in the shape of valuable knowledge, or, at any rate, a valuable suspicion that had lately reached her: the suspicion, in short, which had somehow crept abroad as suspicions will, that West had done a certain thing which another man was supposed to have done. Therefore, when they turned homeward in the soft dusk, her man having been brought to exactly the right frame of mind, she struck with her most languorous voice.

"How is that dear little Charlotte Weyland? It seems to me I haven't seen her for a year, though it was positively only last week."

"Oh! She seemed very well when I saw her last."

So Mr. West, of the lady he was going to marry. For, though he had never had just the right opportunity to complete the sweet message he had begun at the Byrds' one night, his mind was still quite made up on that point. It was true that the atmosphere of riches which fairly exuded from the girl now at his side had a very strong appeal for his lower instincts. But he was not a man to be ridden by his lower instincts. No; he had set his foot upon the fleshpots; his idealistic nature had overcome the world.

Miss Avery, sublimely unaware that Mr. West was going to offer marriage to her rival during the present month, the marriage itself to take place in October, indolently continued:—

"To my mind she's quite the most attractive dear little thing in town. I suppose she's quite recovered from her disappointment over the—hospital, or whatever it was?"

"Oh, I believe so. I never heard her mention it but once."

West's pleasant face had clouded a little. Through her fluttering veil she noted that fact with distinct satisfaction.

"I never met that interesting young Mr. Surface," said she, sweeping the car around a curve in the white road and evading five women in a surrey with polished skill. "But—truly, I have found myself thinking of him and feeling sorry for him more than once."

"Sorry for him—What about?"

"Oh, haven't you heard, then? It's rather mournful. You see, when Charlotte Weyland found out that he had written a certain editorial in the *Post*—you know more about this part of it than I—"

"But he didn't write it," said West, unhesitatingly. "I wrote it myself."

"You?"

She looked at him with frank surprise in her eyes; not too much frank surprise; rather as one who feels much but endeavors to suppress it for courtesy's sake. "Forgive me—I didn't know. There has been a little horrid gossip but of course nearly every one has thought that he—"

"I'm sure I'm not responsible for what people think," said West, a little aggressively, but with a strangely sinking heart. "There has been not the slightest mystery or attempt at concealment—"

"Oh! Then of course Charlotte knows all about it now?"

"I don't know whether she does or not. When I tried to tell her the whole story," explained West, "soon after the incident occurred, she was so agitated about it, the subject seemed so painful to her, that I was forced to give it up. You can understand my position. Ever since, I have been waiting for an opportunity to take her quietly and straighten out the whole matter for her in a calm and rational way. For her part she has evidently regarded the subject as happily closed. Why under heaven should I press it upon her—merely to gain the academic satisfaction of convincing her that the *Post* acted on information superior and judgment sounder than her own?"

Miss Avery, now devoting herself to her chauffeur's duties through a moment of silence, was no match for Mr. West at the game of ethical debate, and knew it. However, she held a very strong card in her pongee sleeve, and she knew that too.

"I see—of course. You know I think you have been quite right through it all. And yet—you won't mind?—I can't help feeling sorry for Mr. Surface."

"Very well—you most mysterious lady. Go on and tell me why you can't help feeling sorry for Mr. Surface."

Miss Avery told him. How she knew anything about the private affairs of Mr. Surface and Miss Weyland, of which it is certain that neither of them had ever spoken, is a mystery, indeed: but Gossip is Argus and has a thousand ears to boot. Miss Avery was careful to depict Sharlee's attitude toward the unfortunate Mr. Surface as just severe enough to suggest to West that he must act at once, and not so severe as to suggest to him— conceivably—the desirability, from a selfish point of view, of not acting at all. It was a task for a diplomat, which is to say a task for a Miss Avery.

"Rather fine of him, wasn't it, to assume all the blame?—particularly if it's true, as people say," concluded Miss Avery, "that the man's in love with her and she cares nothing for him."

"Fine—splendid—but entirely unnecessary," said West.

The little story had disturbed him greatly. He had had no knowledge of any developments between Sharlee and his former assistant; and now he was unhappily conscious that he ought to have spoken weeks ago.

"I'm awfully sorry to hear this," he resumed, "for I am much attached to that boy. Still—if, as you say, everything is all right now—"

"Oh, but I don't know at all that it is," said Miss Avery, hastily. "That is just the point. The last I heard of it, she had forbidden him her house."

"That won't do," said Charles Gardiner West, in a burst of generosity. "I'll clear up that difficulty before I sleep to-night."

And he was as good as his word, or, let us say, almost as good. The next night but one he called upon Sharlee Weyland with two unalterable purposes in his mind. One was to tell her the full inside history of the reformatory article from the beginning. The other was to notify her in due form that she held his heart in permanent captivity.

To Miss Avery, it made not the slightest difference whether the gifted and charming editor of the Post sold out his principles for a price every morning in the month. At his pleasure he might fracture all of the decalogue that was refinedly fracturable, and so long as he rescued his social position intact from the ruin, he was her man just the same. But she had an instinct, surer than reasoned wisdom, that Sharlee Weyland viewed these matters differently. Therefore she had sent West to make his little confession, face to face. And therefore West, after an hour of delightful *tête-à-tête* in the charming little back parlor, stiffened himself up, his brow sicklying o'er with the pale cast of disagreeable thought, and began to make it.

"I've got to tell you something about—a subject that won't be welcome to you," he plunged in, rather lugubriously. "I mean—the reformatory."

Sharlee's face, which had been merry and sweet, instantly changed and quieted at that word; interest sprang full-armed in her deep blue eyes.

"Have you? Tell me anything about it you wish."

"You remember that—last editorial in the *Post?*"

"Do you think that I forget so easily?"

West hardly liked that reply. Nor had he ever supposed that he would find the subject so difficult.

"Well! I was surprised and—hurt to learn—recently—that you had—well, had been rather severe with Surface, under the impression that—the full responsibility for that article was his."

Sharlee sat in the same flowered arm-chair she had once occupied to put this same Surface, then known as little Dr. Queed, in his place. Her heart warmed to West for his generous impulse to intercede. Still, she hardly conceived that her treatment of Mr. Surface was any concern of Mr. West's.

"And so?"

"I must tell you," he said, oddly uneasy under her straightforward look, "that—that you have made a mistake. The responsibility is mine."

"Ah, you mean that you, as the editor, are willing to take it."

"No," said West—"no"; and then suddenly he felt like a rash suicide, repentant at the last moment. Already the waters were rushing over his head; he felt a wild impulse to clutch at the life-belt she had flung out to him. It is to be remembered to his credit that he conquered it. "No,—I—I wrote the article myself."

"You?"

Her monosyllable had been Miss Avery's, but there resemblance parted. Sharlee sat still in her chair, and presently her lashes fluttered and fell. To West's surprise, a beautiful color swept upward from her throat to drown in her rough dark hair. "Oh," said she, under her breath, "I'm glad—so *glad!*"

West heaved a great sigh of relief. It was all over, and she was glad. Hadn't he known all along that a woman will always forgive everything in the man she loves? She was glad because he had told her when another man might have kept silent. And yet her look perplexed him; her words perplexed him. Undoubtedly she must have something more to say than a mere expression of vague general gladness over the situation.

"Need I say that I never intended there should be any doubt about the matter? I meant to explain it all to you long ago, only there never seemed to be any suitable opportunity."

Sharlee's color died away. In silence she raised her eyes and looked at him.

"I started to tell you all about it once, at the time, but you know," he said, with a little nervous laugh, "you seemed to find the subject so extremely painful then—that I thought I had better wait till you could look at it more calmly."

Still she said nothing, but only sat still in her chair and looked at him.

"I shall always regret," continued West, laboriously, "that my—silence, which I assure you I meant in kindness, should have—Why do you look at me that way, Miss Weyland?" he said, with a quick change of voice. "I don't understand you."

Sharlee gave a small start and said: "Was I looking at you in any particular way?"

"You looked as mournful," said West, with that same little laugh, "as though you had lost your last friend. Now—"

"No, not my last one," said Sharlee.

"Well, don't look so sad about it," he said, in a voice of affectionate raillery. "I am quite unhappy enough over it without—"

"I'm afraid I can't help you to feel happier—not to-night. If I look sad, you see, it is because I feel that way."

"Sad?" he echoed, bewildered. "Why should you be sad now—when it is all going to be straightened out—when—"

"Well, don't you think it's pretty sad—the part that can't ever be straightened out?"

Unexpectedly she got up, and walked slowly away, a disconcerting trick she had; wandered about the room, looking about her something like a stranger in a picture gallery; touching a bowl of flowers here, there setting a book to rights; and West, rising too, following her sombrely with his eyes, had never wanted her so much in all his life.

Presently she returned to him; asked him to sit down again; and, still standing herself, began speaking in a quiet kind voice which, nevertheless, rang ominously in his ears from her first word.

"I remember," said Sharlee, "when I was a very little girl, not more than twelve years old, I think, I first heard about you—about Charles Gardiner West. You were hardly grown then, but already people were talking about you. I don't remember now, of course, just what they said, but it must have been something very splendid, for I remember the sort of picture I got. I have always liked for men to be very clean and high-minded—I think because my father was that sort of man. I have put that above intellect, and abilities, and what would be called attractions; and so what they said about you made a great impression on me. You know how very young girls are—how they like to have the figure of a prince to spin their little romances around ... and so I took you for mine. You were my knight without fear and without reproach ... Sir Galahad. When I was sixteen, I used to pass you in the street and wonder if you didn't hear my heart thumping. You never looked at me; you hadn't any idea who I was. And that is a big and fine thing, I think—to be the hero of somebody you don't even know by name ... though of course not so big and fine as to be the hero of somebody who knows you very well. And you were that to me, too. When I grew up and came to know you, I still kept you on that pedestal you never saw. I measured you by the picture I had carried for so many years, and I was not disappointed. All that my little girl's fancy had painted you, you seemed to be. I look back now over the last few years of my life, and so much that I have liked most—that has been dearest—has centred about you. Yes, more than once I have been quite sure that I was in love with you. You wonder that I can show you my heart this way? I couldn't of course, except—well—that it is all past now. And that is what seems sad to me.... There never was any prince; my knight is dead; and Sir Galahad I got out of a book.... Don't you think that that is pretty sad?"

West, who had been looking at her with a kind of frightened fascination, hastily averted his eyes, for he saw that her own had suddenly filled with tears. She turned away from him again; a somewhat painful silence ensued; and presently she broke it, speaking in a peculiarly gentle voice, and not looking at him.

"I'm glad that you told me—at last. I'll be glad to remember that ... and I'm always your friend. But don't you think that perhaps we'd better finish our talk some other time?"

"No," said West. "No."

He pulled himself together, struggling desperately to throw off the curious benumbing inertia that was settling down upon him. "You are doing me an injustice. A most tremendous injustice. You have misunderstood everything from the beginning. I must explain—"

"Don't you think that argument will only make it all so much worse?"

"Nothing could possibly be worse for me than to have you think of me and speak to me in this way."

Obediently she sat down, her face still and sad; and West, pausing a moment to marshal his thoughts into convincing form, launched forth upon his defense.

From the first he felt that he did not make a success of it; was not doing himself justice. Recent events, in the legislature and with reference to Meachy T. Bangor, had greatly weakened his confidence in his arguments. Even to himself he seemed to have been strangely "easy"; his exposition sounded labored and hollow in his own ears. But worse than this was the bottomless despondency into which the girl's brief autobiography had strangely cast him. A vast mysterious depression had closed over him, which entirely robbed him of his usual adroit felicity of speech. He brought his explanation up to the publication of the unhappy article, and there abruptly broke off.

A long silence followed his ending, and at last Sharlee said:—

"I suppose a sudden change of heart in the middle of a fight is always an unhappy thing. It always means a good deal of pain for somebody. Still— sometimes they must come, and when they do, I suppose the only thing to do is to meet them honestly—though, personally, I think I should always trust my heart against my head. But ... if you had only come to us that first morning and frankly explained just why you deserted us—if you had told us all this that you have just told me—"

"That is exactly what I wanted and intended to do," interrupted West. "I kept silent out of regard for you."

"Out of regard for me?"

"When I started to tell you all about it, that night at Mrs. Byrd's, it seemed to me that you had brooded over the matter until you had gotten in an overwrought and—overstrung condition about it. It seemed to me the considerate thing not to force the unwelcome topic upon you, but rather to wait—"

"But had you the right to consider my imaginary feelings in such a matter between yourself and ...? And besides, you did not quite keep silent, you remember. You said something that led me to think that you had discharged Mr. Surface for writing that article."

"I did not intend you to think anything of the kind. Anything in the least like that. If my words were ambiguous, it was because, seeing, as I say, that you were in an overstrung condition, I thought it best to let the whole matter rest until you could look at it calmly and rationally."

She made no reply.

"But why dwell on that part of it?" said West, beseechingly. "It was simply a wretched misunderstanding all around. I'm sorrier than I can tell you for my part in it. I have been greatly to blame—I can see that now. Can't you let bygones be bygones? I have come to you voluntarily and told you—"

"Yes, after six weeks. Why, I was the best friend he had, Mr. West, and—Oh, me! How can I bear to remember what I said to him!"

She turned her face hurriedly away from him. West, much moved, struggled on.

"But don't you see—I didn't know it! I never dreamed of such a thing. The moment I heard how matters stood—"

"Did it never occur to you in all this time that it might be assumed that Mr. Surface, having written all the reformatory articles, had written this one?"

"I did not think of that. I was short-sighted, I own. And of course," he added more eagerly, "I supposed that he had told you himself."

"You don't know him," said Sharlee.

A proud and beautiful look swept over her face. West rose, looking wretchedly unhappy, and stood, irresolute, facing her.

"Can't you—forgive me?" he asked presently, in a painful voice.

Sharlee hesitated.

"Don't you know I said that it would only make things worse to talk about it to-night?" she said gently. "Everything you say seems to put us further and further apart. Why, there is nothing for me to forgive, Mr. West. There was a situation, and it imposed a certain conduct on you; that is the whole story. I don't come into it at all. It is all a matter between you and— your own-"

"You do forgive me then? But no—you talk to me just as though you had learned all this from somebody else—as though I had not come to you voluntarily and told you everything."

Sharlee did not like to look at his face, which she had always seen before so confident and gay.

"No," said she sadly—"for I am still your friend."

"Friend!"

He echoed the word wildly, contemptuously. He was just on the point of launching into a passionate speech, painting the bitterness of friendship to one who must have true love or nothing, and flinging his hand and his heart impetuously at her feet. But looking at her still face, he checked himself, and just in time. Shaken by passion as he was, he was yet enough himself to understand that she would not listen to him. Why should he play the spendthrift and the wanton with his love? Why give her, for nothing, the sterile satisfaction of rejecting him, for her to prize, as he knew girls did, as merely one more notch upon her gun?

Leaving his tempestuous exclamation hanging in mid-air, West stiffly shook Sharlee's hand and walked blindly out of the room.

He went home, and to bed, like one moving in a horrible dream. That night, and through all the next day, he felt utterly bereft and wretched: something, say, as though flood and pestilence had swept through his dear old town and carried off everything and everybody but himself. He crawled alone in a smashed world. On the second day following, he found himself able to light a cigarette; and, glancing about him with faint pluckings of convalescent interest, began to recognize some landmarks. On the third day, he was frankly wondering whether a girl with such overstrained, not to say hysterical ideals of conduct, would, after all, be a very comfortable person to spend one's life with.

On the evening of this day, about half-past eight o'clock, he emerged from his mother's house, light overcoat over his arm in deference to his evening clothes, and started briskly down the street. On the second block, as luck had it, he overtook Tommy Semple walking the same way.

"Gardiner," said Semple, "when are you going to get over all this uplift rot and come back to Semple and West?"

The question fell in so marvelously with West's mood of acute discontent with all that his life had been for the past two years, that it looked to him strangely like Providence. The easy ways of commerce appeared vastly alluring to him; his income, to say truth, had suffered sadly in the cause of the public; never had the snug dollars drawn him so strongly. He gave a slow, curious laugh.

"Why, hang it, Tommy! I don't know but I'm ready to listen to your siren spiel—now!"

In the darkness Semple's eyes gleamed. His receipts had never been so good since West left him.

"That's the talk! I need you in my business, old boy. By the bye, you can come in at bully advantage if you can move right away. I'm going to come talk with you to-morrow."

"Right's the word," said West.

At the end of that block a large house stood in a lawn, half hidden from the street by a curtain of trees. From its concealed veranda came a ripple of faint, slow laughter, advertising the presence of charming society. West halted.

"Here's a nice house, Tommy; I think I'll look in. See you to-morrow."

Semple, walking on, glanced back to see what house it was. It proved to be the brownstone palace leased for three years by old Mr. Avery, formerly of Mauch Chunk but now of Ours.

Sharlee, too, retired from her painful interview with West with a sense of irreparable loss. Her idol of so many years had, at a word, toppled off into the dust, and not all the king's horses could ever get him back again. It was like a death to her, and in most ways worse than a death.

She lay awake a long time that night, thinking of the two men who, for she could not say how long, had equally shared first place in her thoughts. And gradually she read them both anew by the blaze lit by one small incident.

She could not believe that West was deliberately false; she was certain that he was not deliberately false. But she saw now, as by a sudden searchlight flung upon him, that her one-time paladin had a fatal weakness. He could not be honest with himself. He could believe anything that he wanted to believe. He could hypnotize himself at will by the enchanting music of his own imaginings. He had pretty graces and he told himself they were large, fine abilities; dim emotions and he thought they were ideals; vague gropings of ambition, and when he had waved the hands of his fancy over them, presto, they had become great dominating purposes. He had fluttered fitfully from business to Blaines College; from the college to the *Post*; before long he would flutter on from the *Post* to something else— always falling short, always secretly disappointed, everywhere a failure as a man, though few might know it but himself. West's trouble, in fact, was that he was not a man at all. He was weakest where a real man is strongest. He was merely a chameleon taking his color from whatever he happened to light upon; a handsome boat which could never get anywhere because it had no rudder; an ornamental butterfly driving aimlessly before the nearest breeze. He meant well, in a general way, but his good intentions proved descending paving-stones because he was constitutionally incapable of meaning anything very hard.

West had had everything in the beginning except money; and he had the faculty of making all of that he wanted. Queed—she found that name still clinging to him in her thoughts—had had nothing in the beginning except his fearless honesty. In everything else that a man should he, he had seemed to her painfully destitute. But because through everything he had held unflinchingly to his honesty, he had been steadily climbing the heights. He had passed West long ago, because their faces were set in opposite directions. West had had the finest distinctions of honor carefully instilled into him from his birth. Queed had deduced his, raw, from his own unswerving honesty. And the first acid test of a real situation showed that West's honor was only burnished and decorated dross, while Queed's, which he had made himself, was as fine gold. In that test, all superficial trappings were burned and shriveled away; men were made to show their men's colors; and the "queer little man with the queer little name" had instantly cast off his resplendent superior because contact with his superior's dishonesty was degrading to him. Yet in the same breath, he had allowed his former chief to foist off that dishonesty upon his own clean shoulders, and borne the detestable burden without demand for sympathy or claim for gratitude. And this was the measure of how, as Queed had climbed by his honesty, his whole nature had been strengthened and refined. For if he had begun as the most unconscious and merciless of egoists, who could sacrifice little Fifi to his comfort without a tremor, he had ended with the supreme act of purest altruism: the voluntary sacrifice of himself to save a man whom in his heart he must despise.

But was that the supreme altruism? What had it cost him, after all, but her friendship? Perhaps he did not regard that as so heavy a price to pay.

Sharlee turned her face to the wall. In the darkness, she felt the color rising at her throat and sweeping softly but resistlessly upward. And she found herself feverishly clinging to all that her little Doctor had said, and looked, in all their meetings which, remembered now, gave her the right to think that their parting had been hard for him, too.

Yet it was not upon their parting that her mind busied itself most, but upon thoughts of their remeeting. The relations which she had thought to exist between them had, it was clear, been violently reversed. The one point now was for her to meet the topsy-turveyed situation as swiftly, as generously, and as humbly as was possible.

If she had been a man, she would have gone to him at once, hunted him up this very night, and told him in the most groveling language at her command, how infinitely sorry and ashamed she was. Lying wide-eyed in her little white bed, she composed a number of long speeches that she, as a man, would have made to him; embarrassing speeches which he, as a man, or any other man that ever lived, would never have endured for a moment. But she was not a man, she was a girl; and girls were not allowed to go to men, and frankly and honestly say what was in their hearts. She was not in the least likely to meet him by accident; the telephone was unthinkable. There remained only to write him a letter.

Yes, but what to say in the letter? There was the critical and crucial question. No matter how artful and cajoling an apology she wrote, she knew exactly how he would treat it. He would write a civil, formal reply, assuring her that her apology was accepted, and there the matter would stand forever. For she had put herself terribly in the wrong; she had betrayed a damning weakness; it was extremely probable that he would never care to resume friendship with one who had proved herself so hatefully mistrustful. Then, too, he was evidently very angry with her about the money. Only by meeting for a long, frank talk could she ever hope to make things right again; but not to save her life could she think of any form of letter which would bring such a meeting to pass.

Pondering the question, she fell asleep. All next day, whenever she had a minute and sometimes when she did not, she pondered it, and the next, and the next. Her heart smote her for the tardiness of her reparation; but stronger than this was her fear of striking and missing fire. And at last an idea came to her; an idea so big and beautiful that it first startled and dazzled her, and then set her heart to singing; the perfect idea which would blot away the whole miserable mess at one stroke. She sat down and wrote Mr. Surface five lines, asking him to be kind enough to call upon her in regard to the business matter about which he had written her a few weeks before.

She wrote this note from her house, one night; she expected, of course, that he would come there to see her; she had planned out exactly where they were each to sit, and even large blocks of their conversation. But the very next morning, before 10 o'clock, there came a knock upon the Departmental door and he walked into her office, looking more matter-of-fact and businesslike than she had ever seen him.

CHAPTER XXXII

Second Meeting between a Citizen and the Great Pleasure-Dog Behemoth, involving Plans for Two New Homes.

And this time they did not have to go into the hall to talk.

No sooner had the opening door revealed the face of young Mr. Surface than Mr. Dayne, the kind-faced Secretary, reached hastily for his hat. In the same breath with his "Come in" and "Good-morning," he was heard to mention to the Assistant Secretary something about a little urgent business downtown.

Mr. Dayne acted so promptly that he met the visitor on the very threshold of the office. The clergyman held out his hand with a light in his manly gray eye.

"I'm sincerely glad to see you, Mr. Queed, to have the chance—"

"Surface, please."

Mr. Dayne gave his hand an extra wring. "Mr. Surface, you did a splendid thing. I'm glad of this chance to tell you so, and to beg your forgiveness for having done you a grave injustice in my thoughts."

The young man stared at him. "I have nothing to forgive you for, Mr. Dayne. In fact, I have no idea what you are talking about."

But Mr. Dayne did not enlighten him; in fact he was already walking briskly down the hall. Clearly the man had business that would not brook an instant's delay.

Hat in hand, the young man turned, plainly puzzled, and found himself looking at a white-faced little girl who gave back his look with brave steadiness.

"Do you think you can forgive me, too?" she asked in a very small voice.

He came three steps forward, into the middle of the room, and there halted dead, staring at her with a look of searching inquiry.

"I don't understand this," he said, in his controlled voice.

"What are you talking about?"

"Mr. West," said Sharlee, "has told me all about it. About the reformatory. And I'm sorry."

There she stuck. Of all the speeches of prostrate yet somehow noble self-flagellation which in the night seasons she had so beautifully polished, not one single word could she now recall. Yet she continued to meet his gaze, for so should apologies be given though the skies fall; and she watched as one fascinated the blood slowly ebb from his close-set face.

"Under the circumstances," he said abruptly, "it was hardly a—a judicious thing to do. However, let us say no more about it."

He turned away from her, obviously unsteadied for all his even voice. And as he turned, his gaze, which had shifted only to get away from hers, was suddenly arrested and became fixed.

In the corner of the room, beside the bookcase holding the works of Conant, Willoughby, and Smathers, lay the great pleasure-dog Behemoth, leonine head sunk upon two massive outstretched paws. But Behemoth was not asleep; on the contrary he was overlooking the proceedings in the office with an air of intelligent and paternal interest.

Between Behemoth and young Henry Surface there passed a long look. The young man walked slowly across the room to where the creature lay, and, bending down, patted him on the head. He did it with indescribable awkwardness. Certainly Behemoth must have perceived what was so plain even to a human critic, that here was the first dog this man had ever patted in his life. Yet, being a pleasure-dog, he was wholly civil about it. In fact, after a lidless scrutiny unembarrassed by any recollections of his last meeting with this young man, he declared for friendship. Gravely he lifted a behemothian paw, and gravely the young man shook it.

To Behemoth young Mr. Surface addressed the following remarks:—

"West was simply deceived—hoodwinked by men infinitely cleverer than he at that sort of thing. It was a manly thing—his coming to you now and telling you; much harder than never to—have made the mistake in the beginning. Of course—it wipes the slate clean. It makes everything all right now. You appreciate that."

Behemoth yawned.

The young man turned, and came a step or two forward, both face and voice under complete control again.

"I received a note from you this morning," he began briskly, "asking me to come in—"

The girl's voice interrupted him. Standing beside the little typewriter-table, exactly where her caller had surprised her, she had watched with a mortifying dumbness the second meeting between the pleasure-dog and the little Doctor that was. But now pride sprang to her aid, stinging her into speech. For it was an unendurable thing that she should thus tamely surrender to him the mastery of her situation, and suffer her own fault to be glossed over so ingloriously.

"Won't you let me tell you," she began hurriedly, "how sorry I am—how ashamed—that I misjudged—"

"No! No! I beg you to stop. There is not the smallest occasion for anything of that sort—"

"Don't you see my dreadful position? I suspect you, misjudge you—wrong you at every step—and all the time you are doing a thing so fine—so generous and splendid—that I am humiliated—to—"

Once again she saw that painful transformation in his face: a difficult dull-red flood sweeping over it, only to recede instantly, leaving him white from neck to brow.

"What is the use of talking in this way?" he asked peremptorily. "What is the good of it, I say? The matter is over and done with. Everything is all right—his telling you wipes it all from the slate, just as I said. Don't you see that? Well, can't you dismiss the whole incident from your mind and forget that it ever happened?"

"I will try—if that is what you wish."

She turned away, utterly disappointed and disconcerted by his summary disposal of the burning topic over which she had planned such a long and satisfying discussion. He started to say something, checked himself, and said something entirely different.

"I have received your note," he began directly, "asking me to come in and see you about the matter of difference between the estates. That is why I have called. I trust that this means that you are going to be sensible and take your money."

"In a way—yes. I will tell you—what I have thought."

"Well, sit down to tell me please. You look tired; not well at all. Not in the least. Take this comfortable chair."

Obediently she sat down in Mr. Dayne's high-backed swivel-chair, which, when she leaned back, let her neat-shod little feet swing clear of the floor. The chair was a happy thought; it steadied her; so did his unexampled solicitousness, which showed, she thought, that her emotion had not escaped him.

"I have decided that I would take it," said she, "with a—a—sort of condition."

Sitting in the chair placed for Mr. Dayne's callers, the young man showed instant signs of disapprobation.

"No, no! You are big enough to accept your own without conditions."

"Oh—you won't argue with me about that, will you? Perhaps it is unreasonable, but I could never be satisfied to take it—and spend it for myself. I could never have any pleasure in it—never feel that it was really mine. So," she hurried on, "I thought that it would be nice to take it—and give it away."

"Give it away!" he echoed, astonished and displeased.

"Yes—give it to the State. I thought I should like to give it to—establish a reformatory."

Their eyes met. Upon his candid face she could watch the subtler meanings of her idea slowly sinking into and taking hold of his consciousness.

"No—no!" came from him, explosively. "No! You must not think of such a thing."

"Yes—I have quite made up my mind. When the idea came to me it was like an inspiration. It seemed to me the perfect use to make of this money. Don't you see?... And—"

"No, I don't see," he said sharply. "Why will you persist in thinking that there is something peculiar and unclean about this money?—some imagined taint upon your title to it? Don't you understand that it is yours in precisely the same definite and honest way that the money this office pays you—"

"Oh—surely it is all a question of feeling. And if I feel—"

"It is a question of fact," said Mr. Surface. "Listen to me. Suppose your father had put this money away for you somewhere, so that you knew nothing about it, hidden it, say, in a secret drawer somewhere about your house"—didn't he know exactly the sort of places which fathers used to hide away money?—"and that now, after all these years, you had suddenly found it, together with a note from him saying that it was for you. You follow me perfectly? Well? Would it ever occur to you to give that money to the State—for a *reformatory*?"

"Oh—perhaps not. How can I tell? But that case would—"

"Would be exactly like this one," he finished for her crisply. "The sole difference is that it happens to be my father who hid the money away instead of yours."

There was a silence.

"I am sorry," said she, constrainedly, "that you take this—this view. I had hoped so much that you might agree with me. Nevertheless, I think my mind is quite made up. I—"

"Then why on earth have you gone through the formality of consulting me, only to tell me—"

"Oh—because I thought it would be so nice if you would agree with me!"

"But I do not agree with you," he said, looking at her with frowning steadiness. "I do not. Nobody on earth would agree with you. Have you talked with your friends about this mad proposal? Have you—"

"None of them but you. I did not care to."

The little speech affected him beyond all expectation; in full flight as he was, it stopped him dead. He lost first the thread of his argument; then his steadiness of eye and manner; and when he spoke, it was to follow up, not his own thought, but her implication, with those evidences of embarrassment which he could never hide.

"So we are friends again," he stated, in rather a strained voice.

"If you are willing—to take me back."

He sat silent, drumming a tattoo on his chair-arm with long, strong fingers; and when he resumed his argument, it was with an entire absence of his usual air of authority.

"On every score, you ought to keep your money—to make yourself comfortable—to stop working—to bring yourself more pleasures, trips, whatever you want—all exactly as your father intended."

"Oh! don't argue with me, please! I asked you not. I must either take it for that or not at all."

"It—it is not my part," he said reluctantly, "to dictate what you shall do with your own. I cannot sympathize in the least with your—your mad proposal. Not in the least. However, I must assume that you know your own mind. If it is quite made up—"

"Oh, it is! I have thought it all over so carefully—and with so much pleasure."

He rose decisively. "Very well, I will go to my lawyers at once—this morning. They will arrange it as you wish."

"Oh—will you? How can I thank you? And oh," she added hastily, "there was—another point that I—I wished to speak to you about."

He gazed down at her, looking so small and sorrowful-eyed in her great chair, and all at once his knees ran to water, and the terrible fear clutched at him that his manhood would not last him out of the room. This was the reason, perhaps, that his voice was the little Doctor's at its brusquest as he said:—

"Well? What is it?"

"The question," she said nervously, "of a—a name for this reformatory that I want to found. I have thought a great deal about that. It is a—large part of my idea. And I have decided that my reformatory shall be called— that is, that I should like to call it—the Henry G. Surface Home."

He stared at her through a flash like a man stupefied; and then, wheeling abruptly, walked away from her to the windows which overlooked the park. For some time he stood there, back determinedly toward her, staring with great fixity at nothing. But when he returned to her, she had never seen his face so stern.

"You must be mad to suggest such a thing. Mad! Of course I shall not allow you to do it. I shall not give you the money for any such purpose."

"But if it is mine, as you wrote?" said Sharlee, looking up at him from the back of her big chair.

Her point manifestly was unanswerable. With characteristic swiftness, he abandoned it, and fell back to far stronger ground.

"Yes, the money is yours," he said stormily. "But that is all. My father's name is mine."

That silenced her, for the moment at least, and he swept rapidly on.

"I do not in the least approve of your giving your money to establish a foundation at all. That, however, is a matter with which, unfortunately, I have nothing to do. But with my father's name I have everything to do. I shall not permit you to—"

"Surely—oh, surely, you will not refuse me so small a thing which would give me so much happiness."

"Happiness?" He flung the word back at her impatiently, but his intention of demolishing it was suddenly checked by a flashing remembrance of Fifi's definition of it. "Will you kindly explain how you would get happiness from that?"

"Oh—if you don't see, I am afraid I—could never explain—"

"It is a display of just the same sort of unthinking Quixotism which has led you hitherto to refuse to accept your own money. What you propose is utterly irrational in every way. Can you deny it? Can you defend your proposal by any reasonable argument? I cannot imagine how so—so mad an idea ever came into your mind."

She sat still, her fingers playing with the frayed edges of Mr. Dayne's blotting-pad, and allowed the silence to enfold them once more.

"Your foundation," he went on, with still further loss of motive power, "would—gain nothing by bearing the name of my father. He was not worthy.... No one knows that better than you. Will you tell me what impulse put it into your mind to—to do this?"

"I—had many reasons," said she, speaking with some difficulty. "I will tell you one. My father loved him once. I know he would like me to do something—to make the name honorable again."

"That," he said, in a hard voice, "is beyond your power."

She showed no disposition to contradict him, or even to maintain the conversation. Presently he went on:—

"I cannot let you injure your foundation by—branding it with his notoriety, in an impulsive and—and fruitless generosity. For it would be fruitless. You, of all people, must understand that the burden on the other side is—impossibly heavy. You know that, don't you?"

She raised her head and looked at him.

Again, her pride had been plucking at her heartstrings, burning her with the remembrance that he, when he gave her everything that a man could give, had done it in a manner perfect and without flaw. And now she, with her infinitely smaller offering, sat tongue-tied and ineffectual, unable to give with a show of the purple, too poor-spirited even to yield him the truth for his truth which alone made the gift worth the offering.

Her blood, her spirit, and all her inheritance rallied at the call of her pride. She looked at him, and made her gaze be steady: though this seemed to her the hardest thing she had ever done in her life.

"I must not let you think that I wanted to do this only for your father's sake. That would not be honest. Part of my pleasure in planning it—most of it, perhaps—was because I—I should so much like to do something for your father's son."

She rose, trying to give the movement a casual air, and went over to her little desk, pretending to busy herself straightening out the litter of papers upon it. From this safe distance, her back toward him, she forced herself to add:—

"This reformatory will take the place of the one you—would have won for us. Don't you see? Half-my happiness in giving it is gone, unless you will lend me the name."

Behind her the silence was impenetrable.

She stood at her desk, methodically sorting papers which she did not see, and wildly guessing at the meaning of that look of turbulent consciousness which she had seen break startled into his eyes. More even than in their last meeting, she had found that the sight of his face, wonderfully changed yet even more wonderfully the same, deeply affected her to-day. Its new sadness and premature age moved her strangely; with a peculiar stab of compassion and pain she had seen for the first time the gray in the nondescript hair about his temples. For his face, she had seen that the smooth sheath of satisfied self-absorption, which had once overlain it like the hard veneer on a table-top, had been scorched away as in a baptism by fire; from which all that was best in it had come out at once strengthened and chastened. And she thought that the shining quality of honesty in his face must be such as to strike strangers on the street.

And now, behind her on the office floor, she heard his footsteps, and in one breath was suddenly cold with the fear that her hour had come, and hot with the fear that it had not.

Engrossed with her papers, she moved so as to keep her back toward him; but he, with a directness which would not flinch even in this untried emergency, deliberately intruded himself between her and the table; and so once more they stood face to face.

"I don't understand you," he began, his manner at its quietest. "Why do you want to do this for me?"

At this close range, she glanced once at him and instantly looked away. His face was as white as paper; and when she saw that her heart first stopped beating, and then pounded off in a wild frightened pæan.

"I—cannot tell you—I don't know—exactly."

"What do you mean?"

She hardly recognized his voice; instinctively she began backing away.

"I don't think I—can explain. You—rather terrify me this morning."

"Are you in love with ME?" he demanded in a terrible voice, beginning at the wrong end, as he would be sure to do.

Finger at her lip, her blue eyes, bright with unshed tears, resting upon his in a gaze as direct as a child's, Sharlee nodded her head up and down.

And that was all the hint required by clever Mr. Surface, the famous social scientist. He advanced somehow, and took her in his arms. On the whole, it was rather surprising how satisfactorily he did it, considering that she was the first woman he had ever touched in all his days.

So they stood through a time that might have been a minute and might have been an age, since all of them that mattered had soared away to the sunlit spaces where no time is. After awhile, driven by a strange fierce desire to see her face in the light of this new glory, he made a gentle effort to hold her off from him, but she clung to him, crying, "No, no! I don't want you to see me yet."

After another interval of uncertain length, she said:—

"All along my heart has cried out that you couldn't have done that, and hurt me so. *You couldn't.* I will never doubt my heart again. And you were so fine—so fine—to forgive me so easily."

In the midst of his dizzying exaltation, he marveled at the ease with which she spoke her inmost feeling; he, the great apostle of reason and self-mastery, was much slower in recovering lost voice and control. It was some time before he would trust himself to speak, and even then the voice that he used was not recognizable as his.

"So you are willing to do as much for my father's son as to—to—take his name for your own."

"No, this is something that I am doing for myself. Your father was not perfect, but he was the only father that ever had a son whose name I would take for mine."

A silence.

"We can keep my father's house," he said, in time, "for—for—us to live in. You must give up the office. And I will find light remunerative work, which will leave at least part of my time free for my book."

She gave a little laugh that was half a sob. "Perhaps—you could persuade that wealthy old lady—to get out a second edition of her *thesaurus!*"

"I wish I could, though!"

"You talk just like my little Doctor," she gasped—"my—own little Doctor.... I've got a little surprise for you—about remunerative work," she went on, "only I can't tell you now, because it's a secret. Promise that you won't make me tell you."

He promised.

Suddenly, without knowing why, she began to cry, her cheek against his breast. "You've had a sad life, little Doctor—a sad life. But I am going to make it all up to you—if you will show me the way."

Presently she became aware that her telephone was ringing, and ringing as though it had been at it for some time.

"Oh bother! They won't let us have even a little minute together after all these years. I suppose you must let me go—"

She turned from the desk with the most beautiful smile he had ever seen upon a face.

"It's for you!"

"For me?" he echoed like a man in a dream. "That is—very strange."

Strange, indeed! Outside, the dull world was wagging on as before, unaware that there had taken place in this enchanted room the most momentous event in history.

He took the receiver from her with a left hand which trembled, and with his untrained right somehow caught and imprisoned both of hers. "Stand right by me," he begged hurriedly.

Now he hoisted the receiver in the general direction of his ear, and said in what he doubtless thought was quite a businesslike manner: "Well?"

"Mr. Queed? This is Mr. Hickok," said the incisive voice over the wire. "Well, what in the mischief are you doing up there?"

"I'm—I'm—transacting some important business—with the Department," said Mr. Surface, and gave Sharlee's hands a desperate squeeze. "But my—"

"Well, we're transacting some important business down here. Never should have found you but for Mr. Dayne's happening along. Did you know that West had resigned?"

"No, has he? But I started—"

"Peace to his ashes. De mortuis nil nisi bonum. The directors are meeting now to elect his successor. Only one name has been mentioned. There's only one editor we'll hear of for the paper. Won't you come back to us, my boy?"

The young man cleared his throat. "Come? I'd—think it the greatest honor—there's nothing I'd rather have. You are all too—too kind to me—I can't tell you—but—"

"Oh, no buts! But us no buts now! I'll go tell them—"

"No—wait," called the young man, hastily. "If I come, I don't come as Queed, you know. My name is Henry G. Surface. That may make a difference—"

"Come as Beelzebub!" said the old man, testily. "We've had enough of hiring a *name* for the *Post*. This time we're after a man, and by the Lord, we've got one!"

Henry Surface turned away from the telephone, struggling with less than his usual success to show an unmoved face.

"You—know?"

She nodded: in her blue-spar eyes, there was the look of a winged victory. "That was the little secret—don't you think it was a nice one? It is your magnificent boast come true.... And you don't even say 'I told you so'!"

He looked past her out into the park. Over the budding trees, already bursting and spreading their fans of green, far off over the jagged stretch of roofs, his gaze sought the battered gray *Post* building and the row of windows behind which he had so often sat and worked. A mist came before his eyes; the trees curveted and swam; and his visible world swung upside down and went out in a singing and spark-shot blackness.

She came to his side again: in silence slipped her hand into his; and following both his look and his thought, she felt her own eyes smart with a sudden bright dimness.

"This is the best city in the world," said Henry Surface. "The kindest people—the *kindest people*—"

"Yes, little Doctor."

He turned abruptly and caught her to him again; and now, hearing even above the hammering of his own blood the wild fluttering of her heart against his, his tongue unlocked and he began to speak his heart. It was not speech as he had always known speech. In all his wonderful array of terminology there were no words fitted to this undreamed need; he had to discover them somehow, by main strength make them up for himself; and they came out stammering, hard-wrung, bearing new upon their rough faces the mint-mark of his own heart. Perhaps she did not prize them any the less on that account.

"I'm glad that you love me that way—Henry. I must call you Henry now—mustn't I, Henry?"

"Do you know," she said, after a time, "I am—*almost* weakening about giving our money for a Home. Somehow, I'd so like for you to have it, so that—"

She felt a little shiver run through him.

"No, no! I could not bear to touch it. We shall be far happier—"

"You could stop work, buy yourself comforts, pleasures, trips. It is a mad thing," she teased, "to give away money.... Oh, little Doctor—I can't breathe if you hold me—so tight."

"About the name," he said presently, "I—dislike to oppose you, but I cannot—I cannot—"

"Well, I've decided to change it, Henry, in deference to your wishes."

"I am extremely glad. I myself know a name—"

"Instead of calling it the Henry G. Surface Home—"

Suddenly she drew away from him, leaving behind both her hands for a keepsake, and raised to him a look so luminous and radiant that he felt himself awed before it, like one who with impious feet has blundered upon holy ground.

"I am going to call it the Henry G. Surface *Junior* Home. Do you know any name for a Home so pretty as that?"

"No, no, I—can't let you—"

But she cried him down passionately, saying: "Yes, that is *our* name now, and we are going to make it honorable."

From his place beside the sociological bookcase—perhaps faunal naturalists can tell us why—the great pleasure-dog Behemoth, whose presence they had both forgotten, raised his leonine head and gave a sharp, joyous bark.